PETER THE BRAZEN

PETER THE BRAZEN

GEORGE F. WORTS

A MYSTERY STORY OF MODERN CHINA

*"A man whose heart is burning with passion
follows the undulations of a thought."*
—Su-Tong-Po.

WILDSIDE PRESS

TO
DR. AND MRS. W. B. A. MOORE
HONG KONG

INTRODUCTION

JOHN BETANCOURT

George Frank Worts (1892–1967) was an American writer best remembered today for his pulp-era adventurer Peter the Brazen, along with a number of other serials and magazine stories. He also published under the pseudonym "Loring Brent." Born in Toledo, Ohio, Worts learned telegraphy and wireless operation in his youth and spent several years "punching brass"—operating the telegraph—aboard ships in the Pacific. That experience gave his fiction a touch of authenticity when he described the wireless operator's trade, a profession still novel and romantic in the early twentieth century.

Worts began selling fiction to pulp magazines in the 1910s, though at first his output was modest. He briefly attended Columbia University in 1915 but soon left, preferring real-world adventure to academic life. He worked as a newspaper reporter and later as a magazine editor before devoting himself full-time to freelance writing. Like many pulp writers of his generation, Worts supported himself by producing a steady stream of fast-paced tales that catered to the tastes of magazine audiences.

His best-known creation, Peter the Brazen, debuted in 1918 in *Argosy* with the story "Princess of Static." The first six stories in the series were later combined into the 1919 book *Peter the Brazen: A Mystery Story of Modern China* (which you are now reading). Peter Moore, the hero, is both a wireless operator and an adventurer, gifted with extraordinary hearing and an uncanny sense for trouble. The series carried him through a range of dangers in exotic locales, blending technical novelty with crime, espionage, and high adventure.

Worts's place in pulp fiction is secure, though not as widely celebrated as some of his contemporaries. His work displays the classic hallmarks of the pulps: rapid pacing, cliffhanger peril, and a taste for distant settings that offered readers escape from the everyday. His approach anticipated some of the techniques later codified by Lester Dent and other architects of the pulp style, with heroes who were resourceful, bold, and endlessly mobile.

Beyond the "Peter the Brazen" series, Worts wrote the "Singapore Sammy" stories, which offered seagoing adventure in the same spirit, and he contributed to crime and detective magazines under both his real and pen names.

This versatility was typical of pulp writers, who often moved between genres and magazines to meet editorial demand.

Readers who enjoy *Peter the Brazen* will likely also appreciate Worts's other adventure series, as well as the work of Talbot Mundy (especially the "Jimgrim" series), H. Bedford-Jones, and Robert E. Howard's non-fantastic tales. Each combined a sense of the exotic with fast-moving plots and colorful characters, offering the allure of distant places and perilous quests during the golden age of pulp storytelling. Movie-goers will recognize Indiana Jones as one of many modern descendants of Peter Moore and his kind.

PART I

THE CITY OF STOLEN LIVES

"How serene the joy,
when things that are made for each other meet
and are joined;
but ah,—
how rarely they meet and are joined, the things
that are made for each other!"

—SAO-NAN

CHAPTER I

When Peter Moore entered the static-room, picked his way swiftly and un-noticingly across the littered floor, and jerked open the frosted glass door of the chief operator's office, the assembled operators followed him with glances of admiration and concern. No one ever entered the Chief's office in that fashion. One waited until called upon.

But Moore was privileged. Having "pounded brass" for five useful and adventurous years on the worst and best of the ships which minimize the length and breadth of the Pacific Ocean, he was favored; he had become a person of importance. He had performed magical feats with a wireless machine; he had had experiences.

His first assignment was a fishing schooner, a dirty, unseaworthy little tub, which ran as far north sometimes as the Aleutians; and he had immediately gained official recognition by sticking to his instruments for sixty-eight hours—recorded at fifteen-minute intervals in his log—when the whaler *Goblin* encountered a submerged pinnacle rock in the Island Passage and flashed the old C.Q.D. distress signal.

It was brought out in the investigation that the distance at which Peter Moore had picked up the signals of the sinking *Goblin* exceeded the normal working range of either apparatus. When pressed, the young man confessed the ownership of a pair of abnormally keen ears. Afterward, it was demonstrated for the benefit of doubters that Moore could "read" signals in the receivers when the ordinary operator could detect only a far away scratching sound.

Beginning his second year in the Marconi uniform, Peter Moore was recognized as material far too valuable to waste on the fishing boats; and he was stationed on the *Sierra*, which was then known in wireless circles as a supervising ship. Her powerful apparatus could project out a long electric arm over any part of the eastern Pacific, and the duty of her operator was to reprimand sluggards who neglected answering calls from ship or shore stations, and inexperienced men who violated the strict rules governing radio intercourse.

It was whispered that Peter Moore grew tired of the nagging to which his position on the supervisor ship gave him privilege, for he shortly made application for a berth in the China run. Now every operator on the Pacific cherishes the hope that his fidelity will some day be rewarded by a China run, and there are applications always on file for those romantic berths. The Chief granted Peter Moore his whim unhesitatingly; and Moore selected the *Vandalia*, perhaps the most desirable of the transpacific fleet, because she stayed away from San Francisco the longest.

That the supersensitiveness of his ears was not waning was soon proved by his receipt of a non-relayed message, afterward verified, from the shore station in Seattle, when the *Vandalia* lay at anchor in the harbor at Hong-Kong. That was a new record. Marconi himself is believed to have written the young magician a complimentary letter. But Peter Moore showed that letter to no one. That was his nature. He was something of a mystery even to the members of his own profession. Many of the younger operators knew him only as a symbol, a genius behind a key, or as a hand. Professionally speaking, it was his hand that made his personality unique and enviable. There was a queer vitality in the signals sent into the air from a wireless machine when his strong white fingers played upon the key; his touch was as familiar to them as the voice of a friend.

There was a general simmering down of coastwise gossip in the static-room when the frosted glass door of the Chief's office closed behind him. Voices trailed off into curious whisperings. Then—

"But great guns, man, I need you!" boomed the cranky voice of the Chief.

Followed then the low hum of Peter Moore as he explained himself.

"Makes no difference!" the Chief roared. "Can't get along without you. Short handed. Gotta stay!"

In irritation the Chief always abbreviated his remarks quite as if they were radiograms to be transmitted at dollar-a-word rates.

The truth then dawned and burst upon those ardent listeners in the static-room. Peter Moore was resigning! It was incredible.

A more daring head pressed its audacious ear against the snowy glass. This was a fat, excitable little man, long in the service, but destined forever, it seemed, to hammer brass in the Panama intermediate run. A skillful operator, but his arm broke, as wireless men say, whenever faced by emergency. He distinctly heard Peter Moore state in a voice of emotion: "Too much China. God, man, I'll be smuggling opium next!"

"Rubbish!" the Chief snorted.

The Panama Line man waved a pale hand behind him for absolute silence.

"Want a shore station for a while?"

"Intend to rest up and then look around," Moore answered.

"You'll be back. Mark my word. The sea and the wireless house is a winning combination. The old cities—new faces—freedom—"

"I'm tired."

"Pah! You've only begun. When does the *Vandalia* clear for China?"

"Thursday night."

"I'll hold your berth open till Thursday noon. Hoping you'd break in a new operator. Queer chap. Glass eye. 'Member—Thursday noon."

The frosted door went inward abruptly. The intense blue eyes in the pale face of the man who had resigned closed half way upon encountering the blushing eavesdropper. The Panama Line operator moved uncertainly toward a vacant chair. Unaware of the curious stares addressed at him Moore went to the outer door. A wave of exquisite nervousness rippled through the silence of the static-room as the door clicked.

When the rumor reached the *Vandalia*, lying in state at her pier, that Peter Moore had resigned, Captain Jones, after bluntly airing his disappointment, advanced the theory to his chief engineer that Sparks had "taken the East too much to heart. The fangs are in too deep."

"He will be on hand sailing time," added the chief engineer, who had been trying to retire from active duty in the China run for eleven years.

But Moore did not come back to the *Vandalia* for that reason at all.

CHAPTER II

Communication between certain individuals in China and their relatives and friends in Chinatown must, for political and other reasons, be conducted in a secret way. In Shanghai, Moore had made the acquaintance, under somewhat mysterious auspices, of Ching Gow Ong, an important figure in the silk traffic.

Moore, so it was said by those who were in a position to know, had once performed a favor for Ching Gow Ong, of which no one seemed to know the particulars. What was of equal importance, perhaps, was that Ching Gow Ong would have willingly given Moore any gift within his power had Moore been so inclined.

But it appears that Moore was not a seeker after wealth, thereby giving some real basis to the common belief that he possessed that rare thing—a virginal spirit of adventure. He cemented this queer friendship by conveying messages, indited in Chinese script, which he did not read, between Ching Gow Ong and his brother, Lo Ong, officially dead, who conducted a vile-smelling haunt in the bowels of Chinatown.

Peter Moore made his way through the narrowing alleys, proceeded through a maze of blank walls, down a damp stone stairway, and rapped upon a black iron door. It opened instantly, and a long clawlike hand reached forth, accepted the yellow envelope from the operator's hand, and slowly, silently withdrew, the door closing as quickly and as quietly as it had opened.

No words were spoken. His errand done, Peter Moore retraced his steps to the wider and brighter lanes which comprised the Chinatown known to tourists.

He walked slowly, with his head inclined a little to one side, which was a habit he had acquired from the eternal listening into the hard rubber receivers. He had proceeded in this fashion a number of steps up one of the narrow, sloping sidewalks when he felt, rather than perceived, a pair of eyes fastened upon him from a second-story window.

They were the eyes of a young Chinese woman, but he sensed immediately that she was not of the river type. Her fine black hair was arranged in a gorgeous coiffure. Gold ornaments drooped from her ears, and her complexion was liberally sanded with rice powder. Her painted lips wore an expression of malignity.

In the obliquity of the eyes lurked a solemn warning. Then he became aware that she seemed to be struggling, as if she were impeding the movements of some one behind her.

It is safe to say that in his tramps through the winding alleys of Canton, of Peking, of Shanghai, Peter Moore had encountered many Chinese women of her type. There was a sharp vividness to her features which meant the inbreeding of high caste. She was unusual—startling! She looked into the street furtively, held up a heavily jeweled hand—an imperial order for him to stop—and withdrew. He lounged into the doorway of an ivory shop and waited.

It was quiet in Chinatown, for the time was noon and the section was pursuing its midday habit of calm. The padding figures were becoming a trifle obscure, owing to a cold, pale fog that was drifting up from the bay. In a moment the woman reappeared, examined the street again with hostile eyes, held up a square of rice paper, and slowly folded it.

Peter Moore nodded slightly and smiled. It was a habit with him—that smile. The sensitiveness of his nervous system found a quick outlet, when he was nervous or excited, by a disingenuous smile. He proceeded to the shop directly underneath her window, observing it to be Ah Sih King's gold shop. The window was rich in glittering splendors from the Orient. He picked up from the sidewalk a crumpled ball of red paper and stowed it away in his coat pocket.

To an alert observer the indifference with which Moore turned and pretended to study the gold ornaments in Ah Sih King's window might have seemed a trifle too obvious, and the smile on his lips, one might go on to say, was uncalled for.

As he waited, a soft thud sounded at his feet, coincident with a flash of black and white across his shoulder. He covered the object with one foot, as the oily, leering face of Ah Sih King appeared in the doorway. The blanched face surmounted a costly mandarin robe, righteously worn, a gorgeous blue raiment with traceries of fine gold and exquisite gems. At this moment he seemed to exhale an air of faint suspicion.

"Gentleman!" accosted the thin, curled lips in a tone that was well-nigh personal.

"Buy nothing," Peter Moore said curtly.

"You see my—my see you," observed Ah Sih King, reverting, as he deemed fitting, to pidgin.

The wireless operator turned his back impolitely; Ah Sih King did likewise. When he turned again, sharply, the oily smile was gone, a look of concern having crept into his sly, old face, and the slightly bent shoulders of the much slier young man were several strides distant.

A faint hiss, as of warning, issued from the carmine lips of the Chinese woman. Then the window closed noiselessly, and Chinatown, having paid not the slightest heed to the incident, pattered about its multifarious businesses, none the wiser.

There was an indefinable something in this incident which caused creases to appear across Moore's brow. Why had two notes been thrown? The puzzle sifted down to this possibility: Some one behind the Chinese woman had thrown a ball of red paper, a note, into the street.

Then she had beckoned him to wait, had written a second note, perhaps to warn him away. He glanced furtively at the second note, saw that it was written in Chinese, and thereupon decided in return for many favors to call upon Lo Ong for a translation.

Chinatown now was slowly vanishing from view, swallowed by the gray blanket of fog which rolled in from the Pacific through the mouth of the harbor. Retracing his steps through the mist, Moore descended the narrow stone stairway and tapped on the oblong of iron with his heavy seal ring. A shutter clinked, uneasy eyes scrutinized him, and he heard the bolt slide back. He opened the door and entered, restoring the bolt to its place.

The room was low, deep and dark under the flickering light of a single dong, which hung from the ceiling at the end of a roped-up cluster of fine brass chains. The rich, stupefying odor of opium tainted the heavy air. The orange flame, motionless as if it were carved from solid metal, showed the room to be bare except for a few grass mats scattered about in the irregular round shadow under it.

To one of these mats Lo Ong, gaunt, curious, even hostile, retreated, squatting with his delicately thin hands folded over his abdomen. A look of recognition disturbed only for the instant the placidity of the ochre features.

"No come buy?" he intoned, as if Peter Moore had never passed under that piercing gaze before.

"My never come buy," said the wireless man curtly. "Wanchee you come help; savvy?"

"Mebbe can do," asserted Lo Ong, in the voice and manner of one incessantly pursued by favor-seekers. Lo Ong's draped arm, as if it were detached from his body and governed by some extraneous mechanism, indicated a mat. Moore slipped down in the familiar cross-legged attitude, lighted a cigarette and blew the smoke at the belly on the dong.

"You Wanchee cumshaw?" demanded the Chinese, uneasily.

Peter Moore disdained to reply, extracted the two lumps of paper, slid one under his knee and unfolded the other, while Lo Ong looked unfavorably beyond him at the door. Three rows of Chinese markings were scrawled down it. Lo Ong's body commenced to sway back and forth in impatient rhythm.

"Lo Ong," stated Moore, "my wanchee you keep mouth shut—allatime shut—you savvy?"

"Can do," murmured Lo Ong indifferently. He reached for the rice paper, lifting it tenderly in long, clawing fingers, and held it to the flame. He seemed not to believe what he read, for he twisted the paper over, looked at it upside down, then sat down again, his lean fingers convulsing.

"No can do," he muttered, replacing the paper on his visitor's knee. "Mino savvy."

The white forefinger of the wireless operator pointed unwaveringly at the flattened nose. "Read that," he ordered.

Lo Ong glanced the other way, as if the subject had ceased to interest him, and tapped the floor with his knuckles.

"Wanchee money—cumshaw?"

"Lo Ong," declared Moore, losing his patience, "you b'long dead. Now savvy?"

"Mebbe can do," said Lo Ong faintly.

Moore ran his fingers down the first row of fresh markings.

"O-o-ey," commented Lo Ong, shifting uneasily, "'My see you allatime, long ago on ship.' Savvy?"

"What's next?"

"'You no see my. My see you allatime.'"

The long, sloping shoulders seemed to jerk. "Keep away. Savvy?"

"It says that?"

"Take look see," invited Lo Ong, poking his claw nervously down the column. "'Keep away. Keep away.' One—two times. Savvy?"

Peter Moore nodded thoughtfully.

The Chinese, officially dead, replaced the sheet gingerly on his knees, as if it were an instrument of wickedness. His bony fingers twitched a moment.

"High lady," he added nervously; "velly high lady. You stay away. Huh?"

"Wait a minute." Peter extracted the other paper ball, unfolding it near the orange flame. The inner surface was red, the earthly red of porphyry, and cracked and scarred by the crumpling. Nearly obliterated by the lacework of wrinkles and scratches was a scrawl, evidently scarred into the glazed surface by a knife-point. The upper part was unintelligible. On the lower surface he made out with difficulty the single word, *Vandalia*. He carried it to the door, slid back the shutter and let the dim, gray light filter upon it. The other words were too mutilated to be read.

"Hi!"

He returned to Lo Ong's jacketed side. The bony finger was circling excitedly about a smear of black in the lower corner of the rice paper.

"What's this?"

"Len Yang. *Len Yang*! Savvy?"

"O-ho! And who is Len Yang?"

Lo Ong shook his head in agitation. "Len Yang—city. Savvy? Shanghai—Len Yang—fort' day."

"Fourteen days from Shanghai to Len Yang?"

"No. No! *No*! Fort'."

"Forty?"

"O-o-ey." The flattened nose bobbed up and down. "Keep away—ai?"

"Maskee," Peter replied, meaning, broadly speaking, none of your business.

Lo Ong unbolted the door, to hint that the interview was concluded. "You keep away—ai?" he repeated anxiously. Moore grinned in his peculiarly disingenuous way, swung open the black door, and a long, gray arm of the fog groped its way past Lo Ong's countenance.

CHAPTER III

The junior operator toyed with the heavy transmitting key while Peter Moore, who knew the behavior of his apparatus as he would know the caprices of an old friend, adjusted helix-plugs, started the motor-generator, and satisfied the steel-eyed radio inspector that his wave decrement was exactly what it ought to be.

Then the inspector grunted suspiciously and wanted to know if the auxiliary batteries were properly charged. With a faint smile, Moore hooked up the auxiliary apparatus, tapped the key, and a crinkly blue spark snapped between the brass points above the fat rubber coil.

"I reckon she'll do," observed the inspector. "Aerial don't leak, does it?"

"No," said Peter.

The government man took a final look at the glittering instruments, and departed. Wherewith the junior operator swung half around in the swivel-chair and exposed to Peter an expression of mild imploration. Two gray lids over cavernous sockets lifted and lowered upon shining black eyes, one of which seemed to lack focus. Peter recalled then that the Chief had said something about a second operator having only one human eye, the other being glass.

"This is your first trip?"

The sallow face was inclined, and the pallid lips moved dryly.

"I just came from the school. I'm pretty green. You see—"

"I see. We'd better let me take the first trick. I'll sit in till midnight. After that there's very little doing. You may have to relay a position report or so. Be sure and don't work on navy time. The Chief will watch you closely for long-distance. The farther you work, the better he'll like it. How's the air? Have you listened in?"

"Do you mean—static? I heard a little. Seemed pretty far away, though."

Peter adjusted the nickeled straps about his head and pressed the rubber disks tight to his ears. He tilted his head slightly. A distant but harsh rasping, as of countless needle-points grating on glass, occurred in the head phones. This was caused by charges of electricity in the air, known to wireless men as "static." Percolating through the scratching was a clear, bell-like note. The San Pedro station was having something to say to a destroyer off the coast.

With delicate fingers Peter raised the tuning-knob a few points. Dale, the junior operator, hands clutched behind him, stared with the fearful adoration of an apprentice. He seemed to be making a mental notation of every move that Peter made, for future reference.

"Ah—do you mind if I ask a few questions? You see, I'm kind of green."

"Go ahead!" Peter said cordially.

"Where do I eat? With the crew? I hear that lots of these ships make you eat with the crew."

"No. In the main dining-saloon. Mr. Blanchard, the purser, will take care of you. See him at six thirty."

A deep monstrous shudder, arising to a clamor, half roar, half shriek, issued from the boilers of the *Vandalia*.

"It's rather interesting to watch us pull out," said Peter when the noise had ceased. "But be careful. There's no rail around this deck."

He was on his hands and knees at the motor-generator with a pad of sandpaper between his fingers when the tremulous voice of the junior operator sounded in the doorway. "Mr. Moore, there's some excitement on the dock."

Peter followed the narrow shoulders to the starboard side and looked down. The *Vandalia* was warping out from the pierhead with a sobbing tug at her stern. He noted that the head-lines were still fast. A straggling line of passengers' friends, wives, husbands, and sweethearts was moving slowly toward the end of the pier, for a final parting wave.

Something seemed to be wrong at the shore end of the gangplank, for, despite the fact that the ship was swinging out, the plank was still up. In the midst of an excited crowd a taxicab purred and smoked. There was a general parting in the crowd as the door was flung open. Two figures emerged, were lost from sight, and reappeared at the foot of the plank. An incoherent something was roared from the bridge.

One of the figures appeared to be struggling, clutching at the rail. For an instant she seemed to glance in Peter's direction. But her face could hardly be seen, for it was shrouded by a heavy gray veil. A gray hood covered her hair, and a long cloak reached to her shoe-tops.

Patiently urging her was a Chinese woman in silk jacket, trousers, and jeweled slippers. A customs officer tried to break through the mob, but somehow was held back. The gray-hooded figure suddenly seemed to become limp, and the Chinese woman half lifted, half pushed her the remaining distance to the promenade deck.

Peter was then conscious of a staring, lifeless eye fixed upon his.

"What do you make of it, Mr. Moore?" the junior operator wanted to know.

"Of that?" said Peter. "Nothing—nothing at all. By the way, I forgot to tell you that the captain has issued strict orders forbidding subofficers to use the starboard decks. Always, when you're going forward, or aft, walk on the port side."

CHAPTER IV

Peter turned over the log-book and the wireless-house to Dale, a few minutes before midnight.

"Everything's cleared up. The static is worse, and KPH may want you to relay a message or two to Honolulu. If you have trouble, let me know."

"Yes, yes," replied Dale, looking over his shoulder nervously. "I will. Thanks."

Peter left him to the mercies of the static. As he descended the iron ladder to the promenade-deck, he imagined he saw some one moving underneath him. The figure, whoever or whatever it was, slid around the white wall and vanished as his foot felt the deck. He hastened to follow.

As he stepped into the light a low, sibilant whisper reached him. At the cross-corridor doorway he was in time to see the flicker of a vanishing gray garment and a sandaled foot on a naked ankle flash over the vestibule wave-check. He shook open the door and followed.

A vertical stripe of yellow light cleaved the dark of the corridor as a door was quietly shut. He heard the faint, distant click of a door-latch. Counting the entrances to that one, and sure that he had made no mistake, he rapped. The near-by clank of the engine-room well was the reply. He tried the handle. It was immovable. He struck a match. It was stateroom forty-four.

Peter went to the purser's office. Light rippled through the wrinkled green, round window, as he had hoped. He tapped lightly, and a voice bade him to enter.

Blanchard, the purser, dwarfed, perpetually stoop-shouldered, looked up from a clump of cargo reports and blinked through convex, thick, steel spectacles at his interrupter. His eyes were red and dim with a gray-blue, uncertain definition which always reminded Peter of oysters. Blanchard had been purser of the *Vandalia* for thirteen years, and Peter knew that the man possessed the garrulous habits of the oyster as well.

"Well, well!" observed Blanchard in the crisp, brittle accents of senility; "so you're back again, eh? Well, well, well." There was no emphasis laid on the words. They were all struck from the same piece of ancient metal.

"Here I am!" agreed Peter with mild enthusiasm. "The bad penny!"

"Ha, ha! The bad penny returns!" The exclamation died in a futile cough. "What are you prowlin' around ship this time o' night for, eh? After three bells, Sparks. Time for respectable people to be fast asleep. Or, are you leavin' the radio unwatched?"

"I'm looking for information." Peter drew himself by stiffened arms upon the purser's single bunk.

"Lookin' for information?" The thin voice suffered the quavery attrition of surprise. "Funny place to be lookin' for that commodity. What's on your mind? Eh?"

"Chinamen!"

Blanchard tilted the rusted spectacles to his forehead, and the motionless gray orbs seemed to glint with a half-dead light. "Chinamen? What Chinamen?" The spectacles slid back into place.

"One, a woman, came aboard as we were pulling out this afternoon. Who is she? Where is she? Where's she from? Where's she going? Who's with her? That's what I want to clear up."

"Is that all?" squeaked Blanchard. His wrinkled, dried lips were struggling as if with indecision. A veiled, a thinly veiled conflict of emotions apparently was taking place behind that ancient gray mask. "What—what for?" was the final outcome in a hesitant half-whisper.

"My private information," smiled Peter. "Just curious, that's all. Didn't mean to pry open any dark secrets." He made as if to go.

"Sparks! Don't be in a hurry. I'm not so busy."

"Well?"

"What's botherin' you? Maybe I could straighten you out."

"Who are the occupants of stateroom forty-four?" Peter replied.

Again the expression shifted like water smitten by an evil wind.

"Forty-four!" The words were mild explosions.

A long cardboard sheet with blue and red lines was produced from a noiselessly opened drawer.

"The passenger list. We shall see." Blanchard's red, shiny forefinger clawed down the column of names, halting at the numeral forty-four. The space was blank. "You see?"

"Empty?"

"Empty." A restrained note of triumph was unquestionably evident in the purser's cracked voice.

"I'll bother you with just one more question. What is Len Yang?"

A look of doubt, of incredulity bordering upon feeble indignation, settled upon the serrated countenance. But Blanchard only shook his head as if he did not comprehend.

Peter slipped down from the bunk. "Guess I'll take a turn on deck, if the fog's lifted, and roll in. G'night, purser."

Blanchard started to say something, evidently thought better of it, and retrieved his pen. As he dipped the fine point into the red ink by mistake he flung another frown over his shoulder. The wireless man lingered on the threshold, swinging the door tentatively.

"G'night, Sparks."

CHAPTER V

The *Vandalia* was wallowing majestically through long, dead black swells. Peter poked his way up forward to the solitary lookout in the peak and glanced overside. Broad, phosphorescent swords broke smoothly with a rending, rushing gurgle over the steep cut-water. His eyes darted here and there over the void as his mind struggled to straighten out this latest kink.

What facts of significance he might have discovered from Blanchard were overshadowed by the purser's suspicious attitude. Blanchard knew, and Blanchard, for some reason, did not choose to divulge. This made matters more interesting, if slightly more complicated.

He was now reasonably sure of several things, without really having definite grounds for being sure. The malignant-eyed Chinese woman and whoever she had successfully concealed behind her in the loft above Ah Sih King's were now aboard the *Vandalia*. He was quite positive that he had recognized her in the woman who had come aboard in company with the gray-cloaked figure at the last minute before sailing-time.

He recalled the scene on the pierhead, and it occurred to him that the eyes behind the gray veil, before their owner was whisked up to the deck and from his sight, had fastened upon him for a long breath.

"Four bells, all well!" bawled the lookout as four clanging strokes rang out from abaft the wheel-house.

And Blanchard had proved that stateroom forty-four was unoccupied. Peter decided to borrow a master key in the morning, from the chief engineer, perhaps, and investigate stateroom forty-four. And with the feeling that he was on the verge of discovering something which did not exist, he prepared to turn in.

He was not undressed when the lock grated, the door lurched open, and the pale visage of Dale teetered at his shoulder. An attempt at grinning ended in a hissing sob of in-taken breath. The limp frame flung itself in the bunk beside Peter, and Dale's white, perspiring face was buried in palsied hands.

"Feel the motion?" Peter pulled down one of the hands, gently uncovering the expressionless eye.

"I wish I was dead!"

"Want me to finish your trick?"

Dale's face disappeared in the pillow. A moment he was stark. His head partly revolved, profiling a yellow, pointed nose against the white of the linen.

"Static's much worse, Mr. Moore. Frisco's sent me the same message three times now. It's for Honolulu. He says he won't repeat it again." The pale lips trembled in misery. "And there seems to be a funny sort of static in the receivers. The dynamos in the engine-room may cause it."

"That's strange," Peter reflected as he slipped on his blue coat. "There's never been any induction on board as far back as I can remember. Does it hum—or what?"

"No, it grates, like static. Sounds like static, and yet it doesn't. Kind of a hoarse rumble, like a broken-down spark-coil."

Two even rows of white teeth drew in the trembling lip and clung to it. "That awful staticky sound— And the *Rover's* been calling us." He groaned miserably. "I couldn't answer either of them. I was lying on the carpet!"

"Get some sleep," advised Peter. "When you feel better come up and relieve me. If I were you I wouldn't smoke cigarettes when you think it's rough."

"I won't smoke another cigarette as long as I live!"

Peter slipped into his uniform, draped an oil-skin coat about his slender shoulders, and made his way up to the wireless house. The receivers were lying on the floor.

The *Vandalia* was entering a zone of pale, thin mist, which created circular, misty auras about the deck-lights. The tarpaulined donkey-engine beneath the after-cargo booms rattled as the *Vandalia's* stern sank into a hollow, and the beat of the engines was muffled and deeper. A speck of white froth glinted on the black surface and vanished astern.

The wireless-house seemed warm and cozy in the glare of its green and white lights. An odor of cheap cigarette-smoke puffed out as he opened the door.

Peter slipped the hard-rubber disks over his ears and tapped the slider of the tuner. Static was bad tonight, trickling, exploding and hissing in the receivers.

The electric lights became dim under the strain of the heavy motor, as he slid up the starting handle. The white-hot spark exploded in a train of brisk dots and dashes. He snapped up the aerial switch and listened.

KPH—the San Francisco station—rang clear and loud through the spatter of the electric storm. Peter flashed back his okay, tuned for the Kahuka Head station at Honolulu, and retransmitted the message.

Sensitizing the detector, he slid up the tuning handle for high waves. Static, far removed, trickled in. Then a faint, musical wailing like a violin's E-string pierced this. The violin was the government station at Arlington, Virginia, transmitting a storm warning to ships in the South Atlantic. For five minutes the wailing persisted. Sliding the tuning handle downward, Peter listened for commercial wave-lengths.

A harsh grinding, unmusical as emery upon hollow bronze, rasped stutteringly in the head phones. Laboriously, falteringly, the grating was cleaved into clumsy dots and dashes of the Continental Code, under the quaking fingers of some obviously frightened and inexperienced operator. Were these the sounds which had unnerved Dale? For a time the raspings spelled nothing intelligible. The unknown sender evidently was repeating the same word again and again. It held four letters. Once they formed, H-I-J-X. Another time, S-E-L-J. And another, L-P-H-E.

The painstaking intent, as the operator's acute ears recognized, was identical in each instance. Frequently the word was incoherent altogether, the signals meaning nothing.

Suddenly Peter jerked up his head. Out of the jumble stood the word, as an unseen ship will often stand out nakedly in a fog rift. Over and over, badly spaced, the infernal rasp was spelling, *H-E-L-P*.

He waited for the signature of this frantic operator. But none occurred. Following a final letter "p" the signals ceased.

For a minute or two, while Peter nervously pondered, the air was silent. Then another station called him. A loud droning purr filled the receivers. Peter gave the "k" signal. The brisk voice of the transport *Rover* droned:

"I can't raise KPH. Will you handle an M-S-G for me?"

"Sure!" roared the *Vandalia's* spark. "But wait a minute. Have you heard a broken down auxiliary asking for help? He's been jamming me for fifteen minutes. Seems to be very close, K."

"Nix," replied the *Rover* breezily. "Can't be at all close or I would hear him, too. I can see your lights from my window. You're off our port quarter. Here's the M-S-G."

Peter accepted the message, retransmitting it to the KPH operator, then called the wheelhouse on the telephone. Quine, first officer, answered sleepily.

"Has the lookout reported any ship in the past hour excepting the *Rover*?"

"Is that the *Rover* on our port quarter?" Quine's voice was gruffly amazed. Like most mariners of the old school, he considered the wireless machine a nuisance. Yet its intelligence occasionally caught him off guard.

"Only thing in sight, Sparks."

Peter made an entry in the log-book, folded his hands and shut his eyes. The Leyden jars rattled in their mahogany sockets as the *Vandalia* climbed a wave, faltered, and sped into the hollow. Far removed from her pivot of gravity, the wireless house behaved after the manner of an express elevator. But the wireless house chair was bolted to the floor.

Wrinkles of perplexity creased his forehead. Had this stuttering static anything in kind with those other formless events? If not, what terrified creature was invoking his aid in this blundering fashion?

A simple test would prove if the signals were of local origin—from a miniature apparatus aboard the ship. He hoped anxiously for the opportunity. And in less than a half hour the opportunity was given him.

A tarred line scraped the white belly of the life-boat which swelled up from the deck outside the door, giving forth a dull, crunching sound with each convulsion of the engines. The square area above it danced with reeling stars, moiled by a purple-black heaven.

Peter, who had been studying the tarred rope, swung about in the chair and dropped an agitated finger to the silvered wire which rested against the glittering detector crystal. A tiny, blue-red flame snapped from his finger to the crystal chip! The frantic operator was aboard the *Vandalia*!

The broken stridulations took on the coherence of intelligible dots and dashes. The former blundering was absent, as if the tremulous hand of the sender was steadied by the grip of a dominant necessity; the signals clarified by the pressure of terror.

"*Do not try to find me,*" it stammered and halted.

Some maddened pulse seemed to leap to life in Peter's throat. His fingers, working at the base of the tiny instrument, were cold and damp.

"*You must wait,*" rasped the unknown sender, faltering. "*You must help me! You are watched.*"

For a breath there was no sound in the receivers other than the beating of his heart.

Click! Snap! Sputter! Then: "*Wait for the lights of China!*"

The receivers rattled to the red blotter, and Peter rushed out on deck. Slamming the door, he stared at the spurting streams of white in the racing water. Indescribably feminine was the fumbling touch of that unknown sender!

A grating—hollow, metallic—occurred in the lee of the wireless cabin. A footfall sounded, coincident with the heavy collision into his side of an unwieldy figure whose hands, greasy and hot, groped over his. Both grunted.

"'Sthat you, Sparks?" They were the German gutturals of Luffberg, one of the oilers on the twelve-to-six watch. "Been fixin' the ventilator. Chief wondered if you were up. Wants to know why you ain't been down to say hello."

Peter decided to lay a portion of his difficulties before Minion.

CHAPTER VI

The first operator had developed for himself at an early stage of his occupancy of the *Vandalia's* wireless house the warm friendship of the chief engineer. A wireless man is far more dependent for his peace of mind upon the engine-room crew than upon the forward crew. The latter has only one interest in him: that he stick to his instruments; while the engine-room crew strictly is the source from which his blessings flow, his blessings taking the invisible, vital form of electric current.

Wireless machines are gourmands of electricity. They are wastrels. Not one-tenth of the energy sucked from the ship's power wires finds its way through the maze of coils and jars to the antennae between the mastheads.

The *Vandalia's* engine-room equipment was installed long before wireless telegraphy was a maritime need and a government requirement. Hence, her dynamos protested vigorously against the strain imposed upon them by the radio machine. Any electric engine is unlike any steam engine. Steam engines will do so much work—no more. Dynamos or motors will do so much work—and then more. They can be overloaded, unsparingly. But the strain tells. Stout, dependable parts become hot, wear away, crumble, snap.

In the typical case of the *Vandalia*, the question of whether or not the wireless men should be provided with all of the current they required, was narrowed down to individuals.

If Minion had disliked Peter Moore he could have slowed down the dynamos at the critical times when the operator needed the high voltage; but Peter had had encounters with chief engineers before. He had at first courted Minion's good graces with fair cigars, radio gossip and unflagging courtesy. And on discovering that the chief was a sentimentalist at heart and a poet by nature, he had presented him with an inexpensively bound volume of his favorite author. Daring, but a master-stroke! He had not since wanted for voltage, and plenty of it.

He pondered the advisability of taking Minion entirely into his confidence as he followed the sweated, undershirted shoulders to the engine-room galley, and thence across the oily grill of shining steel bars which comprised one of the numerous and hazardous superfloors which surrounded the cylinders.

Minion was nursing a stubbornly warm bearing in the port shaft alley.

The fat cylinder revolved with a pleasant ringing noise, the blurring knuckles of the frequent joints vanishing down the yellow, vaulted alley to a point of perspective, where the shaft projected through the hull. The floundering of the great propellers seemed alternately to compress and expand the damp atmosphere.

The sad, white face of Minion arose from the dripping flanks of the journal as he caught sight of Peter in the arched entrance. A pale smile flickered at his lips.

The chief did not in any wise reflect his monstrously heaving, oil-dripping surroundings. He was a small, deliberate man, with oceans of repressed energies. His skin had the waxy whiteness of a pond lily. An exquisitely trimmed black moustache adorned his mouth. The deep brown eyes of a visionary rested beneath the gentle, scythe-like curves of thin and pointed eyebrows.

"You look worried," vouchsafed Minion as their hands met. His quiet voice had a clarity which projected it nicely through the bedlam of engine-room noises. "Why you up so early—or so late? Anything wrong?"

Peter took out a cigarette and nervously lighted it at the sputtering flame Minion held for him. "Mr. Minion, something's in the wind," he complained, and hesitated. He was at the verge of telling what he had seen on the promenade deck, of the confusion on the pierhead, of the unaccountable behavior of the woman in the window above Ah Sih King's, of the suspicious attitude of Blanchard, of the recent plea for help. Again something checked him.

"Mr. Minion, what is Len Yang? And where is it?"

The scythe-like brows contracted. Minion's lucid, brown eyes rested on his lips, seeming to await an elaboration of the query. His features suddenly had stiffened. His whole attitude appeared on the moment to have undergone a change, from one of friendly interest to a keen defensiveness.

"Len Yang is a city in China. Why?"

The operator suspected that Minion was sparring for time.

"Where is Len Yang?"

"Do you mean, how does one reach Len Yang?"

"Either."

"Mr. Moore"—the suspicion fell from the chief's expression, leaving it calm and grave—"you are not an amateur. You have discretion. The man who controls Len Yang is the *Vandalia's* owner."

"Why, I understood the Pacific and Western Atlantic Transport Line owned her!"

"This man—he is a Chinese. Oh, I've never seen him, Mr. Moore. One of the richest of China's unknown aristocrats, the central power of the cinnabar ring. You have never gone up the river with us to load at Soo-chow?"

Peter shook his head. "Cinnabar from his mine is brought down the Yangtze on junks and transferred at Soo-chow?"

Minion seemed not to be listening. His eyes were stagnant with an appalling retrospect. "A terrible place—horrible! Five years ago I visited Len

Yang. Hideous people with staring eyes, dripping the blood-red slime of the mines! And girls! Young girls! Beautiful—for a while." He sighed. "They work in that vicious hole!"

"Young girls?" Peter exclaimed.

"Imported. From everywhere. I tried to find why. There is no explanation. They come—they work—they become hideous—they die! It is his habit. No one understands. Poor things!"

Peter was staring at him narrowly. "Quite sure he imports them to work in the mines?"

Minion nodded vehemently. "I made sure of that. I went up the river as *his* guest. Trouble with the seepage pumps. Hundreds of them drowned like rats. Len Yang is near the trade route into India. Leprosy—filth—vermin! God! You should have seen the rats! Monsters! They eat them. Poor devils! And live in holes carved out of the ruby mud."

He tore the clump of waste from his left hand and ground it under his heel.

"And in the center of this frightfulness—his palace! Snow-white marble, whiter than the Taj by moonlight. But its base is stained red, a creeping blood-red from the cinnabar. Damn him!"

"No escape?" Peter muttered.

"Escape!" Minion shouted. "*Dang hsin*! They call him the Gray Dragon. He reaches over every part of Asia. That is no exaggeration. Take my advice, Mr. Moore, if you have stumbled upon one of his schemes—*ni chü bà*—don't meddle!"

The white face writhed, and for a new reason Peter smothered the impulse to tell the agitated Minion what he had seen. Their conversation drifted to general shipboard matters. When he left he borrowed the chief engineer's master key on the excuse that he had locked himself out of the wireless cabin.

Besides a stiffening head wind the ship was now laboring into piling head seas. Far beyond the refulgence of the scattered lights stars shone palely. Flecks of streaming white were making their appearance at the toppling wave crests.

A hail of stinging spray, flung inboard by a long gust, struck Peter's face sharply as he struggled forward, rattling like small shot against the vizor of his cap and smarting his eyes. The needle-like drops were icy cold. The elastic fabric of the *Vandalia* shivered, her broad nose sinking into a succession of black mountains. Peak gutters roared as the cascading water was sucked back to the untiring surface.

Gaining the cross entrance, he braced his strength against the forces of wind which imprisoned the door, and crept down the passage.

His heart pounded as his groping fingers outlined the cold iron numerals on the panel. Nervously, he inserted the master key into the door lock, and paused to listen.

Rhythmic snoring moaned from an opened transom near by. What other night sounds might have been abroad were engulfed by the imminent throbbing in the engine-room well.

Stateroom forty-four's transom was closed. The lock yielded. The door yawned soundlessly. A round, portentous eye glimmered on the opposite wall. An odor of recently wet paint and of new bed linen met him. The excited pulsing of his heart outsounded the engines.

He shut the door cautiously, not to awake the occupants of the berths, and fancied he could again hear the warning sibilance of the whisper, but in sleep, perhaps drawn through unconscious lips.

Eagerly, his hand slipped over the enameled wall and found the electric switch. Turning, to cover all corners of the stateroom he snapped on the light.

Stateroom forty-four, through whose doorway he could have sworn to have seen a sandaled foot vanish less than three hours previous, was empty!

The blue-flowered side curtains of the white enameled bunks were draped back in ornamental stiffness. Below the pillows the upper sheets were neatly furled like incoming billows on a coral beach. He threw open the closet door. Bare! Not one sign of occupancy could he find, and he looked everywhere.

As he made to leave the room a small oblong of white paper was thrust under the door. He hesitated in surprise, stooped to seize it and flung open the door. A gust of night, wind—the slamming of a door—and the messenger was gone.

Tremblingly, he unfolded the paper. His eyes dilated. Hastily scrawled in the lower right-hand corner of the otherwise blank leaf was a replica of the blurred sign that had caused such consternation on the part of Lo Ong.

The ideograph had twice been brought to his attention. It was apparently a solemn warning. Should he heed it? He felt that he was watched. But the porthole glowed emptily.

Lighting a cigarette, he dropped down to the bunk, cupped his chin in his palms, and frowned at the green carpet.

He was being frustrated, by persons of adroit cunning. It was maddening. This had ceased to be an adventurous lark. It was to become a fight against weapons whose sole object seemed to be to guard the retreat of some evil spirit.

It occurred to him suddenly that he should be grateful upon one score at least: He had not lost the trail, for the symbols were unchanged.

But from that point the trail vanished—vanished as abruptly as if its design had been wiped off the earth! Sharp eyed and eared, alertness night after night availed him nothing. And not until the twinkling lights of Nagasaki were put astern, when the *Vandalia* turned her nose into the swollen bed of the Yellow Sea, did the traces again show faintly.

CHAPTER VII

That a recrudescence of those involved in the murky affair might be imminent was the thought induced in Peter's mind as the green coast of Japan heaved over the horizon. With each thrust of the *Vandalia's* screws the cipher was nearing its solution. Each cylinder throb narrowed the distance to the shore lights of China—the lights of Tsung-min Island. And then—what?

In a corner of the smoking-room he puffed at his cigarette and watched the poker players as he drummed absently upon the square of green cork inlaid in the corner table. The vermilion glow of the skylight dimmed and died. Lights came on. A clanging cymbal in the energetic hands of a deck steward boomed at the doorway, withdrew and gave up its life in a far away, tinny clatter.

The petulant voice of a hardware salesman, who was secretly known to represent American moneyed interests in Mongolia, drifted through the haze of tobacco smoke at the poker table.

"—that's what I'd like to know. Damn nonsense—saving steam, probably—off Wu-Sung before midnight—if—wanted to throw in a little coal—means I miss the river boat tomorrow—not another—Saturday. Dammit!"

Peter drew long at the cigarette and glanced thoughtfully at the oak-paneled ceiling. Chips clicked. The petulant voice continued:

"—rottenest luck ever had." Evidently he was referring to his losses. "Rotten line—rottener service—miss my man—Mukden—" The voice ceased as its owner half turned his head, magnetized by the intentness of the operator's gaze. Peter glanced away. The salesman devoted himself to the dealer.

The *Vandalia* was bearing into a thin mist. The night was cool, quiet. Had he been on deck Peter would have seen the last lights of Osezaki engulfed as if at the dropping of a curtain.

During the voyage he had haunted the smoking-room, hoping that by dint of patient listening he might catch an informative word dropped carelessly by one of the players. No such luck. The players were out-of-season tourists, bound for South China or India, or salesmen, patiently immersed in the long and strenuous task of killing time.

"—thirty—thirty-five—forty—forty-five—" The fat man was counting his losings.

Faint, padded footsteps passed the port doorway. Peter became aware of an elusive perfume—scented rice powder—

"—seventy-five—eighty—eighty-five—ninety—"

A pale, malignant face was framed momentarily in one of the starboard windows.

Peter blinked, then bounded after. The salesman impeded his progress and grudgingly gave way.

The deck was empty, slippery with the wet of the mist. He was suddenly aware that one of the ports, in the neighborhood of the stateroom he had entered, was ajar. Nervously he halted, gasping as a long, trembling hand, at the extremity of a spectral wrist, plucked at his sleeve. Blanched as an arm of the adolescent moon, it fumbled weakly at his clutching fingers—and was swiftly withdrawn!

The staring eyes of a white, gibbous face sank back from the hole. Below the nose the face seemed not to exist.

Its horror wrapped an icy cord about his heart. He plunged his arm to the shoulder through the round opening, struck a yielding, warm body; descending claws steeled about his wrist and deliberately forced him back.

The brass-bound glass squeezed on his fingers. He wrenched them free, crushed, throbbing, and warmly wet. The anguish seemed to extend to his elbow. Then, suddenly, the gruff, seasoned voice of Captain Jones descended from space behind him. "Sparks, come to my cabin."

Peter followed the brutish shoulders to the forward companionway, endeavoring to clarify his thoughts. Mild confusion prevailed when Captain Jones closed and locked the door of his spacious stateroom behind them and dropped heavily into one of the cumbersome teak chairs.

He was a hardened, brawny chunk of a man, choleric in aspect and temperament, brutal in method, bluntly decisive in opinion. Iron was his metal. "Starboard Jones" was one of the few living men who had successfully run the Jap blockade into Vladivostok during that bloody tiff between the black bear and the island panther.

Reddened sockets displayed keen, blue eyes in a background of perpetual fire. His large, swollen nose had a vinous tint, acquiring purplishness in cold weather. Tiny red veins, as numerous as the cracks in Satsuma-ware, spread across both cheeks in a carmine filigree.

His cabin was ornamented chiefly by hand-tinted photographs from the yoshiwaras of Nagasaki, of simpering, coy geishas. Souvenirs of their trade, glittering fans, nicked teacups, flimsy sandals, adorned the available shelf room. Cigars as brawny and black as if their maker had striven to emulate the captain's own bulk were scattered among papers on his narrow desk.

He reached clumsily for one of these brown cylinders now, neglecting to remove his glance of gloating austerity from the operator's tense face.

"Haven't seen much of you lately, Sparks," he observed, applying a steady match flame to the oval butt. He spoke in his usual tones, with a gruffness that balanced on a razor edge between rough jocularity and official harshness. "What's new? Have one of my ropes?"

Peter studied the glowing end narrowly. "Had a little trouble first night out. No, thanks. Not smoking tonight." His bruised finger-tips were curved up tenderly in his coat pocket.

"What's 'at?" The steel eyes were motionless beneath half-lowered lids.

"Some one used an electric machine. Jammed my signals."

The choleric face dipped knowingly. What Captain Jones did not comprehend he invariably pretended to comprehend. "Noticed anything else?" His ruddy face was now weighty with significance.

Peter sat up abruptly. "What!"

A thick, red forefinger threatened, "Lis'n to me, Sparks, you're a overgrown, blundering bull in a china-shop. You're—"

"Well?" There was a trace of anger in Peter's suave inquiry. His face became stony white. A spot of color appeared at either cheek.

"I mean: Keep your damn nose out of what don't concern you. Savvy?" The heated words spilled thickly from the captain's red lips. "I mean: Butt out of what concerns Chinese women and—and—other words, mind your own particular damn business! Duty on this ship's to mind the radio. What goes on outside your shanty's none of your damn concern!" Captain Jones' mouth remained open, and the butt of the black cigar slid into it.

Peter raised a restraining hand. His lips trembled. His eyes seemed to snap in a rapid fire between the eyes and mouth of the big man slouched down in the chair in front of him. "Wait a minute," he spat out. "Since you do know that somebody is being kidnapped on this ship—"

"What in hell do you mean?"

"Exactly what I say. A Chinese woman, no matter who she is—is hiding some one, a woman, somewhere on this ship. That woman—that woman who's being held—grabbed my hand not five minutes ago. It's your duty—"

"Keep your hands where they belong. You're talking like a fool. Kidnapped? You're crazy. My duty? You're a fool! You're talking baby talk." Captain Jones sprang from his chair. "You're on this ship to tend the wireless," he bawled. "You're under oath to keep your mouth shut. Any one back there?"

"No!"

"Don't you know it breaks a government rule when that room's empty—at sea?"

The mist-laden wind shrilled through the screen door abruptly thrust back. Captain Jones slammed the stout inner door. Peter turned up his coat collar, bound a clean handkerchief about his aching fingers, climbed agilely over the life-rafts, passed the roaring, black funnels, and entered the wireless house.

The low, intermingling whine of Jap stations was broken by an insistent P. and O. liner, yapping for attention. Shanghai stiffly droned a reply, advising the P. and O. man to sweeten his spark.

Peter tapped his detector and grunted. Shanghai was loud—close! The *Vandalia* must be nearing the delta.

"—Nanking Road. Stop. Forty casks of soey—" yelped the P. and O.

Nearing the great river! Out of the mist a faint blur would come—the first lights of China!

"—Thirteen cases of tin—" The P. and O.'s spark remained unsweetened.

Would the lights be Hi-Tai-Sha—Tsung-min?—port or starboard?

Far below decks a bell jangled faintly. The throbbing of the engines was suddenly hushed. The bell sounded distantly, through a portentous silence. Peter glanced at the clock. Half-past twelve.

The silence was shattered by a turbulent, stern lifting rumble as the screws reversed. The *Vandalia* wallowed heavily, and lay with the yellow tide.

Extinguishing the lights, Peter slipped out on deck, leaned over the edge, and peered into the murk. His heart pumped nervously.

At first all was blank. Then a misty, gray-white glow seemed to swim far to port. Murkily, it took form, vanished, reappeared and—was swallowed up again.

But these were not the lights of Tsung-min. The ship was in the river. He knew those lights well. Even now the *Vandalia*, was slipping down with the current abreast of Woo-Sung! The first lights of China! But what was happening? He dashed to the starboard side.

Out of the mist there arose a tall, gaunt specter. A junk. Perhaps a collision was decreed by the evil spirit of the Whang-poo. But the usual shriekings of doomed river men were absent. The gray bulk floated idly with the steamer. The silence of death permeated both craft.

At a loss to account for this queer coincidence, this mute communion, Peter elbowed over the edge, dangerously high above the water, and slid down a stanchion to the promenade deck.

Simultaneously every light on that side of the ship was extinguished. As his feet struck the metal gutter, several unseen bodies rushed past him, aft.

He was grabbed from behind and hurled to the deck. Springing up, he heard the thick breathing of his unknown assailant. He lunged for the sound, met flying fists, smashed his man against the rail. The blow knocked the wind from his antagonist, or broke his back.

Peter did not pause to make inquiries. As the limp body thudded to the wood, the operator sprinted after the vanished figures.

A lone light on the after spur illumined a dim confusion in the cargo well. The stern of the junk was backed against the rail. Oars flashed faintly as the crew of the junk strove to keep her fast against the steamer's side. But where was the crew of the *Vandalia*? Had Captain Jones consented to and perhaps aided in this mid-river tryst?

Another source of illumination sprang into being. A dong was burning yellowly on the junk's poop deck, casting a plenitude of light upon the scene.

As Peter dropped down the precipitous ladder into the well, he made out two figures struggling against the rail. From the junk, imploringly, a giant Chinese with pigtail flapping held out his long arms. Silent, his face was writhing with the supplication to hurry.

Peter drove in between the two figures, one of which suddenly collapsed and lay inert. The other sprang at his neck, sinking long claws into his throat. Slit eyes glinted close. Before his wind was shut off he caught the oppressive fragrance of a heavy perfume. A woman!

He struck the clawing hands loose, and she stemmed a scream between convulsing lips. The woman above Ah Sih King's!

He hurled her back, and she staggered against the iron flank of the well. A chatter of Chinese broke from her lips. Shaking, she extracted an envelope from her satin blouse and pressed it into his hands. Thoughtlessly he stuffed the envelope into his pocket, not reckoning what it might contain.

The junk swung out, closed in with a smart smack, and the giant on her deck crouched to spring. He squealed, a high-pitched ululation of anger. Another sound was abroad, the jangling of the engine-room bell.

Peter struck down the groping hands of the woman and sprang to the rail, bracing his feet on the smooth iron deck-plate as the Chinese leaped. A knife glinted. Peter seized a horny wrist with both hands, bent, and wrenched it. The knife struck the water with a sibilant splash. The *fokie* lost his balance. His legs became entangled.

He gibbered with horror as he slipped—slipped—

The Chinese woman sprang at Peter with the frenzy of a pantheress.

A weltering splash—Peter dimly saw the bobbing head before it was driven below the surface as the junk, yawing in, crowded the swimmer down.

A life? Nothing to the turgid river, draining all effluvia from the yellow heart of this festering land.

With a hissing sob, the woman drove Peter backward, raining blow after blow on his chest. The engines pounded briskly. A boom rattled. Despairingly, Peter's antagonist shifted her tactics, surprised him by flinging herself to the rail.

The junk was veering away as the *Vandalia's* blades took hold.

She poised on the top rail, drew herself together, and leaped!

The junk slid into the mist.

CHAPTER VIII

Peter was conscious of a hot stickiness at his throat where the claws had taken hold. Then he concerned himself with the gray shape that lay quite still on the iron deck at his feet. New enemies from other quarters, he realized, might strike at any instant.

Gathering up the limp form, he climbed the ladder to the darkened promenade deck and up another flight through the tarpaulin cover to the boat-deck. Opening the wireless-house door, he deposited his burden gently upon the carpet, and switched on the light. Then he turned the key in the lock, and examined his find. A long, gray bag of some heavy material swathed the small figure from head to foot. There was no sign of life.

Yelping arose from the river. It was still dark. The sampan coolies were out early. Peter listened, becoming thoughtful as a solution seemed to present itself to his problem.

He went out on deck and beckoned to one of them to stand by.

A swaying coolie in the stern of the nearest craft caught sight of him.

"Hie! Hie!" The wagging paddle became mad. The sampan slipped under the towering shadow and brought up with a smack against the moving black hull.

Peter pried up the tarpaulin life-boat cover, dragged out a coil of dirty rope, made one end fast at the foot of the davit, and tossed the other end overside. The coolie caught it and clung.

Re-entering the wireless cabin, Peter opened his pocket-knife and slit the cord at the head.

A mass of curly, brown hair flowed out upon the carpet. There was a silken lisp of underskirts. A faint sigh.

Peter suddenly turned his head. Black, glassy eyes were riveted upon his from the after window. They vanished.

He jumped up, bolted to the deck, and stood still, listening.

The scuffle of a foot sounded on the port side. Some one was running forward. He plunged after. The footsteps stopped sharply coincident with a dull smash, a frantic grunt. The pursued reeled to the deck, groaning.

Peter pounced upon him, grabbed his collar, and dragged him across the deck into the wireless house.

"Mr. Moore, the captain told me—" whimpered Dale.

Peter knocked him into the chair, opened the toolbox, and extracted a length of phosphor-bronze aerial wire. Binding the wiggling arms to the chair, he made the ends fast behind.

Snapping out the lights, he gathered the gray bag into his arms and deposited it on the deck in the narrow space between the life-boat and the edge. He looked down. The coolie was staring up, clinging to the rope, waiting.

The bag slipped down half-way. A warm moist hand clutched at his wrist. A faint moan issued from the unseen lips. He jerked again. The bag came away free, and he tossed it overboard. The yellow current snatched it instantly from sight.

The hand clung desperately at his wrist. "Don't let them—" began a sweet voice in his ear.

He wrapped his legs around the rope and worked his way over the edge. "Arms around my neck!" he commanded hoarsely. "Hold tight!"

Soft arms enfolded him. They dangled at the edge.

The coarse rope slipped swiftly through his fingers, scorching the palms, seeming to rake at the bones in his hand.

A wild shout came from the wireless house. An echo, forward, answered.

They slipped, twisting, scraping, down the rough strand. His hands seemed hot enough to burst. Maddened blood throbbed at his eyes, his ears, and dried his throat. Dimmed lights of the promenade deck soared upward. A glimmering port-hole followed.

For an eternity they dangled, then shot downward.

Something popped in Peter's ears. His feet struck a yielding deck. He staggered backward, sprawled. The rope was whipped from his hand. The warm arms still clung about his neck.

As the world wheeled, a drunken universe, a sullen voice yelped at his ear. The arms loosened.

The *Vandalia* twinkled closely and was swept into the mist, a blur, a phantom. His hands blazed with infernal fire.

He sat up and looked behind him. The river was murderously dark. Water gurgled under the flimsy bow. The dull tread of feet and a watery flailing behind him advised Peter that the coolie was struggling against the rushing current.

Slowly he became conscious of a weight upon his breast, a low sobbing. A delicate, feminine odor brought him to earth, unraveled his tangled wits.

He was sitting upon the wet floor of the sampan's low cabin. His captive had crept close to him for protection. Protection! He snorted, wondering if the coolie was licensed.

"Hai! Hai! Woo-Sung way." The voice was villainously stubborn.

"Shanghai-way. *Kuai cho*—hurry!" roared Peter. A sigh escaped from the girl. She snuggled closer. "Woo-Sung. *Pu-shih*! Savvy?"

"Hai! Mebbe can do." The sampan reared, braving the direct onslaught of the Whang-poo's swift tide.

A myriad of questions in his brain strove for utterance. But the girl spoke first.

"Who are you?" she whispered. "I am Eileen Lorimer."

"I am—I was the wireless operator of the *Vandalia*."

The coolie paused a moment for breath, then the mad plunging of the paddle sounded again.

"The wireless operator? You heard my call?"

"Been waiting for China's lights—ever since. But how—what?" he demanded.

She was silent a moment. "I know the code. My brother owned a private station. We lived in Pasadena—ages ago. It does seem ages." She stirred feebly. "You don't mind?"

"No, no," he protested.

"I am afraid—such a long time. Weeks? Years?" She shuddered. "I do not know. Oh—I want to go home!"

The coolie broke into a working sing-song as he struggled. The tide should shift before long.

"Were you in the loft above Ah Sih King's?"

"Roped! I broke loose."

"The red note?"

"I scribbled with a nail, and threw it before she knocked me down. That woman was a demon!"

A pale, yellow glow seemed to body forth from the enshrouding mist. Dawn was breaking. Soon the great river would be alight.

"School-teacher," the girl was murmuring. "A wedding present for her—in Ah Sih King's." A small hand fumbled for his, and found it. "In the back room they began gibbering at me. And this demon came. Meaningless words—Ah Sih King leered. Called me the luckiest woman in China."

"But how did you know?"

An empty freighter with propellers flailing half out of water pounded through the yellow mist close to them.

"Hie! Hie!" shrilled the coolie's warning.

Light seeped through the doorway. The outlines of a dark skirt were silhouetted against the scrubbed white floor.

"He said when I saw the lights of China I would go aboard a beautiful ship. She was watching you. Three times our stateroom was changed. Always at night."

"You used a coil?" Peter was professionally interested on this point.

The girl murmured affirmatively. "She had some affliction. A San Francisco doctor said the electric machine would cure it. And I pretended to use it, too. But it broke down that night."

The yellow light grew stronger. Equipment of the cabin emerged: a crock of rice and fish, a corked jug, a bundle of crude chop-sticks bound with frayed twine, a dark mess of boiled sea-weed on a greasy slab.

He looked down. The girl moved her head. Their eyes met.

Timid, gray ones with innocent candor searched him. Shining dark hair rippled down either side of a pale, lovely face. She was younger than he had expected, more beautiful than he had hoped. Her rosebud of a mouth trembled in the overtures of a smile.

His feelings were divided between admiration for her and horror—she had escaped so narrowly. In the realization of that moment Peter shaped his course. His following thought was of finances.

He brought to light a handful of change. Less than one dollar, disregarding four twenty-cent Hu-Peh pieces; hardly enough to pay off the sampan coolie.

His charge sighed helplessly, thereby clinching his resolution. "I haven't a penny," she said.

He explored the side-pocket of his coat, hoping against fact that he had not changed his bill-fold to his grip. His fingers encountered an unfamiliar object.

The struggling pantheress flashed into his mind. And the wrinkled envelope she had drawn from her satin jacket and pressed into his hand. Past dealings with Chinese gave him the inkling that he had been unknowingly bribed.

A scarlet stamp, a monograph, was imposed in the upper right corner of the pale blue oblong.

"Money—Chinese bills. Full of them!" Miss Lorimer gasped. "I saw it. What are they for? And why did that dreadful woman—"

"Jet-t-e-e-ee!" sang the coolie, swinging the oar hard over. The sampan grated against a landing. "Shanghai. *Ma-tou*! *Hān liang bu dung yāng che lāi*!"

Peter was counting the pack. "Fifty one-thousand-dollar Bank of China bills!"

Excited yelpings occurred on the *ma-tou*. The rickshaw coolies were dickering for their unseen fare.

Peter tossed the sampan boy all the coins he had, and left him to gibber over them as he lifted the girl to the jetty. She clung to his arm, trembling, as the coolies formed a grinning, shouting circle about them. More raced in from the muddy bund.

"What are we going to do?" she groaned.

"We are going to cable your mother that you are starting for home by the first steamer," Peter cried, swinging her into the cleanest and most comfortable rickshaw of the lot. "The *Mongolia* sails this afternoon."

"What will become of you?" she demanded.

Peter gave her his ingenuous smile. "I will vanish—for a while. Otherwise I may vanish—permanently."

Miss Lorimer reached out with her small white hand and touched his sleeve. They were jouncing over the Su-Chow bridge, on their way to the American Consulate. "Won't I see you again? Ever?" She looked bewildered and lost, as if this strange old land had proved too much for her powers of readjustment. Her rosebud mouth seemed to quiver. "Are you in danger, Mr. Moore?"

Peter glimpsed a very yellow, supercilious face swinging in his direction from the padding throng.

"A little, perhaps," he conceded.

"Because of me?"

The yellow face reappeared and was swallowed again by the crowd, as a speck of mud is engulfed by the Yangtze.

Miss Lorimer repeated her question. Peter shook his head in an extravagant denial, and helped her down from the rickshaw. They had stopped before the consulate in the American quarter.

"I'm leaving you here," he said.

"But—but I like you!" her small voice faltered. "Aren't you going to explain—anything? Is this—is this all?"

Peter smothered his rising feelings under an air of important haste. "Your way lies there"—he pointed down river. "For the present mine lies here"—and he jerked a thumb in the general direction of Shanghai's narrow muddy alleys.

"Shall I—won't you—gracious!" Miss Lorimer stared into her left hand. Two one-thousand-dollar Bank of China bills were folded upon it. She was confused. When she looked back the young man who had miraculously delivered her from an unguessable fate had been spirited with Oriental magic from her sight.

CHAPTER IX

The bund of Shanghai was striped with the long, purple shadows of coming night, a night which seemed to be creeping out of the heart of the land, ushering with it a feeling of subtle tension, as though the touch of darkness stirred to wakefulness a populace of shadows, which skulked and crouched and whispered, comprising an underworld of sinister folk which the first glow of dawn would send scampering back to a thousand evil-smelling hiding-places.

The rhythmic chant of coolies on the river ended. Mammoth go-downs, where the products of China flowed on their way to distant countries, became gloomily silent and empty. Handsome, tall sikhs, the police of the city, appeared in twos and threes where only one had been stationed before; for in China, as elsewhere, wickedness is borne on the night's wings.

With the descent of the velvety darkness the late wireless operator of the transpacific greyhound, the *Vandalia*, slipped out of an obscure, shadowy doorway on Nanking Road and directed his steps toward the glittering bund, where he was reasonably sure his enemies would have difficulty in recognizing him.

Peter's uniform now reposed on a dark shelf in the rear of a silkshop. He had no desire to be stabbed in the back, which was a probability in case certain up-river men should find him. The Chinese gentleman who conducted the silkshop was an old friend, and trustworthy.

Peter now wore the garb of a Japanese merchant. His feet were sandaled. His straight, lithe figure was robed in an expensive gray silk kimono. Jammed tight to his ears, in good Nipponese fashion, was a black American derby. His eyebrows were penciled in a fairly praiseworthy attempt to reproduce the Celestial slant, and he carried a light bamboo cane.

Yet the ex-operator of the *Vandalia* was not altogether sure that the disguise was a success. If the scowling yellow face he had detected among the throngs on the bund that morning should have followed him to the silk-shop, of what earthly use was this silly disguise?

He padded along in the lee of a money-changer's, keeping close to the wall. By degrees he became aware that he was followed; and he endeavored to credit the feeling to imagination, to raw nerves. A ghostly rickshaw flitted by. The soft chugging of the coolie's bare feet became faint, ceased. A muttering old woman waddled past.

He looked behind him in time to see a gaunt face, lighted by the dim glow of a shop window, bob out of sight into a doorway. Turning again a moment later, he saw the man dive into another doorway.

Peter ran to the dark aperture, seized a muscular, satin-covered arm, and dragged a whispering Chinese, a big, brawny fellow, into the circular zone of the yellow street-light. Quickly recovering from his surprise, the Chinese reached swiftly toward his belt. Peter, hoping that only one man had been set on his trail, gave a murderous yell, and at the same time drove his fist into a yielding paunch.

With a groan the Chinese staggered back against the shop window, caving in a pane with his elbow. Peter raised his fist to strike again.

Then a monumental figure, with a clean turban coiled about his head, strode austerely into the circle of yellow light.

"*Ta dzoh shēn mō szi?*"

"Thief," said Moore simply, indicating the broken shop window.

"Lāo shēn lāo shēn!" growled the sikh. He seized the luckless window-breaker by both shoulders, backed him against an iron trolley-post, and strapped him to it.

With a jovial, "Allah be with you!" Peter Moore continued his stroll toward the bund. Now that the trailer was out of his way for the night at least, he could make his way in peace to the Palace bar and find out what might be in the wind for him.

As he crossed Nanking Road where it joined the bund, a frantic shout, mingled with a scream of fear or of warning, impelled him to leap out of the path of a rickshaw which was making for him at a breakneck speed. A white face, with a slender gloved hand clutched close to the lips, swept past.

Peter gasped in surprise quite as staggering as if the girl in the rickshaw had slapped him across the face. He shouted after her. But she went right on, without turning.

"Licksha?" A grinning coolie dropped the shafts of an empty rickshaw at Peter Moore's heels.

He ceased being angry as a softer glow crept into his veins. The rickshaw turned to the right, following the other, which occupied the center of the almost deserted bund, and speeding like the wind.

"*Ní chü bà!*" shouted Peter Moore. The girl seemed to be headed for the bund bridge. But why? A number of questions stormed futilely in his brain. Why had the girl ignored him? Why had she not gone aboard the *Manchuria*, as she had promised?

The coolie joggled along, his naked legs rising and falling mechanically. The wireless operator drew the folds of the kimono more closely about his throat, for the night air blowing off the Whang-poo was chill and damp.

At the bridge the rickshaw ahead suddenly stopped, waiting. Peter Moore drew alongside, and leaped to the ground.

The near-by street-light afforded him the information that he had made a mistake. Undeniably similar to the girl he had sent away on the *Manchuria* that morning was the young lady in the rickshaw. She had the same white, wistful face, the same alert, appealing eyes, the same rosebud mouth. Any one might have made such a mistake. It was very embarrassing.

"Why are you following me?" she demanded.

"I thought I knew you. I am sorry. I'll go at once."

"No! Wait." Her volte relented. It was a fresh young voice, not indeed unlike that of Miss Lorimer's. She was smiling. "Why are you dressed as a Jap?"

"I am sorry," Peter faltered, retreating. "Mistake. You're not the girl I—I expected. *Sayonara!*"

"*Please* don't run away," said the girl with a soft laugh. "I'm not afraid, or I would have run, instead of waiting, when you followed me. I've just come up from Amoy—alone. And I leave tomorrow for Ching-Fu—alone. You're American!" she murmured. "But why the Jap—disguise? I'm American, too. I used to live in New York, on Riverside Drive. Oh! It must have been ages ago!"

"Why?" asked Peter unguardedly.

"I haven't met one of my countrymen in centuries! And tomorrow I go up the river, 'way beyond Ching-Fu, beyond Szechwan!"

"Bad travelling on the river this time of the year," Peter murmured politely. "She's out of her banks up above Ichang, I have been told."

"Yes," replied the girl sadly. "If I could only have just one evening of fun—a dance or two, maybe—I—I—wouldn't mind half so much. I—I—"

Peter advised himself as follows: I told you so. Aloud he said:

"I believe there's a dance at the Astor Hotel. If we can get a table—"

"Oh, how lovely!" exclaimed the girl. "Do—do you mind very—much?"

"Tickled to death," Peter declared amiably.

CHAPTER X

At a small round table in the end of the room over which hung the orchestra balcony, Peter found himself in the presence of two disarming gray eyes, which drank in every detail of his good-looking young face, including the penciled eyebrows.

Miss Vost—Miss Amy Vost—gave him to understand that she was really grateful for his hospitality, rushed on to assure him that it was not customary for her to meet strange young men as she had met him, and then frankly asked him what he was doing in China. Every time she thought of him her curiosity seemed to trip over the Japanese kimono.

Influenced by his third glass of Japanese champagne, he almost told her the truth. He modified it by saying that he was a wireless operator; that he had missed his ship, and that his plans were to linger in China for a while. He liked China. Liked China very much.

Miss Vost caressed the tip of her nose with a small, pink thumb. She was not the kind who hesitated.

"You can do me a favor," she said, and halted.

The Philippine orchestra burst into a lilting one-step. Miss Vost arched her eyebrows. Peter arose, and they glided off. It developed that Miss Vost was well qualified. There was divineness in her youthful grace; she put her heart into the dance. It seemed probable to Peter Moore that she put her heart into everything she did.

"You spoke about my doing a favor," he suggested, glancing sternly at a dark-eyed Eurasian girl who seemed to be trying to divert his attention.

"There is a man in Shanghai I want you to try to find for me—tonight. Last time I saw him—this morning—he was drunk. He was the first officer on the steamer that brought me up from Amoy. Perhaps you know him. He's only been on the coast a short while. Before that he ran on the Pacific Mail Line between San Francisco and Panama. His name is MacLaurin, a nice boy. Scotch. But he drinks."

"MacLaurin? I know a man named MacLaurin—Bobbie MacLaurin."

"No!" gasped Miss Vost. "I suppose I ought to make that old remark about what a small world it is! Do you know where Bobbie MacLaurin is?"

"No," he murmured. "Why is he drunk?"

"That is a matter," replied Miss Vost, somewhat distantly, "that I prefer not to discuss. Will you try to find him for me? He threatened to be—be captain of the river-boat, the *Hankow*, that I leave on tomorrow for Ching-Fu. I'd rather like to know if he intends to carry out his threat. Will you find out, if you can, if he is going to be sober enough to make the trip—and let me know?" requested Miss Vost, as the music stopped. "I'd rather he wouldn't, Mr. Moore," she added quickly. "But I do wish *you* were going to make the trip. I'd love to have you!"

The ex-operator of the *Vandalia* experienced a warm suffusion in the vicinity of his throat. In the next breath he felt genuinely guilty. As he looked deep into the anxious, appealing gray eyes of Miss Vost, he cursed himself for being, or having the tendencies to be, a trifler; and in his estimation a trifler was not far removed from the reptile class. Yet somehow, damn it, that trip to Ching-Fu on the *Hankow* appealed to him now as a most profitable excursion, for Ching-Fu was only a few hundred li from Len Yang.

Something of the doughtiness of a mongoose marching into a den of monster cobras characterized Peter Moore's intention to penetrate the stronghold of the cinnabar king. He knew that his chances for entering Len Yang were absurdly small. Yet the whole of the Chinese Empire was not particularly safe for him now. The Gray Dragon had paid him the compliment of recognizing in him an enemy. He no longer doubted Minion's warning; the dragon of Len Yang controlled a powerful organization. No part of China was safe. If he desired to run away from this very actual danger in which direction could he run?

"*When menaced by danger,*" runs an old Chinese proverb, "*go to the very heart of it; there you will find safety.*"

It lacked a few minutes of midnight when Peter entered the Palace bar by the bund side. Only a few lights were burning, and the exceedingly long teak bar—"the longest bar east of Suez"—was adorned by a few knots of men only. Tobacco smoke was thick in the place, nearly obscuring the doorway into the hotel lobby.

He scanned the idlers, looking for the cloth of sailormen. His quest was ended. Bobbie MacLaurin was here, disposing of all of the imported Scotch whiskey that came convenient to his long and muscular reach.

In a deep and sonorous voice he was pointing out to a group of uniformed sailors, burdening his point with a club-like forefinger with which he pounded on the edge of the teak bar, that while he rarely drank off duty, he never drank when on. This claim Peter had reason to know was not untrue.

The wireless operator edged his way to MacLaurin's side, and touched his arm, making a whispered remark which the Scotchman evidently did not comprehend. For MacLaurin wheeled on him, and bestowed upon him a red, glassy, and hotly indignant stare.

Bobbie MacLaurin was, in the language of the sea, a whale of a man. His head seemed unnecessarily large until you began to compare it with his body; and his body was the despair of uniform manufacturers, who desire above all things to make a fair percentage of profit. He was like a living monument, two and a half hundred weight of fighting flesh and bones, which, when all of it went into action, could better be compared to a volcano than to a monument. Otherwise he was an exceedingly amiable young giant.

The redness and hotness of the stare he imposed upon the friend of more than one adventurous expedition slowly receded, leaving only the glassiness in evidence. Bobbie fidgeted uneasily.

"Damn my hide!" he roared. "Your face is familiar! It is! It is! Where have I seen that face before? Ah! I know now! I had a fight with you once."

"More than once," corrected Peter Moore, grinning. "The last time was in Panama. Remember? I tripped you up, after you knocked the wind out of me, and you fell, clothes and all, into the Washington Hotel's swimming tank."

"Peter Moore!" gasped Bobbie MacLaurin, and Peter Moore was smothered in log-like arms and the fumes of considerable alcohol.

Extricating himself at length from this monstrous embrace, Peter permitted himself to be held off at arm's length and be warmly and loquaciously admired.

"My old side-kick of the damn old *San Felipe*!" announced Bobbie MacLaurin to the small group of somewhat embarrassed sailors. "The best radio man that God ever let live! He can hear a radio signal before it's been sent. Can't you, Peter? Boys, take a long look at the only livin' man who can fight his weight in sea serpents; the only livin' man who ever knocked me cold, and got away with it! Boys, take a long, lastin' look, for the pack o' you're goin' out o' that door inside of ten counts! God bless 'um! Just look at that there Jap get-up! Sure as God made big fish to eat the little fellows, Peter Moore's up to some newfangled deviltry, or I'm a lobster!"

"Sh!" warned Peter Moore, conscious that in China the walls, doors, floors, ceilings, windows, even the bartenders, have ears.

"Out with the lot of you!" barked MacLaurin. "There's big business afoot tonight. We must be alone. Eh, Peter?"

And Peter was convinced that business could not be talked over tonight. Of one thing only did he wish to be certain.

"You're taking the *Hankow* up-river tomorrow?"

"That I am, Peter!"

"Then we'll take the express for Nanking tomorrow morning."

"Aye—aye! Sir!"

"We'll turn in now. Otherwise you'll look like a wreck when Miss Vost sees you."

"Miss Vost!" exploded MacLaurin. "When did you see Miss Vost?"

"A little while ago, Bob. Shall we turn in now?"

"Miss Vost is why I'm drunk, Peter," said Bobbie MacLaurin sadly.

"So she admitted. Tomorrow we'll talk her over, and other important matters."

"As you say, Peter. I'm the brawn, but you're the brains of this team—as always! The bunks are the order."

When Bobbie MacLaurin's not unmusical snore proceeded from the vast bulk disposed beneath the white bedclothes, Peter Moore again descended to the lobby, let himself into the street, and hailed a rickshaw.

The mist from the Whang-poo had changed to a slanting rain. The bund was a ditch of clay-like mud. Each street light was a halo unto itself.

He lighted a cigarette, suffered the coolie to draw up the clammy oil-skin leg-robe to his waist, and dreamily contemplated the quagmire that was Shanghai.

The rickshaw crossed the Soochow-Creek bridge and drew up, dripping, under the porte-cochère of the Astor House Hotel, where a majestic Indian door-tender emerged from the shadows, bearing a large, opened umbrella.

Contrary to her promise Miss Vost was not waiting for his message. However, she sent back word by the coolie, that she would dress and come down, if he desired her to. Peter pondered a moment. A glimpse of Miss Vost at this time of night meant nothing to him. Or was he hungry for that glimpse? Nonsense!

He dashed off a hasty note, sealed it in an envelope, and gave it to the room-boy to deliver.

He pictured her sleepy surprise as she opened it, and read:

Bobbie seems much put out. We take morning express to Nanking. Try to make it. We'll have tea, the three of us, at Soochow.

At Soochow! There he was—at it again! A trifler.

"Damn my withered-up sense of honor, anyway!" observed Peter Moore to himself, as he climbed into the rain-soaked rickshaw.

CHAPTER XI

With the pristine dawn, Robert MacLaurin arose from his bed like a large, yellow mountain; for his pajamas—every square yard of them—were of fine Canton silk, the color of the bulbous moon when it reposes low on China's horizon.

Satisfying himself at length that the bedroom had another occupant, he drained the contents of a fat, white water-jug, then tossed the jug upon the incumbent of the bedroom's other bed.

At such times as this critical one, the smiling destiny which held the fate of Peter Moore in the hollow of her precious hand was ever watchful, and the white water-jug caromed from his peaceful figure with no more than an unimportant thud. The jug bounded to the floor and ended its career against the hard wall. Peter Moore sat up, rubbing his eyes.

"Dead or alive, Peter?"

"You nearly broke my back."

"Serves you right, old slug-abed! You tucked me in last night with the warning that we pick up the early express for Nanking."

"Quite so," admitted Peter Moore thickly. In the past two days he had managed to set aside altogether four hours for sleep; and he felt that way. He examined his room-mate, but was not surprised at what met his glance.

Bobbie MacLaurin, disregarding the fact that he had not yet shaved, looked as fresh as a rose. His endurance was like that of a range of mountains. His sea-blue eyes were cannily clear, his complexion was transparent and glowing. The ill effects of last night had been absorbed with about as much apparent effort as a gigantic sponge might display in absorbing a dewdrop.

"Chinamen's eyes and Chinamen's knives have been running through my dreams," Peter muttered.

"Cheer up! The pirates are thick above Ichang. We'll both have our bloody necks slit a dozen times before we make Ching-Fu." Bobbie turned from the miniature mirror. His sea-blue eyes glared through a white lake of lather. "Hurry up and shave, you loafer! We'll miss that train."

"I'm not going to shave for six months!"

"Election bet?"

"When your utterly worthless life has been endangered as many times as—"

"What you need is a drink, my lad!"

"When you have evidence that the greatest criminal-at-large wants to have you stuck like a pig—"

MacLaurin swung his big frame about and stared. "You're not serious."

"I am referring to—a Gray Dragon. Ever hear of one?"

The razor in the large, red hand of Bobbie MacLaurin flashed. It came away from his cheek. A broad trickle of crimson spread down the lathered jaw, But he did not curse.

"We must hurry for that train," rumbled his big voice. "We must talk this over. We must hurry, Peter," he said again.

Miss Amy Vost was not in evidence when the two rickshaws rattled up to the platform of the red brick station.

"Perhaps she's waiting for us in the coach, holding seats for us," Peter suggested.

"Just like her," said MacLaurin. "She's a little peach!"

Peter entered the compartment first and scanned the heads. The only tresses in evidence were the long, black, shining ones of a bejeweled Chinese lady. The other passengers were men.

"There will be no tête-à-tête in Soochow," observed Peter Moore to his conscience.

"I'd go to hell for that girl!" declared Bobbie MacLaurin as he sat down at Peter's side. "Now, tell me what you were doing in that Jap rigging. Two years, isn't it, since we were chased out of Panama City by the *spigotties*?"

"I came over on the *Vandalia*."

"And didn't go back, I gather."

"She sailed up-river for Soo-chow yesterday. No, I won't go back. Bobbie, I started something on that ship, and I'm on my way to Ching-Fu—and 'way beyond Ching-Fu—to finish it."

"It will be beautifully finished, Peter! Or your name's not Moore."

"There was a girl, a beautiful girl—"

"There usually is," MacLaurin sighed.

Peter gazed bitterly at the scenery flitting evenly past the window: groves of feathery bamboo, flaming mustard fields, exquisite gardens, and graves—graves beyond count.

"Perhaps she is passing through the Inland Sea by now. Bobbie, I wanted her to go home. She was—she was that kind of a girl. She wanted to stay. Bobbie, that girl could have made a man of me! She—she even told me she—liked me!"

"They have a way of doing that," commented Bobbie sadly.

Several miles rolled by before either of the men spoke.

"Why is Miss Vost making the trip to Ching-Fu?"

"You'll have to find that out, Peter. I was too busy letting her know how bright my life has become since she entered it!"

The square, red jaw swung savagely toward Peter. Of a sudden the sea-blue eyes seemed a trifle inflamed. "She's probably going to Ching-Fu on serious business. She's like that. She's not like you!"

"What do you mean?" said Peter.

"You're going to try to break into Len Yang; that's what I mean! Some day, on one of these reckless expeditions of yours, Peter, you're going to run plumb into a long, sharp knife! If I could head you off, I would."

"You can't, Bobbie. My mind is made up."

"Get out of China. Why enter the lion's den? You're too confiding, too trusting, too young. In duty to my conscience, I oughtn't to let you go. But I know you'd walk or fly or swim if I tried to head you off."

"I certainly would," agreed Peter.

CHAPTER XII

No member of the earth's great brotherhood of dangerous waterways is blessed with quite the degree of peril which menaces those hardy ones who dare the River of the Golden Sands.

Bobbie MacLauren's steamer, the *Hankow*, was the net result of long ship-building experience. Dozens of apparently seaworthy boats have gone up the Yangtze-Kiang, not to return. After years of experiment a somewhat satisfactory river-boat has been evolved. It combines the sturdiness of a sea-going tug with the speed of a torpedo-boat destroyer.

The *Hankow* was ridiculously small, and monstrously strong. Chiefly it consisted of engines and boilers. Despite their security, despite the ship-wrecks and deaths that have been poured into their present design, Yangtze river-boats sink, a goodly crop of them, every season.

But the world of commerce is an arrogant master. There is wealth in the land bordering the upper reaches of the river. This wealth must be brought down to the sea, and scattered to the lands beyond the sea. In return, machinery and tools must be carried back to mine and farm the wealth.

Little is heard, less is told, and still less is written of the men who dare the rapids and the rocks and the sands of the great river. Sometimes the spirit of adventure sends them up the Yangtze. Frequently, as is the case with men who depart unexplainedly upon dangerous errands, a woman is the inspiration, or merely the cause.

Miss Amy Vost, of New York City, but more recently of Amoy, China, province Fu-Kien, was the generator in the case of Bobbie MacLaurin.

When Miss Vost tripped blithely aboard the *Sunyado Maru*, anchored off the breaks of Amoy, and captured, at first blush, the hearts of the entire forward crew, Bobbie MacLaurin was the most eager prisoner of the lot.

Perhaps she took notice of him out of the corner of her glowing young eyes long before he became seriously and mortally afflicted. Certainly the first mate of the *Sunyado Maru* was no believer in the theory of non-resistance.

Had Miss Vost been a susceptible young woman, it is safe to assume that Bobbie MacLaurin would not have accepted command of the *Hankow* from tide-water to that remote Chinese city, Ching-Fu.

He wooed her in the pilot-house—where passengers were never allowed; he courted her in the dining-room; and he paid marked attention to her at all hours of the day and night, in sundry nooks and corners of the generous promenade deck.

Miss Vost sparred with him. As well as being lovely and captivating, she was clever. She seemed to agree with the rule of the philosopher who held that conversation was given to mankind simply for purposes of evasion. By the end of the first week Bobbie MacLaurin was earning sour glances from his staid British captain, and glances not at all encouraging from Miss Vost.

He informed her that all of the beauty and all of the wonder of the stars, the sea, the moonlight, could not equal the splendor of her wide, gray eyes. She replied that the moon, the stars, and the sea had gone to his head.

He insisted that her smile could only be compared to the sunrise on a dewy rose-vine. He threw his big, generous heart at her feet a hundred times. Being fair and sympathetic, she did not kick it to one side. She merely side-stepped.

He closed that evening's interview with the threat that he would follow her to the very ends of the earth. She gave him the opportunity, literally, by observing dryly that her destination was precisely at the world's end—in the hills of Szechuen, to be exact.

He took the breath out of her mouth by saying that he would travel on the same river-boat with her to Ching-Fu, if he had to scrub down decks for his passage. She told him not to be a silly boy; that he was, underneath his uncouthness, really a dear, but that he didn't know women.

When the *Sunyado Maru* dropped anchor off Woo-sung, Miss Vost let Bobbie hold her hand an instant longer than was necessary, and stubbornly refused to accompany him in the same sampan—or the same tug—to the customs jetty. Summarily, she went up the Whang-poo all alone, while Bobbie, biting his finger-nails, purposely quarreled with the staid British captain, and was invited to sign off, which he did.

Through devious subterranean channels Bobbie MacLaurin found that the berth of master on the *Hankow* was vacant, the latest incumbent having relinquished his spirit to cholera. Was he willing to assume the tremendous responsibility? He was tremendously willing! Did he possess good papers? He most assuredly did!

When the Shanghai express rolled into the Nanking station, Bobbie MacLaurin climbed into a rattling rickshaw and clattered off in the direction of the river-front, registering the profound hope that Miss Vost had somehow managed to reach the *Hankow* ahead of him. Peter Moore, who knew China's ancient capital like a book, struck off in a diagonal direction on foot.

He made his way to a Chinese tailor's, who bought from him the Japanese costume and sold him a suit of gray tweeds, which another customer had failed to call for. While not an adornment, the gray tweeds were comfortably European, a relief from the flapping, clumsy kimono.

He wanted to have a little talk with Miss Vost before she saw Bobbie. He had so much affection for Bobbie that he wanted to ask Miss Vost to please not be unnecessarily cruel with him. He did not know that Miss Vost was never unnecessarily cruel to any living creature; for he made the mistake there of classifying all women into the good and the cruel, of which Miss Vost seemed to be among the latter. As a matter of fact, Miss Vost was simply a young woman very far from home, compelled to believe in and on occasion to resort to primitive methods of self-defense.

Peter took a rickshaw to the river. He picked out the *Hankow* among the clutter of shipping, anchored not far from shore, and out of reach of the swift current which rushed dangerously down midchannel. Black smoke issued from her single chubby funnel. Blue-coated coolies sped to and fro on her single narrow deck. Bobbie MacLaurin leaned far out across the rail as Peter's sampan slapped smartly alongside. The coolie thrashed the water into yellowy foam.

"Have you seen Miss Vost?" shouted MacLaurin above the hiss of escaping steam. "We pull out in an hour, Miss Vost or no Miss Vost. That's orders."

Peter, reaching the deck, scanned the pagoda-dotted shore-front. "She'll be here," he said.

Pu-Chang, the *Hankow's* pilot, a slender, grayed Chinese, grown old before his time, in the river service, sidled between them, smiling mistily, and asked his captain if the new tow-line had been delivered. While MacLaurin went to make inquiries, Peter watched a sampan, bow on, floating downstream, with the intention, evidently, of making connections with the *Hankow's* ladder. On her abrupt foredeck was a slim figure of blue and white.

Startled a little by recollection, Peter leaned far out. For a moment he had imagined the white face to be that of Eileen Lorimer. The demure attitude of Miss Vost's hands, caught by the finger-tips before her, gave further grounds to Peter Moore for the comparison. Her youth and innocence had as much to do with it as anything, for there was undeniably an air of youth and extreme innocence about Miss Vost.

Something in the shape of a triumphant bellow was roared from the engine-room companionway. Whereupon the companionway disgorged the monumental figure of Bobbie MacLaurin, grinning like a schoolboy at his first party. He seized Miss Vost by both hands, swinging her neatly to the deck.

She panted and fell back against the rail, holding her hand to her heart, and welcoming Bobbie MacLaurin by a glance that was not entirely cordial.

"The sampan boy hasn't been paid," she remarked, opening her purse. "It's twenty cents."

While MacLaurin pulled a silver dollar from his pocket and spun it to the anxious coolie, Miss Vost turned with the warmest of smiles to Peter. Rarely had any girl seemed more delighted to see him, for which, under the circumstances, he found it somewhat difficult to be grateful.

He experienced again that dull feeling of guilt. He felt that she ought to show more cordiality to Bobbie MacLaurin. Here was Bobbie, trailing after her like a faithful dog, on the most hazardous trip that any man could devise, and he had not been rewarded, so far, with even the stingiest of smiles.

Women were like that. They took the fruits of your work, or they took your life, or let you toss it to the crows, without a sign of gratitude. At least, *some* women were like that. He had hoped Miss Vost was not that kind. He had hoped—

Miss Vost laid her small, warm hand in his, and she seemed perfectly willing to let it linger. Her lips were parted in a smile that was all but a caress. She seemed to have forgotten that the baffled young man who stared so fixedly at the back of her pretty, white neck existed.

It was quite embarrassing for Peter. The feeling of the little hand, that lay so intimately within his, sent a warm glow stealing into his guilty heart.

Then, aware of the pain in the face of Bobbie MacLaurin, a face that had abruptly gone white, and realizing his duty to this true friend of his, he pushed Miss Vost's hands away from him.

That gesture served to bring them all back to earth.

"Aren't you glad—aren't you a little bit glad—to see me—me?" said the hurt voice of Bobbie MacLaurin.

Miss Vost pivoted gracefully, giving Peter Moore a view of her splendid, straight back for a change. "Of course I am, Bobbie!" she exclaimed. "I'm always glad to see you. Why—oh, look! Did you ever see such a Chinaman?"

They all joined in her look. A salmon-colored sampan was riding swiftly to the *Hankow's* riveted steel side. With long legs spread wide apart atop the low cabin stood a very tall, very grave Chinese. His long, blanched face was more than grave, more than austere.

Peter Moore stared and ransacked his memory. He had seen that face, that grimace, before. His mind went back to the shop front, on Nanking Road, last evening, when he was skulking toward the bund from the friendly establishment of his friend, the silk merchant, Ching Gow Ong.

This man was neither Cantonese nor Pekingese. His long, rather supercilious face, his aquiline nose, the flare of his nostrils, the back-tilted head, the high, narrow brow, and the shock of blue-black hair identified the Chinese stranger, even if his abnormal, rangy height were not taken into consideration, as a hill man, perhaps Tibetan, perhaps Mongolian. Certainly he was no river-man.

It seemed improbable that the window-breaker could have been released by the heartless Shanghai police so quickly; yet out of his own adventurous past Peter could recall more than one occasion when "squeeze" had saved him embarrassment.

There was no constraint in the pose of the man on the sampan's flat roof. With indifference his narrow gaze flitted from the face of Bobbie MacLaurin to that of Miss Vost, and wandered on to the stern, sharp-eyed visage of Peter Moore.

Here the casual gaze rested. If he recognized Peter Moore, he gave no indication of it. He studied Peter's countenance with the look of one whose interest may be distracted on the slightest provocation.

An intelligent and wary student of human nature, Peter dropped his eyes to the man's long, claw-like fingers. These were twitching ever so slightly, plucking slowly—it may have been meditatively—at the hem of his black silk coat. At the intentness of Peter's stare, this twitching abruptly ceased.

The sampan whacked alongside. The big man tossed a small, orange-silk bag to the deck. He climbed the ladder as if he had been used to climbing all his life.

"I don't care for his looks," remarked Miss Vost, looking up into Peter's face with a curious smile.

"Nor I," said Bobbie MacLaurin.

The richly dressed stranger vaulted nimbly over the teak-rail, recovered the orange bag, and approached MacLaurin. His head drooped forward momentarily, in recognition of the authority of the blue uniform.

He said in excellent English: "I desire to engage passage to Ching-Fu."

"This way," replied the *Hankow's* captain.

"You seemed to recognize him," said Miss Vost to Peter, when they had the deck to themselves.

"Perhaps I was mistaken," replied Peter evasively. He suddenly was aware of Miss Vost's wide-eyed look of concern.

Impulsively she laid her hand on his arm. She had come up very close to him. Her head moved back, so that her chin was almost on a level with his.

"Mr. Moore," she said in a low, soft voice, "I won't ask you any questions. In China, there are many, many things that a woman must not try to understand. But I—I want to tell you that—that I think you are—splendid. It seems so fine, so good of you. I—I can't begin to thank you. My—my feelings prevent it."

"But—why—what—what—" stammered Peter.

"Oh, Mr. Moore, I know—I know!" Miss Vost proceeded earnestly. "Like all fine, brave men, you are—you are modest! It—it almost makes me want to cry, to think—to think—"

"But, Miss Vost," interrupted Peter, gently and gravely, "you are shooting over my head!"

In the rakish bows of the *Hankow* arose the clank and clatter of wet anchor-chains. A bell tinkled in the engine-room. The stout fabric of the little steamer shuddered. The yellow water began to slip by them. On the shore two pagodas moved slowly into alignment. The *Hankow* was moving.

Miss Vost strengthened her gentle hold upon Peter's reluctant arm. Her bright eyes were a trifle blurred. "Last night, when we met on the bund," she went on in a small voice, "I knew immediately—immediately—what you were. A chivalrous gentleman! A man who would shelter and protect any helpless woman he met!"

"That was nice of you," murmured Peter.

Like Saul of Tarsus, he was beginning to see a bright light.

"And it was true!" Miss Vost plunged on. "Now—now, you are risking your life—for poor, unworthy little me! Please don't deny it, Mr. Moore! I only wanted to let you know that I—I understand, and that I am—g-grateful!" Her eyelids fluttered over an unstifled moistness.

"Bobbie *loves* you," blurted Peter. "He'd do anything in the world for you. He told me so. He told me—"

Miss Vost opened her eyes on a look that was hurt and humiliated. "What?"

"He'd go to hell for you!"

"He's an overgrown boy. He doesn't know what he says. That's nonsense," declared Miss Vost, looking away from Peter. "I know his type, Mr. Moore. He falls in love with every pretty face; and he falls out again, quite as easily."

"You don't know Bobbie, the way I do," said Peter stubbornly.

"I don't have to. I know his kind—a girl in every port."

"No, no. Not Bobbie!"

For a moment it seemed that they had come to an *impasse*. Miss Vost was blinking her eyes rapidly, appearing to be somewhat interested in a junk which was poling down-stream.

She looked up with a wan smile. Tears were again in her eyes. "Mr. Moore," she said in a broken voice, "what you've told me about Mr. MacLaurin, Captain MacLaurin, moves me—deeply!"

"Do try to be nice to Bobbie," begged Peter. "He is the finest fellow I know. He is true blue. He would give his life for your little finger. Really he would, Miss Vost!"

The bright eyes gave him a languishing look.

"I'll try," she said simply.

That night the banks of the great river were gray and mysterious under the effulgence of a top-heavy yellow moon. The search-light on the peak pierced out the fact that a low, swirling mist was creeping up from the river's dulled surface.

The air was damp with the breath of the land. Occasionally the gentle puffs of the wind bore along the water the flavor of queer, indistinguishable odors.

Elbow to elbow, glancing down at the hissing water, Miss Vost and Peter stood for a number of sweet, meditative moments in silence. At length Miss Vost slipped her arm through his.

"Sometimes," she murmured, inclining her head until it almost rested against his shoulder, "I feel lonely—terrible! Especially on such a night as this. The moon is so impersonal, isn't it? Here it is, a great, gorgeous ball of cold fire, shining across China at you and me. In Amoy it seemed to frown at me. Now—it seems to smile. The same moon!"

"The same moon!" whispered Peter as her warm hand slipped down and snuggled in his.

"Don't *you* ever feel lonely—like this?" demanded Miss Vost suddenly.

Peter sighed. "Oh, often. Often! The world seems so big, and so filled with things that are hard to learn. Especially at night!" He wondered what she thought he meant.

"I—I feel that way," Miss Vost's absorbed voice replied. "I try—and try—to reason these things out. But they are so baffling! So elusive! So evasive! Here is China, with its millions of poor wretched ones, struggling in darkness and disease. There are so many! And they are so hard to help. And out beyond there, not so many miles beyond that ridge, lies Tibet, with her millions, and her ignorance, and her disease. And to the left—away to the left, I think, is India.

"If a person would be happy, he must not come to China or India. Their problems are too overwhelming. You cannot think of solutions fast enough, and even while you think, you are overcome by the weariness, the hopelessness, of it all. I wish I had never come to China.

"I happened to be in Foo-Chow not long ago. There is in Foo-Chow a thing that illustrates what I mean. It is called the baby tower. Girls, you know, aren't thought much of in China. At the bottom of the tower is a deep well. Women to whom are born baby girls go to the baby tower—" Miss Vost shuddered. "The babies are thrown into the well. I have seen them. Poor—poor, little creatures—dying like that!"

Miss Vost sniffled for a moment. Brightly she said:

"I like to talk to you, Mr. Moore. You're so—so sympathetic!"

A great, dark shadow bulked up against the rail alongside Peter.

"Good evening, folks!" declared the pleasant bass voice of Bobbie MacLaurin.

"We were just talking about you, Bobbie," said Peter affably. "As I was telling Miss Vost, you're the most sympathetic man I ever knew! Good night, Miss Vost. Night, Bobs!"

CHAPTER XIII

When Peter descended the stairway into the narrow vestibule which served as reception-hall, dining-saloon, and, incidentally, as the corridor from which the *Hankow's* four small staterooms were entered, he had the chilly feeling that the darkness had eyes.

Yet he saw nothing. The cabin was dark. Three round ports glimmered greenly beyond the staircase on the cabin's forward side. The glimmer was occasioned by the refracted rays of the *Hankow's* dazzling searchlight. But these were not the ones he felt.

Gradually his own eyes became accustomed to the pulp-like darkness. He steadied his body against the gentle swaying of the steamer, and endeavored to listen above, or through, the imminent thrashing and clattering of the huge engine.

He examined the four stateroom doors anxiously. As the darkness began to dissolve slightly, Peter, still conscious that eyes were fastened upon him, made the discovery that the stateroom adjoining his was slightly ajar. The moon favored him—Miss Vost's impersonal moon. It outlined against the slit what appeared to be a large, irregular block.

Peter decided that the irregular block was nothing more nor less than the head of a man. To prove that his surmise was correct, Peter quickly shifted the revolver from his right hand to his left, brought it even with his eyes and—struck a match.

In the startling flare of the phosphorus the evil glint of Celestial eyes was instantly revealed in the partly opened door.

With incredible softness the door was closed. Where there had been half-lidded eyes, a positive snarl, and a shock of blue-black hair was now a white-enameled panel.

Peter continued to smile along the barrel, which glistened in the dying flame of the match. He unlocked his door, closed it, and shot the bolt. Switching on the electric light, he cautiously drew back the sheet. Apparently satisfied, he sniffed the air. It was nothing more than stuffy, as a stateroom that has been closed for a week or so is apt to be.

Unscrewing the fat wingbolts which clamped down the brass-bound port-glass, he let in a breath of misty river air. Simultaneously voices came into the room.

Miss Vost and Bobbie MacLaurin were conversing in clear, tense syllables. Peter could not help eavesdropping. They were standing on the deck, directly over his stateroom, only a few scant feet from his porthole, which was situated much nearer the deck than the surging water.

"But I do—I do love you!" Bobbie was complaining in his rumbling voice. "Ever since you set foot on the old *Sunyado Maru* I've been your shadow—your slave! What more can any man say?" he added bitterly.

"Not a great deal," rejoined Miss Vost lightheartedly. She became abruptly serious. "Bobbie, I do like you. I admire you—ever so much. But it happens that you are not the man for me. You don't understand me. You can never understand me. Don't you realize it? You're too sudden—too brutal—too—"

"Brutal! I've treated you like a flower. I want to shield you—"

"But I don't *need* shielding, Bobbie. I'm prudent, fearless, and—twenty-two. I don't need a watch-dog!"

"Good God, who said anything about being a watchdog?" exclaimed Bobbie. "I—I just want—"

"You just want me," completed Miss Vost. "Well, you can't have me."

"You love somebody else, then. That young pup!"

Peter stared sourly at the bilious moon.

"Don't you dare call him a young pup, Robert MacLaurin," retorted Miss Vost resentfully. "He is a fine young man. I admire him and I respect him very, *very* much."

"He can't fool around any girl of mine!"

Peter heard Bobbie sucking the breath in between his teeth, as if he might have pricked himself with a pin. Bobbie had done worse than that.

"A girl of *yours*!" snapped Miss Vost.

Followed low, anxious and imploratory whispers. These were terminated by a long, light, and delicious laugh.

"Bobbie, you're so *funny*!" Miss Vost gurgled.

"I wish I was dead!" declared Bobbie despondently.

"You should go to Liauchow," Miss Vost chirped.

"*Why* should *I* go to Liauchow?" grumbled the bass voice.

"To be happy, you must be born in Soochow, live in Canton and die in Liauchow. So runs the proverb."

"Why should I go to Liauchow?" persisted Bobbie.

"Because Soochow has the handsomest people, Canton the most luxury, and Liauchow the best coffins!"

CHAPTER XIV

Peter Moore's curiosity regarding the motives which were sending Miss Amy Vost into Szechwan, most deplorable, most poverty-stricken of provinces, was satisfied before the *Hankow* had put astern the great turbulent city after which it had been named.

At Hankow the *Hankow* picked up the raft which it would tow all the way up to Ching-Fu. Upon this raft was a long, squat cabin, in and out of which poured incessantly members of China's large and growing family.

There were thin, dirty little men, and skinny, soiled little women, and quantities of hungry, dirty little boys and girls. A great noise went up from the raft as the *Hankow* nosed in alongside, and the new towline was passed and made fast over the bitts.

As the big propeller thumped under them and churned the muddy water into unhealthy-looking foam, Peter Moore and Miss Vost leaned upon the rail, where it curved around the fantail, and discoursed at length, speculating upon the probable destination of that raftful of dirty humanity, and offering problematic answers to the puzzling question as to why were all these people deserting relatively prosperous Hankow for the over-populated, overdeveloped province of Szechwan.

Peter had an inkling that Miss Vost was distressed by the scene.

"Let's take a stroll forward," he suggested.

An urchin, directly below them, stood rubbing his eyes with two grimy fists. His whines were audible above the churning of the engines.

"No, no. I'm quite accustomed to this. Look—just look at that miserable little fellow!"

"He is blind," stated Peter quietly.

"Half of them are blind," Miss Vost replied. Her features were transfixed by a look of sadness. "Wait for me. I'll return in a second."

Peter watched the graceful swing of her shoulders as she strode down the deck to the forward companionway, admiring the slim strength of her silk-clad ankles. She was every inch an American girl. He was proud of her. She returned, carrying a small oblong of cardboard, upon which a photograph was pasted.

Peter found himself looking into the sad, be-wrinkled eyes of a gray-bearded man, a patriarchal gentleman, who stood on the hard clay at the foot of a low stone stairway. His nose, his eyes, his intellectual forehead were distinctly those of Miss Vost. A child in a freshly starched frock, with eyes opened wide in surprise and interest, was firmly clutching one of his trouser-legs.

"My father," explained Miss Vost. "He was stationed at Wenchow then, in charge of the mission. I have not seen him since."

Peter remarked to himself that somehow Miss Vost did not seem to be the daughter of a missionary, nor was the costly way she dressed in key with her remark. Perhaps she divined his thoughts.

"He has money—lots of it. He has a keen, broad mind. But he chose this. When he was first married be brought mother to China. He saw, and realized, China's vast problems. And he stayed. He wanted to help."

Peter gazed into her gray eyes, which seemed to take on a clear violet tinge when she was deeply moved.

"He told me to come to see him because he was growing old. I stopped off in Amoy," said Miss Vost with a ghost of a smile. "A young missionary he wanted me to meet lives there. I met him. But I could not admire that young missionary. He was a—a *poseur*. He was pretending. One reason I like you, Mr. Moore, is because you're so sincere. He was so transparent. And his 'converts' saw through him, too. They were bread-and-butter converts. They listened to him; they devoured his food—then they went to the fortune-tellers! Father could not have known Doctor Sanborn longer than a few minutes—or else he's not the father that he used to be! I inherit his love for sincerity. I—I'm sure he will like you!"

"But—but—" stammered Peter—"I don't expect to go to Wenchow. Better say he'd like—Bobbie!"

"Oh, he'd like anybody that I liked," Miss Vost said lightly. "It—it's really interesting, you know, from Ching-Fu to Wenchow. We take bullock carts—if we can find them. Otherwise we walk. Doesn't it—appeal to you—just a little—to be all alone with me for nearly a hundred miles?"

"Very much indeed," replied Peter earnestly. "But our roads part—at Ching-Fu. I go directly south."

"In search of more adventure and romance? Perhaps—perhaps a girl who is not so silly as I have been? Or—is it India—or Afghanistan?"

"Neither. An old friend!"

"Is that why you are growing a beard—to surprise—*him*?"

"Perhaps," said Peter, absently fingering the bristles. "Don't tell me it's unbecoming or I'll have to shave it off!"

"As if what I thought made a particle of difference!" retorted Miss Vost defiantly.

Peter gave her a thoughtful, a puzzled stare. "I overheard you last night. You broke your promise. You promised to be nice to him."

"I was. Do you mean what I said about Liauchow?"

"You don't realize what you *mean* to Bobbie. My dear, dear girl—"

"I am not your dear, dear girl!"

Peter groaned.

"Does your heart ache, too, Peter?"

"Of course it does! I—I'd like—"

"Then why don't you?"

"It wouldn't be fair, that's why!"

"To—Bobbie?"

"Bobbie, too."

"Then there *is* another girl," Miss Vost cried bitterly. She bit her lip. "You should have told me before."

"I thought it wouldn't be necessary."

Miss Vost dropped her eyes to Peter's hand which was resting on the rail. Her own hand moved over and nestled against it.

"Do—do you l-love her as much as th-this?" Her eyes returned to his face.

"I did think I did!"

"But you're not sure—now?"

"Oh, I thought I was sure! I *am* sure'"

"There's little more to say, then, is there?" Her lids were blinking rapidly as she looked down at the mob of filthy little Arabs on the flat. Her fingers plucked, trembling, at the embroidered hem of a white, wadded handkerchief.

"Bobbie *does* care for you so," observed Peter with unintentional cruelty.

"Oh—oh—*him*!" sobbed Miss Vost, leaving him to stare after her drooping figure as she retreated down the deck.

She seemed on a sudden to be avoiding the entrance to the forward companionway. He wondered why.

The girl stopped, with her hands clenched into white fists at her sides.

From the doorway, smiling suavely and wiping one hand upon the other in a gesture of solicitous meekness, emerged the tall and commanding figure of the Mongolian—or was he a Tibetan? He was attired now in the finest, the shiniest of Canton silks. His satin pants, of a gorgeous white, a *courting* white, were strapped about ankles which terminated in curved sandals sparkling with gold and jewels in the mid-day sun. His jacket, long and perfectly fitting, was of a robin's egg blue. His blue-black queue, freshly oiled, gleamed like the coils of an active hill snake.

He was a picture of refined Chinese saturninity.

Miss Vost, beholding him, was properly impressed. She stepped back, not a little appalled, and swept him from queue to sandal with a look that was not the heartiest of receptions. The Mongolian was speaking in oiled, pleasing accents.

Peter strode toward them.

"He insulted me!" panted Miss Vost. "Like many fine, Chinese gentlemen, he thought, perhaps, that I might be—what do they call 'em—a 'nice li'l 'Melican girl!' Impress him with the fact that I am not, Mr. Moore—please do that!"

She hastened around the forward cabin, out of sight.

The Mongolian was regarding Peter with a cool, complacent smile. His expression was smug, uninjured.

"Looka here, Chink-a-link," Peter advised him, "my no savvy you; you no savvy my. My see you allatime. Allatime. You savvy, Chink-a-link?"

"I comprehend you, my friend," replied the Mongolian in polished accents. "In my case, 'pidgin' is not, let me hasten to say, necessary."

"Very good, Chink; the next time you so much as glance in Miss Vost's direction, you're going to walk away with a pair of the dam'dest black eyes in China! Get that—you yellow weasel?"

"Unfortunately," replied the Mongolian, lifting his fine, black eyebrows only a trifle, "your suggestion—your admonitions—are again, most inappropriate. Miss Vost—do I pronounce it correctly? Miss Vost and yourself are the victims of a misunderstanding."

"Take off your coat, and prove I'm wrong!" shouted Peter. "I'm a better man than you are! Swallow it or—fight!"

Peter's gray tweed coat flopped in a heap upon the ironwood deck.

The Mongolian retired a few feet, with indications of anxiety.

"I—I did not intend to offend her," he retracted. His ropy throat muscles seemed to convulse. His long face flamed hotly red. He burst out, as though unable to control himself: "My savvy allatime you no savvy! *Ní bùh yào tī nà gò hwà! Djan gò chü, ràng ó dzóu!*"

"*Lao-shu,*" laughed Peter. "*Dang hsin!*"

CHAPTER XV

They came to Ichang next noon. Peter was on deck watching the somewhat hazardous procedure of transferring large grass-bound cases of tools from a tidewater steamer to the stern of the flat when he saw the Mongolian emerge from the companionway and walk to the rail, forward. Peter gave him a full stare, but the man did not glance in his direction. He was looking down at the muddy river, and beckoning.

Peter observed a sampan coolie give an answering wave, and the sampan sidled alongside the flat.

The Mongolian returned a few minutes before the *Hankow* hauled in her anchor. He retired to his stateroom and stayed there until late afternoon.

The river above Ichang was swifter, more dangerous, than in its lower course. Except for the junks and an occasional sampan, the *Hankow* had the stream to herself. The yellow waters were tinged with red, dancing and sparkling to a fresh breeze under a fair blue sky. Great blue hills confined the swollen current. This was not the Yangtze of yesterday. It was a maddened millrace, gorged by the mountain rains. Even the gurgle under the sharp-cut waters seemed to convey a menace.

Dikes were broken down. The brown waters had flowed out to right and left, forming quiet lakes where there had been fields of paddy and wheat. The junks from up-river were having a strenuous time of it. Swarms of gibbering coolies manned the long sweeps, striving above all to keep their clumsy craft in safe mid-current.

They were passing a long row of pyramids, green, brown and red. But Miss Vost was staring along the deck.

"The Mongolian!" she muttered. "How he is grinning at you!"

The Mongolian had come upon them, apparently unintentionally. He hesitated and paused when Peter looked up. Peter saw no grin upon his lips. They were set in a firm, straight line. His long arms were folded behind his back, and his eyes were empty of mirth—or malice. They simply expressed nothing. He looked at Peter shortly, and favored Miss Vost with a long stare.

Her eyes faltered. Peter stepped forward.

But the Mongolian bowed, passed them at a slow, meditative walk, and was lost from their sight behind the cabin's port side.

The idea took hold of Peter that the stalker had become the killer. There was a telegraph station at Ichang through which ran the frail copper wires connecting the seventy millions of Szechwan Province with civilization. Had it been possible for the Mongolian to signal his master in Len Yang and receive an answer while the *Hankow* lay at Ichang?

After dinner, curious and nervous, Peter went below. The light was burning over the table of weapons in the main cabin.

The Mongolian's door was slightly ajar, and as Peter descended the stairs, the door closed.

He waited. His heart thumped, louder than the thump of the laboring engine. He walked to his stateroom, opened the door, kicked the threshold, and—slammed the door! He hastened to the table, and hid behind it. Between the table legs he had a splendid view of both doors.

Holding a kris, point down, in front of him, the Mongolian slipped out, tried the adjacent door-knob and entered Peter's room. When he came out, he looked perplexed and angry. He slid the dagger into his silk blouse and looked up the stairway, listening.

His expression of rage passed away; now his look was inscrutable. Stealing across the vestibule, he approached Miss Vost's door, and rapped.

Peter ran his fingers along the edge of the table until they encountered the hilt of a cutlass. He waited.

The Mongolian rapped a little louder. There was no answer. Again he knocked, imperatively. Peter heard Miss Vost's sleepy voice pitched in inquiry. Her door opened an inch or two.

The Mongolian forced his way inside!

Miss Vost uttered a short, sharp scream, which was instantly smothered.

As Peter burst into the room, the Mongolian turned with a snarl, reaching for his silk blouse. Peter clapped his free hand to the muscled shoulder, and dragged him into the corridor.

Miss Vost, in a long, white nightgown, was framed in the doorway, staring sleepily. Her hand was clutched to her lips. Her hair tumbled about her bare shoulders in dark, silky clusters.

Bright steel flashed in the Mongolian's hand. "*Ha-li!*" he muttered.

Peter braced himself, and thrust straight upward, striking with fury. He drove the sword through the Mongolian's right eye.

Miss Vost, a slender pillar of white, stared down at the floundering heap. She seemed to be going mad, with the green light of the electric glittering in her distended eyes.

Bobbie MacLaurin bounded down the steps.

"He tried to come into my room," said Miss-Vost. "He tried to come into my room!"

"I know. I know. But it's all right," soothed Peter, panting. "You must go back to bed. You must try to sleep." He talked as though she were a child. "He was a bad man. He had to—to be treated—this way!"

"You—you look like an Arab. The dark. And that beard. Where is Bobbie?"

"Right here. Right here beside you!"

"You're not hurt—either of you? You're both all right?"

"Yes. Yes. *Please* go to bed!" begged Peter.

"Please!" implored Bobbie.

To them there was something unreligious, something terrible, in the notion of Miss Vost standing in the presence of the grim black heap in the shadow. Nor were her youth and her innocence intended to be bared before the eyes of men in this fashion.

As if a chill river wind had struck her, she shivered—closed the door.

The men carried the limp body, which was unaccountably heavy, to the deck. After a minute there—was a splash. The *Hankow* had not been checked. On the Yangtze formal burial ceremonies are seldom performed.

Peter went to bed at once. He tried to sleep. He counted the revolutions of the propeller. He added up a stupendous number of sheep going through a hole in a stone wall. Every so often the sheep faded away, to be replaced by the fearful countenance of the Mongolian, who was now perhaps ten miles or more downstream.

After a while the engines were checked, turning at half speed for a number of revolutions, then ceasing as a bell rang. The only sound was the soughing gurgle of the water as it lapped along the steel plates, and the distant drone of the rapids.

He heard the splash of an anchor, accompanied by the rumble and clank of chains, forward; and a repetition of the sounds aft. Directly under him, it seemed a loud, prolonged scraping noise took place. The fires were being drawn.

The sounds could only mean that the *Hankow* had reached the journey's end. The trip was over; the *Hankow* was abreast Ching-Fu. She would lie in the current for a few days, before facing about and making for tidewater.

Today would see the last of Miss Vost, a termination of that serio-humorous love affair of theirs, which, on the whole, had been one of his most delightful experiences. He wondered whether or not she would ask him to kiss her good-bye. He rather hoped she would.

On the other hand, he hoped she would do nothing of the kind. Distance was lending enchantment to Eileen Lorimer. He was sure this was not infatuation. She was not the first; he had had affairs; oh, numbers of them! But they were mere fragments of his adventurous life. They were milestones, shadowy and vague and very far away now. Dear little milestones, each of them!

Sometime he would go to Eileen, and get down on his knees before her in humility, and ask her if she could overlook his systematic and hardened faults! When would he do this? Frankly, he did not know.

He dozed off, and it seemed only an instant later when he was awakened by a harsh cry.

The port-hole was still dark. Morning was a long way off.

The cry was repeated, was joined by others, excited and fearful.

Peter sat up in bed, and was instantly thrown back by a sudden lurch. Next came a dull booming and banging. The stateroom was filled with the hot, sweet smell of smoking wood, the smell that is caused by the friction of wood against wood, or wood against steel.

Another pounding and booming. Some one hammered at the door. Peter tried to turn on the electric light. There was no current. He opened the door.

Bobbie, shoeless and collarless, dressed only in pants and shirt, towered over the light of a candle which he held in a hand that shook.

"A collision! Junk rammed us! Get up quick! Don't know damage. Call Miss Vost! Get on deck! Take care of her! My hands filled with this dam' boat."

Peter snatched his clothes, and before he was out of his pajamas the *Hankow* began to keel over. It slid down, until the port-hole dipped into the muddy current. Water slopped in and drenched his knees and feet.

He yanked open the door, not stopping to lace his shoes, and called Miss Vost. She had heard the excitement, and was dressing. The floor lurched again, and he was thrown violently against a sharp-edged post.

Miss Vost's door was flung open, and she stumbled down the sloping floor, bracing her hands against his chest to catch herself.

"We're sinking," she said without fear.

To Peter it was evident that Miss Vost had never been through the capsizing of a ship before. He fancied he caught a thrill of eager, almost exultant, excitement in her voice. In that vestibule, he knew they were rats in a water-trap, or soon would be.

He still felt weak and limp from his fall against the post, and he was trying hard to regain his strength before they began their perilous ascent to the deck.

Miss Vost misunderstood his hesitancy.

"I am not afraid, not a bit!" she declared, holding with both hands the folds of his unbuttoned shirt. "I am never afraid with *you*! When I am in danger, you—you are always near. It—it seems that you were put here to—to look after me. But there is no danger—is there?" She shook him almost playfully.

"Cut out your babbling," he snapped. "Get to that stairway!"

He heard the breath hiss in between her teeth. But she clung to his arm obediently. They sprawled and slipped in the darkness to the stairs. Clinging to the railing, they reached the deck, which was inclined so steeply that they clung to the cabin-rail for support.

In the dark on all sides of them coolies shouted in high-pitched voices. Heavy rain was falling, drumming on the deck. The odor of wood rubbing against steel persisted. They could see nothing. The world was dark, and filled with contusion.

A sharp explosion took place in the bows. Chains screamed through the air and clanged on metal and wood. One of the forward anchor-chains had parted.

The deck was tilted again. Bobbie MacLaurin was not in evidence. Peter shouted for him until he was hoarse. Then he left Miss Vost and groped his way to the starboard davits. The starboard life-boat was gone!

Suddenly the rain ceased. A dull red glow smouldered on the eastern heaven.

Miss Vost was praying, praying for courage, for help. She clung to him, and sobbed. By and by her nerves seemed to steady themselves.

There was nothing to do but wait for daylight—and pray that the gurgling waters might not rise any higher.

The glow in the east increased, and permitted them to see the vague outlines of a looming shape which seemed to grow out of the bows. As dawn came, Peter made out the form of a huge junk, which had pinioned and crushed the foredeck rail under her brawny poop.

Then the remaining anchor-cable snapped like a rotten thread. Dimly they saw the end of the chain whip upward and crash down. A coolie, paralyzed, stood in its way. The broken end struck him in the face. He screamed and rolled down the deck until he lodged against the rail.

Bobbie shouted their names, and scrambled and slipped down.

"We're trying to get up steam. Our only chance. Both forward anchors gone. We'll swing around with the current and lose this damn junk. If the after anchor holds till steam's up—we're safe!" He sped aft.

The steamer shuddered, and they felt her swinging as the scattered shore lights moved from left to right. The junk was acting as a drag. The shore lights became stationary. A gang of coolies with grate bars were trying to pry up the junk's coamings.

Peter was aware then that Miss Vost's arms were clinging about his neck, and that she was whimpering softly in his ear.

Up-river boomed another explosion. The deck seemed to fall from under his feet. Water splashed up over his toes. In the gold-speckled dawn he could see the waters foaming and swirling, and rising higher.

He knew it was suicide to swim the Yangtze rapids, knew the whirlpools which sucked a man down and held him down until his body was torn to shreds. There was no alternative. And the water was now half-way to his knees. He dragged the unresisting girl to the rail.

"Can you swim—at all?"

"A—a little," she chattered.

"Hold to my collar and swim with one hand. Only try to keep afloat."

They slipped into the racing current, were seized, and spun around and around. Above the drone of the waters he heard the roar of a whirlpool, coming rapidly nearer. The firm clutch of Miss Vost's hand on his collar was not loosened. Occasionally he heard her gasp and sputter as a wave washed over her face.

They were swept down. On they went, spinning, snatched from one eddy to another. The roar of the whirlpool receded, became a low growl and mutter.

Now they could see the churning surface covered with torn bits of wreckage. A body, bloated and discolored, spun by, and was caught and dragged under, leaving only an indescribable stench.

After a while the northern shore, a low, brown bank, crept out toward them, like a long, merciful arm. In another minute Peter's bare feet came in contact with slimy, yielding mud. They were in shoal water!

He picked up Miss Vost in his arms, and carried her ashore; and she clung to him, shivering and moaning. He did not realize until afterward that she was kissing him over and over again on his wet lips and cheeks.

Coolies found them, and carried them to a village, and deposited them in a little red clay compound behind a building of straw. A bonfire was kindled. The sun came up, a disk that might have been cut out of red tissue-paper.

Some time later a tall man came into the clearing with a little group of coolies who were pointing out the way. A white patriarchal beard extended nearly to his waist.

He saw Miss Vost and shouted. She leaped up, was enfolded in his arms.

Peter stared at them a moment with a look that was somewhat dazed. He picked himself up, and skulked out of the compound, in the direction of the foaming river.

His mind was not in a normal state just then, or he would not have wanted to cross to Ching-Fu in a sampan. But he did want to cross. In the back of his brain foolish words were urging him: "You must get to Ching-Fu. You must go on to Len Yang. Hurry! Hurry!"

He had no money. A box filled with perforated Szechwan coins now lay at the bottom of the river in what was left of the *Hankow*. Nevertheless, he hailed a sampan as though his pockets were weighted down with lumps of purest silver.

The boat leaked in dozens of places. The paddle, scarred and battered, clung to the stern by means of a rotting leather thong. As Peter looked and hesitated, a long, imperative cry issued from behind him. Possibly Miss Vost wanted him to return.

The coolie stipulated his price, and Peter stepped aboard without a murmur, without looking around, either. The crossing was precarious. They skirted the edge of more than one whirl; they were caught and tossed about in waves as large as houses. Peter kept his eye on the rotting thong, and marveled because it actually held.

Deposited on the edge of Ching-Fu's bund, he confessed his poverty, and offered his shirt in payment. The shirt was of fine golden silk, woven in the Chinan-Fu mills. For more than a year it had worn like iron, and it had more than an even chance of continuing to do so.

Peter stripped off the shirt before a mob of squealing children, and the coolie scrutinized it. He accepted it, and blessed Peter, and Peter's virtuous mother, and called upon his green-eyed gods to make the days of Peter long and filled with the rice of the land.

CHAPTER XVI

With the coming of noon Peter sat down under a stunted cembra pine tree and contemplated the distant rocky blue ridge with a wistful and discouraged air. He removed from his trouser-pocket two yellow loquats and devoured them.

He was dreadfully hungry. His stomach fathered a dull, persistent ache, which forced upon his attention the pains in his muscles and bones. It was their way of complaining against the abuse he had heaped upon them during the past twenty-four hours.

He was beginning to feel weak and dispirited. His was a constitution that arose to emergencies in quick, battling trim; but when the emergency was past, his vitality seemed to be drained.

He looked down the muddy brown road as he finished the second loquat (which he had stolen from a roadside farm in passing) and estimated that Ching-Fu was all of ten miles behind him. Walking through the pasty blue mud in his bare feet, with the rain streaming through his hair and down his beard and shoulders, had been tedious, trying. Several times he had stopped, with his feet sinking in the clay, and cursed the Yangtze with bitterness.

What had become of Bobbie MacLaurin? Had that noble soul been snatched down by the River of Golden Sands?

He cursed the river anew, for Bobbie was a man after God's own heart. Never had there lived such a generous, such a fine and brave comrade. More than once the mule-kick which lurked behind those big, kind, red fists had saved Peter from worse than black eyes.

He would never forget that night on the pier at Salina Cruz, when the greaser had flashed out a knife, bent on carving a hole in Peter's heart—and Bobbie had come up from behind and knocked the raving Mexican a dozen feet off the pier into the limpid Pacific!

Those days were ended now. The adventures, the excitement, the sorrows, and the fiery gladness were all well beyond recall.

Peter leaned back against the thorny trunk of the cembra pine, and sniffed the odors of drenched earth, listened to the drip and patter of the cold, gray rain, and gazed pessimistically at the blue crest of rock which lifted its granite shoulders high into the mist miles away.

He stretched himself, groaned, and staggered on through the mire.

The valley was filled with the blue shades of dusk when he espied some distance beyond him what was evidently a camp, a caravan at rest. The setting sun managed at last to burrow its way through a rift of purple before sinking down behind the granite range, to leave China to the mercies of its long night.

These departing rays, striking through the purple crevice, and setting its edges smolderingly aflame with red and gold, became a narrow, dwindling spotlight, which brought out in black relief the figures of men and mules, of drooping tents and curling wisps of cookfire smoke. The sun was swallowed up, and the camp vanished.

Peter plunged on, with one leg dragging more reluctantly than the other. But he had sensed the odor of cooking food in the quiet air.

A sentry whose head was adorned by a dark-red turban presented the point of his rifle as Peter approached. He shouted, was joined by others, both Chinese and Bengalis, and Peter, not adverse even to being in the hands of enemies as long as food was imminent, was inducted into the presence of a kingly personage, who sat upon a carved teak stool.

This creature, by all appearances a mandarin, of middle age, was garbed in a stiff, dark satin gown, heavy with gold and jewels which flashed brightly in the light of a camp-fire. His severe, dark face was long, and stamped with intelligence of a high order. He wore a mustache which drooped down to form a hair wisp on either side of his small, firm mouth.

As Peter was whisked into his presence he placed his elbow with a slow, deliberate motion upon his knee, and rested his rounded chin in his palm, bestowing upon the mud-spattered newcomer a look that searched into Peter's soul.

A single enormous diamond blazed upon the knuckle of his forefinger.

He put a question in a tongue that Peter did not understand. It was a deep, resonant voice, with the mellow, rounded tones of certain temple-bells, such a sound as is diffused long after the harsh stroke of the wooden boom has subsided. Vibrant with authority, it was such a voice as men obey, however much they may hate its owner. He repeated the question in Mandarin, and again Peter indicated that that was not his speech.

A different voice, yet quite as impelling as the other, caused Peter to look up sharply. The mandarin smiled wisely, but not unkindly.

"The darkness deceived me," he said in English of a strange cast. "I mistook you for a beggar. You are far from the river, my friend. The bones of your steamer lie fathoms deep by now. Why are you so far from Ching-Fu? You were stunned, perhaps?"

"I am only hungry," said Peter boldly. "My way lies into India. There I have friends."

The mandarin studied him dubiously, and clapped his hands, the great diamond cutting an oval of many colors. Coolies were given up by the night, and ran to obey his guttural, musical commands. They returned with steaming bowls of rice and meat, and a narrow lacquer table.

"Come and sit beside me. Your feet must be sore—bleeding. You may call me Chang. So I am known to my British friends on the frontier. I have been ill, a mountain fever, perhaps. In Ching-Fu. I had expected medicine on the river steamer."

He snapped his fingers, and whispered to a coolie whose face was gaunt and stolid in the flickering red glow of the fire.

So while Peter consumed the rice and stew, his bruised feet were bathed in warm water, rubbed with a soothing ointment, and wrapped in a downy bandage.

A blue liquor served in cups of shell silver completed the meal. The aromatic syrup, which exhaled a perfume that was indescribably oriental, sent an exhilarating fire through his veins. It seemed to clarify his thoughts and vision, to oil his aching joints, and remove their pain.

From the corner of his eye he detected the silken folds of the mandarin's lofty tent, in the murky interior of which a fat, yellow candle sputtered and dripped. When his eyes came back to the table, the bowls and cups had been removed, and in their place was a chess-board inlaid with ivory and pearl.

Inspired by the cordial, and the queerness of this setting, Peter felt that he was the central figure of a dream. The pungent odor of remote incense, the distant tinkling of a bell, the stamping and pawing of the mules and the brooding figure in silk and gold at his side, took him back across the ages to the days and nights of Scheherezade.

And the mandarin appeared to be hungry for Peter's companionship. Over the chess-board, between plays, they discoursed lengthily upon the greatness of the vast empire, once she should awake; upon the menace of the wily Japanese; upon the lands across the mountains and beyond the seas, and their peoples, of which Chang had read much but had never visited.

Wood was heaped upon the fire, which flared up and leaped after the crowding shadows.

It was the life that Peter dearly loved.

The mandarin's eyes glowed, and rested upon him for longer spaces. His words and sentences came fewer and more reluctant.

In one of these pauses he seized Peter's hand. And Peter was forthwith given the meagre details of a story, neither the beginning nor the end of which he would ever know. It was the cross-section of a tale of intrigue, of cold-blooded killings that chased the thrills up and down his spine; a tale of loot, of gems that had vanished, of ingots and kernels of gold that had leaked from iron-bound chests.

The mandarin uttered his woe in a quivering voice, shifting from a Bengal patois to Mandarin, and again to reckless English.

Peter was given to understand that in Chang's camp was a traitor, a man who eluded him, whose identity was shielded, a snake that could not be stamped out unless the lives of every one of his attendants were taken!

In a composed voice Chang, the mandarin, was saying:

"You have walked far. You are weary. Another couch is in my tent. You shall sleep there."

The candle was guttering low in its bronze socket when Peter awoke. A cool breeze stirred the tent flaps. A queer feeling oozed in his veins.

He lay still, breathing regularly, searching the corners with eyes that were brighter than a rat's. The low sleep-mutterings of the mandarin continued from the couch across from him.

Slowly the tent flaps were being drawn back. Peter strained his eyes until they ached. He was impelled to shout, to awaken his companion. Yet the visitor might be bent on legitimate business. He would wait. In the final analysis it was Peter's profound acquaintance with the ways of the East which sealed his lips. In the heart of China one does not strike at shadows, or shriek at sight of them. Not always.

At his side between the covers lay a strong, naked dagger. Why the mandarin had provided him with the weapon he did not know.

A gray shadow entered the tent and backed noiselessly against the front pole. Indeed, not a sound was created by his entrance, not even the rustling whisper of bare feet on dry grass. It seemed very ominous, mysterious, and ghostly.

The gray shadow floated into the candle-light, which waved and quivered a little as the still air was disturbed. Peter was conscious that he was being acutely examined. Not a muscle of his face twitched. He continued to breathe regularly, with the heaviness of a man steeped in sleep. Tentatively he permitted his lids to raise.

The intruder's back was toward him. He was bending with slow stealth over the mandarin's face. What was the fellow doing?

Peter caught the glint of metal, or glass. At the same time a powerful, sickening odor spread through the tent.

Peter groped for the naked dagger, bounded up from the couch with a nervous cry, and burled the steel up to its costly jeweled hilt in the foremost shoulder.

Without a sound the man in gray turned part way round, and a shudder ran through him, causing the folds of his garment to flap slightly. He sank down with a sigh like wind stealing through a cavern, and his fingers clawed feebly in the leaping shadow.

Peter detected a tiny glass vial spilling out its dark, volatile fluid upon the dust. He picked it up, but it was snatched from his hand. The dull pig-eyes of Chang stared very close to his, with the stupefaction of sleep still extending the irises into round dark pools. The vial was in his hand, and he was sampling its odor, waving it slowly back and forth under his wide nostrils. He shouted, and turbaned men filed into the tent, and carried the gray figure away.

The hand of Chang rested upon Peter's shoulder, and in a voice that throbbed with the sonorousness of a Buddha temple-gong he said:

"You have rendered me a service for which I can never sufficiently repay you—for I value my life highly! In the morning your mind will have forgotten what has taken place. Try to sleep now. You will obey—promptly!"

The candle sputtered and jumped, as if it were striving mightily to lengthen its golden life if only for another minute; and went out.

From Chow Yang to Lun-Ling-Ting all the land could not provide costlier raiment than Peter found at his bedside when the long, high-keyed cries of the mule men opened his eyes upon another morning.

When camp was broken up, long before the sun became hot, he was given a small but able mule; and he rode down the valley toward India at Chang's side. They moved at the head of a long, slow train, for here bandits were not feared, despite the loneliness of the land through which they were traveling. Farms became more scattered, more widely separated by patches of broken, barren rock; and, finally, all traces of the microscopic cultivation which gave Szechwan Province its lean fruitfulness were left behind them.

The mandarin rode for many miles in silence, occasionally changing reins, looking steadily and gloomily ahead of him, with his attention riveted, it seemed, upon the sharp and ceaseless clatter of his mule's hoofs and the twisting rock road.

Peter's mind was fixed upon the problem which crept hourly nearer. His head was cast between his shoulders as if the weight of a sorrowful world rested upon that narrow, well-proportioned skull, with its covering of shining light hair.

He loved his task as a man might love a selfish and thoughtless woman, who demanded and craftily accepted all that he could give, to the last ounce of his gold and the final drop of his blood. It was a thankless task, yet it had grace.

It was well past mid-morning before Chang spoke the first word.

"A grateful dream came into my sleep last night. For years I have fought in the darkness with a man who has the heart of Satan himself. He has robbed me. Time after time he has sent into my camp his spies. Some were more adroit than others. But none so adroit as the coolie from Len Yang."

Peter repressed his surprise, and merely winked his eyes thoughtfully a number of times. Chang went on:

"In this dream last night a young man was given into my keeping whose spirit and manliness have not yet been soiled. His gratitude was immediate. In return for the acts which grew out of that gratitude, I am prepared to give him anything that is mine, or in my power, whether he desires wealth, or position, or my friendship."

"The young man," said Peter gravely, "desires neither wealth nor position. If he has been of service to the man who befriended him, that is enough."

"Should he desire a favor of any kind—"

"Then help him to reach his enemy, who is your enemy, who is the Gray Dragon of Len Yang!"

"In jest—"

"In all seriousness!" said Peter.

"It is death to enter Len Yang!"

"My mind is made up, mandarin!"

They had entered a narrow ravine, and on both sides of the slender trail rose up sharp elbows of hard rock. Peter's head was inclined a little to the right in an attitude he unconsciously assumed when listening for important words of man or wireless machine.

"It is the folly of adventurous youth," rang out the melodious and sincere voice of the mandarin. "It is a quest for a grail which will end in a pool of your own blood! Come into India with me!"

"But I decided—long ago—mandarin!"

"Your life is your life," said the mandarin sadly. "The City of Stolen Lives is beyond the mountain. *Ch'ing*!"

CHAPTER XVII

A road as white and straight as a silver bar led directly between the black, jutting shoulders of the hills to the gates of Len Yang.

Peter, with his heart beating a wild symphony of anticipation and fear, drew rein.

The small mule panted from the long desperate climb, his plump sides filling and caving as he drank in the sharp evening air.

Close behind the city's faded green walls towered the mountain ranges of Tibet, cold, gloomy, and vague in the purple mystery of their uncertain distances. They were like chained giants, brooding over the wrongs committed in the City of Stolen Lives, sullen in their mighty helplessness.

In the rays of the swollen sun the close-packed hovels enclosed within the moss-covered walls seemed to rest upon a blurring background of vermilion earth.

As Peter clicked his tongue and urged the tired little animal down the slope, he recalled the fragment of the description that had been given him of this place. Hideous people, with staring eyes, dripping the blood-red slime of the cinnabar-mines—leprosy, filth, vermin—

His palace! It stood out above the carmine ruck like a cube of purest ivory in a bleeding wound. Its marble outrivaled the whiteness of the Taj Mahal. It was a thing of snow-white beauty, like a dove poising for flight above a gory battlefield. And it was crowned by a dome of lapis lazuli, bluer than the South Pacific under a melting sun! But its base, Peter knew, was stained red, a blood-red which had seeped up and up from the carmine clay.

The gate to the city was down, and by the grace of his blue-satin robe Peter was permitted to enter.

And instantly he was obsessed with the flaming color of that man's unappeased passion. Red—red! The hovels were spattered with the red clay. The man, the skinny, wretched creature who begged for a moment of his gracious mercy at the gate, dripped in ruby filth. The mule sank and wallowed in vermilion mire.

Scrawny, undernourished children, naked, or in rags that afforded little more protection than nakedness, thrust their starved, red-smeared faces up at him, and gibed and howled.

And above all this arose the white majesty of his palace—the throne of the Gray Dragon!

Peter urged the mule up the scarlet alley to a clearing in which he found coolies by the thousands, trudging moodily from a central orifice that continued to disgorge more and more of them. The dreadful, reeking creatures blinked and gaped as if stupefied by the rosy light of the dying day.

Some carried lanterns of modern pattern; others bore picks and shovels and iron buckets, and they seemed to pass on interminably, to be engulfed in the lanes which ran in all directions from the clearing.

It was as though the earth were vomiting up the vilest of its creatures. And in the same light it was consuming others of equal vileness. Down into the red maws of the shaft an endless chain of men and women and children were descending.

Quite suddenly the light gave way, and Peter was aware that the night of the mountains was creeping out over the city, blotting out its disfigurements, replacing the hideous redness with a velvety black.

At the shaft's entrance a sharp spot of dazzling light sprang into being. It was an electric arc light! Somehow this apparition struck through the horror that saturated him, and he sighed as if his mind had relinquished a clinging nightmare.

Professionally now he gave this section of Len Yang another scrutiny. Thick cables sagged between stumpy poles like clusters of black snakes, all converging at the mine's entrance. His acute ears were registering a dull hum, indicating the imminence of high-geared machinery or of dynamos.

At the further side of the red shaft, now crusted with the night's shades, and garishly illuminated by the diamond whiteness of the frosty arc, he made out a deep, wide ditch, where flowed slowly a ruddy current, supplied from a short fat pipe.

Peter believed that electric pumps sucked out the red seepage waters from the mine and lifted them to the bloody ditch.

On impulse he lifted his eyes to the darkening heavens, and he knew now that the threads of this, his greatest adventure, were being drawn to a meeting point; for he detected in the sun's last refracted rays the bronze glint of aerial wires! What lay at the base of the antenna he could guess accurately. He hastened to the base of the nearest aerial mast—a pole reaching like a dark needle into the sky—and found there a low, dark building of varnished pine with a small door of eroded, green brass.

The rain-washed pine, the complete absence of windows, and the austerity of the massive brass door contributed to a personality of dignified and pessimistic aloofness. The building occupied a place to itself, as if its reserve were not to be tampered with, as if its dark and sullen mystery were not meant for the prying eyes of passing strangers.

Peter knocked brazenly upon the door, and it clanked shallowly, giving forth no inward echo. He waited expectantly.

It yawned open to the accompaniment of grumbled curses in a distinctly tenor whine.

A man with a white, shocked face stared at him from the threshold. The countenance was long, tapering, and it ended nowhere. Dull, mocking eyes with a burned-out look in them stared unblinkingly into Peter's face.

Peter could have shouted in recognition of the weak face, but he compressed his lips and bowed respectfully instead.

"What the hell do you want?" growled the man on the threshold.

"May Buddha bring the thousandth blessing to the soul of your virtuous mother," said Peter in solemn, benedictive tones. "It is my pleasure to desire entrance."

"Speak English, eh?" shrilled the man. "Dammit! Then come in!" And to this invitation he added blasphemy in Peter's own tongue that made his heart turn sour. It was the useless, raving blasphemy of a weakling. It was the man as Peter had known him of old. But a little worse. He still wore what remained of his Marconi uniform, tattered, grease-stained coat and trousers, with the ragged white and blue emblems of the steamship line by which he had been employed before he had disappeared. His bony hands trembled incessantly, and his face had the chalky pastiness native to the opium eater.

Peter, reflecting upon the honor which that uniform had always meant for him, felt like knocking this chattering, wild-eyed creature down and trampling upon him. But he bowed respectfully. The door clanged behind him, and his eye absorbed in an instant the details of the ponderously high-powered electrical apparatus.

"Speak God's language, eh?" whined the man. "Sit down and don't stare so. Sit down. Sit down."

"A mandarin never seats himself, O high one, until thrice invited."

"Thrice, four, five times, I tell you to sit down!" he babbled. "Men, even rat-eaters like you, who speak my language, are too rare to let go by. Mandarin?"

He stepped back and eyed his guest with stupid humor.

"I say, men who speak my language are rare. Nights I listen to fools on this machine, and tell them what I please. What is the news from outside? What is the news from home?"

"From where?"

"From America!" He stumbled over the words, and took in his breath with a long, trembling hiss between his yellow teeth.

"It is many years since I visited that strange land, O great one! It is many, many years, indeed, since I studied for the craft which you now perform so honorably."

"You—what was that?"

"I, too, studied to your honorable craft, my son. But it was denied me. Buddha decreed that I should preach his doctrines. It is my life to bring a little hope, a little gladness into the hearts—"

"You stand there and tell me that you know the code?" cried the white-faced man shrilly.

"Such was my good fortune," Peter replied gravely.

"Well, I believe you're a dam' liar, you Chink!" scoffed the other, who was swinging in nervousness or irritation from side to side.

Peter shrugged his shoulders, and permitted his gaze to fondle the monstrous transmission coil.

"I'll show you!" railed the man. "I'll give you a free chance, I will! Now, listen to me. Tell me what I say." He pursed his lips and whistled a series of staccato dots and dashes.

"What you have said," replied Peter in a deep voice, "is true, O high one!"

"What did I say?"

"You said: 'China, it is the hell-hole of the world!' Do I speak the truth?"

Peter thought that this crazy man—whose name had formerly been Harrison—was preparing to leap at him. But Harrison only sprang to his side and seized his hands in a clammy, excited grip. Tears of an exultant origin glittered in the man's eyes, now luminous.

"You stay with me, do you hear?" he babbled. "You stay here. I'll make it worth your while! I'll see you have money. I'll see—"

"But I have no need of money, O high one!" interrupted Peter in a somewhat resentful tone, striving to mask his eagerness.

"You stay!" cried Harrison.

"Lotus eater!" Peter said, knowing his ground perfectly.

"What if I am?" demanded Harrison defiantly. "So are you! So are we all! So is everybody who lives in this rotten country!"

"To the sick, all are sick," Peter quoted sorrowfully.

"Rot! As long as I must have opium, there's nothing more to be said. Now, I pry my eyes open with matches to stay awake. With you here—"

His thin voice trailed off. He had confessed what Peter already knew. It was the blurted confession, and the blurted plea, of a mind that was half consumed by drugs. A diseased mind which spoke the naked truth, which caught at no deception, which was tormented by its own gnawings and cravings to such an extent that it had lost the function of suspecting. Suspicion of a low, distorted sort might come later; but at its present ebb this mind was far too greedy to gain its own small ends to grope beyond.

The lids of Harrison's smoldering eyes drew down, and they were blue, a sickly, pallid blue. With their descent his face became a death-mask. But Peter knew from many an observation that such signs were deceptive; knew that opium was a powerful and sustaining drug; knew that Harrison, while weak and stupid and raving, was very much alive!

"There is little work to be done," went on the thin voice. "Only at night. Say you will stay with me!" he pleaded.

Peter permitted himself to frown, as if he had reached a negative decision. Harrison, torn by desire, flung himself down on his ragged knees, and sobbed on Peter's hand. Peter pushed him away loathfully.

"What is my task?"

Harrison sank back on his heels, oblivious of the wet streak which ran down from his eyes on either side of his thin, sharp nose, and delved nervously into his pocket. He withdrew a lump of black gum, about the size of a black walnut, broke off a fragment with his finger-nails, and masticated it slowly. He smirked sagely.

"He won't care. Why should he care?"

"Who, my son?"

"That man—that man who owns Len Yang, and me, and these rat-eaters. All *he* wants is results."

"Ah, yes. He owns other mines?"

"What does *he* care about the mines? Of course he directs the other mines by wireless. He owns a sixth of the world. *He* does. He is rich. Rich! You and I are poor fools. He gives me opium"—Harrison glared and gulped—"and he does not ask questions."

"Wise men learn without asking questions, my son," said Peter gravely.

"Certainly they do! He knows everything, and he never asks a question. Not a one! He answers them, *he* does!"

"You have asked him questions?"

"I? Humph! What an innocent fool you are, in spite of that gold on your collar! Have I seen him to ask questions?"

"That is what I meant."

"Not I. He is no fool. You may be the Gray Dragon for all of me. No one in Len Yang sees him. No one dares! It is death to see that man! Didn't I try? But only once!"

"You did try?"

"That was enough. I got as far as the first step of the ivory palace. Some one clubbed me! I was sick. I thought I was going to die! There is a scar on my neck. It never seems to heal!"

The senile whine trailed off into a thin, abusive whimper. His bony jaws moved slowly and meditatively. He went on:

"He is crazy, too. Women! Beautiful women for the mines! Men—men—men everywhere know the price he will pay. In pure silver!"

"He pays well, my son?"

"A thousand taels, if he is satisfied. That is where this hole got its name. You know the name—the City of Stolen Lives? It should be the City of Lost

Hope. For none ever leave. The mines swallow them up. What becomes of them?"

"Ah! What does become of the stolen lives?"

The sunken eyes stared playfully at him. "What is a thousand taels to him? He is rich, I tell you! They say his cellar is filled with gold—pure gold; that his rooms and halls run and drip with gold, just as his rat-eaters run and drip with the cinnabar poison. And the wireless—he has stations, and this is the best. Mine is the best. I see to that, let me tell you!"

"To be sure!"

"These hunters, these men who know his price for beautiful women—he will have none other—and who are paid a thousand taels—"

"Where did you say these stations are?"

"In all parts. There is a station in Afghanistan, between Kabul and Jalalabad, and one in Bengal, in the Khasi Hills, and another in northern Szechwan Province, and one in Siam, on the Bang Pakong River—"

"A station on the Bang Pakong?"

"Yes, I tell you. All over. These hunters find a woman, a lovely girl; and they must describe their prize in a few words. He is sly! The fewer the better. If the words appeal to him, he has me tell them to come. Lucky devils! A thousand taels to the lucky devils! Some day I myself may become a hunter."

"It is tempting," agreed Peter. "But why does he want beautiful young girls for his mine, my son?"

Harrison ignored the question.

"Tonight I will listen. You can watch me. Then you can see how simple it is. It is time."

Peter was aware that the door had opened and closed behind his back, and now he heard the faint scraping of a sandaled foot, heavy with the red slime. A Chinese, in the severe black of an attendant, stood looking down at him distrustfully. His eyebrows were shaved, and a mustache drooped down to his sharp, flat chin like sea-weed.

He asked Harrison a sharp question in a dialect that smacked of the guttural Tibetan.

"He wants to know where you came from," translated Harrison irritably.

"From Wenchow. A mandarin. He should know."

The man in severe black bowed respectfully, and Peter looked at him frigidly.

Harrison slipped the Murdock receivers over his ears, and his voice went on in a weak, garrulous and meaningless whimper.

"Static—static—static. It is horrible tonight. I cannot hear these fellows. Ah! Afghanistan has nothing, nor Bengal. Hey, you fool, I cannot hear this fellow in Szechwan. He has a message. Yes, you, I cannot hear him. Not a word! He is faint, like a bad whisper. They will beat me again if I cannot hear!"

He tried again, forcing the rubber knobs against his ears until they seemed to sink into his head.

"Have you good hearing?"

"I will try," said Peter.

"Then sit here. You must hear him, or we will both be beaten. This fellow goes straight to *him*."

Peter slipped into the vacated chair and strapped down the receivers. A long, faint whisper, as indistinguishable as the lisp of leaves on a distant hill, trickled into his ears. Ordinarily he would have given up such a station in disgust, and waited for the air to clear. Now he wanted to establish his ability, to demonstrate the acuteness of hearing for which he was famous.

Behind him the black-garbed attendant muttered, and Peter scowled at him to be silent.

With deftness that might have surprised that wretch, Harrison, had his wits been more alert, he raised and closed switches for transmission, and rapped out in a quick, professional "okay."

He cocked his head to one side, as he always did when listening to far-away signals, and a pad and pencil were slid under his hand.

The world and its noises and the tense, eager figures behind him, retreated and became nothing. In all eternity there was but one thing—the message from the whispering Szechwan station.

His pencil trailed lightly, without a sound, across the smooth paper.

A message for L. Y. An American girl. Brown hair. Eyes with the moon's mystery. Lips like a new-born rose. Enchantingly young.

The blood boiled into Peter's brain, and the pencil slipped from fingers that were like ice. There was only one girl in the world who answered to that description. Eileen Lorimer! She had been captured again, and brought back to China!

He grabbed for the paper. It was gone. Gone, too, was the black-garbed attendant, hastening to his master.

Harrison was pawing his shoulder with a skinny, white hand, and making noises in his throat.

"You lucky fool! He'll give you *cumshaw*. God, you have sharp ears! Only one man I ever knew had such sharp ears. He always gives *cumshaw*. *Na-mien-pu-liao-pa*! You must divide with me. That is only fair. But—what difference? Here you can enter, but you can never leave. You have no use for silver. I have."

The face of Eileen Lorimer swam out of Peter's crazed mind. Miss Vost, that lovely innocent-eyed creature, fitted the same description!

Peter stared stupidly at the massive transmission key, and disdained a reply. Miss Vost—and the red mines! He shuddered.

Harrison was whining again at his ear. "He says yes. Yes! Tell that fellow yes, and be quick. The Gray Dragon will give him an extra thousand taels for haste. Oh, the lucky fool! Two thousand taels! Tell him, or shall I?"

How could Peter say no? The ghastly white face was staring at him suspiciously now.

While he hesitated Harrison pushed him aside, and his fingers flew up and down on the black rubber knob. "Yes—yes—yes. Send her in a hurry. A thousand taels bonus. The lucky devil!"

Out of Peter's anguish came but one solution, and that vague and indecisive. He must wait and watch for Miss Vost, and take what drastic measures he could devise to recapture her when the time came.

The pallid lips trembled again at his ear. "Here! You must divide with me. A bag of silver. *Yin*! A bag of it! Listen to the chink of it!"

Peter seized the yellow pouch and thrust it under his silken blouse. He was beginning to realize that he had been exceptionally lucky in catching the signals of the Szechwan station. He was vastly more important now than this wretch who plucked at his arm.

"Give me my half!" whined Harrison.

Peter doubled his fist.

"Give me my half!" Harrison clung to his arm and shook him irritably.

Peter hit him squarely in the mouth.

CHAPTER XVIII

As night melted into day and day was swallowed up by night, the problem which confronted Peter took on more serious and baffling proportions. His hope of entering the ivory palace was dismissed. It was imperative for him to give up the idea of entering, of piercing the lines of armed guards and reaching the room where the master of the City of Stolen Lives held forth until some later time.

That had been his earlier ambition, but the necessity of discarding the original plan became hourly more important with the drawing near of the girl captive.

If he could deliver Miss Vost from this dreadful city, that would be more than an ample reward for his long, adventurous quest.

He could not sleep. Perched on an ancient leather stool upon the roof of the wireless building, he kept a nightly and a daily watch with his eyes fixed upon the drawbridge. A week went by. Food was carried up to him, and he scarcely touched it. The rims of his eyes became scarlet from sleeplessness, and he muttered constantly, like a man on the verge of insanity, as his eyes wandered back and forth over the red filth, from the shadowy bridge to the shining white of the palace.

Drearily, like souls lost and wandering in a half world, the prisoners of Len Yang trudged to the scarlet maws of the mine and were engulfed for long, pitiless hours, and were disgorged, staggering and blinking, in Tibet's angry evening sun.

The woeful sight would madden any man. And yet each day new souls were born to the grim red light of Len Yang's day, and clinging remorsefully to the hell which was their lot, other bleeding souls departed, and their shrunken bodies fed to the scarlet trough, where they were washed into oblivion in some sightless cavern below.

It was a bitterly cold night, with the wind blowing hard from the ice and snow on the Tibetan peaks, when Peter's long vigilance was rewarded. A booming at the gate, followed by querulous shouts, aroused him from his lethargy. He looked out over the crenelated wall, but the cold moonlight revealed a vacant street.

The booming and shouting persisted, and Peter was sure that Miss Vost had come, for in cities of China only an extraordinary event causes drawbridges to be lowered.

He slipped down the creaking ladder into the wireless-room. Harrison was in a torpor, muttering inanely and pleadingly as his long, white fingers opened and closed, perhaps upon imagined gold.

Peter opened the heavy brass door, and let himself into the deserted street. The jeweled sandals with which Chang had provided him sank deep into the red mire, and remained there.

He sped on, until he reached the black shadow of the great green wall. Suddenly the bridge gave way with many creakings and groanings and Peter saw the moonlight upon the silvery white road beyond.

A group of figures, mounted on mules, with many pack-mules in attendance, made a grotesque blot of shadow. Then a shrill scream.

Hoofs trampled hollowly upon the loose, rattling boards, and the cavalcade marched in.

A slim figure in a long, gray cloak rode on the foremost mule. Peter, aided by the black shadow, crept to her side.

"Miss Vost! Miss Vost!" he called softly. "It is Peter, Peter Moore!"

He heard her gasp in surprise, and her moan went into his heart like a ragged knife.

Peter tried to keep abreast, but the red clay dragged him back. Behind him some one shouted. They would emerge into the sharp moonlight in another second.

"Help me! Oh, help me!" she sobbed. "He's following! He is too late!"

She was carried out into the moonlight. At the same time, countless figures seemed to rise from the ground—from nowhere—and in every direction Peter was blocked. The stench of Len Yang's miserable inhabitants crept from these figures upon the chill night air.

Naked, unclean shoulders brushed him; moist, slimy hands pressed him back. But he was not harmed; he was simply pushed backward and backward until his bare foot encountered the first board of the bridge which was still lowered.

Behind him an order was hissed. He placed his back to the surging shadows. Coils of heavy rope were unfolding. The drawbridge was being raised.

Down the white road, veering drunkenly from one side to the other, came a leaping black dot.

The drawbridge creaked, the ropes became taut, and the far end lifted an inch at a time.

Peter shouted, but no one heeded him. His breath pumped in and out of his lungs in short, anguished gulps. He leaped out upon the bridge, and shouted again. The creaking ceased; the span became stationary.

The drunken dot leaped into the form of a giant upon a galloping mule which swept upon them in a confusion of dust. Hoofs pounded on the bridge; the giant on the mule drew rein, and to Peter it was given to look upon the face of the man he thought dead. The raging eyes of Bobbie MacLaurin swept from his face to his muddy feet.

"Moore! Where have they taken her?" ripped out the giant on the mule.

"Dismount and follow me. To the white palace! Are you armed?"

"And ready to shoot every dam' yellow snake in all of China!"

He jumped heavily to the boards, and Peter caught the gleam of steel-tipped bullets in the narrow strap which was slung from shoulder to waist.

The foreman of the rope-pullers dared to raise his head, and Bobbie kicked him with his heavy-shod foot in the stomach, and the coolie bounded up and backward, and lay draped limply over the side.

As they ran under the broad, dark arch into the street, he gave Peter in one hand the thick butt of an army automatic, and in the other a half-dozen loaded clips.

And they began blazing their way to the palace steps. Weird figures sprang up from the muck, and were shot back to earth.

They reached the hill top, and the green moon of Tibet scored the roof of the white palace.

A handful of guards, with rifles and swords, rushed down the broad, low flight.

The two men flung themselves upon the clay, while high-powered bullets plunked on either side of them or soughed overhead. The two automatics blazed in shattering chorus. The guards parted, backed up, some ran away, others fell, and Peter felt the sudden burn of screaming lead across his shoulder. He slipped another clip of cartridges into the steel butt; they leaped up and raced to the white steps. A rifle spurted and roared in the black shadow. Bobbie groaned, staggered, and climbed on. Now they were guided by a woman's sharp cries issuing from an areaway. And they stopped in amazement before a majestic white-marble portal.

With two coolies struggling to pinion her arms, the girl was kicking, scratching, biting with the fire of a wildcat, dragging them toward the broad, white veranda.

Bobbie shot the foremost of them through the brain, and the other, gibbering terribly, vanished into the shadow.

Peter caught Miss Vost by one hand and raced down the steps. Bobbie, holding his head in a grotesque gesture, ran and staggered behind them.

Bobbie waved his free arm savagely. "Don't wait for me! Get her out of this place! Don't take your eyes from her till you reach Wenchow!"

He wheeled and shot three times at a figure which had stolen up behind him. The figure spun about and seemed to melt into a hole in the earth.

Peter wrapped his arm about Bobbie's waist and dragged him down the hill. Miss Vost, as he realized after that demonstration in the areaway, could handle herself.

The bridge was up. Lights glowed from hovel ways like evil red eyes. Peter released the rope and the bridge sprang down to the road with a boom that shook the solid walls. Bobbie's mule nosed toward them, and Peter all but shot the friendly little animal!

Between Peter and Miss Vost, who was chattering and weeping as if her heart was breaking, their wounded companion was lifted into the saddle. They crossed the bridge, and the bridge was whipped up behind them.

Not until they attained the brow of the hill did they look back upon the gloomy walls, now black and peaceful under the high clear moon. And it was not until then that Peter marveled upon their easy escape, upon the snatching up of the bridge as they left. Why had no shots been fired at them as they climbed the silver road?

They trusted to no providence other than flight. All night long they hastened toward the highway which led to Ching-Fu—and India. And they had no breath to spare for mere words. At any moment the long arm of the Gray Dragon might reach out and pluck them back.

Only once they paused, while Peter ripped out the satin lining of his robe and bound up the wound in Bobbie's dazed head.

Miss Vost sat down upon a moss-covered rock and wept. She made no effort to help him, but stared and wiped her eyes with her hands.

A misty, rosy dawn found them above the valley in which ran the connecting road between Ching-Fu and the Irriwaddi.

Miss Vost was the first to see the camp-fires of a caravan. She laughed, then cried, and she tottered toward Peter, who stood there, a lean weird figure in his tattered blue robe and his tangled beard.

She extended her arms slightly as she approached, and her gray eyes were luminous with a soft and gentle fire.

Bobbie staggered away from the mule's heaving sides, with one hand fumbling weakly at the satin bandage, and in his eyes, too, was the look that rarely comes into the eyes of men.

In a single glance Peter could see to the very depths of that man's unselfish soul. It was like glancing into the light of a golden autumn morning.

Miss Vost lifted both of Peter's hands, and one was still blue from the back-fire of the automatic. She lifted them to her lips and kissed them solemnly. With a little fluttering sigh she looked up at Bobbie, standing beside her and towering above her like a strong hill.

They looked long at one another, and Peter felt for a moment curiously negligible. He had cause to feel that his presence was absolutely unessential when, with a happy, soft little laugh, Miss Vost sprang up and was crushed in the cradle of Bobbie's great arms.

Peter looked down into the green valley with tears standing in his grave, blue eyes. The caravan was slowly winding out upon the trail. In five weeks it would leave Kalikan, the last soil of China, on the frontier of India.

Peter felt exceedingly happy as he hastened down the hillside to catch the caravan.

PART II

THE BITTER FOUNTAIN

She bends over her work once more:
"I will weave a fragment of verse among the flowers of his robe,
and perhaps its words will tell him to return."

—LI-TAI-PE

CHAPTER I

The newly arrived wireless operator of the Java, China, and Japan liner, *Persian Gulf*, deposited his elbows upon the promenade deck-rail, and cast a side-long glance at the Chinese coolie who had taken up a similar position about a bumboat's length aft. And the coolie returned his deliberate stare with a look of dreamy interest, then quickly shifted his glance to the city which smoldered and vibrated across Batavia's glinting, steel-blue harbor.

Without turning his head the wireless man continued to watch sharply the casual movements of this Chinese, quite as he had been observing him since they had left Tandjong Priok in the company's launch and come out to the *Persian Gulf* together.

He had suspected the fellow from the very first, and he was prepared, on the defensive; yet he was willing and eager to take the offensive should this son of the yellow empire so much as show the haft of his kris, or whisper a word of counsel in his ear. The latter he feared quite as much as the former, for it would mean many things.

As the fellow sidled a little closer, Peter was aware that the man was making queer signals with his slanting eyes for the purpose of attracting his attention, without arousing the curiosity or interest of any persons who might be observing the two.

Whereupon Peter turned on his left heel, walked to the other's side and gave him a stare of deliberate hostility.

The coolie moved backward a few inches by flexing his body; his feet remained as they were. And as Peter ran his eye from the black crown hat to the faded blue jacket, the black-sateen pants, which were clipped about the ankles, giving them a mild pantaloon effect, and to the black slippers with their thick buck-soles, the coolie smiled.

It was a smile of arrogance, of self-satisfaction. Indeed, it was the smile of a hunter who has winged his prey, and smiles an instant to watch it squirm before administering the death-shot.

"You wanchee my?" inquired Peter succinctly.

"You allatime go Hong Kong way?" replied the coolie, his smile becoming a little more civil, while he measured Peter's length, breadth, and seemed to estimate his brawn.

It was a foolish question, for the *Persian Gulf*, as everybody in Batavia knew quite well, made a no-stop run from the Javanese port to Hong Kong. Peter indicated this fact impatiently.

"No go Hong Kong way?" persisted the coolie, not relaxing that devilish grin. "*Maskee* Hong Kong. *Nidzen yang giang*?"

The wheezy old whistle of the *Persian Gulf* told the world in unmistakable accents that sailing time was nigh. The *Persian Gulf* was not a new boat or a fast boat, and she sailed in the intermediate service south of Java. Yet she was stout, and typhoons meant very little to her as yet.

"Why not?" demanded Peter in the tones of an interlocutor.

The coolie simply lifted the flap of his blue tunic, and Peter was given the singular glimpse of a bone-hafted knife, the blade of which he could guess lay flat against the man's paunch.

Still the Chinese smiled, without avarice. Plainly he was stating the case as it was known to him, reciting a lesson, as it were, which had been taught him by one skilled in the ways of killing and of espionage.

The facts of this case were that Peter Moore should immediately postpone or give up entirely his trip to Hong Kong for reasons best known to the powers arrayed against him. And strangely enough, Hong Kong was one of the two cities in China where Peter had pressing business.

It made him furious, this knowledge that the man of Len Yang had picked up the trail again.

So Peter glanced up and down the deck to see if there would be any witness to his act, and there was only one, a passenger. The Chinese was still smiling, but by degrees that smile was becoming more evil and sour. He was perplexed at the wireless operator's furtive examination of the promenade deck. Yet he was not kept in the dark regarding Peter's intentions much longer than it would have taken him to utter the Chinese equivalent of Jack Robinson.

With an energetic swoop, Peter seized him by the nearest arm and leg, and in the next breath the coolie was shooting through an awful void, tumbling head over heels like a bag of loose rice, straight for the oily bosom of Batavia's harbor!

So much for Peter's slight knowledge of jiu-jitsu.

He was angrily at a loss to account for the appearance of this trailer, for he had been watchful every moment since escaping from the green walls of that blood-tinted city, and he was positive that he had shaken off pursuit. Yet somewhere along that trail, which ran from Len Yang to Bhamo, from Rangoon to Penang, and around the horn of Malacca, his escape had been betrayed.

The spies of Len Yang's master must have possessed divining rods which plumbed the very secrets of Peter's soul.

In Batavia Peter attended to a task long deferred. He despatched a cablegram to Eileen Lorimer in Pasadena, California, advising her that he was still on top, very much alive, and would some day, he hoped, pay her a visit.

He wondered what that gray-eyed little creature would say, what she would do, upon receipt of the message from far-away Java. It had been many long months since their parting on the rain-soaked bund at Shanghai. That scene was quite clear in his mind when he turned from the Batavia cable office to negotiate his plan with the wireless man of the *Persian Gulf*.

Peter found the man willing, if not positively eager, to negotiate—a circumstance that Peter forecasted in his mind as soon as his eyes had dwelt a fleeting moment upon the pudgy white face with its greedy, small, black eyes. The man was quite willing to lose himself in the hills behind Batavia until the *Persian Gulf* was hull down on the deep-blue horizon, upon a consideration of gold.

Peter could have paid his passage to Hong-Kong, and achieved his ends quite as handily as in his present role of wireless operator. But his fingers had begun to itch again for the heavy brass transmission-key, and his ears were yearning for the drone of radio voices across the ethereal void.

It was on sailing morning that he was given definite evidence in the person of the Chinese coolie that his zigzagged trail had been picked up again by those alert spies of Len Yang's monarch.

He steamed out to the high black side of the steamer in the company's passenger-launch, gazing back at the drowsy city, quite sure that the pursuit was off, when he felt the glinting black eyes of the coolie boring into him from the tiny cabin doorway.

His suspicions kindled slowly, and he admitted them reluctantly. It was the privilege of any Chinese coolie to stare at him, quite as it was the privilege of a cat to stare at a king. But the seed of mistrust was sown, and it was sown in fertile soil.

Peter ignored the stare, however, until the launch puffed up alongside the sea-ladder, then he gave the coolie a glance pregnant with hostility and understanding.

Taking the swaying steps three at a time, Peter hastened to his stateroom, emerging about five minutes later in a white uniform, the uniform of the J. C. & J. service, with a little gold at the collar, bands of gold about the cuffs, and gold emblems of shooting sparks, indicative of his caste, upon either arm.

He looked for the coolie and found him on the starboard side of the promenade deck. The subsequent events have already been partly narrated.

CHAPTER II

The coolie plunged into the water with a weltering splash which sent a small spiral of spray almost to the deck. For a moment the man in the water pedaled and flailed, vastly frightened, and gasping, above the clang of the engine-room telegraph, for a rope. The black side of the *Persian Gulf* started to slide away from him.

"You better make for shore!" shouted Peter between megaphonic hands.

Several boatmen were poling in the coolie's direction, but all of them refrained from slipping within reach of the thrashing hands. A Javanese boatman can find more amusing and enjoyable scenes than an angry Chinese coolie flailing about in the water; but he must travel many miles to find them.

"Swim to the *ma-fou*," Peter encouraged him. He knew there were sharks in that emerald pond.

His attention then was diverted by a flutter of white at his elbow. He turned his head. The lonely passenger, a girl, was smiling mischievously into his face. But in her very dark eyes there was a blunt question.

"Why did you do that?" she asked in a voice that rang with a low musical quality. Her voice and her beauty were of the tropics, as were the features which, molded together, gave form to that beauty; because her hair and eyes were of a color, dark like walnut, and her olive skin was like silk under silk, with the rosy color of her youth and fire showing underneath.

She was rather startling, especially her deep, dark and restless eyes. It was by sense rather than by anything his eyes could base conclusions upon that Peter realized her spirited personality, knew instinctively that radiant and destructive fires burned behind the sombre, questioning eyes. The full, red lips might have told him this much.

And now these lips were forming a smile in which was a little humor and a great deal of tenderness.

Why there should be any element of tenderness in the stranger's smile was a point that Peter was not prepared to analyze. He had been subjected to the tender smiles of women, alas, on more than one occasion; and it was part of Peter's nature to take these gifts unquestioningly. He was not one to look a gift smile in the mouth! Yet, if Peter had looked back upon his experience, he would have admitted that such a smile was slightly premature, that it smacked of sweet mystery.

And it is whispered that richly clad young women do not ordinarily smile with tenderness upon young ruffians who throw apparently peaceful citizens from the decks of steamers into waters guarded by sharks.

To carry this argument a step farther, it has always seemed an unfair dispensation of nature that women should fall in love so desperately, so suddenly, so unapologetically and in such numbers with Peter the Brazen.

The phenomenon cannot be explained in a breath, or in a paragraph, if at all. While he was good to look upon, neither was Peter a god. While he was at all times chivalrous, yet he was not painstakingly thoughtful in the small matters which are supposed to advance the cause of love at a high pace. Nor was he guided by a set of fixed rules such as men are wont to employ at roulette and upon women.

Peter did not understand women, yet he had a perfectly good working basis, for he took all of them seriously, with gravity, and he gave their opinions a willing ear and considerable deference.

The rest is a mystery. Peter was neither particularly glib nor witty. Instinctively he knew the values of the full moon, the stars, and he had the look of a young man who has drunk at the fountain of life on more than one occasion, finding the waters thereof bitter, with a trace of sweetness and a decided tinge of novelty.

Life was simply a great big adventure to Peter the Brazen; and he had been shot, stabbed, and beaten into insensibility on many occasions, and he was not unwilling for more. He dearly loved a dark mystery, and he had a certain reluctant fondness for a woman's bright, deceptive eyes.

As from a great distance he heard the jeers of the Javanese boatmen and the flounderings of the coolie as he looked now into the dark, deep eyes of this pretty, smiling stranger.

"Why did you do that?" she repeated softly.

"Because I wanted to," returned Peter with his winning smile.

"But there are sharks in there." This in a voice of gentle reproof.

"I hope they eat him alive," said Peter, unabashed.

"You threw him overboard just because you wanted to. And if you want to, I'll go next, I suppose."

"You might," laughed Peter. "When I have these spells I simply grab the nearest person and over he goes. It is a terrible habit, isn't it?"

"Perhaps he insulted you."

"Or threatened me."

"Ah!" Her sigh expressed that she understood everything. "May I ask: Who are you?"

"I? Peter Moore."

"I mean, your uniform. You are one of the ship's officers, are you not?"

"The wireless operator. Shall we consider ourselves properly introduced?"

"My name is Romola Borria. I presume you are an American—or British."

"American," informed Peter. "And you? Spanish *señorita*?"

"I have no nationality," she replied easily. "I am what we call in China, a 'B.I.C.'"

"Born in China!"

"Born in Canton, China. Father: Portuguese; mother: Australian. Answer: What am I?" She laughed deliciously, and Peter was moved.

They lingered long enough to see the coolie drag himself up on the shore unassisted, and then separated, the girl to make ready for lunch and to request the steward to assign them to adjoining seats at the same table, and Peter to take a look at the register, the crew, and what passengers might be on deck.

The passengers, lounging in steamer-chairs awaiting the call to tiffin, and the deck crew, strapping down the forward cargo booms and battening the forward hatch, Peter gave a careful inspection, retaining their images in an eye that was rapidly being trained along photographic lines.

It was a comparatively simple matter, Peter found, to remember peoples' faces; the important point being to select some striking feature of the countenance, and then persistently drive this feature home in his memory. He knew that the human memory is a perverse organ, much preferring to forget and lose than to retain.

So he looked over the crew and found them to be quite Dutch and quite self-satisfied, with no more than a slight but polite interest in him and his presence. Wireless operators, as a rule, are self-effacing individuals who inhabit dark cabins and have very little to say.

He called at the purser's office and helped himself to the register, finding the name of Romola Borria in full, impulsive handwriting, giving her address as Hong Kong, Victoria; and a long list of Dutch names, representing quite likely nothing more harmful than sugar and coffee men, with perhaps a sprinkling of copra and pearl buyers.

Peter then investigated the wireless cabin, which was situated aft on the turn of the promenade deck, and commanding a not entirely inspiring view of the cargo well and the steerage.

Assuring himself that the wireless machine was in good working order, Peter hooked back the door, turned on the electric fan to air the place out, and with his elbows on the rail gave the steerage passengers a looking over.

He did not look far before his gaze stopped its traveling.

Directly below him, sitting cross-legged on a hatch-cover, was a Chinese or Eurasian girl whose face was colorless, whose lips were red, and whose eyes, half-lidded, because of the dazzling sunlight, were of an unusual blue-green shade.

Had Peter wished to make inquiries regarding this maiden, he would have found that she was from the Chinese settlement in Macassar, and on her way to Canton, to pay a visit to a grandmother she had never seen. But it was Peter's nature to spin little dreams of his own whenever he contemplated exotic young women, to place them in settings of his own manufacture.

Her blue-black hair was parted in a white line that might have been centered by the tip of her tiny nose and an unseen point on the nape of her pretty neck.

Peter could not know, as he studied her, how this innocent maid from Macassar was destined to play an important and significant part in his life, entering and leaving it like a gentle and caressing afternoon monsoon. His guess, as he looked away, was that she was a woman of no caste, from her garb; probably a river girl; more than likely, worse. Yet there was an undeniable air of innocence and youth in her narrow shoulders as she slowly rocked. Peter could see the tips of bright-red sandals peeping from under each knee, and he guessed her to be about eighteen.

She caught sight of Peter, who had folded his arms and was resting their elbows idly upon the teak rail, and their eyes met and lingered. A light, indescribably sad and appealing, shone in the blue-green eyes, which seemed to open larger and larger, until they became round pools of darting, mysterious reflection. It was a moment in which Peter was suspended in space.

"I am afraid that wireless operators are not always discreet," purred a low, sweet voice at his side.

Peter smiled his grave smile, and vouchsafed nothing. The girl in the steerage had returned to her sewing and was apparently quite oblivious of his presence. And still that look of demure, wistful appeal stood out in his memory.

Romola Borria was murmuring something, the context of which was not quite clear to him.

"Eh? I beg pardon?"

"It is quite dreadful, this traveling all alone," she remarked.

"Yes," he admitted. "Sometimes I bore myself into a state of agony."

"And it breeds such strange, such unexplainable desires and caprices," the girl went on in her cultivated, honeyed tones. "Strangers sometimes are so—so cold. For instance, yourself."

"I?" exclaimed Peter, supporting himself on the stanchion. "Why, I'm the friendliest man in the world!"

Romola Borria pursed her lips and studied him analytically.

"I wonder—" she began, and stopped, fretting her lip. "I should like to ask you a very blunt and a very bold question." Her expression was darkly puzzled.

"Go right ahead," urged Peter amiably, "don't mind me."

"Why I speak in this way," she explained, "is that since I ran away from Hong Kong—"

"Oh, you ran away from Hong Kong!"

"Of course!" She said it in a way that indicated a certain lack of understanding on his part. "Since I ran away from Hong Kong I have been looking, looking for such—for such a man as you appear to be, to—to confide in."

"Don't you suppose a woman would do almost as well?" spoke Peter, who, through experience, had grown to dislike the father-confessor role.

"If you don't *care* to listen—" she began, as though he had hurt her.

"I am all ears," stated Peter, with his most convincing smile.

"And I have changed my mind," said Romola Borria with a disdainful toss of her pretty head. "Besides, I think the Herr Captain would have a word with you."

The fat and happy captain of the *Persian Gulf* occupied the breadth if not the height of the doorway, wearing his boyish grin, and Peter hastened to his side with a murmured apology to the girl as he left her.

He merely desired to have transmitted an unimportant clearance message to the Batavia office, to state that all was well and that the thrust-bearing, repaired, was now performing "smoot'ly."

Dropping the hard rubber head-phones over his ears, Peter listened to the air, and in a moment the silver crash of the white spark came from the doorway.

Romola Borria stared long and venomously at the little Chinese maiden, who was sewing away industriously as she rocked to and fro on the hatch. Immersed in her own thoughts the girl, removing her quick eyes from the flying needle, glanced up at the deep-blue sky, and, smiling, shivered in a sort of ecstasy.

CHAPTER III

At dinner Peter met the notables. It seemed the fat and handsome captain had taken a fancy to him. And it was as Peter had deduced earlier. These passengers were stodgy Dutchmen, each with a little world of his own, and forming the sole orbit of that little world. For the most part they were plantation owners escaping the seasonal heat for the cool breezes of a vacation in Japan, boastful of their possessions, smug in their Dutch self-complacency, and somewhat gluttonous in their manner of eating.

The fat captain beamed. The fat plantation owners gorged themselves and jabbered. The three-piece orchestra played light opera that the world had forgotten. The company became light-hearted as more frosty bottles of that exotic drink, *arracka*, were disgorged by the *Persian Gulf's* excellent ice-box. And all the while, speaking in light, soothing tones, Romola Borria gazed alluringly into the watchful eyes of Peter Moore.

At length the chairs were pushed back, and Peter, with this fairy-like creature in a dinner-gown of most fetching pink gossamer clinging to his arm, took to the deck for an after-dinner Abdullah.

They chatted in low, confiding tones of the people in the dining-room. They whispered in awe of the Southern Cross, which sparkled like frost on the low horizon. She confessed that at night the moon was her god, and Peter, feeling exalted under the influence of her exquisite charm, the touch of the light fingers upon his arm which tingled and burned under the subtle pressure, became bold and recited that verse of "Mandalay" wherein "I kissed her where she stood."

It was quite thrilling, quite delicious, and altogether quite too fine to last.

After a while, when they were passing the door of the wireless cabin, Romola squeezed his arm lightly and expressed a desire to have him send a message, a message she had quite forgotten. When Peter replied that such a message would be costly, involving an expensive retransmission by cable from Manila to Hong Kong, she only laughed.

Peter snapped on the green-shaded light and handed her pad and pencil. Dropping lightly to the couch which ran the length of the opposite wall, she nibbled at the pencil's rubber, and her smooth brow was darkened by a frown of perplexity.

Peter, lowering the aerial switch, sent out an inquiring call for the Manila station. The air was still as death. A dreary hush filled the black receivers, and then, through this gloomy silence trickled a far-away silver voice, the brisk, clear signals of Manila.

He swiveled half around, and the girl nervously extended the pad of radio blanks.

The message was directed to Emiguel Borria, the Peak, Hong Kong, and it contained the information that she would reach the Hong Kong anchorage on the following Tuesday morning. The last sentence; "Do not meet me."

Peter inclined his eyebrows slightly, but not impertinently, counted the words and flashed them to the operator at Manila.

This one shot back the following greeting:

"Who are you? Only one man on the whole Pacific has a fist like that."

Peter changed the manner of his sending, resorting to a long and painful "drawl."

"I am a little Chinese waif," Peter spelled out slowly, and smiled, adding: "Good hunting to you, Smith!" He signed off.

The silvery spark of Smith was quick in reply.

"If you are Peter Moore, the Marconi people are scouring the earth trying to find you. Are you Peter Moore?"

"In China," replied Peter breezily, changing back to the inimitably crisp sending for which he was famous, "we bite off people's noses who are inquisitive. Good night, old-timer!"

The voice of Manila screamed back in faint reprisal, but Peter dropped the nickeled band to the ledge, and pivoted quickly, to face the girl.

It was startling, the look she was giving him. Perhaps he had completed the transmission before she was aware. At all events, when Peter turned with a smile, her eyes bored straight into his with a distorted look, a look that seemed cruel, as if it might have sprung from a well of hate; and hard and glinting and black as polished jade.

All of this vanished when she caught Peter's eyes, and it was as the passage of a vision, unreal. In its place was an expression of demureness, of gentle, almost fondling meekness. Had she been staring, not at him, but beyond him, over the miles to a detestable scene, a view of horror? It seemed more than likely.

Then he observed that the door of the wireless room was closed. He made as if to open it, but she interrupted him midway with a commanding gesture of her white, small hand.

"Lock it, and sit down here beside me."

Somewhat dazed and greatly flabbergasted, Peter obeyed.

He locked the door, then sat down beside her. She moved closer, took his hand, wrapped both of hers tightly around it, and leaned toward him until the breath from her parted lips was upon his throat, moist and warm, and her eyes were great shining balls of limpid mystery and dancing excitement, so close to his that he momentarily expected their eyelashes to mingle.

She caught her breath, and then, for such dramatic circumstances, made a most ridiculous remark. She realized that herself, for she whipped out:

"It is a foolish question. But, Mr. Moore, do you believe in love at first sight?"

Peter's tense look dissolved into a smile of giddy relief. He was expecting something quite frightful, and the clear wit of him found a ready answer.

"Foolish?" he chuckled. "Why, I'm the most devout worshiper at the shrine! The shrine brags about me! It says to unbelievers: Now, if you don't believe in love at first sight, just cast your orbs upon Peter Moore, our most shining example. Allah, by Allah! The old philanderer is assuredly of the faith!"

"I am quite serious, Mr. Moore."

"As I was afraid, Miss Borria. Seriously, if you must know it, then here goes: As soon as I saw you I was mad about you! Call it infatuation, call it a rush of blood to my foolish young head, call it anything you like—"

"Why don't you stop all this?" she broke him off.

"All what?" he inquired innocently.

"This—this life you are leading. This indolence. This constant toying with danger. This empty life. This sham of adventure-love that you affect. It will get you nothing. I know! I, too, thought it was a great lark at first, and I played with fire; and you know just what happens to the children who play with fire.

"At first you skirt the surface, and then you go a little deeper, and finally you can do nothing but struggle. It is a terrible feeling, to find that your wonderful toy is killing you. Certain people in China, Mr. Moore, are conducting practises that you of the western world frown upon. And blundering upon these practices, as perhaps you have, you believe you are very bold and daring, and you are thrilled as you rub elbows with death, in tracing the dragons to their dens."

"Dragons!" The syllables cracked from Peter's lips, and his wits, which were wandering in channels of their own while this lecture progressed, suddenly were bundled together, and he was alert and keenly attentive.

"Or call them what you will," went on the girl in a low-pitched monotone. "I call them dragons, because the dragon is a filthy, wretched symbol."

"You have some knowledge of my encounters with—dragons?" put in Peter as casually as he was able.

"I profess to know nothing of your encounters with anybody," replied the girl quietly and patiently. "I base my conclusions only on what I have seen. This morning I saw you throw a Chinese coolie into the harbor at Batavia. It happens that I have seen that coolie before, and it also happens that I know a little—do not ask me what I know, for I will never tell you—a little about the company that coolie keeps."

"I guess you are getting a little beyond my depth," stated Peter uncomfortably. "Would you mind sort of summing up what you've just said?"

"I mean, I want to try to persuade you that the life you have been living is wrong. At the same time, I want you to help me, as only you can help me, in putting a life of wretchedness behind me. It is asking a great deal, a very great deal, but in return I will give you more than you will ever realize, more than you can realize, for you cannot realize the danger that surrounds your every movement, and will continue to surround you until they—*they*—are assured that you have decided to forget them."

Peter shook his head, forgetting to wonder what an officer might think upon finding the door locked. Would the jovial little captain be quite so jovial viewing these incriminating circumstances? Not likely. But Peter had dismissed the fat captain from his mind, together with all other alien thoughts, as he concentrated upon the amazing words of this exceedingly amazing and beautiful girl. She was looking down at the chevron of gold sparks on his sleeve.

"I can tell you but one more thing of consequence," she continued. "It is this: Together we can stand; divided we will fall, just as surely as the sun follows its track in the heavens. I have a plan that will offend you—perhaps offend you terribly—but there is no other way. When *they* know that we have decided to forget them, we can breathe easily. Our secrets, grown stale, are not harmful to them."

"I am always open to any reasonable inducement," Peter said dryly.

The eyes meeting his were quite wild.

"How would you like to go to some lovely little place to have money, to live comfortably, even luxuriously, with a woman of whom you could be justly proud, and who would bend every power with the sole view of making you happy?"—she was blushing hotly—"and all this woman would demand in return would be your loyalty, your respect—and later your love, if that were possible."

"But this—this is—astounding!" Peter exclaimed.

"I expected you to say that. But let me assure you, I have thought this over. I have given it every possible consideration, and now I know there is no other way. I want to leave China. I want to go away forever and ever. I must leave."

Her shoulders jerked nervously.

"My life has been miserable—so miserable. And I am not brave enough to go through with it alone. I am afraid, terribly afraid. And afraid of myself, and of my weakness. I must be encouraged, must have some one to make me strong and brave, and afterward to take the good in me and bring it out, and kill the bad."

She relinquished Peter's hand and thumped her chest with small fists.

"There is good in me; but it has never been given a chance! I want a man who will bring that good out, a man who will make me fine and true and honorable. For such a man I would give everything—my life!" She lowered her voice. "I would give my best—my love. When I saw you lift the coolie, after he showed you his knife, I thought you were such a man; and when I looked into your face I believed I had found such a man. The rest—remains—for you to say."

"Where do you want me to t-take you?" demanded Peter.

"Ah! That is of so little importance! To Nara—Nagoya—to Australia—America."

She shrugged, as if to say, "and little I care."

"Now I am offering you only two rewards for that sacrifice—your safety against *them*—and money. You can name your price. I feel that you will come to love me; but that can come, if it cares, any time. When you want me—I will be waiting. I want you to consider this now. Now! Will you? Tell me that you will!"

"I—I don't know what to say!" stammered Peter in a husky voice. "Are—you are not joking, are you, Miss Borria? You can't be! But this is so serious! Shocking! Why, you never saw me before! Why should you pick me for such a thing when you never saw me? You don't know me. You don't know what a brute I might be. Why, I might be married for all you know—"

"I am reasonably sure," said the girl with some of her former serenity.

"But this—this is unbelievable!" cried Peter. "You never saw me before today. Why, you're a nice girl. You're not the kind of girl who runs away with a man at first sight. You're not in love with me at all. Not at all. Miss Borria—"

A flame of hot suspicion shot athwart Peter's mind. He seized her hands, glared into her eyes, dragged her to her feet.

"See here!" he clamored. "Tell me what you really want. What's your game, eh? You're a wise little bird, you are. I may look stupid, I may not see all the way through this talk you've been giving me. You're holding back. What is it? Come on! Out with it!"

She was not disturbed in the least at his harshness, nor did she seemingly disapprove of the rough way he handled her.

"I am married," she said simply.

CHAPTER IV

To Peter this revelation was like the addition of a single grain to a bucket brimming with sand.

"Well, what of it?" he barked.

"To a man who is fat and untidy, a man old enough to be my father, who treats me as if I were a thief, or a dog. I loathe him. And he detests me. You see"—she smiled ironically—"we are not very happy. I ran away from him a month ago, from Hong Kong. I ran as far as Singaraja, and now I have to go back because I have not the courage to stay away. A stronger will would make me give him up. Would make me go away, and stay. And I grabbed at you."

"As a drowning man would grab at a straw."

"Not at all! Perhaps, let us say, I had pictured such a man as you. And then you came. He will beat me when I return."

"No!"

"Yes!" She pressed down the gauzy stuff which came up almost to her throat in the form of a high "V." And across the rounded white curve of her chest were four angry red stripes, the marks of a whip.

He shuddered. "This is terrible."

"Will you help me—now?"

"What can I do? What can I do?" He was striving to adjust himself to this exceedingly difficult situation. "But I don't understand how you can place all this confidence in me."

"Because when I saw you I knew you were a man who stopped at nothing."

"But why—why does he beat you? It—it's incomprehensible!"

He stared at the beautiful face, the long, white appealing face, and the deep, dark eyes with their fringe of long lashes. If ever a girl was meant to be loved and protected it was this one.

"I know I am asking a great deal, far more than I have any right, and not taking you into consideration at all. But you will help me. You must. Have I talked to you in vain? Do—do you think I would make you unhappy?"

"That's not the question, not the question at all. But you don't know me. We are perfect strangers!"

That is what Peter had been trying to get out of his system all of this time. Had he been thinking connectedly at this trying moment, not for the life of him would he have uttered those words. He had convinced himself that he was above and beyond all shallow conventions. And in an unguarded moment this thought, which had been in and out of his mind, popped out like a ghost from a closet. We are perfect strangers!

"So is every man a stranger to his wife. What difference does time make? Very little, I think. A day—a week—a month—a year—twenty!—you and I would still be strangers, for that matter. Who can see into any man's heart?"

She stopped talking, and kneaded her hands as if in anguish.

"And think! Do think of me!"

"I am thinking of you," said Peter constrainedly.

"We can go to Nara, if you like, to the little inn near the deer-park, and be so happy—you and I. Think of Nara—in cherry-blossom time!"

"I can't see the picture at all," said Peter dryly. "But since you've elected me to be your—your Sir Galahad, I'll tell you what I will do."

Nervously the girl was fumbling at her throat, where, suspended by a fine gold chain, hung a cameo, a delicately carved rose, as red as her lips, and as life-like. She nodded, quite as though her life hung by that gold thread and depended at the high end upon his decision.

"Your husband's nationality?" he asked abruptly.

"He is a Portuguese gentleman, my father's cousin."

"It would be possible for me, perhaps, to aid a lady in distress by punishing the cause of it."

"You mean—"

"I will gladly undertake to thrash the gentleman, if it would do any good."

"No, no! That would not do."

"Then there's no choice for me. Either I must accept or decline your invitation."

"I pray you will! I have told you frankly and quickly, because time is valuable. We have none to lose. A steamer leaves for Formosa and Moji the morning after we arrive—at daybreak. We would scarcely have time to complete our plans, and embark."

Peter raised his eyebrows. "Complete our plans?" he intoned.

"Yes. We must raise money. You see, there is money, thousands of dollars, always in that house. It would be necessary to—to take whatever of it we needed. That is why I will need you, too."

"I think," declared Peter with decision, "that we had better call this a misdeal, and play another game for a while. In the first place, I will not run away with you, because it is against my principles to run away with a strange young woman. In the second place, stealing for pleasure is one of the seven deadly sins that I conscientiously avoid.

"Now that I have aired my views, now that I have proved to you I'm not as fine and brave as you hoped me to be, let's shake hands and part the best of friends—or the worst of enemies."

The girl rose from the chair into which she had dropped when Peter began his say. Alternately she was biting her upper and lower lips in nervousness or irritation. She put her back to the door and braced her hands against the white enameled panels. Her breast was heaving. She was desperately pale, and little dots of perspiration shone on her white forehead. And she was limp, as though his last remark had drained the final drop of vitality from her.

"I—I won't give you up," she said in a small, husky voice. "Besides, you are wrong, wrong in saying and believing that stealing his money would not be for a good cause. He is a brute, a monster, and worse than a thief. I cannot tell you how he gets his money. I would not dare to whisper it. You will be doing a fine and splendid thing in taking his money. You will be freeing me! Does that sound like heroics? I don't care if it does! But with that money you can buy my soul out of bondage. You can make me happy. Won't you? Won't you do—that—for me?"

Peter stood there like a block of ice—melting rapidly! But he said nothing. His thoughts were beyond the expression of clumsy words.

Her dumb hand found the key, turned it. The door opened, and a sweet breath of the cool sea air crept into the small room.

For a moment her white, distraught face hung down on her breast like that of a child who has been scolded without understanding why. Then she darted out of the room.

CHAPTER V

When Peter snapped off the switch he found that he was trembling, trembling from his knees to his neck. With a feeling akin to guilt he wiped the sweat from his face and walked unsteadily to the rail which overhung the cargo-well.

He lighted an Abdullah, and watched the little smoke pool, which the wind snatched and tossed up into the booms and darkness.

It must have been a nightmare, this scene just past. What an incredible, a preposterous request for a woman to make! And the more thought he fed to the enigma the more incredible and unreal it became.

It was too big and complex a thought to hold all together in his tired brain now. In the morning he would tackle it with some zest, with an inner eye washed clean by a long sleep. Just now he felt the need of relaxation, and as he smoked, his thoughts flitted afar, to come back now and then, irresistibly drawn by the vivid picture painted in his mind by Romola Borria.

His eyes, commanders of his thoughts, traveled out over the stern, which rose and sank with a ponderous, wallowing sound in the heaving ground swells, and he made out the weaving and coiling, the lustrous but dim windings of the phosphorescent wake.

As he became more accustomed to the shadowy, pointed darkness of the steerage cabins, he became aware of a small figure crouching on the hatch-cover near the starboard rail. He studied this intently, and at length he made out the long, black queue of the Chinese girl who had stared at him in such bewitching fashion a little earlier in the day.

And his mind was carried back at the thought of this small maiden to the grim and red Tibetan city, whose memories now were scarcely more than a confused and hideous dream. He pictured again the splendors of the blue-domed white palace which reposed like a beast of prey atop the red filth disgorged by the cinnabar mine.

Peter's heart thumped in youthful resentment as the thought of that evil spirit came to him now. When would he meet the Gray Dragon face to face? When would he again penetrate the stronghold of that unhappy red city? Who could say? Probably never.

The small Chinese girl on the hatch-cover had found him staring at her, and with a little shiver of surprise Peter made the discovery that she was smiling archly at him; and she inclined her head. She was beckoning? It seemed so, indeed.

Because Peter was a youth of deep and subtle understandings, he did no more than nod slightly, and forthwith descended the companion-ladder to the well, and crossed the well to her side.

Her eyes were given a queer little twinkle by the near-by electric which burned dimly over the door of the engine-room galley, and she motioned him to be seated. He squatted, Chinese fashion, and she took a deep, sighing breath, holding out her hands with a quick gesture.

Across her wrists and drooping to her knees and beyond them into the shadow was a strip of heavy, deep-blue silk. All down its length were stitched small, round dots of dark red. Peter knew this for a sarong, an ornamental waist-sash, affected by most Javanese gentlemen and many Australians and New Zealanders.

While he hesitated, she laid this in his lap with a shy impulsiveness.

"It is yours, sar," she informed Peter in English of a very strange mold. She spoke in a rather high-pitched, bell-like voice, pure and soft, and tinkling with queer little cadences. "It is yours, sar. I made it for you."

Indubitably the girl was Eurasian. Asiatic features predominated, with the exception of her eyes, which were more round than oblique, from which circumstance Peter could surmise that her Aryan blood, provided she was a half-caste, came from her mother's side; the predominance of the Mongolian in her features being due to an Asiatic father, a Chinese.

The colorless face, relieved by the bright color of her lips, the slightly oblique eyes, told him that; yet her accents were those of a Javanese, a Malay from the south.

"You made this—for me?" replied Peter, surprised.

"Oh, yes, sar," said the tinkling little voice.

"Well, that is fine. It is beautiful," he said, feeling his way with prudence. "And how much do I owe you, small one?"

She shook her head indignantly.

"It is a geeft," she informed him. "I am no longer poor, my lord. I can now give geefts. I like you. I give this to you."

Peter was moved momentarily beyond speech.

"You are very fine, *busar satu*," went on the tiny, musical voice. "So is this sarong. You will wear it, great one, around thy middle?"

"Around my middle, to be sure, small one," laughed Peter; "until my middle is clay, or until the sarong is no more than a thread."

"Well said, *busar satu*!" The girl giggled, bobbing her small head in happy approval. "It is twice blessed: with my love and with my foolish blood, for I pricked my finger on the wicked needle. But I covered that spot with a red mata-ari (sun). You can never, never tell."

"Assuredly not!" cried Peter gaily.

"Let the sarong be wound about thy middle," commanded the Chinese maiden. "Arise, sar, and wind it about thy middle."

And Peter did rise, winding the sarong about his lean waist twice, allowing one end to dangle down on his left side in a debonair and striking fashion. If set off his slim figure in a rather bizarre way.

"It's bully!" he exclaimed, pirouetting with one hand on his head after the style of the matador.

"It is bully!" she echoed, in such quaint reflection of his exclamation that Peter laughed outright. "Now, sit down again, sar," she invited. And when Peter had again disposed himself at the side of this light-hearted young person, she went on:

"I am coming a long, long way to visit my aged grandmother (may the green-eyed gods grant her the twelve desires!) who lives Canton-way. My dear father sells opium. He has grown rich in that trade, even though the stupid eyes of the Dutch *babis* are on him all the while. When I have seen my ancient grandmother, and given her geefts, I will go home, to the south, Macassar-way."

"Now, where, oh where, do I fit in this scheme?" was what Peter thought. "What have I that this maiden desires?"

"Ah, *busar satu!*" the maiden was saying, deftly and unaffectedly patting the sarong. "It is bully! And now—"

"And now—" intoned Peter calmly, for even as a life pays for a life, and an eye for an eye, and a tooth for a tooth, so does a gift pay for a gift.

"And now," went on the maid from Macassar, whose father had grown rich in the opium-trade under the very eyes of the Dutch, "tell me but one thing, my lord—is Hong Kong safe for such as I?"

"When one is young and virtuous," spake Peter in the drone of an ancient fortune-teller, "one keeps her eyes pinned on the front. One hears nothing; and one becomes as discreet of tongue as the little blue sphinx at Chow-Fen-Chu."

"Those are the words of Confucius, the wise one," retorted the little bell-like voice with a tinkling laugh. "I need no guide, then? I have heard that China is unsafe. That is why I asked."

"Small one," replied Peter, with a smile of gravity and with much candor in his blue eyes, "in China, such a one as you are as safe as a Javanese starling in a nest of hungry yellow snakes. You will travel by daylight, or not at all. You will go from Kowloon to your venerable grandmother by train. You will carry a knife, and you will use it without hesitation. Have you such a knife?"

The small head bowed vehemently.

"In Hong-Kong you will go aboard a sampan and be rowed Kowloon-way, from whence the train runs by the great river to Canton."

"That will be safe, that sampan?"

"I will make it safe, small one. For I will go with you as far as Kowloon, if that is what you wish."

"And does the brave one admire my sarong?" the small voice wavered.

"It shames my ugly body," said Peter. "Now run along to bed—*kalak*!" And he clapped his hands as the small figure bobbed out of sight, with her long, black pigtail flopping this way and that.

CHAPTER VI

It came to Peter as he climbed up the iron-fretted steps to the lonely promenade-deck that life had begun to take on its old golden glow, the luster of the uncertain, the charm of women who found in him something not undesirable.

At this he smiled a little bit. He had never known, as far back as the span of his adventures extended, a woman who deemed his companionship as quite so valuable a thing as the mysterious and alluring Romola Borria, the husband-beaten, incredible, and altogether dangerous young woman who passionately besought him to accompany her on a pilgrimage of forgetfulness into the flowery heart of dear old Japan.

Ascending the ladder to the unoccupied deck, he was conscious of the sweet drone of the monsoon, which blew off the shores of Annam over the restless bosom of the China Sea, setting up a tuneful chant in the *Persian Gulf's* sober rigging, and kissing his cheeks with the ardor of a despairing maiden.

Peter the Brazen decided to take a turn or two round deck before going to his bunk, to drink in a potion of this intoxicating, winelike night. The wheel of fortune might whirl many times before he was again sailing this most seductive of oceans.

And he was a little intoxicated, too, with the wine of his youth. His lips, immersed in the fountain, found very little bitterness there. Life was earnest and grave, as the wiseacres said; but life was, on the whole, sublime and poignantly sweet. A little bitterness, a little dreary sadness, a pang at the heart now and again, served only to interrupt the smooth regularity, the monotony, to add zest to the nectar.

When he had finished the cigarette, he flung the butt over the rail into the gushing water, which swam south in its phosphorescent welter, descended between decks to the stateroom that had been assigned to him, and fitted the key to the lock.

He felt decidedly young and foolishly exalted as he closed the door after him and heard the lock click, for to few men is it given to have two lovely young women in distress seek aid, all in the span of a few hours. Perhaps these rosy events had served merely to feed oil to the fires of his conceit; but Peter's was not a conceit that rankled anybody. And there were always volunteers, hardened by the buffets of this life, to cast water upon that same fire.

So, humming a gay little tune, Peter snapped on the light, bathing the milk-white room in a liquid mellowness, opened the port-hole, wound his watch, hung it on the curtain-bar which ran lengthwise with his berth, pushed the flowered curtains at either end as far back as they would go, in order to have all the fresh air possible, and—

Peter gasped. He declared it was absolutely impossible. Such things did not happen, even in this world of strange happenings and of stranger stirrings below the surface of actual happenings. His self-complacencies came shattering down about his ears like mountains of senseless glitter, and he stooped to recover the object which was lying upon, almost ready to tumble from, the rounded, neat edge of the white berth.

A rose of cameo! The hot breath from his lips, which drooped in astonishment and chagrin, seemed to stir the delicate petals of the exquisitely carved red rose which reposed in its mountain of soft gold in the palm of his trembling hand. The fine gold chain, like a rope of gold sand, trickled between his fingers and dangled, swinging from side to side.

The impossible thought pounded at the door of his brain and demanded recognition. Romola Borria had been a visitor to his room. But why? He had no secrets to conceal from the prying ears of any one, not now, at all events, for he had destroyed all evidences depending upon the excursion he had made from Shanghai to Len Yang, and from Len Yang to Mandalay, to Rangoon, to Penang, Singapore, and Batavia.

Naturally, his first impulsive thought was that Romola Borria was somehow entangled with those who ruled the destinies of the hideous mountain city, which crouched amidst the frosty emerald peaks on the fringe of Tibet. He had felt the weight of that ominous hand on other occasions, and its movements were ever the same. Night stealth, warnings chalked on doors, the deliberate and cunning penetration of his secrets; all of these were typical machinations of the Gray Dragon, and of those who reported back to the Gray Dragon.

No one would break into his stateroom who was not the tool of Len Yang's unknown king. Thus the finger of accusation was brought to bear tentatively upon Romola Borria.

Yes, it was incredible that this girl, with those scarlet stripes across her breast, could in any way be complicated with the wanton designs of the beast in Len Yang. Yet here was evidence, damning her, if not as a wilful tool of the cinnabar king, then at least as a room-breaker. Why had she come into his room? And how?

He searched the room, then dragged his suit-case from under the bunk to the middle of the blue carpet, and spilled its contents angrily upon the floor. It took him less than ten seconds to discover what was missing; not his money, nor the few jewels he had collected in his peregrinations, for they were untouched in the small leather bag.

Peter looked again, carefully shaking each garment, hoping, and refusing to hope, that the revolver would make its appearance. It was an American revolver, an automatic, a gift from Bobbie MacLaurin. And now this excellent weapon was missing.

He felt that eyes were upon him, that ears were listening slyly to his breathing, that lips were rustling in bated whispered comments upon the fury with which he took this important loss.

Snapping off the light, he plunged down the murky corridor, with the guilty rose cameo clutched in his sweating hand, and came at length to the purser's office. This dignitary was absent, at midnight lunch probably; so Peter rifled the upper drawer in the desk, and brought out the passenger-register, finding the name and room number he sought after an instant of search.

Carefully he replaced the ledger in its original position, closed the drawer, and darted back up the corridor.

In front of a room not far from his own he paused and rapped. His knock, sharp and insistent, was one of practice, a summons which would not be mistaken by the occupants of adjoining staterooms, nor was it likely to disturb them.

After a moment, light showed at the opened transom. Some one rustled about within, and in another instant the door opened far enough to admit a head from which dark masses of hair floated, framing a face that was white and inquisitive.

At sight of her midnight visitor Romola Borria opened her door wide and smiled a little sleepily. She had paused long enough in arising to slip into a negligee, a kimono of blackest satin, revealing at the baglike sleeves and the fold which fell back from her throat a lining of blood-red silk.

One hand was caught up to her throat in a gesture of surprise, and the other was concealed behind her, catching, as Peter surmised, nothing if not his own automatic revolver, which had been loaded, ready for instant use, immediately the safety-catch was released.

She stared at him softly, with eyes still mirroring the depths of the sleep from which he had so rudely aroused her, her delicate red lips forming a curious smile. And she continued to smile more gently, more tenderly, as she became quite conscious of his presence.

"You have come to tell me that you will go to Japan with me," she stated.

Peter shook his head slowly, and with equal deliberateness lifted up the small object in his hand until the light from the ceiling-lamp fell directly upon it.

"My cameo!" she exclaimed with a start of surprise. "Where did you find it?" She reached impulsively for the ornament, but Peter closed his fingers upon it firmly.

"You have something to give me in return, I think," he said sternly.

She was staring at the closed hand with something of despair and fright, as if reluctant to believe this truth, while her fingers groped at her throat to verify a loss apparently not before detected.

She stepped back into the room and said:

"Close the door. Come inside."

He thought: If she had wanted to shoot me, she had plenty of chance before. A shot in this room, a murder would fasten evidence upon her, and besides, it would instantly arouse the occupants of the adjoining staterooms, if not one of the deck crew on watch.

So he entered and closed the door, presenting a full view of his broad, white-uniformed back, and the gaudy-blue sarong about his waist. He took more time than was necessary in closing the door and sliding the bolt, to give her every opportunity to arrange this scene she desired.

But the girl was only drawing the curtains over the port-hole, to keep out prying eyes, when he turned about.

She sat down on the edge of her berth, with her small white feet almost touching the floor, and the huge blue automatic resting upon her knees. It was unlikely that she did not appreciate fully the seductive charm of the red and black gown which adapted itself in whatever pose to the youthful curves of her body; and she permitted Peter to sit down on the narrow couch opposite and to examine her and perhaps to speculate for a number of seconds before she seemed to find her speech.

Meekly her dark eyes encountered his.

"I was afraid," she explained in a voice, low but free in her remarkable self-possession. "I knew you would not care, and I hoped that you would have a revolver in your room. So I went there. How did I get in? I borrowed a pass-key from the purser on the plea that I had left mine in my room. I hoped you would not miss it until we reached Hong Kong, and I intended to return it then and explain to you.

"My life," she added deprecatingly, "is in some slight danger, and, like the small fool that I am—even though I am fully aware that no one in the whole world cares whether I am living or dead—well, Mr. Moore, for some reason I still persist in clinging to the small hope."

She smiled wanly and earnestly, so Peter thought. A dozen impulses militated against his believing a word of this glib explanation; his common sense told him that he should seek further, that the explanation was only half made; and yet it cannot be denied that she had gone unerringly to his greatest weakness, perhaps his worst fault, his belief in the sincerity of a woman in trouble.

"Why didn't you ask me?" he demanded in his most apologetic voice, as though he had wronged her beyond repair. "Why didn't you tell me you were in danger? I'd have loaned you the revolver willingly—willingly!"

"I did try to find you," she replied; "but the wireless room was dark. You were nowhere on deck."

Peter was aware that for some reason Romola Borria did not prefer to share the secret of her real or fancied danger with him. He felt a little dissatisfied, cheated, as though the straightforward answer for which he had come had been turned into the counterfeit of evasion.

The situation as it now had shaped itself demanded some sort of decision. Without the whole truth he was reluctant to leave, and it was imprudent to remain any longer.

Romola, in this constrained pause in their conversation, feeling perhaps the reason for his silence, lowered her dark lashes and drew up her feet until they were concealed by the red folds of the kimono, and she drew the satin more closely about her soft, white throat.

"You have decided nothing, then?" she parried.

"What decision I might have formed," he said, a trifle coolly, "has been put off by—this. You see, I must admit it, this—this rather complicates things for me. I'm in the dark altogether now, you see. I wanted to help you, however I could. And then—then I find this cameo."

She nodded absently, fingering the groove in the automatic's handle.

"I'm afraid I took too much for granted," she said in a low voice. "Don't you suppose my curiosity was aroused when you threw the coolie overboard? I said nothing; rather, I asked you no questions; and I thought that a man who was self-poised enough to meet his enemies in that way would be—what shall I say?—charitable enough to overlook such a—" She paused. "When I confessed that you and I are facing a common enemy, that the same hands are eager to do away with both of us, I thought that bond was sufficient, was strong enough, to justify what might shock an ordinary man. I mean—"

"I think I understand," Peter took her up in contrite tones. "I'll ask nothing more. In the morning we will talk the other matter over. I must have a little time. For the present, I want you to keep the revolver, and—here is the cameo. Forgive me for being so unreasonable, so—so selfish."

He leaned over. She seemed uncertain a moment, then caught the gold chain lightly from his hand.

"And—your revolver," she said. "Those are the terms of the agreement, I believe."

"No, no," he protested. "I have no use for it; none whatever. You keep it."

But quite as resolutely Romola Borria shook her head and extended the automatic, butt foremost, to him. "I insist," she said.

"But you say you're in danger," he argued.

"No. Not now. I have something else that will do quite as well. If it is written that I am to die, why give Death cause to be angry? I am a fatalist, you see. And I want you to take back your revolver, with my apologies, and quite without any more explanation than I have given you, please."

"But—" began Peter.

"Look," she said.

In the small space of the stateroom he could not avoid bending so low as to sense the warmth of her skin, in order to study the object toward which she was directing his gaze. A sense of hot confusion permeated him as her fingers lightly caressed his hand; her physical nearness obsessed him.

She had drawn back the fluffy pillow, and on the white sheet he glimpsed a long, bright, and exceedingly dangerous-looking dagger, with a jewel-incrusted hilt.

The singular thing about this knife was the shape of the blade, which was thin and with three sides, like a machinist's file. It would be a good dagger to throw away after a killing because of the triangular hole it would leave as a wound, a bit of evidence decidedly incriminating.

Peter straightened up, round-eyed, accepted the automatic, and slipped it into his pocket, smoothing his coat and the sarong over the lump, and approached the door.

For a moment his heart beat in a wild desire, a desire to take her in his arms as she stood so close and so quiet beside him, smiling wistfully and a little sadly; and unaccountably she seemed to droop and become small and limp and pitifully helpless in the face of him and of all mankind.

"Good night, Mr. Moore, and thank you so—much," she murmured. "And I do hope you will forgive me for being a—a thief."

He thought that she was on the point of kissing him, and his eyes swam and became of a slightly deeper and more silky blue than a moment before. But she faltered back, while the faintest suggestion of a sigh came from her lips.

In the next instant, as the door closed quietly behind him, Peter was mighty glad that neither he nor she had yielded to impulse. He was not, in the light of the literal version, the owner of a wholly untarnished record, for he had given in to weakness, as most men do give into weakness.

But he was above temptation now, not because temptation was put behind him, but because he had had the strength to resist; and it was his full, deep desire to hold himself until that girl, far across the Pacific, who inspired the finest and best in him, should bear the name he bore.

It was a splendid thing, that feeling. It gave him courage and confidence, and took him quite light-heartedly, with head erect and shoulders back, out of the dreariest of his moments.

So, quick in a new and buoyant mood, Peter joggled the key in the lock of his stateroom door, slipped in, and was before long dreaming of a cottage built for two, of springtime in California, albeit snoring almost loud enough to drown out the throb of the *Persian Gulf's* old but still useful engines.

CHAPTER VII

Because of the fatigue which possessed his every muscle, fatigue springing from the arduous, the trying hours now past, Peter the Brazen was sleeping the slumber of the worthy, when, at a somewhat later hour in the night, some time before dawn crept out of the China Sea, a figure, lean and gray, flitted past his stateroom on the narrow orlop deck, peered in the darkened port-hole, and passed on.

Awakened by an instinct developed to a remarkable degree by his training of the past few months, Peter established himself upon one elbow and looked and listened, wondering what sounds might be abroad other than the peaceful churn of the engine.

Quite as intuitively he slipped his hand under the pillow and encountered the reassuring chill of the blued steel. Half withdrawing this excellent weapon, he shifted his eyes, alternately from the door to the port-hole, conscious of an imminent danger, a little stupefied by his recent plunge into the depths of sleep, but growing more widely awake, more alert and watchful, with the passage of each instant.

The port-hole loomed gray and empty, one edge of it licked by the yellow light of some not far distant deck-lamp. With his eye fastened upon this scimitar of golden light, Peter was soon to witness an unusual eclipse, a phenomenon which sent a shiver, an icy shiver, of genuine consternation up and down his backbone.

As he watched, a square of the yellow reflected light was blotted out, as though a bar of some nature had cast its shadow athwart that metallic gleam. This shadow then proceeded to slide first up and then down the brass setting of the port-hole, and the shadow dwindled.

As Peter sat up on the edge of his cot, gripping the square butt of the automatic in his hand and tentatively fingering the trigger, the origin of the shadow moved slowly, ever so slowly, into the range of his perplexed and anxious vision.

What appeared at first glance to be a cat-o'-nine-tails on a rather thick stem, Peter made out to be, as he built some hasty comparisons, the Maxim silencer attached either at the end of a revolver or of a rifle; for the black cylinder on the muzzle was circumscribed at regular intervals with small, sharp depressions, the clinch-marks of the silencing chambers.

As this specter crept up and over the edge of the port, Peter, with a deliberate and cold smile, raised the automatic revolver, slipped out of the berth with the stealth and litheness of a cat, crept into the corner where the stateroom door was hinged, and leveled the weapon until his eye ran along the dark obstruction of the barrel.

Slowly and more slowly the silencer moved inward until the blunt end of it was registered precisely upon a point where Peter's head would lie if he were sleeping in a normal attitude.

This amused him and perplexed him. All Peter wanted to see was the head or even the eye of this early morning assassin, whereupon he would take immediate steps to receive him with a warm cordiality that might forestall future visitations of a kindred sort.

In the space between heart-beats Peter stopped to inquire of himself who his visitor might be. And even as he stopped to inquire, a bright, angry, red flame spurted straight out from the mouth of the silencer, and Peter would have willingly gambled his bottom dollar that the bullet found its way into his pillow, a wager, as he later verified, upon which he would have collected all of the money he was eager to stake.

The lance of yellow-red flame had occasioned no disturbance other than a slight smack, comparable with the sharp clapping of a man's hands.

In the second leaping flame Peter was far more interested. Having delivered himself of one shot, the assassin could be depended upon to make casual inquiries, and to drop at least one more bullet into the darkness between the upper and lower berths, to make a clean job of it.

And it was on the appearance of the inquiring head that Peter relied to repay the intruder in his own metal, that metal taking the form of a wingless messenger of nickel-sheathed lead.

But the visitor was cautious, waiting, no doubt, for sounds of the death struggle, provided the shot had not gone directly home, its home being, as Peter shuddered to think, his own exceedingly useful brain.

He waited a little longer before his guest apparently decided that the time was come for his investigation; and thereupon a small, square head with the black-tasseled hat of a Chinese coolie set upon it at a rakish angle was framed by the port-hole.

Smirking nervously, Peter released the safety catch and brought pressure to bear slowly and firmly upon the trigger.

Click! That was all. But it told a terrible story. The weapon was out of commission, either unloaded or tampered with. And Peter's panic-stricken thoughts leaped, even as the square head leaped away from the window, to the Borria woman, to the cause of his desperate helplessness.

Romola Borria, then, had tampered with this revolver. Romola Borria had plotted, that was sure, with the coolie outside the port-hole for his assassination. That explained the visit to his room. That explained her perturbation over his discovery of her visit, of her sly and cool evasions and dissimulations.

It was with these thoughts hammering in his brain that Peter dropped out of range of the deadly porthole and squirmed, inching his way into the doubtful shelter provided by the closet. At any instant he expected another red tongue to burn the now still darkness above his head, to experience the hot plunge of a bullet in some part of his slightly clad anatomy. And then— death? An end of the glorious adventures whose trail he had followed now for well upon ten years?

And still the death bullet was withheld. Groping about in the darkness with one hand as he loosened the magazine clip on the butt, and finding that the clip of cartridges had been removed, he finally discovered the where-abouts of the suit-case, and dragged it slowly toward him, with his eyes pinned upon the vacant port.

Fumbling among the numerous objects contained in the suit-case, his fingers encountered at length a cartridge clip. He slipped this into the maga-zine, and indulged in a silent grunt of relief as the clip moved up into place. He drew back the rejecting mechanism, and heard the soft, reassuring *snick* of the cartridge as it slid from the magazine into the chamber.

Then sounds without demanded his attention, the sounds of a tussle, of oaths spoken in a high, feminine tongue, in a language not his own.

Peter would have shouted, but he had long ago learned the inadvisability of shouting when such grim business as tonight's was being negotiated.

Slipping on his bath-robe, he opened the door and tentatively peered out into the half-light of the orlop deck from the cross corridor vestibule-way, for indications of a shambles.

They were gone. The deck was deserted. But he caught his breath sharp-ly as he made out a long, dark shape which lay, with the inertness of death, under his port-hole, blending with the shadows. He rolled the man over upon his back, and dragged him by the heels under the deck-light, and, dragging him, a dark trail spread out upon the boards, and even as Peter examined the cold face, the spot broadened and a trickle broke from it and crept down toward the gutter.

Stabbed? More than likely. Pausing only long enough to reassure himself that this one was the assassin whose square head had been framed by the port, Peter looked for a wound, and shortly he found the wound, and Peter was not greatly astounded at the proportions thereof.

It was a small wound, running entirely through the neck from a point below the left ear to one slightly below and to the right of the locked jaw. Upon close scrutiny the death wound proved to be small and thorough and of a triangular pattern.

Just why he had expected to find that triangular wound Peter was unable to explain even to himself, but he was quite as sure that Romola Borria's hand was in this latest development as he had been sure a moment before that her steady, small hand had deliberately removed the clip of cartridges from the butt of the automatic, to render him helpless in the face of his enemies.

Silently contemplating the stiffening victim of Romola Borria's triangular dagger, Peter heard the rustle of silk garments, and looked up in time to observe the slender person of Romola Borria herself, attired exactly as he had left her a few hours previous, detach itself from the corridor vestibuleway which led to his stateroom. She approached him.

A thousand questions and accusations swam to his lips, but she was speaking in low, impassioned tones.

"I knocked at your door. God! I thought he had killed you! I was afraid. For a moment I thought you were dead."

"You stabbed him," said Peter in an expressionless voice.

She nodded, and drew a long, sobbing breath.

"Yes. He tried to shoot you. I saw him pass my window. I was waiting. I watched. I knew he would try. Oh, I'm so glad—"

"You knew? You knew that?"

"Yes, yes. He was the—the mate of the coolie you threw overboard in Batavia. You know, they always travel in pairs. You didn't know that?"

"No; I did not know. But I could have defended myself easily enough if it had not been for—"

"Your clip of cartridges? Can you forgive me? Can you ever forgive me for taking them out? I took them out. Oh, Mr. Moore, believe me, I am concealing nothing! I did remove the clip, and in my carelessness I forgot to give them back to you when you left my room."

"I see. Have you them?"

"Yes."

"Please give them to me. You have not by any chance, in another of those careless moods of yours, happened to tamper with the bullets, have you?"

"Mr. Moore—" she gasped, clutching her white hands to her breast in indignation.

"You *are* clever," said Peter sarcastically. "You're altogether too damn clever. What your game is, I'm not going to take the trouble to ask. You—you—"

"Oh, Mr. Moore!" She caught his arm.

He cast it away.

"Didn't tamper with the bullets, eh?" he went on in a deep, sullen voice. "Well, Miss Borria, here is what I think of your word. Here is how much I trust you."

And with a single motion Peter whipped all seven cartridges from the clip and tossed them into the sea. He snarled again:

"You *are* clever, damn clever. Poor, poor little thing! Still want to go to Japan with me, my dear?"

"I do," stated the girl, whose eyes were dry and burning.

"Sure! That's the stuff," railed Peter bitingly; "whatever you do, stick to your story."

He grabbed her wrist, and her glance should have softened granite.

"For example," he sniffed; "that neat little cock-and-bull story you made up about your cruel, brutal husband. Expect me to believe that, too, eh?"

"Not if you don't care to," said the girl faintly.

Peter knocked away her hand, the hand which seemed always to fumble at her throat in moments of strain. He pulled down the black kimono and dragged her under the light, forcing her back against the white cabin. He looked.

The white, soft curve of her chest was devoid of all marks. It was as white as that portion of a woman's body is said to be, by the singing poets, as white as alabaster, and devoid of angry stripes.

Peter seized both limp wrists in one of his hands.

"By God, you *are* clever!" he scoffed. "Now, Miss Enigma, you spurt out your story, and the true story, or, by Heaven, I'll call the skipper! I'll have you put in irons—for murder!"

She hung her head, then flung it back and eyed him with the sullen fire of a cornered animal.

"You forget I saved your life," she said.

As if they were red hot, Peter dropped her hands, and they fell at her sides like limp rags.

"I—I—" he stammered, and backed away a step. "Good God!" he exploded. "Then explain this; explain why you took the clip from my automatic. Explain why you put up that story of a brutal husband, and showed me scars on your breast to prove it—then washed them off. And why—why you killed this man who would have murdered me."

"I will explain what I am able to," she said in a small, tired voice. "I took the clips from the revolver because—because I didn't want you to shoot me. I know *their* methods far better than you seem to; and I knew I could handle this coolie myself far better than you could; and I wanted to run no risk of being shot myself in attending to him.

"As for the 'brutal-husband story,' every word of that is the truth. If you must know, I used rouge for the scars. Since you are so outspoken, I will pay you back in the same cloth. There are scars on my body, on my back and my legs."

Her face was as red as a poppy.

"And I killed this man because—well," she snapped, "perhaps because I hate you."

Had she cut him with a whip, Peter could not have felt more hurt, more humiliated, more ashamed, for gratitude was far from being a stranger to him.

He half extended his arms in mute apology, and, surprised, he found her lips caressing his, her warm arms about his neck. He kissed her—once—and put her away from him; and that guiding star of his in California could be thankful that Romola Borria's embrace was rather more forgiving than insinuating.

"We must get rid of this coolie," she said, brushing the clusters of dark hair from her face. "I will help you, if you like. But over he goes!"

"But the blood."

"Call a deck-boy. Tell him as little as you need. You are one of the ship's officers. He will not question you."

He hesitated.

"Can you forgive me for this—way I have acted, my—my ingratitude?"

"Forgiveness seems to be a woman's principal role in life," she said with a tired smile. "Yes. I am sorry, too, that we misunderstood. Good-night, my dear."

And Peter was all alone, although his aloneness was modified to a certain extent by the corpse at his feet. The dead weight he lifted with some difficulty to the railing, pushed hard, and heard the muffled splash. Quickly he got into his uniform, slipped his naked feet into looped sandals, and sought the forecastle.

The occupants of this odorous place were sawing wood in an unsynchronous chorus. No one seemed to be about, so he seized a pail half filled with sujee, a block of holystone, and a stiff broom.

With these implements he occupied himself for fully a half-hour, until the spots on the deck had faded to a satisfactory whiteness. The revolver with Maxim silencer attached he discovered, after a long search, some distance away in the deck-gutter.

He meditated at length upon the advisability of consigning this grim trophy to the China Sea. Yet it is a sad commentary upon his native shrewdness that Peter had not yet recovered from his boyish enthusiasm for collecting souvenirs.

At last he decided to retain it, and he dropped it through the port-hole upon the couch, thereupon forgetting all about it until the weapon was called to his attention on the ensuing morning.

With all evidences of the crime removed, he replaced the pail, the stone, and the broom in the forecastle locker, and sneaked back to his stateroom. He locked the door, barricaded the port-hole with the pink-flowered curtains—those symbols which had reminded him earlier of springtime in California—and examined his pillow.

It had been an exceedingly neat shot. The bullet had bored clean through, had struck the metal L-beam of the bunk, and rebounded into a pile of bedclothes. Dented and scorched, Peter examined this little pellet of lead, balancing it in the palm of his hand.

"Every bullet has its billet," he quoted, and he was glad indeed that the billet in this case had not been his vulnerable cerebrum.

Snapping off the light, he drew the sheet up to his neck and lay there pondering, listening to the whine of the ventilator-fan.

The haggard, distressed face of Romola Borria swam upon the screen of his imagination. This woman commanded his admiration and respect. Despite all dissemblings, all evasions, all actual and evident signs of the double-cross, he confided to his other self that he was glad he had kissed her. What can be so deliciously harmless as a kiss? he asked himself.

And wiser men than Peter have answered: What can be so harmful?

CHAPTER VIII

Night brings counsel, say the French. Only in sleep does one mine the gold of truth, said Confucius.

When Peter was aroused by the golden dawn streaming through the swinging port-glass upon his eyes the cobwebs were gone from his brain, his eyes were clear and of a bright sea-blue, and he was bubbling with enthusiasm for the new-born day.

His ablutions were simple: a brisk scrubbing of his gleaming, white teeth, a dousing of his hands and face in bracing, cold water, with a subsequent soaping and rinsing of same; followed by a hoeing process at the mercy of a not-too-keen Japanese imitation of an American safety-razor.

Assured that the deck below his port-hole was spotless, he ventured to the dining-room, half filled and buzzing with excitement.

He was given to understand by a dozen gesticulating passengers that some time in the course of the night a deck-passenger, a Chinese coolie, from Buitenzorg to Hong Kong, or Macao, had fallen overboard, leaving no trace.

It was whispered that the helpless one had been done away with by foul means. And Peter became conscious during the meal that his fat and jovial little captain was looking at him and through him with a glance that could not be denied or for long avoided.

Wondering what his Herr Captain might know of the particulars of last night's doings, Peter sucked a mangosteen slowly, arranging his thoughts, card-indexing his alibis, and making cool preparations for an official cross-questioning. Clever lying out of his difficulty was the order, or the alternative for Peter was the irons.

When the fat fingers of Mynheer the Captain at length dabbled in the lacquered finger-bowl, after rounding out his fourth pomelo, Peter got up slowly and walked thoughtfully to the foot of the staircase. Here the captain caught up with him, touched his elbow lightly, and together they proceeded to the promenade-deck, which was shining redly in places where the wetness of the washing down had not yet been evaporated by the warm, fresh wind.

Mynheer the Captain fell into place at Peter's side, gripped his fat Javanese cigar between his teeth, and caught his fat wrists together stolidly behind his back, and his low, wide brow slowly beetled.

"Mynheer," he began in a somewhat constrained voice, low and richly guttural, "it iss known to you vat took place on der ship some dam during der nacht? Ja?"

"I overheard the passengers talking about a coolie falling overboard last night, sir," replied Peter guardedly. As long as no direct accusation came, he felt safer. He was reasonably sure, basing his opinion of skippers on many past encounters, that this one would go typically to his subject. In his growing cock-sureness, Peter expected no rapier-play. It would be a case, he felt sure, of all the cards on the table at once; a slam-bang, as it were.

"You know nodding of dot business, young man?"

"Nothing at all, Myn Captain."

"Dot iss strange. Dot iss strange," muttered the captain as they rounded the forward cabin and made their way in slow, measured strides down the port side. "I haf seen you come aboard yesterday, mynheer; und I haf seen you t'row over der side a coolie, a coolie who wass wit' der coolie who dis'ppeared last nacht. Why did you t'row him over der side, eh?"

"He threatened me with his knife," replied Peter without an instant's hesitation. "*Mynheer*, he was a bad Chink, a killer."

"*Ja. Tot ver vlomme!* All of 'em are bad Chinks."

"Why should he stab me?" intoned Peter. "I never saw him before. I am a peaceful citizen. The only interest I have on this ship, Mynheer Captain, is the wireless apparatus."

"*Ja?* Dot iss gude to hear, young man. I haf liked you—how does one say it?—immensely. Der oder man wass no gude. He is gude rittance. You intend to stay wit' us. Ja?"

"I hope so," said Peter heartily and with vast relief.

"You like dis ship, eh?"

"Very much, indeed."

"And I vant you to stay, young man. I vant you to stay joost as long as you feel like staying. But I vant to ask you one t'ing, joost one t'ing."

"I'll do anything you say, sir."

The fat, jovial skipper of the *Persian Gulf* eyed Peter with beady, cunning eyes, and Peter was suddenly conscious of a sinking sensation.

"Joost one t'ing. Better, first I should say, ven you t'row overboard der coolies you dislike, it vould be best not to keep—vat are dey called—der soufenirs. Sooch t'ings as peestols."

"But, *mynheer*—"

The fat hand waved him to silence.

"Bot' of dem vas bad Chinks. I know. I know bot' of dose coolies a long, long time. T'ieves and blood men. *Tot ver vlomme!* It iss gude rittance, as you say. Young man, I haf nodding but one more t'ing to tell you. I say, I like you—immensely. I vant you very much to stay. But der next time coolies are to be t'rown over der side, I will be pleased to haf you ask my permission."

Peter stared hard at the fat little man, with a quick glaze of gratitude over his eyes. The skipper left him, doubling back in the direction of the wheel-house. And something in the unsteadiness of the broad, plump shoulders gave to Peter in his perplexity the not inaccurate notion that the fat little man had enjoyed his joke and was giggling to such an extent that it almost interfered with his dignified strut.

Before buckling down to the day's business he made sure of one thing. Gone from his stateroom was the revolver with its Maxim silencer.

Because the wireless room at sea is a sort of lounging-room for those passengers who are bored from reading, or poker, or promenading, or simply are incompetent to amuse themselves without external assistance, Peter ignored the dozen pair of curious and interested eyes which were focussed on his white uniform as he passed, with those telltale chevrons of golden sparks at the sleeves, strode into the wireless cabin, hastily closed the door, locked it, and thereupon gave his attention to the void.

He was not surprised to hear the shrill yap of the Manila station dinning in the receivers, and having no desire to allow his fair name to be besmirched by what might be professional inattention to duty, he gave Manila a crackling response, and told him to shoot and shoot fast, as he had a stack of business on hand, which was the truth.

Steamship and commercial messages were awaiting his nimble fingers, a half-dozen of them, in a neat little pile where the purser had left them to attract his attention as soon as he came on duty.

Manila's first message, with a Hong Kong dateline, and via the Philippine cable, was a service message, directed to Peter Moore, "probably aboard the steamer *Persian Gulf*, at sea." The context of this greeting was that Peter should report directly upon arrival in Hong Kong to J. B. Whalen, representative of the Marconi Company of America, residence, Peak Hotel.

Following this transmission the Manila operator was anxious to know whether or not this was Peter Moore at the key; that he had been given instructions by the night man, who claimed to be a bosom companion of Peter Moore's, to make inquiries regarding Peter Moore's whereabouts during the past few months.

He further expressed a profane desire to know, provided the man at the key was Peter Moore, how in Hades he was, *where* in Tophet he had been keeping himself, and *why* in Gehenna he had so mysteriously vanished from the face of this glorious earth.

"But why all the hubbub about Peter Moore?" flashed back Peter to the inquisitive Manila operator, who was only about two hundred miles distant by now and rather faint with the coming up of the sun.

"Are—you—Peter—Moore?" came the faint scream.

"No, no, no!" shrieked the voluptuous white spark of the *Persian Gulf*.

"Is—he—on—board?"

"No, no, no!" rapped Peter making no effort to disguise that inimitable sending of his.

"You—are—a—double-barreled liar!" said the Manila spark with vehement emphasis. "No operator on the Pacific has that fist. You might as well try to disguise the color of your eyes!"

Manila tapped his key, making a long series of thoughtful little double dots, the operator's way of letting his listener know he is still on the job, and thinking. Then:

"Why did you leave the *Vandalia* at Shanghai?"

"I never left the *Vandalia* anywhere," retorted Peter. "I've just come up from Singapore and Singaraja way. I am taking the *Persian Gulf* to Hong Kong, and back to Batavia."

"No—you're—not," stated Manila's high-toned spark. "You're going to be pinched as soon as you land in Hong Kong for deserting your ship at Shanghai. That's a secret, for old friendship's sake."

It was now Peter's turn to tap off a singularly long row of little double dots.

"It may be a secret, but only a thousand stations are listening in," he said at length. "But, thanks, old-timer, just the same. If they pinch Peter Moore in Hong Kong, they will have to extradite him from Kowloon. In other words, they will have to go some. Besides, what Peter does in Shanghai cannot be laid against him in Hong Kong. The law's the law."

A savage tenor whine here broke in upon Manila's laughing answer, the *Hi! Hi! Hi!* of the amused radio man; and Peter listened in some annoyance to the peremptory summons of a United States gunboat, probably nosing around somewhere south of Mindanao.

"Stand by, Manila," shrilled this one. "Message for the *Persian Gulf.*" He broke off with a nimble signature.

"Good morning, little stranger," roared Peter's stridulent machine. "You're pretty far from home. Won't you get your feet wet? The ocean's pretty dewy this morning. Well, what do *you* want? Shoot it, and shoot fast. Peter Moore's at the key, and the faster you shoot them the better Peter likes them."

The gunboat stuttered angrily.

"A message for Peter Moore, operator in charge, steamer *Persian Gulf,* at sea. Report immediately upon arrival in Hong Kong to American consul for orders. (Signed) B. P. Eckles, commanding officer, U. S. S. *Buffalo.*"

To which Peter composed the following pertinent reply:

"To Commander Eckles, U. S. S. *Buffalo,* somewhere south of Mindanao. What for? (Signed) Peter Moore."

The promptness of the reply to this indicated that the recrudescence of Peter Moore, dead or alive, was of sufficient interest to command the presence of the gunboat's commander in the wireless house. In effect, Peter now realized that his confession had got him into considerable hot water.

Back came the *Buffalo's* nervous answer: "To Peter Moore, operator in charge, steamer *Persian Gulf*, at sea. Orders. Obey them. (Signed) B. P. Eckles."

Peter cut out the formalities. "Please ask the commander what's the trouble."

And out of the void cracked the retort: "He says, ask the American consul at Hong Kong."

There seemed nothing much to do aside from attending to the accumulated business on hand. In Hong Kong he could only decide which of the two he would honor first, the Marconi supervisor or the American consul; for in strange lands one falls into the custom of complying with the requests of his countrymen.

But Peter was beginning to feel a little of the old-time thrill. It was fine to have the fellows recognize that lightning fist of his; fine to have their homage. For the stumbling signals of both Manila and the *Buffalo* were homage of the most straightforward sort.

For Peter Moore as wireless operator was swift of the swiftest; he despatched with a lightning lilt, and the keenness of his ears, for which he was famous on more than one ocean, made it possible for him to receive signals with rarely the necessity for a repeat.

Manila, obeying orders, was standing by, and Peter, tightening a screw to bring the silver contacts of the massive transmission-key in better alignment, despatched his string at the highest speed of which he was capable. As long as his listeners knew he was Peter Moore, he might as well give them, he decided, a sample of the celebrated Peter Moore sending.

For five minutes the little wireless cabin roared with the undiminishing *rat-tat-tat* of his spark explosions, and Manila, a navy man of the old school, rattled back a series of proud okays.

Proud? Because Peter Moore, of the old *Vandalia*, of the *Sierra*, and a dozen other ships, was at the key. And an operator who said "okay" at the termination of one of Peter's inspired lightning transmissions had every right to be proud, as any wireless operator who has ever copied thirty-three words a minute will bear me witness.

CHAPTER IX

When Peter emerged from the wireless room, having completed his business for the morning, he found Romola Borria with elbows on the rail gazing thoughtfully at a small Chinese girl who sat cross-legged on the hatch cover immersed in her sewing.

And Peter marveled at the freshness of Romola Borria's appearance, at the clarity of her sparkling brown eyes, the sweet pinkness of her complexion, and the ease and radiance of her tender smile.

"You look troubled," she said, as her smile was replaced by a look of tender concern. "What is it?" She lowered her voice to a confidential undertone. "Last night's affair, *desu-ka*?"

Peter shook his head with a grave smile.

"I am discovered, Miss Borria. That is to say, I have just given myself away to the Manila navy station, not to speak of the commander of a gunboat, not far from us, off the coast of Mindanao. It seems"—he made a wry face—"Peter Moore is not popular with the authorities for deserting a certain ship in Shanghai."

"The *Vandalia*!" said the girl, and suddenly bit her lip, as though she would have liked to retract the statement.

Peter sank down on his elbows beside her, until his face was very close to hers, and his expression was shrewd and cunning.

"Miss Borria," he remarked stiffly, "I told you last night you're clever; and now you've given me just one more reason to stick to my guns; one more reason to believe that you know more than you're supposed to know. Now, let's be perfectly frank—for once. Let's not erase any more rouge stripes, so to speak. Won't you please tell me just what you do know about my activities in this neighborhood?"

His outflung gesture indicated the whole of Asia.

The girl pursed her lips and a hard twinkle, like that of a frosty arc-light upon diamonds, came into her eyes. "Yes, Mr. Moore," she said vigorously, "I will. But you must promise—promise faithfully—to ask no questions. Will you do that?"

Peter nodded with a willingness that was far from assumed.

Romola Borria placed the tips of her slender, white fingers together and looked down at them pensively. "Well," she said, looking up and raising her voice slightly, "you escaped from the liner *Vandalia* in the middle of the

Whang-poo River, at night, in a deep fog, in a sampan, with a young woman named Eileen Lorimer in your arms. This occurred after you had delivered her from the hands of certain men, whom I prefer to call, perhaps mysteriously, by the plain word *them*.

"You sent this young lady home on the *Manchuria*, or the *Mongolia*, I forget just which. That night on the bund near the French legation, you met, quite by accident, another young lady who found your companionship quite desirable. Her name was Miss Amy Vost, a bright little thing."

"You don't happen to know," put in Peter ironically, "what Miss Lorimer had for breakfast this morning, by any chance?"

"At last accounts she was studying for a doctor's degree in the university at San Friole, Mr. Moore."

"Indeed!" It was on the tip of Peter's tongue to tell this astounding Romola Borria that she was nothing short of a mind-reader. Instead, he nodded his head for her to continue.

"As I was saying, you met Miss Vost, quite by accident, and danced with her at a fancy dress ball at the Astor House. You wore the costume of a Japanese merchant, I believe, thinking, a little fatuously, if you will permit me, that those garments were a disguise. A little later in the bar at the Palace Hotel, after you left Miss Vost, you met a sea captain, ex-first mate of the Toyo Kisen Kaisha steamer, the *Sunyado Maru*. He was an old friend.

"With Captain MacLaurin and Miss Vost you made a trip on the Yangtze-Kiang in a little river steamer, the *Hankow*, which foundered in the rapids just below Ching-Fu. This occurred after you had stabbed and killed one of their most trusted spies.

"When the *Hankow* sank, you followed what now appears to be your professional habit of a trustworthy gallant, by taking a lady in distress into your arms, and swam the whirlpools to the little village across the river from Ching-Fu. Then Miss Vost was met by her father, an incurable missionary from Wenchow, and by devious routes, well known to *them*, you joined a caravan, owned by a garrulous old thief who calls himself a mandarin, the Mandarin Chang, who told you many lies, to amuse himself—"

"Of course they were lies, Mr. Moore. Chang is one of *his* most trusted henchmen. He even permitted you to kill one of his coolies. The coolie would have died anyway; he was beginning to learn too much. But it tickled Chang, and *him*, to let you have this chance, to see how far you would go. And Chang had orders to help you reach Len Yang. It gave you confidence in yourself, did it not?"

"I don't believe a word," declared Peter in a daze. He refused to believe that Chang, kindly old Chang, was in league with that man, too.

"Then you entered Len Yang, the City of Stolen Lives, and *he* watched you, and when you heard a difficult wireless message on the instruments at the mine, *he* gave you a present of money—five hundred taels, wasn't it?—

hoping, perhaps, that you would 'give up your foolishness,' as he expressed it, and settle down to take the place of the opium-befuddled wireless man you fooled so cleverly. *He* valued you, Mr. Moore, you see, and he was not in the least afraid of you!

"A dozen times, yes, a hundred times, he could have killed you. But he preferred to sit back and stroke those long, yellow, mandarin mustaches of his, and watch you, as a cat watches a foolish mouse. I can see him laughing now. Yes! I have seen him, and I have heard him laugh. It is a hideous, cackling laugh. Quite unearthly! How he did laugh at you when you rescued Miss Vost, dear little clinging Miss Vost, from the jaws of his white palace!

"But he let you go; and he and his thousand sharpshooters who lined the great, green walls, when you and Captain MacLaurin and Miss Vost galloped bravely out, with one poor little mule! A thousand rifles, I say, were leveled upon you in that bright moonlight, Mr. Moore. But *he* said—*no!*"

Peter looked up at the stolid rigging of the *Persian Gulf*, at the sunlight dancing brightly on the blue waves, which foamed at their crests like fresh, boiling milk; at the passengers sleeping or reading in their deck chairs; and he refused to believe that this was not a dream. But the level voice of Romola Borria purred on:

"Then you joined a caravan for India, and, for a little while, they thought your trail was lost. But you reappeared in Mandalay, attired as a street fakir; and you limped all the way to Rangoon. Why did you limp, Mr. Moore?"

"A mule stamped on my foot, coming through the Merchants' Pass into Bengal."

"It healed rapidly, no doubt, for you were very active from that time on. You took passage to Penang, to Singapore, doubling back to Penang, and again to Singapore, and caught a blue-funnel steamer for Batavia."

"But, Miss Borria," writhed Peter, "why, with all this knowledge, hasn't he done away with me? You know. *He* knows. You've had your chance. You could have killed me in your stateroom last night. Please—" And Peter cast the golden robe of the adventurer temporarily from him, becoming for the moment nothing more than a terribly earnest, terribly concerned young man.

"I gave you an inkling last night," replied Romola Borria composedly. "Until you left Batavia *he* believed that you had given up your nonsense. The coolie you threw overboard in Batavia was there, not to stab you, but to warn you away from China. Those warnings, of which you have had many, are now things of the past. You have thrown down the glove to him once too often. He is through toying.

"It was great fun for him, and he enjoyed it. He treats his enemies that way—for a while. You have now entered upon the second stage of enmity with him. Last night was a sample of what you may expect from now on. Only the sheerest luck saved you from the coolie's bullet—and my almost-too-tardy intervention."

Peter gave her a hard, thoughtful and a thoroughly respectful stare.

"I take it," he said, "that you are a special emissary, a sort of minister plenipotentiary, from the Gray Dragon. As a matter of fact, you are here simply to persuade me to correct my erring ways; to persuade me to give you my promise for *him* that I will put China and Len Yang forever out of my plans."

"Express it any way you please, Mr. Moore. I have told you about all that I am able. I know this game, if you will permit me, a little, just a little better than you do, Mr. Moore. I know when fun stops and downright danger begins. The moment you put your foot in China, you are putting your foot in a trap from which you can never, never so long as you are permitted to live, extricate yourself. And, believe me, seriously, that will not be for long. A day? Perhaps. An hour? Very likely not any longer than that.

"Call me a special emissary if you choose. Perhaps I am. Perhaps I am only a friend, who desires above everything else to help you avoid a most certain and a most unpleasant death. I have given you your opportunity. From my heart I gave you, and I still do give you, the chance to leave—with me. Yes; I mean that. Your promise, backed by your word of honor, is a passport to safety for both of us. Your refusal, I might as well confess, means to me—death! Won't you stop and consider? Won't you say—yes?"

Peter's head had snapped back during this epilogue; his white-clad shoulders were squared, and his blue eyes were lighted by a fire that might have made a Crusader envious.

"You may report to him," said he, "that I have listened to his proposal; that I have considered it calmly; and that, as long as the gauntlet is down—it is—*down*! I want but one thing: a man's chance at that beast. You can tell him just that from me, Miss Borria. I am sorry."

She seemed on the point of uttering a final word, a word that might have been of the greatest importance to Peter the Brazen; but the word never got beyond her lips.

Into her eyes crept a look of despair, of mute horror. She half raised her hand; withdrew it. Her shoulders sagged. She staggered to a deck chair, and sank into it, with her head back, her eyes closed, her long, dark lashes lying upon cheeks that had become marble.

Standing there with his eyes glued to the blue of the sea, Peter the Brazen felt the confidence oozing from him as water oozes out of a leaky pail. He felt himself in the presence of a relentless power which was slowly settling down upon him, crushing him, and overpowering him.

It occurred to him as his thoughts raced willy-nilly, to flash a call of help to the gunboat which prowled south of Luzon, a call which would have met with a response swift and energetic.

Yet that impulse smacked of the blunderer. It would put an end forever to his high plan, now boiling more strongly than ever before, in the back of his racked brain: to meet and some day put down the beast in Len Yang.

A bright, waving hand distracted his attention from the sea. The maid from Macassar was endeavoring to attract him. He looked down with a pale, haggard smile.

"You have not forgotten—Kowloon, *busar satu*?" said her tinkling little voice.

"Not I, small one!" Peter called back in accents that entirely lacked their accustomed gaiety.

CHAPTER X

During the remainder of the voyage Romola Borria did not once, so far as Peter was aware, leave her stateroom. Her meals were sent there, and there she remained, sending out word in response to his inquiries that she was ill, could see no one—not that Peter, after that latest astounding interview, cared particularly to renew the friendship. He was simply thoughtful.

Yet he felt a little angry at his demonstration of frank selfishness, and not a little uneasy at the uncanny precision of her recital of his recent history, an uneasiness which grew, until he found himself waiting with growing concern for the rock-bound shore-line of Hong Kong to thrust its black-and-green shoulders above the horizon.

The *Persian Gulf* anchored outside at night, and in the morning steamed slowly in amidst the maze of masts, of sampans and junks, which latter lay with their sterns pointing grotesquely upward, resembling nothing so closely as great brown hawks which had flown down from a Brobdingnagian heaven, to select with greater convenience and fastidiousness what prey might fall within reach of their talons.

Peter was aware that many of these junks were pirate ships, audacious enough to pole into Victoria Harbor under the very guns of the forts, under the noses of battleships of every nation.

When the launch from quarantine swung alongside, Peter went below and changed from the uniform to a light, fresh suit of Shantung silk, a soft collar, a soft Bangkok hat, and comfortable, low walking shoes, not neglecting to knot about his waist the blue sarong.

The steerage passengers were lined up when he came above a little later, sticking out their tongues for the eagle-eyed doctors, and giggling at a proceeding serious enough, had they known it, to send every mother's son and daughter of them back to the land whence they came, if they displayed so much as a slight blemish, for Hong Kong was then in the throes of her latest cholera scare.

Satisfied at length that the eyes and tongues of the steerage and deck passengers gave satisfactorily robust testimony, the doctors came up to the first-class passengers, who stood in line on the promenade deck; and Peter saw the change that had come over Romola Borria.

Her face bore the pallor of the grave. Her large, lustrous eyes were sunken, and lines seemed to have been engraved in a face that had previously been as smooth and fair as a rose in bloom.

He felt panic-stricken as she recognized him with an almost imperceptible nod, and he stared at her a trifle longer than was necessary, with his lips slightly ajar, his nails biting into his palms, and he sensed rather than saw, that her beauty had been transformed into one of gray melancholy.

At that juncture, a tinkling voice shrilled up at him from the after cargo-well, and Peter turned to see his small charge, the maid from Macassar, smiling as she waited for him beside a small pile of silken bundles of the rainbow's own colors. He had not forgotten the Eurasian girl, but he desired to have a parting word with Romola Borria.

He called over the rail, and instructed her of the black pigtail to wait for him in a sampan, and he yelled down to one of the dozens of struggling and babbling coolies, whose sampans swarmed like a horde of cockroaches at the ladder's lower extremity.

Romola Borria, alone, was awaiting him, adjusting her gloves, at the doorway of the wireless cabin when he made his way back to that quarter of the ship. She greeted him with a slow, grave smile; and by that smile Peter was given to know how she had suffered.

Her face again became a mask, a mask of death, indeed, as her lids fluttered down and then raised; and her eyes were tired.

He extended his hand, trying to inject some of his accustomed cheerfulness into the gesture and into the smile which somehow would not form naturally on his lips.

"This—is *adieu*—or *au revoir*?" he said solemnly.

"I hope—*au revoir*," she replied dully. "So, after all, you refuse to take my counsel, my advice, seriously?"

Peter shrugged. "I'm rather afraid I can't," he said. "You see, I'm young. And you can say to yourself, or out loud without fear of hurting my feelings, that I am—foolish. I guess it is one of the hardships of being young—this having to be foolish. Wasn't it today that I was to become immortal, with a knife through my floating ribs, or a bullet in my heart?

"As I grow older I will become more serious, with balance. Perish the thought! But in the end—shucks! Confucius, wasn't it—that dear old philosopher who could never find a king to try out his theories on—who said:

> *"The great mountain must crumble.*
> *The strong beam must break.*
> *The wise man must wither away like a plant."*

She nodded.

"I am afraid you will never become serious, Mr. Moore. And perhaps that is one of the reasons why I've grown so—so fond of you in this short while. If I could take life—and death—as stoically, as happily, as you—oh, God!"

She shut her eyes. Tears were in their rims when she opened them again.

"Mr. Moore, I'll make a foolish confession, too, now. It is—I love you. And in return—"

"I think you're the bravest girl in the world," said Peter, taking her hands with a movement of quick penitence. "You—you're a brick."

"I guess I am," she sighed, looking moodily away. "A brick of clay! Perhaps it is best to walk into the arms of your enemies the way you do, with your head back and eyes shining and a smile of contempt on your lips. If I only could!"

"Why speak of death on a day like this?" said Peter lightly. "Life is so beautiful. See those red-and-yellow blossoms on the hill, near the governor's place, and the poor little brats on that sampan, thinking they're the happiest kids in the world. What hurts them, hurts them; what pleases them, pleases them. They're happy because they don't bother to anticipate. And think of life, beautiful old life, brimming over with excitement and the mystery of the very next moment!"

"If I could only see that next moment!"

"Ugh! What a dreary monotony life would become!"

"But we could be sure. We could prepare for—for—well—" She threw up her head defiantly. "For death, I'll say."

"But please don't let's talk of death. Let's talk of the fine time you and I are going to have when we see each other again."

"Will there be another time, Peter?"

"Why, of course! You name that time; any time, any place. We'll eat and drink and chatter like a couple of parrots. And you will forget all this—this that is behind us."

Her teeth clicked.

"Tonight," she said quickly. "I'll meet you. Let me see. On the Desvoeux Road side of the Hong Kong Hotel balcony, the restaurant, upstairs, you know."

"Right!" agreed Peter with enthusiasm. "Will we let husband go along?"

Her face suddenly darkened. She shook her head.

"I will be alone. So will you, at seven o'clock. You'll be there, without fail?"

A coolie guarded her luggage near by impatiently. They could hear the sobbing of the J. C. J. passenger launch as it rounded the starboard counter.

"I forget," said Peter, with his flashing smile. "I'll be dead in an hour. The steel trap of China, you know."

"Please don't jest."

"I'll tell you what I will do. I'll put a tag on my lapel, saying, deliver this corpse to the Desvoeux Road balcony of the Hong Kong Hotel restaurant at seven sharp tonight! Without fail! C. O. D.!"

These last words were addressed to the empty wireless cabin doorway. The white skirt of Romola Borria flashed like a taunting signal as she hastened out of his sight with the boy who carried her grips.

CHAPTER XI

Wearing a slight frown, Peter made his way through piles of indiscriminate luggage to the port ladder, where his sampan and the maid from Macassar were waiting.

As he descended this contrivance he scanned the other sampans warily, and in one of these he saw a head which protruded from a low cabin. The sampan was a little larger than the others, and it darted in and out on the edge of the waiting ones.

The head vanished the instant Peter detected it, but it made a sharp image in his memory, a face he would have difficulty in forgetting. It was a long, chalk-white face, topped by a black fedora hat—a face garnished at the thin gray lips by a mustache, black and spikelike, resembling nothing more closely than the coal-black mustache affected by the old-time melodrama villains.

An hour of life? Did this man have concealed under his black coat the knife which had been directed by the beast in Len Yang to seek out his heart, to snuff out his existence, the existence of a trifling enemy?

As Peter reached the shelving at the foot of the ladder the thought grew and blossomed, and the picture was not a pleasant one. The man in the sampan, as Peter could judge by his face, would probably prove to be a tall and muscular individual.

And then Peter caught sight of another face, but the owner of it remained above-board. This man was stout and gray, with a face more subtly malignant. It was a red face, cut deep at the eyes, and in the region of the large purple nose, with lines of weather or dissipation. Blue eyes burned out of the red face, faded blue eyes, that were, despite their lack of lustre, sharp and cunning.

The hand of its owner beckoned imperiously for Peter, and he shouted his name; and Peter was assured that in the other hand was concealed the knife or the pistol of his doom.

With these not altogether pleasant ideas commanding his brain he jumped into the sampan in which the maid from Macassar was smilingly waiting.

Peter saw that his coolie was big and broad, with muscles which stood out like ropes on his thick, sun-burned arms and legs. He gave the coolie his instructions, as the sampan occupied by the red-faced man was all the while endeavoring to wiggle closer. Again the man called Peter by name, peremptorily, but Peter paid no heed.

"To Kowloon. Chop-chop!" shouted Peter. "*Cumshaw*. Savvy?" He displayed in his palm three silver dollars and the coolie bent his back to the sweep, the sampan heeling out from the black ironside like a thing alive.

Behind them, as this manoeuvre was executed, Peter saw the two duly accredited agents of the Gray Dragon fall in line. But Peter had selected with wisdom. The coolie verified with the passage of every moment the power his ropy muscles implied. Inch by inch, and yard by yard, they drew, away from the pursuing sampans.

Then something resembling the scream of an enraged parrot sang over their heads, and he instinctively ducked, turning to see from which of the sampans this greeting had come.

A faint puff of light-blue smoke sailed down the wind between the two. Which one? It was difficult to say.

They were beginning to leave the pursuit decidedly in the lurch now. Peter's coolie, with his long legs braced far apart on the running-boards, bent his back, swaying like a mighty metronome from port to starboard, from starboard to port, whipping the water into an angry, milky foam.

The pursuers crept up and fell back by fits and starts; slowly the distance widened.

The girl crouched down in the cabin, and Peter, with his automatic in his hand, waited for another tell-tale puff of blue smoke.

Finally this puff occurred, low on the deck of the larger craft. The bullet plunked into the water not two feet from the sweep, and the coolie, inspired by the knowledge that he, too, was inextricably wrapped up in this race of life and death, sweated, and shouted in the savage "Hi! Ho! Hay! Ho!" of the coolie who dearly loves his work.

Satisfied as to the origin of both bullets, Peter took careful aim at the yellow sampan and emptied his magazine, slipping another clip of cartridges into the oblong hole as he watched for the result.

The yellow sampan veered far from her course, and a sweep floated on the surface some few yards aft. Then the sampan lay as if dead. But the other plunged on after.

This exciting race and the blast of Peter's automatic now attracted the earnest attention of a gray little river gunboat, just down from up-stream, and inured to such incidents as this.

A one-pound shell snarled overhead, struck the water a hundred yards further on, near the Kowloon shore, and sent up a foaming white pillar.

The pier at Kowloon loomed close and more close. It was unlikely that the gunboat would follow up the shot with another, and in this guess, Peter, as the French say, "had reason."

The fires under the gunboat's boilers were drawn, and there was no time for the launching of a cutter.

A great contentment settled down upon Peter's heart when he saw that the oncoming sampan could not reach the pier until he and his charge were out of sight, or out of reach, at least.

He examined his watch. The gods were with him. It lacked three minutes of train-time.

It was only a hope that he and the girl would be safe on board the Canton train before the red-faced man could catch up.

The sampan rubbed the green timbers of the Kowloon landing stage. Peter tossed up the girl's luggage in one large armful, lifted her by the armpits to the floor of the pier, and relieved himself hastily of four dollars (Mexican), by which the grunting coolie was gratefully, and for some few hours, richer.

They dashed to the first-class compartment, and Peter dragged the girl in beside him.

"To Canton, too?" she inquired in surprise.

Peter nodded. He slammed the door. A whistle screamed, and the station of Kowloon, together with the glittering waters of the blue bay, and the white city of Hong Kong, across the bay, all began moving, first slowly, then with acceleration, as the morning express for Canton slid out on the best-laid pair of rails in southern China.

Had his red-faced pursuer caught up in time? Peter prayed not. He was tingling with the thrill of the chase; and he turned his attention to the small maiden who sat cuddled close to his side, with hands folded demurely before her, imprisoning between them the overlap of his flaunting blue sarong.

"We are safe, brave one?" she was desirous of knowing.

He patted her hand reassuringly, and she caught at it, lowering her green-blue eyes to the dusty floor, and sighing.

Peter might have paused in his rapid meditations long enough to be aware that, here he was, dropped—plump—into the center of another ring of romance; nothing having separated him from his last love but two misdirected revolver shots, the warning boom of a gunboat's bow cannon, and a mad chase across Victoria Bay.

Holding hands breaks no known law; yet Peter was not entirely aware that he was committing this act, as his eyes, set and hard, stared out of the window at the passing pagodas with their funny turned-up roofs.

His mind was working on other matters. Perhaps for the first time since the *Persian Gulf* had dropped anchor to the white sand of Victoria Harbor's bottom, he began to realize the grim seriousness of Romola Borria's warning. He was hemmed in. He was helpless.

An hour to live! An hour alive! But he was willing to make the very best of that hour.

Absently, then by degrees not so absently, he alternately squeezed and loosened the small, cool hands of the maid from Macassar. And she returned the pressure with a timid confidence that made him stop and consider for a moment something that had entirely slipped his mind during the past few days.

Was he playing quite squarely with Eileen Lorimer? Had he been observing perhaps the word but not the letter of his self-assumed oath? On the other hand, mightn't it be possible that Eileen Lorimer had ceased to care for him? With time and the miles stretching between them, wasn't it quite possible that she had shaken herself, recognized her interest in him as one only of passing infatuation, and, perhaps already, had given her love to some other?

A silly little rhyme of years ago occurred to him:

Love me close! Love me tight! But
Love me when I'm out of sight!

And perhaps because Peter had fallen into one of his reasoning moods, he asked himself whether it was fair to carry the flirtation any further with the girl snuggled beside him. He knew that the hearts of Oriental girls open somewhat more widely to the touch of affection than their Western sisters. And it was not in the nature of women of the East to indulge extensively in the Western form of idle flirtation. The lowering of the eyelids, the flickering of a smile, had meaning and depth in this land.

Was this girl flirting with him, or was hers a deeper interest? That was the question! He took the latter view.

And because he knew, from his own experience, that the hearts of lovers sometimes break at parting, he finally relinquished the cool, small hands and thrust his own deep into his pockets.

There was no good reason, apart from his own selfishness, why he should give a pang of any form to the trustful young heart which fluttered so close at his side.

"Where does your aged grandmother live, small one?" he asked her briskly, in the most unsentimental tones imaginable.

"I have the address here, *birahi*," she replied, diving into her satin blouse and producing a slip of rice paper upon which was scrawled a number of dead-black symbols of the Chinese written language.

"A rickshaw man can find the place, of course," he said. "Now, look into my eyes, small one, and listen to what I say."

"I listen closely, *birahi*," said the small one.

"I want you to stop calling me *birahi*. I am not your love, can never be your love, nor can you ever be mine."

"But why, *bi*—my brave one?"

"Because—because, I am a wicked one, an *orang gila*, a destroyer of good, a man of no heart, or worse, a black one."

"Oh, Allah, what lies!" giggled the maid.

"Yes, and a liar, too," declared Peter venomously, permitting his fair features to darken with the blackest of looks. Was she flirting with him? "A man who never told the truth in his life. A bad, bad man," he finished lamely.

"But why are you telling such things to me, my brave one?" came the provocative answer.

She *was* flirting with him.

Nevertheless, he merely grunted and relapsed again into the form of meditative lethargy which of late had grown habitual if not popular with him.

A little after noon the train thundered into the narrow, dirty streets of China's most flourishing city, geographically, the New Orleans of the Celestial Empire; namely, Canton, on the Pearl River.

As Peter and his somewhat amused young charge emerged into the street he cast a furtive glance back toward the station, and was dumfounded to glimpse, not two yards away, the man with the red, deeply marked face. His blue eyes were ablaze, and he advanced upon Peter threateningly.

It was a situation demanding decisive, direct action. Peter, hastily instructing the girl to hold two rickshaws, leaped at his pursuer with doubled fists, even as the man delved significantly into his hip-pocket.

Peter let him have it squarely on the blunt nub of his red jaw, aiming as he sprang.

His antagonist went down in a cursing heap, sprawling back with the look in his washed-out eyes of a steer which has been hit squarely in the center of the brow.

He fell back on his hands and lay still, dazed, muttering, and struggling to regain the use of his members.

Before he could recover Peter was up and away, springing lightly into the rickshaw. They turned and darted up one narrow, dirty alley into a narrower and dirtier one, the two coolies shouting in blasphemous chorus to clear the way as they advanced.

After a quarter of an hour of twisting and splashing and turning, the coolies stopped in front of a shop of clay-blue stone.

Paying off the coolies, Peter entered, holding the door for the girl, and sliding the bolt as he closed it after her.

He found himself in the presence of a very old, very yellow, and very wrinkled Chinese woman, who smiled upon the two of them perplexedly, nodding and smirking, as her frizzled white pigtail flopped and fluttered about in the clutter on the shelves behind her.

It was a shop for an antique collector to discover, gorged with objects of bronze, of carved sandalwood, of teak, grotesque and very old, of shining red and blue and yellow beads, of old gold and old silver.

On the low, narrow counter she had placed a shallow red tray filled with pearls; imitations, no doubt, but exquisite, perfect, of all shapes; bulbular, pear, button, and of most enticing colors.

But the small girl was babbling, and a look of the most profound surprise came slowly into the old woman's face. A little pearl-like tear sparkled in either of her old eyes, and she gathered this cherished grand-daughter from far away Macassar into her thin arms.

At that sight Peter felt himself out of place, an intruder, an interloper. The scene was not meant for his eyes. He was an alien in a strange land.

As he hesitated, conjuring up words of parting with his little friend, he gasped. Peering through the thick window-pane in the door was the red-faced man, and his look sent a curdle of fear into Peter's brave heart. Would he shoot through the pane?

The girl, too, saw. She chattered a long moment to her wrinkled grand-mother, and this latter leaped to the door and shot a second strong bolt. She pointed excitedly to a rear door, low and green, set deep in the blue stone.

Peter leaped toward it. Half opening this, he saw a tiny garden surround-ed by low, gray walls. He paused. The maid from Macassar was behind him. She followed him out and closed the door.

"*Birahi*," she said in her tinkling voice, and with gravity far in advance of her summers, "we must part now—forever?"

He nodded, as he searched the wall for a likely place to jump. "It is the penalty of friendship, *birahi*. You do not mind if I call you *birahi* in our last moment together?"

"No. No."

"I am curious, so curious, my brave one, about the red-faced man, and the one with the black coat. But we women are meant for silence. *Birahi*, I have played no part—I have been like a dead lily—a burden. Perhaps, if you are in great danger—"

"I am in great danger, small one. The red toad wants my life, and you must detain him."

"I will talk to him! But the others, the black-coated one—what of them? They would like the feel of your blood on their hands, too!"

Peter nodded anxiously. He was thinking of Romola Borria.

"I will do anything," declared the maid from Macassar patiently.

"Has your grandmother a sampan, a trustworthy coolie?"

"Aie, *birahi*! She is rich!"

"Then have that coolie be at the Hong Kong landing stage with his sam-pan at midnight. Have him wait until morning. If I do not come by dawn he will return immediately to Canton. By dawn, if I am not there, it will mean—"

"Death?" The small voice was tremulous.

Peter nodded.

"If the *fokie* returns with that message, you will write a short note—"

"To one you love?"

"To one I love. In America. The name is Eileen Lorimer; the address, Pasadena, California. You will say simply, 'Peter Moore is dead.'"

"Ah! I must not say that. It will break her heart! But you must go now, my brave one. I will talk to the red toad!"

The green door closed softly; and Peter was left to work out the problem of his escape, which he did in an exceedingly short space of time. Even as he took the fence in a single bound he fancied he could hear the panting of the red-faced man at his heels.

He found himself in a crooked alleyway, which forked out of sight at a near-by bend. Speeding to this point, he came out upon a somewhat broader thoroughfare. He looked hastily for a rickshaw but none was in sight.

So he ran blindly on, resorting at intervals to his old trick of doubling back, to confuse his pursuers. He did this so well that before long he had lost his sense of direction, and the sun having gone from the sight of man behind a mass of dark and portentous clouds.

At length he came to the City of the Dead, and sped on past the ivy-covered wall, circling, doubling back, and giving what pursuit there might have been a most tortuous trail to follow.

He was hooted at and jeered at by coolies and shrieking children, but he ran on, putting the miles behind him, and finally dropped into a slow trot, breathing like a spent race-horse.

At the pottery field he found a rickshaw, estimated that he still had time to spare to make the Hong Kong train, and was driven to the station. Dead or alive, he had promised to deliver himself to Romola Borria at the Hong Kong Hotel at seven.

Visions of the malignant face of his red-featured enemy were constantly in his mind.

But he breathed more easily as the train chugged out of the grim, gray station. He sank back in the seat, letting his thoughts wander where they would, and beginning to feel, as the miles were unspun, that he was at least one jump ahead of the red death which had threatened him since his departure from the friendly shelter of the *Persian Gulf*.

CHAPTER XII

The shadows were lengthening, the sky was of a deeper and vaster blue, when the train came to a creaking stop in the Kowloon Station.

Peter emerged, scanning the passengers warily, but catching not a glimpse of his red-faced enemy. What did that one have in store for him now? This chase was becoming a game of hide-and-seek. But in Hong Kong he would feel safer. Hong Kong was a haunt of civilized men and of able Sikh policemen, who detested the yellow men of China.

He took the ferry-boat across the bay to the city, which rose tier upon tier of white from the purple water; and he made his way afoot to the American consulate.

With auspicious celerity the sad-eyed clerk bowed him into the presence of an elderly gentleman with white side whiskers and an inveterate habit of stroking a long and angular nose.

This personage permitted his shrewd, grave eyes to take in Peter from his blond hair to his tan walking shoes, and with a respectful mien Peter prepared his wits for a sharp and digging cross-examination.

"I have been advised," began the American consul, giving to Peter's blue eyes a look of curiosity in which was mingled not a little unconcealed admiration, as he might have looked upon the person of Pancho Villa, had that other miscreant stepped into his gloomy office—"I have been advised," he repeated importantly, "by the commander of the auxiliary cruiser *Buffalo* that you contemplated a visit to Hong Kong."

He sank back and stared, and it took Peter several moments to become aware that the content of the remark was not nearly so important as its pronunciation. The remark was somewhat obvious. The American consul desired Peter to make the opening.

Peter inclined his head as he slowly digested the statement.

"I was told by Commander Eckles to report to you," he replied respectfully, "for orders."

The American consul laid his hands firmly upon the edge of the mahogany desk.

"My orders, Mr. Moore, are that you leave China immediately. I trust—"

"Why?" said Peter in a dry voice.

"That is a matter which, unfortunately, I cannot discuss with you. The order comes, I am permitted to inform you, from the highest of diplomatic quarters. To be exact, from Peking, and from the American ambassador, to be more specific."

It was crystal clear to Peter that the American consul was not cognizant of what might be behind those orders from the American ambassador; yet his face, for all of its diplomatic masking, told Peter plainly that the American consul was not entirely averse to learning.

"Have I been interfering with the lawful pursuits of the Chinese Empire?" he inquired ironically.

The American consul stroked his long nose pensively.

"Well—perhaps," he said. "On the whole, that is something you can best explain yourself, Mr. Moore. If you should care to give me your side of the question, ah—"

"I haven't a thing to say," rejoined Peter. "If the United States Government chooses to believe that my presence is inimical to its interests in China—"

"Pressure might have been brought to bear from another quarter."

"Quite so," admitted Peter.

"Now, if you should desire to make me acquainted with your pursuits during the past—ah—few months, let us say, it is within the bounds of possibility that I might somehow rescind this drastic—ah—order. Suffice it to say, that I shall be glad to put my every power at your aid. As you are an American, it is my duty and my pleasure, sir, if you will permit me, to do all within my power, my somewhat restricted power, if I may qualify that statement, to reinstate you in the good graces of those—ah—good gentlemen in Peking."

It was all too evident that, back and beyond the friendly intentions of this official, was a hungry desire for information regarding this young man whose dark activities had been recognized by the high powers to an extent sufficient to set in motion the complicated and bulky wheels of diplomacy.

Peter shook his head respectfully, and the consul permitted his reluctantly admiring and inquisitive gaze to travel up and down the romantic and now international figure.

"I am able to say nothing," he expressed himself quietly. "If the American ambassador has decreed that I ought to go home—home I go! I'll confess right now that I did not intend to go home when I stepped into this office, but I do respect, and I will respect, the authority of that order."

"If the President, for example, should request you to continue—ah—what you have been doing, for the good, let us say, of humanity, you would continue without hesitation, Mr. Moore?"

Peter gave the long, pale face a sharp scrutiny. Did this innocent-faced man know more than he intimated, or was he merely applying the soft, velvet screws of diplomacy, endeavoring to squeeze out a little information?

"I certainly would."

The consul rose, with a bland smile, and extended his hand.

"It has been gratifying to know one who has become such a singular, and, permit me to add, such a trying figure, in diplomatic circles, during the past week. Good-day, sir!"

Peter walked down Desvoeux road in a state of mental detachment. A week! Only a week had passed since he had sailed from Batavia, a week since he had thrown overboard the emissary of the Gray Dragon. He concluded that in more than one way could his presence be dismissed from the land of darkness and distrust.

How had the Gray Dragon brought pressure upon the American ambassador, a man of the highest repute, of sterling and patriotic qualities? The answer seemed to be, that the coils of the Gray Dragon extended everywhere, like an inky fluid which had leaked into every crevice and crack of all Asia.

He was still under orders to pay a visit to J. B. Whalen, the Marconi supervisor. That cross-examination he was glad to postpone.

He called at the office of the Pacific Mail, and found that the *King of Asia* was due to leave for the United States the following morning at dawn. He made a deposit on a reservation.

CHAPTER XIII

The hour lacked a few minutes of seven when Peter ascended in the lift to the second floor of the Hong-Kong Hotel and made his way between the closely packed tables to the Desvoeux Road balcony.

Romola Borria was not yet in evidence.

He selected a table which commanded a view of the entrance, toyed with the menu card, absent-mindedly ordered a Scotch highball, and slowly scrutinized the occupants of the tables in his neighborhood. He felt vaguely annoyed, slightly uneasy, without being able to sift out the cause.

For a moment he regretted his audacity in encountering the curious eyes of Hong Kong society, a society in which there would inevitably be present a number of his enemies. It cannot be denied that a number of eyes studied him leisurely and at some pains, over teacups, wine-glasses, and fans.

But these were for the larger part women, and Peter was more or less immune to the curious, bright-eyed glances of this sex.

His attire was somewhat rakish for the occasion; and it appeared that sarongs were not being sported by the more refined class of male diners, who affected as a mass the sombre black of dinner jackets. At all Hong Kong hotels the custom is evening dress for dinner, and Peter felt shabby and shoddy in his silk suit, his low shoes, his soft collar.

An orchestra of noble proportions struggled effectively in the moist, warm atmosphere somewhere in its concealment behind a distant palm arbor with "Un Peu d'Amour," and also out of Peter's sight, an impassioned and metallic tenor was sobbing:

> *"Jaw-s-s-st a lee-e-e-edle lof-f-ff—*
> *A le-e-e-edle ke-e-e-e-e-s—"*

And Peter in his perturbation wished that both blatant orchestra and impassioned tenor were concealed behind a sound-proof stone wall.

He was tossing off the dregs of the highball when there occurred a low-voiced murmur at his side, and he arose to confront the pale, worn face of Romola. She gave him her hand limply, and settled down across from him, her eyes darting from table to table, and occasionally nodding rather stiffly and impersonally as she recognized some one.

"You see"—he smiled at her, as she settled back and fostered upon him a look of brooding tenderness—"you see, my dear, I am here, untagged. Nearly twelve hours have passed since you sounded that note of ominous warning. I have yet to feel the thrill, just before I die, of that dagger sliding between my ribs."

She accepted this with a nod almost indifferent.

"Simply because I have persuaded them to extend your parole to one o'clock. If you linger in China, you have—and need I say that the same applies to me—six more hours in which to jest, to laugh, to love—to live!"

"For which I am, as always in the face of favors, duly grateful," said Peter in high humor. "None the less I have this day, since we parted this morning, indulged in one pistol duel between sampans, with one of your admirable confrères—"

"Yes, I heard of that. But it stopped there. You winged his sampan coolie."

"And at the Canton station, if I may be pardoned for contradicting, I encountered the red-faced one. To tell you what you may already know, I punched him in the jaw, dog-gone him!"

She seemed to be distressed.

"You must be mistaken."

Peter shook his head forcibly. "A choleric gentleman born with the habit of reaching for his hip-pocket," he amplified.

She studied him with wide, speculative eyes. "He must be from the north. Some of them I do not know. But all of them have been informed."

"To permit me to live and love until one tomorrow morning?"

She nodded.

The aspiring and perspiring orchestra and the impassioned tenor had again reached the chorus of "Un Peu d'Amour."

I could ge-e-e-eve you al-l-l my life for the-e-e-s—"

"Badly sung, but appropriate," commented Romola Borria.

Peter's countenance became a question mark.

"It may mean that I am giving you all my life for—this," she explained.

"For these few minutes, when we were to chatter, and make love, and be happy?" Peter demanded indignantly. "My dear—" He reached out for her hand, and she let him fondle it, not reluctantly. "I'd give all my life, too, for these few minutes with you. Do you know—you're perfectly adorable tonight! There's something—something irresistible about you—to me!"

"To you?"

"Yes," he said in a deep voice, and sincerely. "I'd come all the way 'round the world, and lay my life at your feet—thus." And he placed his knuckles on the white cloth, as if they were knees.

"Ah! But you don't mean that!"

"When I'm in love, I mean everything!"

"I know. You are fickle. Miss Lorimer—Miss—Vost—Romola—they come, they love, they are gone, quite as fatefully and systematically as life follows death, and death follows life."

"I do wish you wouldn't talk about death in that flippant manner," he gibed, wondering how under the sun he might get her out of this gloomy mood.

"But death is in my mind always—Peter. When you have gone through—"

"Romola, I refuse to be lectured."

"Very well; I refuse to talk of anything but love and death."

"Excellent, my own love! Tell me now how it feels when *you* are in the heavenly condition."

"Most hopeless, Peter; because death, you see, is so close upon the heels of my love."

"Meaning—me?"

"No—my heart. The death of love and the death—of life follow my love. Now I want to pick up the threads of a moment ago. Peter, don't hold my hand. That woman is—staring. You said—you said, you would come away around the world to see me, to help me, possibly, if I were in trouble. You weren't serious."

"Cross my heart!"

"On the *Persian Gulf* that day—that day I told you something of your recent adventures and your apparently miraculous escapes, I intended to ask you—"

"Seeress, I am all ears—"

"I intended asking you a favor, a most important one, an alternative—"

"The trip to Nara?"

"Yes; an alternative to that. Tell me truly how much at heart you hate the man at Len Yang. Wait. Don't answer me yet. At heart, do you really hate him, as you pretend, or are you simply bowing down to your vanity, to the pride you seem to take in these quixotic deeds? For one thing, there is very little money in what you are doing. If you should approach these adventures a little differently, perhaps, you might put yourself in a position to be rewarded for the troubles you take, the dangers you risk. I mean that."

"I admit I'm not a money hater," frowned Peter, striving without much success to feel her trend.

"It would be so easy for you to make all the money you need in only a few years by—how shall I say it?—by 'being nice.' Wait! I have not finished. You said I was a special emissary from him. You hit the mark more squarely than you thought. Oh, I admit it! I was sent to Batavia to meet you, to intercept you, and, to be quite frank, to ask you your terms."

"From *him*?"

"Yes. He has observed you. He can use you, and oh!—how badly he wants you and your boldness and that unconquerable fire of yours! He needs you! He wants you, more than any man he has known! And he will pay you! Name your price! A half million gold a year? Bah! It is a drop to him!"

"Don't," begged Peter in a whisper. "Please—don't—go on."

His face had become almost as white as the tablecloth, and his lips were trembling, ashen.

"God! I put my confidence in you, time after time, and each time you show me treachery, deeper, more hideous, than before. Please don't continue. I'm trying, as hard as I know how, to appreciate your position in this wretched mess—and trying to find some excuse for it. For you! And it's hard. Damned, brutally hard. Let's part! Let's forget! Let's be just memories to each other—Romola!"

Her face, too, had lost its color, like life fading from a rose when the stem is snapped. Her hand sought her throat and groped there, as it always did in her moments of nervousness, and she drummed on the cloth with a silver knife. She stared curiously at him, with the other light dying hard.

"Then I can only hope—a slender hope—to bring you back to the favor I asked you originally, and I place that before you now, my request for that favor—my final hope. You cannot refuse that. You cannot! You profess to be chivalrous. Now, let me—test you!"

CHAPTER XIV

"Romola, I said no to Nara long ago."

She threw up her head.

"A woman should need to be informed but once that her love is not wanted. This is not what I meant."

"Ah! Another scheme! Your little brain is nothing short of an idea machine. Remarkable! Go on."

"No," she said, rather sullenly, at this flow of bitterness, "a variation of my plan. If you will not accompany me to Nara, then I must go alone. I must have money. Do you understand? I am penniless. The *King of Asia* leaves for Japan tomorrow, at dawn. I will never return to China. Will you—help me?"

"What do you mean by that? Will I break into the house and help you rob?"

"There is no other way. The money is in a desk, locked. I am not strong enough to break the lock. You can. Then, too, there are some papers of mine—"

"Romola, will this give you the contentment you desire?" he said sternly.

"I—I think so. I hope so."

"Then I will help you."

"Oh, Peter, how can I—"

He lifted his hand. "You see, my dear, you can't frighten me—easily. You can't bribe me, Romola. But you can appeal to my weakness—"

"A woman in distress—your weakness!" But there was no mockery in either her voice or her eyes. It was more like a whisper of regret.

"Romola, will you answer a question?"

"I'll try!"

"Why are beautiful women—girls—from all parts of the world stolen—to work in that mine?"

Romola looked at him queerly. "I do not know, Peter."

They attacked the dinner, and by deft stages Peter led the conversation to a lighter vein. It was nearly ten when they left, the dining-room was all but deserted and they departed in high spirits, her arm within his, her smile happy and apparently genuine.

"We must wait until midnight," she informed him. "He will be asleep; the servants will have retired."

Peter suggested a rickshaw ride through the Chinese city to while away the hours in between, but the girl demurred, and amended the suggestion to a street-car ride to Causeway Bay. He consented, and they caught a car in front of the hotel, and climbed to seats on the roof.

He felt gay, excited by the thrill of their impending danger. She was moody. In the bright moonlight on the crystal beach at Causeway Bay he tried to make her dance with him. But she pushed his arms away, and Peter, suddenly feeling the weight of some dark influence, he knew not what, fell silent, and they rode back to the base of the peak road having very little to say.

At a few minutes past midnight they alighted from sedan chairs in the hairpin trail beside the incline railway station at the peak, and as they faced each other, the moon, white and gaunt, slipped from sight behind a billowing black cloud, and the heavens were black and the night was dark around them.

She took his arm, leading him past the murky walls of the old fort, and on up and up the sloping, rocky road, dimly revealed at intervals by points of mysterious light.

They came at length to a high, black hedge, and, groping cautiously along this for a number of yards, found a ragged cleft. He held the branches aside while she climbed through with a faint rustle of silken underskirts. He followed after.

By the dim, ghostly glow of the clouds behind which the moon was floating he made out ominous shapes, scrawny trees and low, stunted bushes.

Hand in hand, with his heart beating very loudly and his breath burning dry in his throat, they approached the desolate, gloomy house—her home!

A low veranda, perhaps a sun-parlor, extended along the wing, and toward this slight elevation the girl stealthily led him, without so much as the cracking of a dry twig underfoot, peering from left to right for indications that their visit was betrayed.

But the house was still, and large and gloomy, and as silent as the halls of death.

They climbed upon the low veranda. The girl ran her fingers along the French window which gave upon the hedged enclosure, and drew back upon greased hinges the window, slowly, inch by inch, until it yawned, wide open.

He followed her into a room, dark as black velvet, weighted with the indescribable, musty odors of an Oriental abode, and possessed of an almost sensuous gloom, a mystic dreariness, a largeness which knew no dimensions.

As Peter cautiously advanced he was impressed, almost startled, by the sense of vastness, and he was aware of great, looming proportions.

Close at hand a clock ticked, slowly, drearily, as if the release of each metallic click of the ancient cogs were to be the last, beating like the rattling heart of a man in the arms of death. This noise, like a great clatter, seemed to fill all space.

And he was alone.

Suddenly a yellow light glowed in the dark recesses of the high ceiling, and Peter sprang back with his hand on the instant inside his coat, where depended in its leather shoulder-sling the automatic.

Across the great room the girl raised a steady hand, indicating a desk of gigantic size, of ironwood or lignum-vitae.

He found himself occupying the center of an enormous mandarin rug, with letterings and grotesque designs in rich blood-reds, and blues and yellows and browns. He gave the room a moment's survey before falling to the task.

The walls of this cavern were of satin, priceless rugs, which hung without a quiver in the breathless gloom. Massive furniture, chairs, tables, settees, of teak, of ebony and dark mahogany, with deep carvings, glaring gargoyles and hideous masks, were arranged with an apparent lack of plan.

And against the far wall, with a face like the gibbous moon, stood a massive clock of carved rosewood, clacking ponderously, almost painfully, as if each tick were to be its last.

Peter crouched before the desk, examining the heavy lock on the drawer, and accepted from the girl's hand a tool, a thick, short, blunt chisel. He inserted the blunt edge of this instrument in the narrow crack, and—

A muffled sob, a moan, a stifled cry!

He sprang to his feet, with his hand diving into his coat, and the fingers he wrapped about the butt of the automatic were as cold as ice.

Romola Borria was cringing, shrinking as if to efface herself from a terrible scene, against the French window, and staring at him with a look of wild imploration, of horror, of—death!

From three unwavering spots along the wall to his left glittered the blue muzzles of revolvers!

Peter dropped to his knees, leaped backward, pointed by instinct, and fired at the lone yellow light in the ceiling.

Darkness. An unseen body moved. Metal rattled distantly upon wood. And metal clanked upon metal. Darkness, black as the grave, and as ominous.

A white, round spot remained fixed upon his retina, slowly fading. The face of the clock. The hands, like black daggers, had pointed to ten minutes of one. Ten minutes of life! Ten minutes to live! Or—less?

Silence, broken only by the reluctant *click-clack, click-clack* of the rosewood clock.

If he could reach the window! Then a low, convulsed sobbing occurred close to his ear. The girl groped for his arm. She was shaking, shaking so that his arm trembled under it.

"Your final card!" he whispered. "The final trick! God! Now, damn you, get me out of this!"

"I can't. I—I— Oh, God! Kill me! I gave you every chance. They forced me—forced me to bring you here. They would have strangled me, just as they strangled the other!" She seemed to steady herself while he listened in growing horror.

"Safe!" he groaned. "Safety for you. Death—for me! You—you led me into their hands, and I—I trusted you. I trusted you!"

She laid a cold, moist hand over his lips, this devil-woman.

"Hush! If they, if he, so much as guessed that I cared for you, that I loved you, it would mean my death. I was forced—forced to bring you here. Don't you understand? And if he even guessed. But you had your chance. You had your chance!"

Almost hysterically she was endeavoring to extenuate her crime, her treason.

"Stand up and face them. Meet your death! Escape is—impossible! Impossible! They are watching you like a rat. In a moment they know you can stand this strain no longer! Face them, I say! Show them that—"

Peter pushed her away from him in loathing, and she lay still, only whimpering.

Yet the devils of darkness—where were they? And slowly, yet more slowly, the rosewood clock ticked off its seconds. It should be nearly one. At one—

A fighting chance?

CHAPTER XV

On his hands and knees he crouched, and began crawling, an inch at a time, toward the French window, dragging the automatic over the thick satin carpet. He reached the window. It was still ajar. Far, far below twinkled the lights of Hong Kong, of ships anchored in the bay, and the glitter of Kowloon across the bay. Out there was life!

A board creaked near him, toward the heart of that darkened vault. He spun about, aimed blindly, fired!

The floor shook as an unseen shape collapsed and writhed within reach of his hand. In his grasp, was the oily, thick queue of a coolie.

And suddenly, as he groped, the wall spat out angry tongues of corrosive red flame.

A white-hot iron seemed to shoot through the flesh of his left arm. The pain reached his shoulder. His left arm was useless—the bone cracked!

Groaning, he pushed himself back. His knees struck the sill, slid over, and he felt the coarse, peeled paint of the veranda. He reached the ledge—dropped to the ground, and in dropping, the revolver spilled from his hand as it caught on a projecting ledge of the floor, bounded off into the darkness.

He groveled to retrieve it, muttering as his hands probed through the tufted grass.

Light glimmered in the room above. There occurred sounds of a struggle, of feet scraping, a muffled oath, a short scream.

Peter leaped back, looking up, prepared to dash for the road.

A yellow light within the room silhouetted the slender figure of Romola Borria against the French window. Her arms went out in frantic appeal to the darkness, to him.

"Wait!" she cried in an awful voice. "I love you! Wait!"

At that confession, a hand seemingly suspended in space was elevated slowly behind her. The hand paused high above her head. A face appeared in the luminous space above her head, an evil face, carved with a hideous brutality, wearing an ominous snarl; and above the writhing lips of this one was a black growth, a mustache, pointed, like twin black daggers.

Emiguel Borria, ardent tool of the Gray Dragon? Emiguel Borria, husband of the girl Romola?

Emiguel Borria, in whose lifting hand Peter now caught the glint of a revolver, attempted to crowd the girl to one side. But she held her ground, and then this woman who had on a half-dozen successive occasions tricked and deceived Peter, who had deliberately and on her own confession lured him into this trap, upset, womanlike, the elaborate plan of her master.

In a frenzy she spun upon Emiguel Borria, seized the white barrel of the revolver in her two hands and forced it against his side. Tiny red flames spurted out on either side of the cylinder and smeared in a smoky circle where the muzzle was momentarily buried in the tangled black coat. And Emiguel Borria seemed to sink into the great room and entirely out of Peter's sight.

Romola leaned far into the darkness.

"Run! Run! For your life!"

And as Peter started to run, out of the compound for the dubious safety of the cloistered road, other men of the Gray Dragon, posted for such a contingency, let loose a shower of bullets from adjoining windows.

But the gods were for the time being on the side of Peter. These shots all went wild.

Shuddering, with teeth chattering and eyes popping, Peter dove through the matted hedge, dashed into the street, and down the street, lighted at intervals with its pin-points of mysterious light.

He came to the incline station, and his footsteps seemed weighted, dragging. And the clock in the station, as he dashed past, showed one o'clock.

He plunged down the first sharp twist of the hair-pin trail, fell, picked himself up dusty and dizzy, with his left arm swinging grotesquely as he ran.

And behind him, riding like the dawn wind, he seemed to feel the presence of a companion, of a silent rickshaw which rattled with a grisly occupant; and a voice, the voice of Romola Borria, shrill and terrible in his ear, cried: "Wait! Oh, wait!"

But the spectre was more real than Peter could imagine.

It was quite awful, quite absurd, the way Peter stumbled and plunged and fell and stumbled on down the hill; past the reservoirs which glittered greenly under their guardian lights.

How he managed to reach Queen's Road in that dreadful state I cannot describe. He dashed down the center of the deserted road, with rudely awakened Sikhs calling excitedly upon Allah, to stop, to stop!

But on he sped, straight down the center of the mud roadway, past the Hong Kong Hotel, now darkened for the night, and past the bund.

Would the sampan be waiting? Otherwise he was now bolting headlong upon the waiting knives of the Gray Dragon's men. No sampan in the whole of Victoria Harbor was safe tonight, but one. Would the one be waiting? Upon that single hope he was staking his safety, his dash for life.

He sped out upon the jetty.

Where could he seek refuge? The *Persian Gulf?* The *King of Asia?* The transpacific liner lay far out in a pool of great black, glittering under sharp, white arc-lights forward and aft as cargo was lifted from obscure lighters and stowed into her capacious hold.

Yet he must go quickly, for in all China there was no safety for him this night.

A shadow leaped out upon the jetty close upon his heels. But Peter did not see this ghost.

The sampan coolie, asleep upon the small foredeck of his home, shivered and muttered in his strange dreams. By his garb and by the richness of the large sampan's upholsterings Peter guessed this to be the craft sent to him by the small Chinese girl.

Peter leaped aboard, awakening the *fokie* with a cry.

Dark knobs arose from the low cabin hatchway, and by the yellow lamps of the jetty Peter made these out to be the heads of the maid from Macassar and her old grandmother.

A *dong* was burning in the cabin, and Peter followed the girl into the small cabin of scrubbed and polished teak, while the old woman gibbered in sharp command to the *fokie*.

Crouching like a beast at last cornered, Peter, by the shooting rays of the *dong*, glared dazedly into an angry red face, a face that was limned and pounded by the elements, from which stared two blue, bloodshot eyes.

The girl said nothing as she nestled at his side, and Peter permitted his head to sink between his hands.

Yet, strange to say, the red-faced man did not fire, made no motion of stabbing him.

Peter looked up, snarling defiance.

"You've got me cornered," he whispered harshly. "It's after one o'clock. The parole is up. Why prolong the agony? Damn you, I'm unarmed!" He shut his eyes again.

Again there was no premonitory click, no seep of steel upon scabbard.

The red-faced man seized his shoulder, shook him.

"Say, you young prize-fighter," he sputtered, "you drunk? Crazy? Or just temporarily off your nut? Who in thunder said anything about prolonging the agony? What agony are you talking about? Why the devil 've you been dodging me all over South China today? You dog-gone young wildcat, you! I've got an assignment for you. The *King of Asia's* wireless man is laid up in the Peak Hospital with typhoid. I want you to take her back to Frisco! Blast your young hide, anyhow!"

The wizen face of the girl's grandmother appeared in the hatchway. She seemed annoyed, angry. She said something in the Cantonese dialect, which Peter did not understand.

"A sampan is following," translated the girl in her tiny voice, "but we are nearly there. In a moment you will be safe."

"Where?" demanded Peter, staring over the red-faced man's shoulder for a glimpse of the other sampan.

"The *King of Asia*," she told him. "In a moment, *birahi*, in a moment." Her tones were those of a little mother.

But Peter was staring anxiously into the red face, trying to decipher an explanation.

"I told the red-faced one to be here, too, at midnight," the girl was whispering in his ear. "He came. He is a friend. Your fears were wrong, *birahi*."

The sampan lurched, scraping and tapping along a surface rough and metallic.

The yellow face of the old woman again appeared in the hatchway. A bar of keen, white light thrust its way into the cabin. It came from somewhere above. No longer could Peter hear the groan and swish of the sweep, and the cabin no longer keeled from side to side. He guessed that the sampan was alongside.

The old woman motioned for him to come out.

"I am not coming aboard; I am going back to my hotel," said the red-faced man. "You will not leave this ship? You will promise me that?"

"I will promise," said Peter gravely. "You, I presume, are Mr. J. B. Whalen, the Marconi supervisor?"

The red-faced man nodded. As if by some prearranged plan, Whalen, after slight hesitation, climbed out of the cabin, leaving Peter alone with this very small, very gentle benefactor of his. He wanted to thank her, and he tried. But she put her fingers over his lips.

"You are going to the one you love, *birahi*," she said in her tinkling little voice. "Before we part, I want you—I want you to—" and she hesitated. "Come now, my brave one," she added with an attempt at briskness. "You must go. Hurry!"

Peter found the side ladder of the *King of Asia* dangling from the upper glow of the liner's high deck. He put his foot on the lower rung and paused. A vast number of apologies, of thanks and good-byes demanded utterance, but he felt confused. The slight relaxation of the past few minutes had left him exhausted, and his brain was encased in fog.

He remembered that the little maid from Macassar had wanted him to do something, possibly some favor. The glow high above him seemed to swim. His injured arm was beginning to throb with a low and persistent pain. And the climb to the deck seemed a tremendous undertaking.

"You were saying," he began huskily, as she reached out to steady the ladder. "You wanted me—"

"Just this, my brave one." And she reached up on tiptoes and kissed him ever so lightly upon his lips. "When you think of me, *birahi*, close your eyes and dream. For I—I might have loved you!"

Half-way up the black precipice, Peter stopped and looked down. For a moment his befuddled senses refused to register what now occupied the space at the ladder's end.

The sampan was no longer there; another had taken its place, a sampan long and as black as the night which encompassed it.

Wide, dark eyes stared up across the space into his, and these were set in a chalky-white face, grim, fearful—startling!

It was Romola Borria. Her white arms were upheld in a gesture of entreaty. Her lips were moving.

Peter descended a step, and stopped, swaying slightly.

"What—what—" he began.

"He is dead!" came the whisper from the small deck. "I killed him! I killed him! Do you hear me? I am free! Free! Why do you stare at me so? I am ready to go. But you must ask me! I will not follow you. I will not!"

And Peter, clutching with a sick and sinking feeling at the hard rope, found that his lips and tongue were working, but that no sound other than a dull muttering issued from his mouth. Momentarily he was dumb—paralyzed.

"I am not a tool of the Gray Dragon," went on the vehement whisper. "I am not!"

And to Peter came full realization that Romola Borria was lying, or endeavoring to trick him, for the last time.

"Go back—there," he managed to stammer at last. "Go back! I won't have you! I'm through with this damned place."

Painfully he climbed up a few rungs.

Then the voice of Romola, no longer a whisper, but loud, broken, despairing, came to him for the last time:

"You are leaving me—leaving me—for her—for Eileen!"

Peter made no reply. He continued his laborious climb; first one foot, then a groping few inches upward along the hard rope with his right hand, and then the other foot. Nor did he once again look down.

He finally gained the deck. It was blazing with incandescent and arc-lights. Under-officers and deckhands were pacing about, giving attention to the loading. Donkey engines hissed, coughed, and rattled, as the yellow booms creaked out, up and in with their snares of bales and crates which vanished like swooping birds of prey into the noisy hatchways.

Peter took in the bustling scene with a long sigh of relief. He still heard that lonely, anguished voice; the black sampan still rested on his eyes, heaving on the flood tide upon which the great ship strained, as if eager to be gone. And out there—out there—beyond the black heart of mystery and the night, was the clean dawn—the rain-washed spaces of the shimmering sea.

But he could not look down again. He would not. For a while—or for-ever—he had had his fill of China. Before him now lay the freedom of the open sea, the sunshine of life—and his homeland!

Peter the Brazen had drunk all too indulgently at the bitter fountain.

CHAPTER XVI

In the months which had passed since their romantic parting on the bund at Shanghai, Peter the Brazen had founded all of his roseate notions of Eileen Lorimer upon the one-sided data furnished by those spirited few hours.

He had thought of her as a lonely little creature, sole inhabitant of a world apart, to which he would some time go and claim her.

He had not taken into his calculations at any time such prosaic objects as parents, brothers, sisters, and, more vital than all, other young men who might have found the same qualities in Eileen to adore as had attracted and bound him.

When, from a long-distance telephone-booth in the Hotel St. Francis, he finally was connected with the Lorimer residence in Pasadena, it was to hear the gruff, masculine accents of a person who claimed to be her father, and who was brusque and impulsive in his inquiries regarding Peter's identity.

Peter did not know, or realize, that Mr. Lorimer would have willingly cut off his right hand for the young man who had restored his daughter to him nearly a year before. He was simply struck more or less dumb, with a schoolboy sort of feeling, when he was aware that, five hundred miles overland, a gruff father wanted righteously to know his business.

By adroit parrying, without giving out his identity, Peter at length secured the information he wanted. Romola Borria had been truthful; Eileen was attending the university at San Friole.

With her San Friole address jotted down in the back of his red note-book, Peter endeavored to be connected with Miss Lorimer by telephone. After a trying pause the long-distance operator advised him that the residence in question did not possess a telephone.

Quartering what remained of his capital by the costly Pasadena call, Peter resorted to the telegraph stand, and waited in the lobby for an answer.

The first of the several bits of unpalatable news he was to be given during the day was delivered to him as he waited, when, unnoticed at first, a Chinese gentleman, a Mr. San Toy Fong, a passenger from Shanghai on the *King of Asia*, came out of the dining-room and occupied a chair at his side, cordially and candidly revealing an identity which Peter had suspected during the entire voyage.

"Mr. Moore," the emissary began in a low, confident voice, "I am returning to China tonight on the *Chenyo Maru*. Before I sail, if there is some message—"

Peter shook a slow decision. "I'm through with China, through with Len Yang, through with wireless. I intend settling down on my little ranch near Santa Cruz. That may save your trailers annoyance."

The polished Chinese gentleman smiled. "Evidently you are not aware that your little ranch is no longer in your possession. You see, Mr. Moore, when we are interested in a person, we take pains to exhaust the tiniest details. Your ranch was sold about three months ago; in a moment of absent-mindedness, perhaps, you neglected to pay the taxes. However, if you but say the word—"

"Thank you," Peter headed him off in a tired and indifferent voice. "You've saved me a trip for nothing. After all, the property is probably better off in other hands. Now I have nothing in the world to worry about but myself. *Bon voyage*, Mr. Fong! And my respects to—"

But San Toy Fong had departed.

After an exasperating wait, a bell-boy brought to Peter a telegraphic reply to his San Friole message, which read:

"Take the twelve-thirty train. Will meet you at station."

And it was signed by Eileen Lorimer.

Peter was again conscious of his diminishing funds when he peeled off a bill at the railroad ticket-window and paid the round-trip fare. But any thoughts upon his possible financial embarrassment were set aside as the train rolled out into the open country, and his mind pictured his reception at the hands of the young woman who meant quite as much to him as life.

He pictured a dozen greetings, each different and each the same, with Eileen in every case weeping with joy at beholding him, and wrapping her slim, warm arms about his neck.

He became more nervous and excited as the villages passed by, and presently the trim concrete structure lettered in gold and black as San Friole came into sight around a curve.

Alighting, he gave his grips to a boy with instructions to have them checked; and he looked eagerly among the crowd of students for the lovely face of Eileen.

At length he discovered her, and simultaneously she must have discovered him; for she elbowed her way through the mob, flushed and breathless, and seized his hands, looking at him with eyes that seemed to glow.

And to Peter the Brazen she was quite the same Eileen as the girl of a year ago; no older, and quite as lovely, with the same pretty flush in her cheeks, the same rosebud mouth, the same sweet and lovable expression.

The little speech he had prepared on the train would not leave his lips; and he could only look, with the color heating his cheeks, as Eileen smiled tenderly and a little meekly, as she had smiled when they parted at the consulate in Shanghai over a year before.

He began to realize, even as he considered and reconsidered his motive, that she was mutely begging him not to kiss her at this time. Perhaps the pressure of her fingers, a subtle pressure away from her instead of toward her, gave him this understanding.

He became aware gradually of another presence, as he was jostled from this side to that by other new arrivals, conscious of the sidelong look that Eileen was giving another man.

With a slight feeling of resentment, Peter examined this interloper, finding himself gazing into the unfriendly, tanned face of a man of about his own age, with keen, sharp, brown eyes, a dimple in his chin, and a thick, blue book under his arm. Through a maze Peter heard his name spoken, then the words "Professor Hodgson;" and he found himself shaking hands briskly with the invader.

Then Peter excused himself, returning with the baggage-checks, and he discovered both Eileen and Professor Hodgson examining him with the frank curiosity that one might bestow upon some wandering minstrel, a foreigner, an alien. He felt, as the odd member of any triangle is sure to feel, that he was a lone bird; that Eileen and her glowering professor were drawn together by some bond unknown to him, but whose nature he warmly resented.

And thus began the crumbling of the rosy crystalline little world that Peter had created for the sole occupation of Eileen Lorimer.

As the three walked slowly down the station platform, he felt the tension, the exaggerated repugnance, which any outdone suitor is bound to feel toward his successful rival. He felt sick and useless, and somehow he wished he was back aboard the train again. He had blown his dream-bubble, rapturously contemplating the shining, dancing, multicolored surface as it expanded and became of size. And this bubble had been rudely pricked.

He felt Eileen's light hand upon his arm, and he heard her voice suddenly become weighted with feminine importance. She was saying:

"Mr. Moore and I have a great deal to talk over. You will excuse me, won't you, until tonight?"

Professor Hodgson, frowning, nodded courteously. "Perhaps Mr. Moore would like to go, if he cares to stag it. I'm afraid every girl in town has been invited by now."

"Stag what?" queried Peter in a dry voice.

"There's to be a St. Valentine's ball tonight," enthused the girl. "St. Valentine's Day is the fourteenth, you know. I'm sure you'd enjoy it! You'll go, won't you?"

"But—but—" stammered Peter. "I had hoped that you and I could spend the evening by ourselves."

"Oh, but I couldn't do that!" cried Eileen, with reproach in her big, gray eyes. "Professor Hodgson invited me ages ago! Can't we talk this afternoon and tomorrow. I'll cut classes all day. Please go! I'll give you every other dance! The professor won't mind. He's an old dear!"

The old dear frowned a shade more darkly, and Peter derived some encouragement from the sign.

"I'll go on that condition," said Peter gaily. "Every other dance with Miss Lorimer!"

"That's fine!" Professor Hodgson rejoined. "Have you a costume?"

"Your wireless uniform!" cried Eileen. "You look wonderful in that!"

Professor Hodgson was preparing to remove his dour look from their vicinity. "I'll be around at eight," he said. "See you later, Mr. Moore."

"So-long!" Peter retorted affably, and Eileen squeezed his arm ever so lightly.

"I want to talk to you all afternoon!" she declared with her adorable smile, when the professor was out of earshot. "Shall we take a car-ride?"

They climbed into the front seat of an open car, and Peter was glad when the girl linked her arm through his and snuggled close to his side.

"I want you to tell me everything from the very beginning," she said with a bright smile. "I want to know why you left me so suddenly in Shanghai. I had a hundred questions to ask. You were mean!"

"You can begin wherever you please," said Peter amiably.

"Then, why," demanded Eileen, giving him a hungry little look, "didn't you let me stay in Shanghai?"

"Because I was in love with you," Peter replied abruptly. "You were in danger. So was I. I wanted to get you out of China as quickly as possible, because, you see, my dear, the man who had his agents kidnap you, and who was having you transported to China on the *Vandalia*, would have recaptured you without difficulty. Do you mind if I tell you, Eileen, that it broke my heart when I realized that we wouldn't see one another for goodness knows how long a time?"

Eileen glanced pensively at the green lawns and the flower-gardens which flowed past the car, and her eyes returned to his face with a question in them. Her hand snuggled into his.

"Tell me the truth, Peter. You thought I was just an innocent, helpless little thing, now didn't you? You said to yourself, 'I'll get myself into all sorts of trouble with her on my hands.' Didn't you say that to yourself, Peter?"

"I did. You're right. You were not made for that place. If you'll let me, I'll tell you what you were made for."

"You needn't," said Eileen with a sigh. "Because I know. You are going to tell me that I am just the right size for a bungalow for two, of which you are the second, and that I need some big man like yourself to have around, to shield and protect me, to smooth and round off the sharp corners of this harsh old life."

"How did you guess?" gasped Peter.

"Maybe your eyes said that when you told me to go home that day, and maybe other men have told me the same thing! Anyway, that is what you have come here to tell me—or haven't you?—that you are all ready now to leave behind the terribly wicked and adventurous life you've been leading, and settle down, and live respectably forever after! Isn't that the truth?"

"You're something of a mind-reader."

"No, I'm not. But I have sense. Peter, I still think, just as I thought that terrible night when you slid down the rope from the *Vandalia* with me dangling from your neck, that dreadful night on the Whang-poo in the fog, that you're the finest and bravest man on earth. That's why I let you make love to me on the bund; because—well, because I wanted you to come back!"

"In return," Peter responded with enthusiasm, "I have kept you next to my heart all of that time, thinking of you every time I felt discouraged, looking upon you always as a refuge, exactly as you say, when China got the best of me."

"Has China got the best of you, Peter?"

"It has! I was chased out of the Yellow Empire with a broken arm, by agents of the same man who tried to kidnap you. I removed the splints only this morning. Since I saw you, I have paid a visit to the dreadful red city where you were being taken, escaped, and made my way through India and the Straits Settlements and back to Hong Kong."

"And they shot you!"

He nodded, and she shivered again, while the fingers against his palm stirred.

"I've put China behind me forever, I hope, and now, a little older, a little wiser, and very weary, I've come to lay the same worthless old heart at your dear little feet!"

"And the worthless old feet will have to kick the dear, big heart aside," said Eileen sadly. "Oh, Peter," she exclaimed, suddenly contrite as she saw the look of pain that came into his face, "you know I wouldn't hurt you for anything in the world! But I am in earnest, deadly in earnest, Peter! I refuse positively to have you consider me any longer as a poor, helpless, clinging little thing, made only to be petted and protected! I'm not like that, Peter! If you'd only written, I would have told you. You're not afraid of anything in the world; nor am I! I love adventure quite as much as you do, Peter, and the moment you told me, back there in Shanghai, that I must hurry home because it wasn't safe, I made up my mind that I would equip myself to go into some of those wonderful adventures with you! Professor Hodgson, the Chinese language professor, is an expert shot with a revolver, and I've wheedled him into giving me lessons. That's for self-protection. Then the Japanese woman who is general chambermaid in my rooming-house is teaching me jiu-jitsu.

"In addition to that, I'm studying for a doctor's degree. When the course is finished I am going to join you in China. We'll invade that dreadful mining city alone, just you and I, and we'll make it the most wonderful place in China! You see, Peter, I intend to be a medical missionary; and you won't have to worry your dear old brain about me the least bit. If you won't take me, I'll go by myself!"

"Sweetheart," Peter declared with difficulty, "you are talking through your hat!"

She shrugged and smiled. "Won't you take me?"

"You know I'd fetch you the man in the moon if you wanted him badly enough!"

"And you'll get that silly old notion of a bungalow for two out of your head?"

"I'll try. It will be a hard job. And, Eileen—"

"Yes, Peter?"

"You don't care about this Professor Hodgson, do you?"

"Oh, no, Peter! Once or twice he's tried to make love, and you could see, couldn't you, how furious he was when we left him?"

"I thought my goose was cooked," sighed Peter.

"Silly old goose!" said Eileen, squeezing his thumb.

With shaken but immeasurably higher notions of this girl, whose appealing gray eyes suffocated him with longing, Peter helped his charge to alight when the end of the car line was reached, and at her suggestion they tramped through the blossoming California fields, back to the village, talking seriously most of the way upon that ardent subject which lay warmly upon both of their young hearts.

CHAPTER XVII

There was a noticeable ripple when Eileen Lorimer walked into the ball-room that evening in the winsome attire of a Quaker maid, with Professor Hodgson, as Pierrot, on one side, and the tall, commanding figure of Peter the Brazen, in a spick-and-span white-and-gold uniform of the Pacific Mail Line, on the other.

For Peter the Brazen, in any garb, was that type of man at whom any normal woman would have looked twice—or, if only once, just twice as long.

Knotted about his lean waist was a flaunting blue sarong. The sarong gave to his straight, white figure the deft touch of romance. It verified the adventurous blue of his deep-set eyes, and the stubborn outward thrust of his tanned, smooth-shaven jaw.

When the young women of Eileen's acquaintance, to whom had been whispered some of the details of this man's thrilling past, crowded about for introductions, Peter had little difficulty in filling the remaining half of his program.

And when the music started for the second event Peter recovered his flushed and glowing Quaker maiden from the reluctant arms of Professor Hodgson, upon whom had fallen, like a dark shroud, a gloom heavy and profound, and the man who had that morning said good-bye forever to China and the wireless game and to ships and the sea, found himself floating in and out upon a sea of gold, with a sprite from elf-land dazzling him with her rosebud smile.

He would have liked to shock their beholders then and there by kissing her squarely upon that smile! And all the while, from the side line, Professor Hodgson, the professor of Chinese, watched their every movement with a face as long and as gray as an alley in the fog.

A little later in the evening, when Peter looked for his partner, a Miss Somebody or Other, whose penciled name had been smudged on his program so that it had become an unintelligible blue, he looked in vain.

He looked then among the dancers for the face of his Quaker maiden, and, unable to see her in the syncopating throng, elected to hunt for her, despite the known fact that she was in the company of his defeated rival, the professor.

Peter searched the refreshment room futilely, and decided that the pair had probably retired to the palm garden, where Eileen was possibly engaged to the best of her ability in soothing the ruffled feelings of her revolver and Chinese instructor.

As Peter parted the golden velvet hangings which shrouded the entrance to the dimly lighted conservatory, he espied a half-dozen couples disposed on as many small benches under the drooping fronds in varied attitudes of tête-à-tête.

The curtains fell in alignment behind him; he caught the angry glare of two brown eyes from a bench, and realized that Eileen's versatile professor was not yet pacified. At Professor Hodgson's side, with her back toward Peter, was a young woman attired in Quaker costume. Her head was not intimately close to that of the young professor; but it was close.

As Peter started to cross the waxed floor to her side, he saw Hodgson's head dip low; saw the girl apparently yield herself into his arms; and as Peter stopped, stock-still, he saw the long arms of the professor wrap themselves about the slim shoulders, drawing the hidden face toward him until the lips met his.

In that dreadful instant the heart of Peter the Brazen deliberately skipped a beat. Black swam into his eyes, and he trembled, then became stiff, as his gaze was glued to that ghastly pantomime. He hesitated, then leaped across the intervening distance.

Both Eileen and her professor leaped up.

Her face was white, and her fingers clutched in convulsion at her throat; but Peter's face was equally as white and strained as hers.

He stared in pain and utter disbelief, while a smile slowly crept over the features of Eileen's professor. She seemed about to faint, and sank back, with eyes tightly closed, against Hodgson's breast.

Peter tried to speak, but a moment passed before he could find words.

"Eileen—Eileen," he muttered, "you said—you told me—oh, God!"

He wheeled and dashed out of the hall, as he proposed to dash out of her life, with terrible, sinking thoughts in his brain, and his heart pounding dismally against his ribs. He recovered his coat and hat in the cloak-room.

Hardly had he vanished than Eileen, recovering slowly from her daze, sprang after. But Hodgson detained her, gripping her arm.

She seemed to realize for the first time what had been done, and to the profound astonishment of the several round-eyed couples, she wiped her hand fiercely across her mouth, the recent repository of the professor's sudden and unexpected kiss.

"You—beast!" she stammered. "You—you saw him come in! How dared you! How dared you! I thought you were a—gentleman—you—you beast!"

Her professor merely grinned, as though the tragedy were a comedy of the most amusing order.

"One stolen kiss—" he chuckled.

And Eileen slapped him smartly across the mouth. She started to bolt for the door, but he dragged her back, clinging to her struggling hand. "You— one of that band!" she cried.

"Oh, let me apologize," he laughed, rubbing the red mark about his mouth with his free hand. "If your hero resents my robbing him of one stingy, little kiss— Band? What band?" But there was no question in his eyes.

"Stop him!" cried Eileen shrilly. "Oh, please, somebody call him back!"

A sophomore, always willing to aid a lady in distress, sprang to the chase, and Eileen, breaking loose, stumbled after him out upon the dance floor. A waltz was under way, and the floor was jammed.

They tried to break through, but were thrust aside by laughing dancers, who seemed to take this to be a new and diverting game.

They tried again, and now Professor Hodgson, smiling blandly, came upon the scene and interposed further interference. Dodging past him and narrowly avoiding collision with a whirling couple close to the wall, Eileen scurried down the side in the direction of the cloakroom, with big, hot tears burning down her flushed cheeks.

When she reached the cloak-room she searched it in anxious haste for the Marconi cap, the light-blue overcoat. Both were missing.

With the sophomore atow, and conscious of the romantic nature of his errand, she ran into the moonlit street, looking up and down the black-shad-owed sidewalk for signs of the straight, tall figure.

Down the street, perhaps a quarter of a mile distant, she made out the motionless streamer of lights of a train, the San Francisco train.

With her gray Quaker dress flapping, and the clutter of white petticoats hindering the rhythm of her knees and ankles, Eileen sped down the middle of the road with the excited sophomore bringing up a mad rear.

The fate of her life lay in the train's waiting. She knew what Peter Moore would do. And if she could not stop him, she would be nothing less than his murderer. Had the evidences of her apparent infidelity been less damning she knew that Peter Moore would have waited, would have listened to her explanation, and believed her.

If she could only reach the train, she could tell him, could compel him to wait, and thereupon have it out with that cad Hodgson. It would be folly to pursue by later train, because Peter, as was customary with that young philanderer, had neglected to leave his forwarding address.

But Eileen never reached the train. The engine screamed scornfully when she was less than a block distant. The red and green tail-lights were dwindling away along the throbbing rails when she arrived at the station.

The night had swallowed up her love and her high hopes. Before long, miles, and thousands of miles, would soon stretch between her and her lover.

With a broken sob she wilted upon the station steps, while the sophomore stood awkwardly above her, bursting with questions, misty-eyed with youthful sympathy and fidgeting in acute discomfort.

And thus was Peter the Brazen swept out of her life and into his next adventure.

CHAPTER XVIII

At about five o'clock the next afternoon Peter, in his hotel bedroom, called for a pitcher of ice-water, the major portion of which he disposed of before considering the next move.

Afternoon sunlight, entering by the single large window, mapped out a radiant oblong of red on the heavy carpet. The long, insolent shriek of a taxicab arose from the square. The bedroom was redolent of the sour odor of last night's cigarette smoke. He had forgotten, for perhaps the first time in his memory, to throw open the window upon retiring. As he arose stiffly from the bed an empty brown bottle bounded to the floor with a thump, and the latter riotous portion of last evening came slowly back to him. He had decided to do something. What had he made up his mind to do? He sat down on the edge of the bed with his head in his hands and frowned. He remembered now.

He was going back to China!

With a throbbing head and a recurrence of the sticky feeling in his mouth, he stripped off his pajamas, went into the bath-room, and shivered and grunted under an icy shower for five minutes, by which time some of the despondency which last night's affair had brought over him was shaken, his headache was loosened a bit, his wits were more clearly in hand, and the warm blood was shooting through him.

After a brisk rub-down he dressed quickly—he had barely had time enough to recover his suit-cases from the San Friole baggage-room when he had fled—and put in a call for the Marconi office.

Shortly he had the chief operator on the wire, and he explained briefly that out-of-town business had interfered with his calling the day before, but that he would drop around for a conference bright and early the next morning. He added that he intended to take the *King of Asia* back to China.

When he entered the chief operator's cubicle, the chief operator looked into the face of a man who had aged, a white, sad face, the face of a man who had found the sample of life he had tasted to be a bitter mouthful.

"Back again, as I live!" he chirruped, pumping Peter's hand exuberantly. "Where now, Peter?"

"China," said Peter; "my old love, the *King of Asia*, sails tomorrow. Can I have her?"

"Sure thing! By the way, here's a special delivery letter for you in the mail that hasn't been assorted—a nice square envelope. Looks to me like a wedding invitation!"

Peter examined the square, white envelope.

A wedding invitation with a San Friole canceling stamp.

Absently he dropped it into his pocket.

Making his way to the St. Francis he found that San Toy Fong had departed for parts unknown. So he sat down at a desk in the writing-room, and penned a brief note, addressing it in care of Ah Sih King. He knew that the letter would reach San Toy Fong as rapidly as a grape-vine telegraph could deliver it to him. He knew that it would be opened, coded and transmitted to the second coil of the vast, hidden government, wherever he might be—from Singapore to Singapore.

The import of that note was simply that he, Peter Moore, was returning to China, and promised to interfere in no way with the band's activities. If he should change his mind, he added, he would file notice of such decision with the duly accredited agents of Len Yang's monarch at the Jen Kee Road place, in Shanghai.

The purple shoulders of the Golden Gate were sinking into the silver-tipped waves when Peter, having despatched his clearance message, left the tireless cabin for a look at the glorious red sunset and a breath of the fresh Pacific air.

A room steward, who had just ascended the iron ladder, approached, touching his cap with a deferential forefinger. "A letter addressed to you, sir. Found it in the corridor outside your stateroom. Must have fallen from your pocket."

The wedding invitation with a San Friole date-mark!

With nerveless fingers Peter drew out, not an envelope, but a stiff card. And he stared at the card in the red twilight, and groaned in pain and astonishment.

Have I said that this was St. Valentine's Day? In the color of the dying sun, and painted carefully by hand, was a tiny heart, bleeding.

And that was the only message.

PART III

THE GREEN DEATH

*"Oh! Chiang Nan's a hundred li, yet in a moment's spac
I've flown away to Chiang Nan and touched a dreaming face."*

—TS'EN-TS'AN

CHAPTER I

A young man can get himself into trouble in China. He may refuse to eat the food that is pushed into his mouth at a Chinese banquet by the perfectly well-intentioned man sitting beside him. In that case he will hardly do more than arouse the contempt of his beneficiary and his host. He simply shows that he lacks good Chinese table manners, for at a Chinese banquet it is proper to stuff food into your companion's mouth, no matter how full his stomach may be.

Another way to offend the Chinese is to refuse a gift.

But these are minor things. The surest method to arouse the suspicion, dislike and animosity of China is deliberately to keep your affairs shrouded in mystery. Discuss your important business secrets in loud shouts; no one will pay the slightest attention. But whisper mysteriously in your friend's ear, and spies will attend you! Leave a note-book filled with precious data plainly in view upon your dressing-table, and your room-boy won't for the life of him peek into it. Lock that same note-book away in a dressing-table drawer, and your room-boy will move heaven and earth to find out what it's all about!

The time of the day was mid-forenoon; the time of the year was spring. The low, mournful voice of a temple gong floated across the race of brown water. River *fokies*, on sampans and junks, were singing their old work song, the *Yo-ho—hi-ho!* of the ancient river, as their naked, broad backs bent to the sweeps. A pleasant breath of perspiring new earth was drifting down the great stretch of yellow water on a light, warm wind.

Peter had taken his favorite stand on the upper-boat deck, where the wireless shack was situated, with one hand wrapped loosely about a davit guy, the other thoughtfully rattling a cluster of keys in his pocket.

Spring is for youth, and Peter was young; yet he did not reflect in any way the mood of the new season. He felt gloomy and depressed. Life seemed an empty, a dreary thing to Peter, because he could see himself getting no-where.

In spite of the sweet candor of the young spring day, one of the first sounds that came to his ears as he stood there, in the shadow of the life-boat, was the brazen clamor of a death cymbal. One of China's four hundred millions had died in the night; now his spirit was being escorted to the seventh heaven of his blessed forefathers, by the death cymbal, clashing with a sober din to drive the devils away from his late abode.

The shadow of the life-boat was rather unaccountably attenuated; Peter turned around and looked into the bland, unsmiling face of Jen, a Chinese deck-boy. Pig-tails were coming back in style again. About six inches of wispy, purple-black braid extended downward from Jen's white cap. His face was quite yellow, and his eyes were green. An understandable light came and flickered across their satiny surface as Peter looked inquiringly into them.

"Wanchee my?" he asked.

The deck-boy took a cautious and all inclusive look of the broad, gray deck, bending head to look past the giant funnels, the first of which stood about twenty feet forward of them.

"Stay allatime on *King Asia*?" inquired the Chinese, moiling his hands together and bowing slightly.

Peter gave him a blue-eyed, indolent stare.

"Maybe. Maybe not," he said. "What's on your mind, Jen?"

"You tell me what going do," replied the yellow one meaningly. "Can do?"

"Mebbe can do," replied Peter, folding his hands. "You run up to the place on Jen Kee Road as soon as you catchee sampan. Tell man-man if I decide to do anything I will drop in and tell him. You don't know, Jen, but he knows that my word is good. If I decide to go up-river I'll tell man-man. If I decide to do nothing, I'll say nothing to man-man."

"Allee light, allee light," said Jen, backing away a few steps. "You tell man-man, eh?"

As Peter watched the retreating skinny shoulders bob up and down as they went away from him toward the after ladder, he felt just a little more undecided than he had five minutes earlier. He went into the wireless-room, to straighten up the apparatus before locking the door for the visit in Shanghai.

As he was locking the tool-box—the Chinese river thieves would steal anything they could lay hands on—he heard his name called in a silvery voice accompanied by a man's pleasant laugh, and he went out on deck to find that Mr. Andover, with the twins in tow, was all dressed up for a trip ashore.

The twins and Anthony Andover were passengers, bound on a sight-seeing trip through the East, and as Peter Moore was a very impressionable young man, it is only natural that the twins be discussed first, in virtue of their loveliness.

Peter had first contemplated Peggy and Helen Whipple in the *King of Asia's* dining-room. It would have been a rather impossible thing not to see Peggy and Helen Whipple, if you were young, and with fair eyesight.

At the first dinner after leaving the Golden Gate Peter had gone into the dining-room rather early, as he skipped tiffin (by reason of an empty pocket) and was ravenously hungry.

He had looked up over his first spoonful of mulligatawny à la Capron to meet the clear, undistilled, brown-eyed gaze of Peggy Whipple, who had seated herself at the captain's table. In that liquid, brown-eyed gaze had lurked a sparkle of mischief, a slightly arrogant look of inquisitive scrutiny, and perhaps a playful invitation.

As Peggy Whipple gave him that mischievous, liquid-brown glance when he was in the act of lifting a level soupspoonful to his lips, he did not, as a man might do under the circumstances, spill the soup upon the table-cloth, or back into the dish; nor did he pause in the work of lifting the liquid to his mouth.

He did not have to look at the spoon to guide its passage to his mouth. Without spilling a drop, he captained the spoon to its destination, maintaining his clear, deep-blue eyes upon the beautiful brown ones of the young passenger. And, without lowering his eyes once, he lifted the loaded spoon up twice in succession.

This skillful management brought a smile to the pretty face of the girl. Perhaps she had expected him to spill the soup under her glance; it was to be expected; more than probably the thing had happened in past episodes of Peggy, for she was distractingly fair to look upon, and her turned-up nose should have disarmed any man.

Her hair was golden and sleek and drawn back straight from her low, white forehead and knotted together in the back, calling attention to a neck that was slim and beautifully proportioned. Pink and white and gold described her. She seemed to bristle with a sort of fidgety energy, as if she had so much youth and loveliness stored up in her that she had a tremendous time keeping it all within bounds.

After Peter had slowly, but not at all insolently or impudently, taken all of this in, in the time required to stow away three heaping spoonfuls of mulligatawny à la Capron, by dead reckoning, she looked away from him with a little pout.

Peter followed her glance. He had not noticed the other girl before. It was evident that they were of the same blood, but the other girl seemed older. She, too, had sprung from a brown-eyed ancestry, and she, too, was blond and pink and lovely, with the prettiest fingers and finger-nails Peter had seen for some time.

Her glance, arising to meet his, was brown and very calm; unlike her sister, she appeared to be grave, more of the deliberate, thoughtful type.

It was in the shop of a Japanese silk merchant on Motomatchi Chome that he had met them for the first time. Several times on the trip across he had passed them on the deck, always escorted by proud young men.

They were the most popular girls on shipboard. Beauty rarely travels in pairs; these were unusual twins.

Once, as Peter was swinging down the ladder from topside, he came upon Peggy alone, looking rather blue. It may have been that she was simply in repose; and the contrast gave him that impression. Her eyes dreamingly encountered his, and the mischievous light flickered in them and instantly went out.

She ran her eyes down the white uniform with the gold emblems of his profession at the lapels, dropped her eyelids demurely, and seemed to wait. He hesitated, and she stood still; but he passed on, leaving her staring after him with a little pout. Obviously the twins had traveled much!

CHAPTER II

It was on the night that the *King of Asia* cleared Nagasaki for the short run across the Yellow Sea into the flow of the Yangtze-Kiang that Peter was sought out by that pleasant young man, Anthony Andover.

Ordinarily passengers were not allowed in the sacred quarters of the wireless house. However, those who possessed daring spirits came up anyway. Peggy Whipple came up there soon after that meeting on deck, with permission from nobody, and Peter gave her about fifteen minutes of his extremely important time on the average of nine times a day, permitting her to adorn the extra chair in the wireless shack, where she unconsciously revealed in her sudden and unexpected shiftings of posture, several inches of adorable silken ankle. I think Peggy was sadly in need of an elderly chaperone, and I am somehow under the impression that Peggy very badly wanted Peter to make love to her. How he resisted her speaks volumes for his quaint, mid-Victorian views regarding woman.

And at the end of the fifteen minutes, after regaling her with tales of the lands she was about to visit, he dismissed her, kindly but with great firmness, and she was as obedient as a lamb.

Anthony Andover, who knew more about plows perhaps than the Egyptians, gave him something else to think about. He looked up from his instruments that evening to see a young man of medium height, slim of build, and rather pale and sharp of mien.

"My name is Anthony Andover," he said in a brisk and business-like voice. "I wonder if I could have a talk with you."

Peter told him to sit down, and he removed the heavy nickeled headpieces from his ears. He expected an important radio from the Shanghai Station; but that could wait. He wondered what Anthony Andover might have on his mind.

"Mr. Moore, I'm in something of a devil of a fix, and I think you're the man who can get me out of it."

"Shoot," said Peter, lighting a yellow cigarette and passing the box. "Chinks?" Trouble to Peter always meant Chinks; they were his symbol of danger.

"No, no! You see, all of my life I've been—well, a city man. The biggest adventure I ever had was a fist fight with my foreman. Now—"

"Did you lick him?" asked Peter with concern.

Anthony nodded reminiscently. "Blacked his eyes and busted his nose!"

"Good for you! Go ahead with your story."

"I've met a girl on the steamer, and according to her way of looking at things, I lack about five thousand different parts of being a hero. You know the girl. That's why I'm bothering you like this."

"Not bothering me a bit. Who's the girl?"

"Peggy." Anthony caressed the word as if it were honey. "Peggy Whipple. Of course, the first thing I want to make sure of is, am I stepping on anybody's toes? If I am, I'll just go ahead, and play my own game my own way. If it's to be a case of a fight—"

"Hold on a moment," interrupted Peter. "I don't quite follow you. Whose toes do you think you're stepping on?"

"Well, Peggy comes up here to the wireless shack so much, that I—I—"

"Oh, not a bit of it, old man. Peggy's a nice girl. I like her. That's all."

"I—I'm mighty glad," said Anthony earnestly. "You know, she's pretty mad about you, but as long as you're not interested the way I am, well—" He bit his lip nervously, and went on: "I think you'd agree with me that it would be rather foolish of her, and very disappointing and disillusioning later on for her to marry the kind of a man she thinks she wants to marry. She has a notion that the man she marries must be a cross between Adonis, and—and Diamond Dick! She wants a man who carries six-shooters in all his pockets, and who fears neither God, man, nor the devil!"

"A regular hell buster!"

"That's it! Down in her heart I think she cares for me a little bit. But I'm nothing but a plain, ordinary business man. I never did anything devilish in my life. There's nothing romantic about me. Look at this necktie! Did you ever see a hero wearing a plain black four-in-hand? Never! Did you ever see a hero wearing nice tan oxfords without a spot of mud on them? If I can somehow manage to make her think for a few minutes that I've got heroic stuff in me, she may listen to a little sense. She tells me—rather she threw it in my face—that you are going to take Helen and her on a sight-seeing trip into some of the darkest holes in Shanghai. You know the ropes, and there's no danger, of course."

"None at all," said Peter.

"Well, I want to know if you'll let me go along. I'll stand every expense; I've got money to burn! Let me in on it, and—"

"But there isn't going to be a chance for anybody to be a hero. I'm going to take those girls to the safest place in Shanghai. A New England church would be a cavern of iniquity alongside of it!"

Anthony laid his fingers along his knees.

"Well, couldn't you stir up something? That's my idea. I'll leave it to you to crack up some danger, not real danger, of course—we can't let those girls get near any real danger. But we can start a fake fight—or something—and give me a chance to play the hero, to rescue Peggy in my arms; that sort of stuff, you know." He looked at Peter foolishly.

Peter stroked his nose. "It might be done," he said. "I'll see what I can do."

Anthony arose, extended his hand, and said: "Of course, I'll need a revolver."

"Load it with blanks," advised Peter. "You know, some people think it's bad luck to kill a Chink."

Anthony was eyeing him curiously. "Do you?" he asked.

Peter nodded his head slowly. "Sometimes," he said.

CHAPTER III

Anthony and the twins called for Peter as soon as they could tear themselves away from the many fascinating incidents attendant upon coming to an anchorage in the Whang-poo-Kiang.

It was late in the afternoon when the first company tug came down-river from Shanghai for passengers. And it was nearly dusk, the golden-brown evening of China, when they were decanted upon the public landing stage at the International Concession.

Anthony was for going directly to the Hotel Astor for dinner, but at Peter's suggestion he and the twins boarded a street-car for the ride to Bubbling Wells.

Peter stood for a number of moments in indecision as the Bubbling Wells tram went up the bund with the slow flood of victorias, rickshaws, and wheelbarrows. It was now about seven o'clock, with the sun hidden under a horizon of dull bronze. Street lights were coming on, twinkling in a long silver serpent along the broad thoroughfare, rising in a grotesque hump over the Soochow bridge, and becoming lost in the American quarter.

He would meet Anthony and the twins in the dining-room. Whoever got there first would wait. He expected to be there long before his three friends came back from Bubbling Wells.

A rickshaw coolie was wheedling him at his elbow but he paid no attention. His eyes were searching the street. It took him several seconds to reconcile himself to the fleeting apparition. What was this girl doing in Shanghai?

The rickshaw had passed, proceeding at unabated speed in the direction of Native City.

The rickshaw boy was still making guttural sounds, softly plucking at his sleeve. The shafts of the rickshaw were close to his feet. But Peter was still undecided.

"Allee right," said Peter, briskly. "French concession."

That was the direction in which the other rickshaw was headed.

He climbed aboard, and they veered out into the north-bound traffic. The girl in the rickshaw was about one block in the lead, and had no intention evidently of accelerating her coolie's pace or of turning back. She had left all decision to him, and his decision was to ask her a few questions.

His coolie trotted heavily, looking neither to the right nor left, with his pigtail snapping from side to side, as his head bent low.

"Follow *lan-sî* veil—savvy?"

"My savvy," returned the coolie, heading toward the narrow alley of filth and sputtering oil *dongs*, breathing the odor of refuse, of cooking food.

Peter's heart was beginning to respond to the excitement. Did she have some message to convey to him that she could not trust to the openness of the bund at the jetty?

Suddenly the rickshaw ahead swerved sharply to the right into an alley that was perfectly dark. Its single illumination was a pale-blue light which burned before a low building set apart from the others at the far end.

Here the first rickshaw stopped. A ghostly figure seemed to float to the ground. There was a clink of coins. A door opened, letting out a wide shaft of orange light which spattered across the paving, flattening itself against the grim wall of the building across the way.

Peter caught the bronze glint of wires on the roof under a pale moon.

He knocked sharply on the door, and stood to one side. It was a habit he had learned from long experience—that trick of stepping to one side when he knocked at a suspicious door. The door moved outward a few inches. A long, yellow face, with a thick, projecting under lip, peered out. Peter pushed the man aside and entered.

He found himself in a low corridor of smoked wood, with fat candles disposed along the walls at intervals of several yards, on a narrow, lacquered rail. One of three doors was open.

A match was struck, the head glowing in a semi-circle of sputtering iridescence before the wood itself kindled. The hand holding the match was trembling; the weak flame fluttered to such an extent that he was denied momentarily a glimpse of the owner of the hand.

A whisper was conveying an order to him. "Please shut the door, Mr. Moore."

He reached for the door and closed it firmly in the face of the man who had let him into this place.

When he turned, the trembling hand was applying the match flame to the wick of an open lamp, a rather ornate *dong*. As the flame rose higher, casting its steady, mild luminance, he caught a glitter of metal, of polished rubber; one end of the room was almost filled with machinery.

"Romola Borria!"

She seemed to have undergone a great change. The beautiful face that had lured him once into the jaws of death was dominated now by a wistful and tender sadness, as though this girl had gone through an epoch of self-torture since they had last been together.

Yet she was still beautiful; it was as if her beauty had been refined in an intense fire. Her mouth was sad, her great brown eyes glowed with an inexpressible sadness, and her face, once oval and proud, seemed narrower, whiter, and, by many degrees, of a finer mold.

She was examining him broodingly; there was a reluctant timidity in her eyes; it was such a look as you may see years afterward in the woman you once have cast aside for some other, perhaps not quite so worthy.

"Well, you have found me, Peter," she said in a faint and tired voice, coming slowly toward him.

"Yes," he admitted, lamely: "I saw you passing the jetty. I followed—naturally. I have just come from America."

"Oh." Her voice expressed no surprise. "You came for me, Peter?"

"I thought you were dead," he confessed.

"Well, I am a hard one to kill!" A tiny smile flickered across her fine lips. "You are not married—to Eileen?"

"No—and never!" he said dully.

"But you must be in love! You are always in love—with some one."

"I am in love with no one."

"Not even—"

"I am in love with no one."

"Nor am I," said Romola Borria quietly. It seemed to come from her as a vast and reluctant confession. "I loved only one man, and my love for him is quite dead. If I should rake over the embers—oh, but I have raked them over, Peter, many, many times—and I have found not one single small ember glowing! When love dies, you know, it requires a great fire to rekindle it. Oh, I have suffered!"

"He—is dead?"

She smiled again, rather ironically. "Can a man live with a bullet in his heart?"

"I—I saw. I thought—but what does it matter what I thought?" He was trying to inject some of his old spirit into his voice. It was rather difficult, this business of laughing at the funeral of love. "Romola, you are more beautiful!"

"I have suffered," she said, in the same restrained voice.

He turned away with a shrug. He, too, had suffered, but in a somewhat different light. He was examining with a professional eye the heap of apparatus which was arranged in splendid order along the back of the small room.

"I am studying. You see, Peter," she explained, in the same rather recriminatory tones, "I was rather fond of you at one time—"

"Romola, please—"

"And because it was your profession I became interested in it. I heard the message you sent last night—to—to the place on Jen Kee Road. I was quite worried for a while."

"That was why you happened along the bund about the time the boat came up-river?"

"Perhaps." She smiled vaguely.

"You wanted to find out if I still cared enough for you to—"

"Follow me? Yes, Peter; I think that was why."

"Then you didn't know I was on my way to China?"

"No, Peter, I knew nothing."

"Aren't you connected with my good friend, the man with the sea-lion mustaches, in Len Yang?"

Romola gave a short gasp. "I never was connected with him."

"But you told me you were—back there on the *Persian Gulf*!"

She shook her head slowly, with a gentle firmness.

"No. I did not tell you that. I have seen him; yes. But I was never in his employ. It was Emiguel Borria, my late and—may I say?—my unlamented husband, who made me do those things. Peter—"

Her attitude seemed to undergo some sort of subtle change, as if she were bitterly amused. "You say you are not in love. Then what of the little golden-haired girl—the two little golden-haired girls—you left this afternoon on the bund?"

"They and the young man are passengers on the *King of Asia*. I brought them ashore to give them an insight into China-as-it-really-is."

"They are in very capable hands, then, Peter. Aren't you running some risk, though? Isn't there some chance that the men in the Jen Kee Road place may take it into their heads—"

"I am on my word of honor, Romola. I have come back to China, not to start trouble, but simply because—well, why are you in China?"

"Because I haven't the will to leave, perhaps. I stay here in the same spirit that a man or a woman lingers before a dreadful oil painting, like the shark picture of Sorolla; it is terrible, but it is fascinating. I cannot leave. If I did, I would come back, as you come back, time after time. Is that why you've come back?"

"Exactly."

"And you imagine you're running no risk with the two golden-haired maids in tow?"

Peter shook his head thoughtfully. "Perhaps I shouldn't have exposed them to danger. But they were determined, and it's partly to help the young man. Anthony is a plain American business man. He's in love with the youngest. And she, a hero worshipper. He wants to demonstrate himself."

She interrupted in a whisper. "Peter, tell me, why is it? What have you ever done? What do you say? Why—why is it?"

Peter the Brazen was looking at her blankly.

She made a gesture of resignation with her beautiful white hands.

"Well, never mind. Tell me more about Anthony."

"Anthony believes that if he can demonstrate his valor to Peggy, she will come to his arms. He really is a fine, upstanding fellow. I had intended bringing them to Ching Tong's place out Bubbling Wells way, harmless enough and watched by the police of nine nations. Ching Tong, being a friend who will put himself out for me, will play the part of a very bad villain. Anthony's revolver is loaded with blanks. Mine isn't, but that's just my cowardly nature. You can never tell what might turn up, you know."

"Naturally. Go on."

"I intend to have Ching Tong stage a very realistic fight down in his cellar, in which Anthony can overpower eight or ten Chink giants, escape out of the window with the fainting Peggy in his arms, and—and—"

"Simple enough," admitted Romola, with a mild frown. She drew him to a broad, low bench. "Somehow," she went on, "your idea rather appeals to me, too. I liked Anthony's looks—what I saw of him. And I rather liked the two little girls—twins, aren't they?"

Peter nodded. "The heavenly twins!"

"I think I'd quite agree with that plan, Peter, if you didn't happen to be in such disrepute in this neighborhood. You must realize that the Gray Dragon's men are watching you. Of course, you didn't recognize your rickshaw coolie. He is one of the Gray Dragon's men—naturally. Don't you think you are exposing those two nice girls unnecessarily to danger?"

Peter lighted two cigarettes, and passed one of them to Romola. She accepted it with an air of abstraction and puffed slowly, blowing out a thin stream of pale smoke.

"But circumstances are changed now. You see, I am on the fence—perfectly safe."

"They are still anxious for you to come with them?"

"That's it. They sent a representative last trip all the way to San Francisco."

"Of course you refused? Peter—" Her soft, white hand was resting on his; her red lips were very close to his face. "Why don't you join them? You and I!"

"You and I?"

She nodded earnestly.

Peter drew back a few inches. "I said 'no' when you asked me that before. No, I'll have nothing to do with that band—never! Going out into the wilderness, up into the mountains on some of their risky errands—with you—might have appealed to me. Not now!"

"Peter, I am afraid I still love you!"

"And yet, Romola, I'm not afraid of falling in love with you—again! But let's not speak of joining that man in Len Yang. What you're offering is—too tempting. I might give in! You are altogether too fascinating!"

"Am I?"

"I've told you that before."

"Then you will go up-river with me?"

"No—never! Why, you almost make me suspect that you're still in that beast's employ."

"I never was. I told you that."

"You've said many things that didn't stand the acid, Romola."

He stood up, looking down at her with whimsical tenderness. She was very beautiful, and when she took on that forlorn air she had the appearance of a helpless, small girl. He wondered if he would ever regret his refusal.

"Ching Tong must have time to make arrangements, and I have a dinner engagement at the Astor House with Anthony and the heavenly twins. Can't you and I have tea tomorrow afternoon?"

Romola came to him and put her two hands on his shoulders. "No," she said. "We must not be seen together. It may mean danger for you. I've been thinking over your plan to convert Anthony into an adventurer. Why not bring them all here. I have seven servants, all Chinese, and they would give their lives for me. Let me see—" She bit her upper lip thoughtfully.

"You can tell them that this place is—well, the heart of the Chinese smuggling trade. It's ridiculous, but it will appeal to them. I will dress up as a Chinese woman—oh, I've done it dozens of times in the past—and I shall be very mysterious. That will seem much more romantic to Peggy than a mere opium den. And it will be safer. I know Ching Tong's shop. It might do, if you were an ordinary person, Peter, but such an adventure should be provided with at least five times as many exits! I have them here."

Peter looked at her doubtingly, although the idea appealed to him. Outriding his admiration of the idea, however, was a recurrence of his old impression of Romola Borria. He knew that he never had been a match for her cunning, her esoteric knowledge of China.

"I have plenty of make-up pots. I'll paint up these *fokies* to look like bandits! I'll have knives in their belts. And I'll plan the rehearsal before you come. Everything will be arranged." She seemed to hesitate. "You—you won't bring that dreadful automatic revolver of yours loaded—will you?"

Peter smiled faintly.

CHAPTER IV

A light spring rain was drizzling down when Peter ordered four rickshaws of the proud Sikh who stood guard over the porte cochère of the Astor House. Long bright knives of light slithered across the wet pavement from the sharp arc lights on the Soochow bridge. The ghostly superstructure of a large and silent junk was thrown in silhouette against the yellow glow of a watchman's shanty across the dark canal, as it moved slowly in the current toward the Yellow Sea.

It was a desolate night. The streets were deserted except for an occasional rickshaw with some mysterious bundled passenger, the footfalls of the coolies sounding with a faint squashing as of drenched sandals, slimy with the heavy sludge of the back-village streets. The world was lonely and awash.

Peter busied himself with Peggy's comfort when the first rickshaw, dripping and wet, rattled up. He drew the waterproof robe up under her chin and fastened the loops, then tucked it in under her feet. Her cheeks were glowing with the pink of her excitement.

Anthony meanwhile gave similar attention to the other twin.

Peter glanced at his watch as they climbed in. He wondered how Anthony might be taking his first and relatively unimportant lap of their adventure, and he instructed his coolie, in "pidgin," to drop behind.

Clear gray eyes shone with a confident reassurance.

"You mustn't hit too hard, and be careful if you shoot your revolver to discharge it in the air. At close range even the wads from the blank cartridges are rather deadly."

Anthony's clear voice came across to him: "Of course."

They stopped at length before the rambling structure which was the abode of Romola Borria. The lamp was extinguished, probably beaten out long before by the pelting rain. Only a pale glow emanated from the place, this from a tiny upstairs window, covered over with oiled paper, and the only sounds were the ceaseless drip of the rain and the low gibberings of the coolies as they examined the coins given them in the greasy light of the rickshaw lanterns.

Peggy, slipping her arm through Peter's and hugging him close to her, trembled with the excitement of anticipation.

"We must not be separated," he warned them in a whisper. "Whatever happens—Peggy and Helen—stand close to us. In case of trouble, each of you stand behind whichever of us is nearest. Don't scream. Don't show any money. Peggy, put your pocketbook in your shirt-waist. Now—ready?"

"Yes!" came the threefold whispering chorus.

He raised his knuckles, and brought them down sharply—three times rapidly, twice slowly. Silence followed, the bristling silence of an aroused house.

Slowly the door gave way, and a villainous-looking old Chinese in black beckoned with a long snake-like finger for them to enter.

Only two candles now were burning on the lacquered rail in the smoky corridor. Curtains at the rear parted; there was a sweep of heavy silken garments, and a white-faced and beautiful woman made her way toward them.

Deft employment of the make-up pot and painstaking searchings through a great number of trunks had blended a picture that was all but melodramatic.

Romola Borria's wonderful dark hair was arranged in a great heap which sloped backward from her head. Her face was chalk white, from a bath in rice powder; her fine lips were curled in the most sinister of smiles; and her eyes glowed with a splendid abandon. She looked wicked; she radiated cruelty.

And the twins gasped in sweet horror. It is probable that twin trickles of icy excitement chased up and down their twin spines. Anthony gaped, and his gray eyes expressed an unbounded infatuation.

With a gracious stealth she moved beyond them, not once lowering her magnificent eyes, and shot a huge brass bolt in the door.

They formed an expectant, a worshipful semicircle. In a low voice Peter made the introductions, dwelling at fastidious length upon the tremendous villainy of this slender sorceress, who swept him all the time with a proud and disdainful fire. She nodded stiffly at intervals.

"The Princess Meng Da Tlang has a word to say to you." He bowed profoundly.

"It is only this," said Romola Borria in tones as rich as the Kyoto temple gong, "what you have thus far seen, and what you are about to gaze upon, must always—forever—remain a secret within your hearts. Follow me." Romola, or the Princess Meng Da Tlang, floated down the dim corridor with a further silken rustle of skirts, and drew back the curtain at the far end.

The quartette filed into a large and lofty room, flickering under the pallid flames of candles. The wax dripping from some of these hung like icicles or stalactites from the shallow bronze cups, and they illuminated a scene that was bizarre.

The walls were burdened with heavy rugs which responded with a waxen sheen to the mystic light of the candles, and they were of the sombre hues of the China that passed its zenith many centuries ago. They served to give this place a solemn air of vast dignity and richness.

Along the inner wall, placed so that it squarely commanded the doorway, grinned a huge green image of Buddha, surrounded by a clutter of brass candlesticks and mounted on a splendid throne of brass filigree underneath which red flames were burning.

The odor of costly incense was heavy and sweet, the smoke from a brazier arising in a thin, motionless blue spar which, when it had climbed up through the air for a distance of about four feet, broke into a sort of turquoise fan and this drifted on up to the ceiling in heavy wisps. The incense pot was very old, of black lacquer and brass, greened with blotches of erosion.

And above the green image of Buddha, before which the Princess Meng Da Tlang was now kneeling and moaning in a faint voice, reposed a very realistic skull and cross-bones. Across the forehead of this hideous reminder of the hereafter was a deep green notch, attesting in all probability to the cause of the luckless owner's death.

"Please be seated—there," Romola requested.

Her graceful, ivory-white arm indicated with a queenly gesture a heavily carved ebony bench, and her guests filed expectantly to this seat.

Peggy, with a long sigh, dragged Peter into the corner. "I'm almost scared. Oh, oh, isn't this simply romantic!" she whispered.

Helen and Anthony gravely occupied the space on the other side of them. The Princess Meng Da Tlang was moving gracefully toward the doorway through which they had entered.

"I—I'm really a little afraid!" whispered Peggy, with her lips so close to Peter's ear that he could feel her warm breath against his neck. "Put your arms around me—please!" Peter slipped his arm behind her and around her. He squeezed her. "Oh," sighed Peggy, "this is grand!"

Helen gave her a sidelong look of surprise. "Peggy, I think you're hardly discreet."

"Let me die while I'm happy!" grinned Peggy. She turned a wistful face to Peter. "Did you ever put your arm around another woman before?" she whispered.

"Heaven forbid!" groaned Peter. "Don't I act like an amateur?"

"No; you don't!"

Romola was holding back the curtains while a troop of four men, muddy and wet, as if from long travel, moved silently into the large room.

"Mongolian smugglers," Peter whispered.

The four large men crossed the room with dignified tread, depositing four small bundles wrapped in blue silk at the altar of Buddha. Then they removed straw-matting rainproofs which dangled from their broad shoulders to their muddy sandals. They were garbed in black silk and fastened at the belt of each was a kris, curved and flashing where the golden candle light skimmed along the whetted steel.

After depositing their slight burdens they bowed low before the altar, muttered deep in their throats, arose and salaamed gravely, until the four pigtails flapped on the heavy blue rug at Romola's bare feet. She wore no sandals, which was probably the custom among pirate princesses. When the men were gone, Romola drew back a rug which hung close to the altar, revealing a small cupboard flush with the wall. Even Anthony looked at the black door and the brass hasp with his gray eyes round in wonder and interest.

After disposing of the four silken parcels, Romola addressed them in a mysterious voice: "Those packages contain gems; diamonds, rubies, pearls from the Punjab, from Bengali, from Burma."

"Can we see them?" pleaded Helen in rapt tones.

"Aw, please!" inserted Peggy in an angelic whisper.

Romola raised both of her hands as if in horror. "They would tempt even a saint," she muttered.

"Be careful," warned Peter, laying his lips to Peggy's pink ear, "the princess has a terrible temper. She has been known to strangle a man for less than that!"

"I don't believe it!" retorted Peggy. "I think the princess is just too sweet for anything."

Romola gave Peter a look of indolent inquiry. She arose abruptly.

"You must have some of my spiced wine. It is really delicious. *P'êng-yu* Moore, we won't bother the servants; won't you help me?"

Peggy folded her hands demurely in her lap. "I hope it isn't intoxicating," she murmured.

Romola had moved graciously across the room, where in a bronze jardinière protruded the dusty, slender necks of tall bottles. She knelt before this. "Nearer," she whispered, as he followed suit. "Peter, tell me—"

"Yes, Romola?"

"What does this little girl mean to you?"

Peggy's clear voice sounded: "Peter, my throat is dusty!"

"In a minute, Peggy," he called back. Lowering his voice again: "She's merely a child. But why—"

"Peter, I've gone to more trouble tonight than you realize, perhaps—"

"What do you want me to do?"

"I want you to stop making love to that innocent child."

The innocent child's sweet voice was clamoring again. "Peter, the Sahara Desert is a flowing river compared with my throat!"

"All right, Peggy; in a minute."

"You said once that you—loved me."

"I still stand by my guns. But I don't love any one now. You're a temptress, Romola. Why, you are a princess! I never saw you more beautiful than tonight!"

"Peter, can't you realize what a dreary life I've led since that night you ran away from me in Hong Kong? Won't you—for me—because I want it—because I want *you*—reconsider, won't you stop, and think, and—"

"We're getting back to forbidden grounds, Romola."

"Oh, God! I know, I know! But what is there left in my life? Why, what is there left in yours? Perhaps you are the best operator on the whole Pacific Ocean; you've had that reputation now—how long—five years? But it is aimless! Where are you drifting? What will become of you as the years pass? You must be nearly thirty now, Peter. I? I am younger, but I have suffered more. The only happiness I have known has been with you."

Peggy's voice became petulant. "Peter, is that cork *awfully* obstinate?"

"In a minute," he said absently.

"Do you remember those wonderful days and evenings we spent together on the Java Sea, on the old *Persian Gulf?* Do you remember those evenings, Peter, under the moon and the Southern Cross?"

"I remember a great deal of treachery!"

"But there is to be no more treachery," she said passionately. "Think, Peter, think! You are penniless—I have only a little money; it will not last long. What follows? Do you know what happens to white women when they are stranded, penniless, friendless, in this country?" She shivered. "And it would be such a simple thing to do——to go with me—to him. We would be together forever then—you and I! Tibet! The Punjab! The merchant's trail into Bengal! You and I with our caravan—in the blue foot-hills!"

"I'm sorry," confessed Peter sadly.

Romola hung her head with a bitter sigh.

Peggy pitched her voice: "Smash the neck, Peter; I don't mind a little broken glass!"

Romola was pushing two silver cups along the floor to him.

He spilled an amount of the sparkling golden liquid on the carpet, where it formed a dark, round stain. With slightly unsteady hands he conveyed the cups across the room, and Peggy, without another word, following a rather vexed: "Thank you, m'lord," emptied the cup in a single swallow. She licked her lips daintily, and her eyes were sparkling.

As Peter moved into the seat beside her, he saw the curtain over the doorway slowly drawn back by an unseen hand. He looked smilingly toward Romola, and her eyes were fixed on the moving curtain, her face rigid in surprise and concern. The thing seemed to puzzle her.

White metal flashed coldly. A lean hand and arm appeared, and a short, fat knife, the haft sparkling with drops that resembled blood, was projected into the room, point down, quivering, in the wood, not five feet from Romola's lacquered bench!

CHAPTER V

"Is this a part—" began Peter.

"No, it is not."

Romola's face seemed thin with her growing anxiety. Obviously the tossed knife was not a part of the evening's performance.

"A part of what?" Peggy was inquiring.

"Oh, another joke of the Mongolian smugglers," he explained.

There was a sudden and astounding explosion in the midst of them. The flame of a revolver bathed the whole room in reddish-yellow for an instant. Smoke was rising, the pungent, pale-blue, nitrous smoke of so-called smokeless powder. Anthony Andover had arisen, had delivered his shot at the waving curtain.

Peter gave a grunt of disapproval. "Why did you do that—"

"Look!"

The candle directly above the curtains had flickered out; in fact, on closer examination Peter discovered that the candle had been split in crude halves, one of the white fragments lying on the rug not far from the incense burner. This proved one point conclusively. Anthony Andover had put real bullets, not blank cartridges, into the six chambers of his revolver. He had reseated himself calmly beside Helen, who was staring at him with eyes like pools.

Peggy found her voice first. "Gracious! Why did you do that? It was only in fun—that dagger, I mean. Why, you might have killed somebody!"

Anthony shrugged his shoulders. "I'm not so sure about that."

"This is really a most dangerous spot," added the Princess Meng Da Tlang in a mysterious voice. But she was looking at Peter with deliberate meaning.

He accepted what he supposed was intended to be a cue, crossed to the far side of the room, and approached the curtains prudently. He drew the nearest one back inch by inch until the wall of the corridor was given back to them blankly. So far it was quite empty.

Dropping his hand leisurely into his coat-pocket, he sauntered into the hall. As he dropped the curtains behind him, glancing swiftly up and down the apparently deserted hallway, he heard the familiar sound again of a gently closed door.

The sound seemed to originate from the direction of the street. He looked about for the old watchman, and he nearly stumbled over him in the half-darkness as he approached.

Peter struck a match, and a gasp of horror came from his lips. The man was dead—stabbed!

Was this killing a part of an elaborate plan? He would not have permitted himself to walk with such apparent innocence into a snare if he had not relied upon the word of that band. His experience had been that their code was a peculiar one whose foundation was the word of honor. For the first time that evening he began to regret a little his arrogance in defying the request of their messenger to report his intentions immediately upon landing to the men in the place on Jen Kee Road.

He dragged the body into the darkest corner, where he covered it with a mat.

Laboring above his keen anxiety regarding the intention of the band was an eagerness to keep away from the two girls the sense of death, of danger, which seemed to pervade this house.

A way would have to be found to break through the line outside; perhaps they would be compelled to wait for daylight. Again sliding the bolt which had been pushed back by the last trespasser, Peter slowly paced the length of the hall in the meditation of active and acute worry. He was still undecided when he pulled back the rug which cloaked the entrance into the large room.

The room was in total darkness!

CHAPTER VI

An eye, red like the play of fire about a distant volcano crater, glowed a number of paces in front of him. But not a candle, of the dozens that had been burning when he last went out of this room, was now lighted.

The scarlet glow he took to be the illumination under the altar of Buddha. He heard a long sigh, a vague murmur of voices.

"Light the candles," he ordered angrily.

"What is the matter?" This was Anthony's voice; it sounded very drowsy.

A tiny flame appeared as if suspended by an unseen cord and moved to the candle rail. One wick glowed; another; then another.

"Moore—Moore—" This was again the sleepy voice of Anthony.

A garish, gray figure arose and stumbled into the candle-light. It was Anthony. His eyes were half shut. He seemed desperately sleepy, and gibbering as if in a dream.

Peter turned savagely upon the girl. She seemed to cower away from him, half lifting her hands as though in fear that he would strike her.

"Romola! Damn you—"

"Peter, I—I—" Her faint voice trickled off into a sigh of anguish.

"Drugs?" he demanded.

She shook her head anxiously.

"No, no. I—I—"

"What have you done to these people? What have you—"

She lifted up her head imperiously. "You are forgetting—" she began.

He had the fingers of her left hand between his, crushing them. She dropped her head. Her fine lips were quivering. "What am I forgetting?"

Anthony had grasped his elbow. "It's not right, Moore; not right to talk to the princess like this. She's really noble. She's fine!"

"You're drunk, Anthony!"

"No, no, no," he babbled. "Sleepy; that's all. Oh, that wine! Perfectly fine! Makes you feel like climbing a moonbeam!"

"So it appears. Where are the girls?"

"Over here. Say—say, Moore, when does the fight start? I—I'm just itching to get at somebody!"

"You'll have your chance in a moment. And it isn't in fun. Understand?"

"Of course I understand! Isn't my gun loaded with bullets? Are we in a trap?"

"We are! And according to my calculations there's exactly one way out. I think you and the girls will have no difficulty in breaking through. Make a dash for it. Run for all you're worth!"

"Hold on there," remonstrated Anthony, as his eyes lost a trifle of their sleepy look. "What's to become of you? Going to make a break for it, too?"

Peter shook his head. "It's me they're after. I can look out for myself, Anthony; this business isn't quite a novelty in my line. You must get out—and get quick!"

"And leave you behind? Not Anthony! I stick!"

Anthony was flashing a length of highly polished gunmetal in his fist.

Romola with a trembling hand was applying a taper to the other candles. Peter, observing that the twins were, to all appearances, sound asleep, approached her.

She paused in her work, holding the taper above her head, so that its gaunt rays flickered on his face. "Because you loved me so?"

Her shoulders drooped, and her head rolled backward slightly, as though she were very tired. She nipped her lower lip between pearl-white teeth.

"Because I love you so?" she repeated dully.

"In some respects," he said bitterly, "you are like a certain snake in India. You can't lock those damned snakes up! They can always find a tiny hole, a slit in the cage, and—out they slip!"

"Ah, Peter—" Romola dropped the taper to the bronze altar, where it flickered a moment and went out. She fondled his reluctant hand between cold fingers. Her face became utterly miserable, and there were sparkling tears in her eyes. "My heart is your heart. I have given my love to you. I would give my life for you!"

He drew away from her slowly, turning his head to avoid the anguish in her eyes.

He went on briskly: "If my death is arranged for tonight—"

He stopped to watch her. She was fumbling at her waist. A little silver of light appeared. The thing was a slim stiletto. Her teeth were clicking as she extended the handle toward him. Their eyes met. In hers was shining a brute command. In his slowly came shock, amazement. She placed her fingers slowly over her heart; her hand slipped down and fell again at her side.

"There!" she murmured.

"Is—is my end so close?" he whispered.

She nodded slowly. "You are in great danger. This may be your final opportunity. See? I am offering no resistance. Why—why do you hesitate?"

With the tiny blade lying like a flame of pure silver across the palm of his hand, Peter experienced a moment troubled and exceedingly awkward. That threat, perhaps, was hardly more than the spilling out of bitterness which she had created in him.

In silence he handed the thing back to her almost furtively; and she accepted it without removing her shining gaze from his. Somehow she seemed to have come out victorious in a conflict that had had nothing to do with knives, with broken promises. And with the restoration of the dagger the spell seemed to be swept aside.

Turning abruptly, with a slight straightening of his shoulders, he walked away from her.

Anthony was like a guardian angel, a statue gravely symbolic of protection, standing over the golden heads, with the revolver dangling from his hand and shooting out metallic gleams. Their eyes were tightly closed; the twins were sleeping as if drugged.

They heard a low, hushed scream.

"Peter—*ni kan!*"

Peter turned quickly, searching both entrances. At first he was conscious of no intrusion. Then a yellow face, long, narrow, with a stub of purple-black hair protruding behind, and which for a moment he took to be a part of the curtain, slowly withdrew, arising upward—vanishing!

The phantom was not unlike the wisps of yellow smoke from a greenwood fire, despatched by a lazy dawn wind. The face of Jen, the deck steward!

CHAPTER VII

Apparently Anthony had not observed this specter.

Peter seized his arm, the left one. "We must start. Wake them up."

Anthony shook a nervous negative. "I've tried. That wine!"

"*Arracka*. Comes from Java. Tastes like May wine, and is stronger than cognac." He was tilting Peggy's chin, shaking her head. No response. He tried the same experiment with Helen, and begot identical results.

Romola Borria had vanished.

Peter stepped out first, supporting his limp freight with his left arm, and in his right brandishing a revolver. He hoped it wouldn't be necessary and he was sure that underneath the splendid varnish of Anthony's fine bravado larked the belief that this entire evening was nothing more than an exciting romantic game.

In the pinch, would Anthony react after the fashion of heroes-to-the-manner-born, or would the sight and smell of blood, if it Was written that blood be shed, unnerve him, make him out to be what he was at heart, the secretary of a prosperous and peaceful plow company?

On his part, Anthony was still babbling incoherently but earnestly, impressing upon Peter the undeniable virtues of the golden wine. He was not prepared, although the nickeled revolver still flashed in his unoccupied hand, for the tumultuous event which was being shaped for the two of them around the corner.

They did not attain the outer door. Out of the drab recesses leaped dusky shadows. There seemed to be a large number of jostling men; perhaps only three or four were at hand by actual count; the insufficient lighting and their shocking and determined appearance lent them plurality.

A sparkling flame roared from the hand of the foremost of these before Peter could bring his hand out of his pocket.

Anthony's nickeled revolver went off twice, from his hip, and the giant faltered, going back shapelessly among the shadows from which he had emerged.

Peter's original scheme to hack a way through the line underwent hasty revision. Escape would have to be made by different channels, and his only choice was the device nearest at hand. It was a long chance, an aimless one, perhaps, fraught with new, dangers and complications. But he did not hesitate.

Beating off a hand that pawed for his shoulder, he flung open the door which faced the dwelling's entrance, and pushed the reluctant Anthony inside.

Peter locked the door, throwing a bench across it for temporary barricade, then lit candles, wondering if any one would have had enough foresight to disconnect the aerial wires. He dropped his burden to the divan against the side wall, and examined Anthony, who had gone very pale. He was shaking, and his gray eyes seemed to have climbed half way out of his head. He propped Peggy tenderly beside her sister, and laid an unsteady hand upon Peter's shoulder. He seemed to be fighting down a very definite fear.

Peter was backing toward the apparatus. "Watch the door. If any one tries to break in, shoot straight at the sound! You're not hurt, are you? Did that fellow get you?"

Anthony shivered all over. "Christ!" he muttered. His lips were white. "That man! I shot him! He's dead! Dead!"

"And we are still alive," said Peter quietly.

He sat down at the instrument table, fixed silvery disks to his ears, twanged the detector wire and made a few quick alterations in connections. Fortunately his inspection of the equipment earlier in the day had given him a grasp of its arrangement. In an instant he had the tuner adjusted, was listening, with those keen ears of his focussed for the ethereal voices which might be abroad at this untimely hour. Distant splashes of heat lightning occurred faintly, like the quivering of sensitive metal.

Casting a glance over his shoulder, to make sure that Anthony was following instructions, he rearranged levers and lowered the heavy switch which drew upon the storage batteries underneath the table.

He tapped the large brass key experimentally. A hissing blue spark lighted up the walls and his features in a ghostly glow. Tightening the vibrator at the terminus of the rubber-covered coil, he spelled out an inquiry in the International Code. Any station within hearing would answer that call.

He wondered if the Shanghai station was closed up for the night, or if by any chance his assistant on the *King of Asia* would be on the job.

Peter waited for several anxious moments, with no sound in the telephones other than the faint spattering of the lightning down the coast. Then his inquiry was given a response, startlingly harsh and close.

The station might have been across the street, the signals were beating in his ears so loudly. The operator was having some difficulty adjusting his spark; it was rough, ragged, like the drumming of hailstones on a metal roof.

A series of test letters followed, exasperatingly slow. "V—V—V—V— What station is that? This is the *Madrusa*."

Peter hesitated, although interference was unlikely. He felt tremendously relieved. The *Madrusa's* rough spark meant more to him than help close by. He knew the *Madrusa* well; a gray, swift gunboat, lying close to the water, whose purpose was to sweep the lower Whang-poo and Yangtze clear of pirates. She could spit streams of bullets for hours without let-up. And the knowledge of her closeness to this death-trap keyed him up, not entirely because she was manned by British sailors who would rather fight than eat. His hand reached out for the key.

"Who is on watch? This is Peter Moore. That you, Johnny Driggs?"

If the man at the *Madrusa's* key did happen to be Jonathan Driggs, he could afford to breathe more easily. Driggs was another man who had found in China the irresistible attraction, and who for some years had sat behind the radio machines of many ships that plied these yellow waters.

"Yes! Yes! Yes!" roared the *Madrusa's* spark. "Where are you? What are you doing up at this time of night playing with a baby coil?"

For the next three minutes the spitting blue spark flared and jumped as Peter spelled out his plight. He sketched their predicament by abbreviated code, and he impressed upon his friend the necessity for utter secrecy, hoping that the night had no other ears.

"Damn it!" replied the quick fingers of the gunboat's operator. "Damn it! But I can't get shore leave! Impossible—you can guess why! Our gunnery officer, Lieutenant Milton Raynard, is jumping to go! He'll fetch you five or six sailors. He knows the lay of the land, and I've sketched him a map of the locality from your description. Cinch! They'll be off at once, soon as they can get the engine started in the launch. Don't give up the ship, old boy! Don't—"

Peter dropped the receiver, walked over to the divan and endeavored to awaken the girls, slapping their hands, shaking them. They did not appear to be drugged. Evidently they had underestimated the power of the smooth, yellow *arracka*. Faint color glowed in their cheeks, and under the treatment Peggy slowly opened one very sleepy brown eye.

It drooped again. She muttered something that was not intelligible. It had something to do with a princess, and even that word was indistinct.

Anthony lifted a cautioning hand. "Some one's outside," he whispered. Slowly, as they watched it, the knob described a single revolution. Anthony lifted his revolver. "Who is there?"

"Let me in!" It was Romola Borria.

"Open the door," said Peter quietly, stepping aside.

Anthony removed the bench, twisted the key.

"You must not go with them," Romola whispered.

"Shut the door—put the bench back," directed Peter. He followed Romola across the room.

Evidently she had read the spark. "Let these people go—yes! But you remain. You will—or won't you?"

Peter looked skeptical. "Why should I? I've decided that life is pretty sweet, after all! Why haven't Jen and his gang broken in here? Why is he waiting? Have you told him help is coming?"

She shrugged impatiently. "I have not seen Jen. I have talked with no one."

"Then you will stay in this room until we leave?"

"But why did you send for them? It was foolish! How will you explain?"

"They are friends. Such men ask no questions."

"But there was no need!" She made a despairing gesture with her hands. "Your friends could have gone safely. Jen has no interest in—*them*!"

Peter nodded indifferently. "But my ship sails."

"Very good. But you must not leave this house until sunrise."

"When the sailors come from the *Madrusa* I shall walk out of here—"

"And into the arms of death, Peter!"

Peter lighted a cigarette and puffed thoughtfully in silence. Romola's gaze was upon his lips, as though the next words he would utter meant to her the difference between life and death.

And what he might have said was forestalled by a heavy battering at the outer door. These deep vibrations seemed on the sudden to stir Peggy out of her sleep. She sat upright, digging fists into tired eyes.

"Gracious! Where's everybody?"

The hammering ceased, and a high-pitched crash followed an instant of hush.

"The men from the *Madrusa*!" cried Anthony. He dragged the bench away; flung the door open with a grand gesture.

And into the room strode a blandly smiling Chinese, magnificent in gold and blue and red. He was flanked by three large and watchful coolies, armed with clubs.

"Mr. Moore; I am the man from the Jen Kee Road place!" He radiated a splendid calm.

Peggy cowered against her sister, with a look of sleepy mystification, while Anthony, glancing to Peter for command, was fingering his revolver in anxious indecision. Already one of the coolies was sidling toward him.

"You were a deck coolie this morning," Peter replied.

The Chinese took a step toward him. Peter felt Romola cringe at his side. He wondered at this.

"Shall we wait until sunrise, or—"

A sudden babble of men's voices on the other side of the partition checked the Chinese, while a look of misunderstanding came over his bland countenance.

"Moore! Moore! Where are you?" These were the rich tones of a man accustomed to command.

And instantly the small room seemed to be overflowing with the white and blue of uniforms.

Peggy stood straight up with a wondering gasp. Confronting her was a tall and handsome youth with the gold-and-black epaulets of his majesty's service at the shoulder-straps of his splendid white uniform. A cutlass in a nickeled case hung from a polished leather belt, and depending from it also was an empty leather holster. Gripped threateningly in his right hand was a blue revolver.

The shrill voice of the man from the Jen Kee Road place rose sharply above the momentary tumult.

In this quick confusion a pale, obnoxious odor, like opium fresh from the poppy, yet with the savor of almonds, flooded Peter's throat. He was vaguely aware of a fumbling in his coat-pocket. Explosions sounded as from afar and a vast redness settled down and encompassed the world.

The interval of dark was surprisingly short-lived. Swimming in and out of his distorted vision was a face. He was conscious for a while of no other impression. The face reeled, came closer—danced away from him! Bright eyes sparkled, leaped, and hung motionless.

He inhaled a new perfume, deliciously like flowers in a summer meadow. It injected fresh life into him. His hands found power, and he clutched at a soft wrist. The owner of this face was talking eagerly.

"We are alone—alone!"

With great effort he found he could incline his head a little. He was struggling. Hot vapors clogged his brain. Where were the girls, Anthony, the young lieutenant from the *Madrusa*?

"Where are they?"

"Safe."

He could recognize the features now distinctly; yet they stirred up in him no longer a feeling of repugnance, but a vague longing.

"Romola!"

"Yes, Peter. You are feeling stronger?"

"What am I doing here? What is this place?"

"We are in the cellar."

It was very dim, with an odor of moldy dampness. The rock foundation, the walls, and floor were perspiring whitely.

Peter's brain became clogged again. The voice came to him softly but quite distinctly, with each word clear and emphatic:

"He is waiting outside. They will not dare come into my house again!"

"I am dizzy. Who will not dare? Who is outside?" he demanded feebly.

"The man from the Jen Kee Road place. He is waiting outside that window. No, No! He cannot see. It is covered with silk."

Peter fell back against the arm. "What does he want?"

"Your answer. I told him to wait. I promised him; I will hold the candle to the window."

"But I am dizzy," he groaned. "I do not understand."

"Once—means 'yes.' Twice—means 'no.'"

He delivered every ounce of his mental energy against the drug in his brain; it was like struggling against the tide. "Once—means 'yes?' Twice—means 'no?'" The meaning suddenly became clear to him. "The up-river trip?"

She nodded slowly, anxiously. "And twice—means death, also, Peter!"

He tried to drag himself erect, tried to twist his head, and he sank back with a bitter groan. "You drugged me!"

"There was no other way. I could not let you go into the night—into death!"

A bitter smile came to his white lips. "I am quite powerless?"

"I—I am afraid you are, Peter."

"If I decide yes—or if I decide no—how can I defend myself?"

"You are quite helpless," she confessed in a whisper. "No. You cannot defend yourself." Her expression showed an inward struggle. "You are in my hands. You are in my arms! Yes! What have you to say?"

The smile of bitterness came and flickered again over his pale lips. He tried to throw back his head, but the redness was settling down upon him again. "What shall I say?" he muttered. "I say—two lights! I say—no! *No!*"

The fingers at his neck were icy. Gently he was lowered to the pavement.

Romola had taken the candle down from the rafter, and she went swiftly to the tiny window. She raised her hand, once, then pinched out the flame between her fingers.

CHAPTER VIII

Foggy consciousness. A roaring like that of the ocean on a rockbound coast. He seemed to be floating in a medium of ice. Once his dragging arm scraped a wet, slippery timber. The journey seemed to be taking him down—down—into the earth, and slowly he began to rise.

Gradually he became aware of innumerable pinpoints of light in a shield of purple darkness. These might have been stars, or the lights of a great city. Next he heard the low gurgle of water, as of a stream splashing through wilderness.

He felt very faint, but the vapor clouds in his brain were beginning to clear away. Next he was badly shaken up, yet he was conscious of no pain. Remorseful eyes stared into his from the face of a candle-white spectre, and in the background a tall, half-naked giant swayed from side to side in a pink glow.

Where, then, were Jen and his Chinese?

He vaguely sensed the dawn; it came to him as an old experience, a sort of groping memory out of a gloriously romantic past. And the swaying giant he decided in a moment of rare clarity to be a sampan coolie.

The pink glow increased, became pale yellow, while a deep blueness figured in it. A swollen sun came and paved a bloody path across a lake of roiled brown, and the water hissed with a white foam.

His jaws were aching; a queer emptiness in his chest caused him long and perplexing speculation. There were shouting voices aloft, and a gleaming black wall slowly took form above him. He made out the pointed heads of rivets.

"Are you awake?" The voice, low and sibilant, emerged from the candle-white face.

He had been dreaming, too, during this fantastic journey. Once he had plainly distinguished a field of waving corn. He seemed to be back in California.

"Eileen," he murmured, surprised at the feebleness of his voice.

"No, no," came the reply. "It is Romola. I—I am leaving you!"

"Ah! Where is Jen?"

Bellowing inquiry came down to them: "Who is that? What do you want?"

The girl called back: "The wireless operator. He is sick. Drop the ladder. Send down some one to carry him."

The sampan was swinging about, and the coolie was paddling like mad.

"River boat—for Ching-Fu?" Peter gasped.

"No. The *King of Asia*. Peter—can you understand? I am leaving you! This is good-bye! I—I—we will never see each other again. I—I couldn't turn you over to that man!"

"But the candle—" Peter was miserably confused. "You raised it—once! I said no!"

Romola seemed to become rather hysterical. "I tricked them, Peter! Oh, won't you understand? I do love you, Peter! I couldn't give you to them!"

"No," he muttered; "I don't understand. I—I'm dizzy."

The voice was bellowing again.

"Is that Peter Moore? What's happened to him?"

"He's sick—sick! Send down a watchman. Hurry! This tide is carrying us away!"

Something bounded into the sampan. A brown coil was flattened against the gleaming black wall.

But Peter could not understand. He was back again in the cellar under Romola's house, mumbling insanely about a candle-light. Perhaps he dreamed that hot lips were pressed lingeringly against his own. Over and over he heard a fading voice; it was saying: "Good-by!—*Ch'ing*!"

The glaring sun was in his face. He shut his eyes. The lips seemed to be torn from his in a cry of anguish. Strong arms encircled his waist, and he was no longer aware of the motion of the sampan.

It was late in the day when Peter opened his eyes again, closed them, and stared at the mattress and springs of a bunk over his head. He was lying on his back in his stateroom. Smoky afternoon sunlight, reflected from a shimmering surface, sparkled and bubbled against the white enameled wall.

His head was aching a little, and there were numerous jumping pains in various parts of his body. He had been dreaming. All of these things that had come and gone with the fading of the night were figments of a slumbering brain. The last portion of the dream which he could visualize distinctly was his act of arising from a wireless machine in a house that had gone mad, to confront a tall Chinese who wore a ridiculously stubby pigtail, like that of Jen, the deck-steward.

He sat up, governed by a sudden worry. Where were the Whipple girls and Anthony? What had become of that dashing British lieutenant, Milton Raynard?

Peter arose hastily from bed, and examined a pale and gaunt countenance in the small mirror above the wash-stand. Dark lines had come under his eyes, and the deep-blue pupils seemed to kindle with a peculiar brilliancy. He had seen that look in other eyes, and another fragment of the dream came back to him. He licked his dry lips, tasting a flavor not unlike that of opium fresh from the poppy, and of almonds.

He filled the wash-basin with cold water, took a long breath, and immersed his face for a half minute. Gasping, he came out of it with pink starting into his cheeks, and his mental faculties somewhat better organized.

When he emerged from his stateroom, attired in a fresh white uniform, with his gold-and-white cap set at a jaunty angle on his head, he looked like a different man. His skin was glowing, and a youthful heart was sending recuperative tingles all over his body.

Peter took a turn about the promenade deck in search of Anthony, and was hailed by his room-boy, who had some mail for him.

He dropped these missives absently into his pocket, made further inquiries, and learned that Anthony and the Misses Whipple had come to the steamer shortly before sunrise in the launch belonging to the river gunboat *Madrusa*.

Then he knocked at Anthony's door. A tired snore, emanating from the transom, broke into a sleepy complaint.

The door opened; Anthony stared at him as if in the presence of a ghost. "Great Scott! I thought you were dead!" He rubbed his eyes to accelerate wakefulness.

Peter chuckled. "What happened? Both girls safe?"

"How did you get here alive?"

"I came down by sampan. The princess detained me."

Anthony shivered. "We thought you were with us. Somebody put out all the lights!" He shivered again. "Raynard wanted to go back—so did I. We didn't dare! The girls, you know." He dropped his head, as if ashamed.

"How is Peggy?"

Anthony frowned, hesitated. "Peter, she—she thinks you're a quitter! She thinks you ran away at the big moment!"

Peter grinned. "That can be cleared up. Did you enjoy—the game? Did you succeed? That's all I'm worrying about."

Anthony looked at him suspiciously. "That was not a put-up job. Why—I shot a man!" He became anxious. "Will there be a row?"

"Not a bit—if you keep your mouth shut."

"Oh, I'll do that! But that dead Chink! Ugh!"

"Forget him," advised Peter cheerfully. "I still don't know what Peggy had to say."

"What do you mean?" Anthony gave him a blank stare.

"Does she think—"

A light of understanding came into Anthony's clear gray eyes. "Oh, I made a little mistake," he confessed weakly. "It—it isn't Peggy; it's Helen! We're engaged! You see, Helen is such a—a quiet and reserved sort of girl.

Just my kind! Peggy—well, you know, I decided she was a little too—too wild!"

A long, low gray launch was chugging alongside when Peter made his way back to the promenade-deck. At the upper extremity of the companion-ladder which reached down to the river's surface was standing a slim and youthful figure in blue, with wisps of golden hair flying about in the soft spring breeze.

She leaned anxiously and expectantly over the rail as a tall and commanding young man in the white uniform of his majesty's naval service climbed up eagerly toward her. The young officer leaped gracefully over the rail, seized both hands of the girl, and his eyes were shining.

Peter's deep-blue eyes unaccountably took on an expression of moist sadness; yet he was grinning.

He climbed up to the boat-deck, unlocked the wireless room, and for the first time recalled the mail in his hip-pocket. Leisurely he scanned the post-cards first, highly colored ones, which had been forwarded from the San Francisco Marconi office, emanating from friends scattered in many parts of the world. One was from Alaska; another from Calcutta, India, from that splendid fellow, Captain Bobbie MacLaurin.

He opened the letter, and his eyes fell upon familiar handwriting. He suddenly felt shocked; the sentences began swimming. The letter was from Eileen, dated Nanking. Words stood out whimsically, like thoughts assailing a tired brain, clamoring for recognition.

> …You are the stubbornest man!… Do you imagine I ever cared for that puppy? Why, Peter—why didn't you wait? I'd have scratched his eyes out! Of course, he kissed me! But the point is, my dear, I didn't realize until it was all over…. I suppose I should have jumped into the ocean when you left me so angrily. But I didn't. I came to China on the *Empress of Japan*. I am now at the Bridge Hotel, in Nanking, on my way to Ching-Fu, where you may find me. Just to show you that I can have adventures, too!

"Great guns!" said Peter. He wondered if he could catch the Nanking express; there was a Chinese steamer leaving Nanking for up-river tomorrow noon.

There was a humble voice at his elbow. A deck-boy was grinning dreamily at him; a queer flicker darted across his green eyes, vanished.

"Jen!" exclaimed Peter, glimpsing an abbreviated pigtail.

"Aie!" said the deck-boy.

"The man from the Jen Kee Road place!"

The deck-steward seemed puzzled. "My no savvy," he said. His look became dreamy again, reminiscent.

"But you can speak English as well as 'pidgin,'" declared Peter, frowning. "You did last night!"

"My savvy 'pidgin,'" said Jen brightly. "China allatime funny place! China no can savvy allatime funny people! Funny!"

"What's that?" snapped Peter. He was baffled and angry. Had Jen played the leading part in the mysterious and grim comedy of last night, or was he only a work coolie, a deck-steward, harmless, innocuous, babbling happily in his limited knowledge of a strange language?

The deck-boy was pointing up-river with a long, yellow finger.

Peter stared. And he saw nothing, nothing but a great red sun with its lower half enveloped in a glowing pool of green and red smoke into which arose the black spars of ships from all over the world.

CHAPTER IX

The sky was clearing. Rain had ceased dripping from the bulging black clouds, and a slender rod of golden sunlight pierced through and marked a path upon the red bricks of the inn courtyard. Hazy in the green-and-purple distance could be glimpsed the yellow withers of the western range. Cooking smells, the sour odor of fish-and-rice chow, were wafted from the braziers of village housewives.

Peter loafed against a spruce post, and moodily contemplated the stamping animals in the enclosure. His hat was in his hand, and the mountain breeze assailed his blond hair, which, rumpled and curly, gave him something of the appearance of a satyr at ease. He was worried. He had, an hour before, come to Ching-Fu from the boat; and Eileen had left Ching-Fu for a trip to Kialang-Hien, a village of the third order some fifty *li* distant, the morning before. Whether to follow or wait was the question.

Somewhere afield a valiant bronze gong called infidels to the feet of an insufferable clay god.

Peter's flow of thought was interrupted. Unnoticed a girl—at first glance the virtuous daughter of a mandarin—was approaching. Her abruptness and her appearance caught him so completely off guard that he held his breath and stared at her rather wildly. And she in turn, as if fascinated, stared back as wildly at him.

His first guess was inaccurate. She was no mandarin's daughter, this one. She was young and exquisitely slim, with wisdom and sadness written upon her colorless face, and he was informed by a single glance at her exploring bright eyes and the straightness of her fine black brows, that she was half-breed, Eurasian.

Those shining eyes, not unlike twin jade beads, were sparkling. Her lips were thin and as red as betel. Her garb was satin, bright with gold filigree and flashing gems; and her dainty feet were disfigured rather than adorned by bright-red sandals. Her feet, however, were not the "feet of the lily," for the lithe grace of her stride was ample proof that they had not been bound.

The dying sun outlined through the folds of her bizarre garment ankles straight, slender, and probably naked.

Rosy color moved swiftly into her satiny complexion while, with a pretty, inquisitive frown, she scrutinized him; and then, with a flick of her black eyelashes, she ran toward the arched doorway, leaving Peter to ponder, and scratch his blond head, and demand amazing explanations of himself.

It was a dominating trait in Peter never to lose time securing information that was interesting to him; but the old proprietor, with his wise and varnished smile, could vouchsafe very little of consequence.

The young woman, he admitted, was named Naradia. She was accompanied by her husband, a young Chinese of high birth, who manifested no more signs of activity to an outward world than a baffling secretness.

The two of them had arrived from down-river on a sailing junk the week before. The husband's name was Meng, he believed, and since he had come, the old man declared, many strange and warlike faces had mysteriously appeared in Ching-Fu.

Such visitors were not uncommon in the villages which bordered the merchants' trail, from the Yangtze to the Irriwaddi, but Peter's interest was kindled. As he made off in the direction of the most reliable village mule-seller, he decided that the secretive young bridegroom, Meng, might be worth cultivating.

From a soft-tongued and hardened swindler Peter procured a mule, and arranged to have the animal in the caravansary at daybreak. It was his intention to start for Kialang in search of Eileen with the first tender glow of dawn.

After dining he waited in the compound for a glimpse of the mysterious Meng, or his ravishing bride, Naradia. Unsuccessful, he returned to his room. His Chinese valet was brewing jasmin-tea when Peter opened and shut the bedroom door. His pajamas were neatly laid out upon his couch, and the rugs were neatly furled back. He detected the acrid and pleasing odor of incense as he crossed the room.

The boy glanced up meekly from the charcoal brazier. "Wanchee tea now?"

"Yes." Peter slipped out of his tunic.

The boy dropped on his knees to unlace Peter's boots.

Peter lighted a cigarette, stretched himself out upon the rugs, and the boy brought him a steaming cup.

"Wake me—daylight—sure," cautioned Peter, lifting the cup.

"*Tsao*," murmured the boy.

When the boy was gone Peter removed the automatic from his raincoat pocket. The metal glittered pleasantly in the yellow light from the suspended lamp. The cup of tea had served to waken him. He released the cartridge clip from the automatic's handle and stared thoughtfully at the glowing lead balls.

He became conscious of a sound, alien and untimely. The door was rattling softly. He studied it with interest; the wooden handle was turning slowly, first to the right, then to the left.

The phenomenon puzzled him. His eyes were sparkling a little as he quietly restored the clip of cartridges.

Creeping to the hinged side of the door, he waited, breathing silently.

With a squeak the door swung in quickly. A lean, yellow hand, gripping a nickel-plated pistol, was thrust inside.

Peter shot three times directly through the wood panel.

The white pistol thudded to the planks, while the yellow hand seemed to be jerked backward by an electric force. Soft footsteps retreated. Peter jerked open the door and stepped out.

The corridor was empty. Some few feet toward the stairway an oiled wick, jutting from a tiny bronze cup which was bracketed to a scantling, burned and sputtered.

Under the door across the way a thin streak of yellow light indicated that the mysterious young Chinese and his bride had not yet retired.

As Peter was examining the floor for blood stains the door budged inward sufficiently to panel the terrified face of the Eurasian girl he had seen earlier in the evening. At sight of him she shut the door hastily.

Perplexed, he went to the stairway and peered into the stark blankness which swam up to the third step below him. He was at a loss to account for the air of serenity which still dwelt in the inn. Surely the three revolver shots had been overheard; yet the place was as silent as the grave, and quite as ominous. Where were the servants, the caravan boys, the muleteers, the traders and merchants? He dismissed as absurd the theory that the walls of his room were stout enough to muffle the short-barreled blasts.

An isolated sound, a swish of discreet garments, a prudent grating sound, as of a window lifted or a chair moved, then came to him, and unquestionably it came from his own room.

Peter left the staircase to its gloomy shadows.

The room was unoccupied. Basing his next action upon sound and tried experience, Peter put out the lamp and hazarded a glimpse out of the window.

A sharp, round moon was perched high in a star-studded heaven, fairly illuminating a muddy street and the low-thatched roofs of nearby dwellings. A horse whinnied and stamped in the enclosure, and from a distance rose the moody growl of the rapids.

Irritated and nervous, Peter felt for the couch and sank down in the blackness, with the revolver dangling idly across one knee.

At that instant he was thrilled to the roots of his hair by a scream, strangely muffled.

Peter indulged in a shiver as he stole to the door on tiptoe, opened it quietly, and looked out. There was terror in that scream; it was the outcry of a human in the clutch of real horror.

The door across the way was slightly ajar, letting out an orange effulgence which lighted the boards, the opposite wall, and the grimy ceiling. Indistinctly he discerned a motionless clump, and, catching the white flicker of steel he sprang across, wrapping his fingers about a struggling wrist.

Immediately the orange light was broadened, then darkened by a tall figure, but Peter's back was turned.

An eager sigh, as if heartfelt relief, was given out by the second shadow.

The knife, under Peter's pressure, dropped to his feet, and, quite sure that the time was now past to ask polite questions, Peter brought down the butt of the revolver with a smart slap where the long black pigtail joined a fat little head. With a throaty gurgle his victim joined the shadows of the floor.

A soft, white hand was laid upon Peter's right arm, and he found himself glaring into the blanched face of the girl Naradia. Her small fingers hardened upon the flesh of his hand, and he was aware that she was staring imploringly across his shoulder.

Peter spun about and for the first time was aware of the presence of the indolent figure in the doorway. The glow of a cigarette was at the man's lips, but the darkness prevented scrutiny.

The rapid procession of mysterious events had unnerved Peter. The silent and indolent presence of the stranger in the doorway put the spark to his long-withheld indignation. He lifted the revolver's nose menacingly.

The cigarette glowed a bright red, as if in amazement.

"You," he snapped, "whoever you are—pick this man up. Carry him into my room. And you," he added sharply to the girl, "follow him!"

The cigarette fell to the planks, and the tall man put his heel upon it. The careless movement gave Peter his first glimpse of the man's profile. The man smiled faintly. He took the unconscious assailant of Naradia by the heels and dragged him into Peter's room.

CHAPTER X

A match hissed; the flame of the lamp rose up slowly.

With a flutter of skirts the girl followed, her head inclined, as though she was humiliated or greatly embarrassed. She went to the couch and faced him, while an attempt at calmness and a determined fear struggled to control her expression. Her attire was negligee, of pink Japanese silk, open at the throat, and revealing a neck and shoulders as white and smooth as bleached ivory.

Peter closed the door and shot the bolt.

The man who smiled so confidently had rolled the knife carrier with his face to the wall. Then he crossed to the couch and took a stand beside the girl, seemingly at ease under Peter's sharp and thorough inspection.

As Peter examined the slender, colorless face he imagined for an instant that the man, also, was Eurasian. But that impression he quickly realized was incorrect. The man simply was of a high order of Chinese intelligence, with smooth, dusky skin, thin, stubborn lips, a straight forehead, and eyes which were dark, watchful and sad.

Yet these eyes seemed to twinkle now, shifting without a trace of fear from the unwavering gun-barrel in Peter's hand to the unwavering glint in Peter's blue eyes.

And there was something undeniably imperial in the young Oriental's bearing. Perhaps this was caused by his attitude, or the Oriental richness of his garb. He might have been an Asiatic prince, or a sheik fresh from the desert, or a maharaja, from a jungle throne. A glittering cluster of gems—diamonds and rubies—hung from a fine gold chain which encircled his bronzed neck. His tunic was of satin, the color of the tropical sea; his breeches were spotlessly white, and his slippers were Arabian, with up-curled toes.

"Well?" asked the young Asiatic, when Peter's gaze finally descended to the scarlet slippers.

"I am waiting," said Peter, impatiently.

Black eyebrows went up inquiringly. "I am a merchant—from Shanghai."

"What you are or who you are is of no importance," returned Peter in a voice of cordial doubt. "Perhaps you've aroused my idle curiosity; at all events, I want you to tell me why you were late in coming to your wife's assistance."

"His life is more precious," she interceded, hastily.

The Oriental waved his hand, as if the answer were absurd. "You anticipated me by three seconds," he replied. "I was drowsing. I thought I had dreamed the scream. May I say—I am very grateful?"

Peter's expression was dubious, but he nodded at length as though partly satisfied. "Perhaps you can tell me what became of the man who opened my door?"

The man's face was frankly bewildered. "I am at a loss to account for any man entering your room—unless by mistake," he said with genuine concern. "I think you are crediting me with an interest in an affair that I know nothing of. Unless—unless—" He hesitated and paused, searching Peter's eyes with a glance suddenly startled. "Can it be possible—?" he muttered. "I judge by your accent that you are an American. I have spent the past four years myself in America—at Harvard. Somehow—" He paused again, and smiled faintly.

Suddenly the smile departed, was displaced by the most murderous of grimaces. He was looking beyond Peter. His right hand flashed into his blue tunic. And before Peter could turn or dodge, he sprang past him, colliding with an object which grunted and instantly cried out in agony.

Peter turned in time to see a thin knife plunge into the throat of a swarthy Chinese, whose face was round as the Mongolian moon, and as yellow.

The Chinese wiped his knife coolly on the fallen man's black jacket. "Why, my good friend, should he attack you, unless—" He paused again, and searched Peter's face with those keen brown eyes, no longer sad.

"Unless what?" he asked, bluntly. "This man is from Len Yang."

He heard the girl utter a sharp gasp, and a queer light was dawning in the other's face.

"Unless you are"—he hesitated—"unless you are the one man in the world I wish you might be." He laughed. "Are you—Peter Moore, known in some parts of China as—Peter the Brazen?"

Peter nodded slowly.

With a delighted cry the young Oriental sprang to him and seized his hand. "Do you hear, Naradia?" he exclaimed. "This is *Peter Moore!*"

And Peter permitted his suspicions to drift, as he thought of the dead man on the floor, and of the reason why he died. He was compelled to admit that the stranger had saved his life.

"We must talk this over," the young Chinese was muttering. "Why, I could not have arranged it more suitably!" He seemed to collect himself then. "Before we talk, let us get rid of this man."

He picked up the dead coolie by the waist, lifted him easily to the window, and dropped him, as if he were a sack of rice, into the mud. He whistled twice. Immediately three shadows were given up by the caravansary. These gathered up the dead man and vanished.

"They will dispose of him," said the stranger, helping himself to a cigarette. He paused with the flaring match in his fingers and looked at Peter quizzically. "My name is Kahn Meng. And I am *not* from Shanghai."

Peter nodded agreeably, although the explanation explained nothing.

"I have returned to China to attack and capture the city of Len Yang. I came from there originally. Exactly five years ago I galloped over the great drawbridge to study the classics in Peking. Fortunately I met a man. He was an American missionary. He said to me: 'Kahn Meng, the classics are dead. Betake yourself to America, where you will find the fountain of modern knowledge.' Of course, the missionary was a Harvard man."

Peter frowned slightly.

"What you don't understand probably, Mr. Moore, is why I can leave Len Yang and return at will. I can't. I escaped from Len Yang at night. I am returning with a thousand men at my back. Those men have occupied this village. My conscience forbids my confessing to you how many of the spies of Len Yang have been fed to the hungry river since my arrival.

"You understand, the monster of Len Yang, as I affectionately call him, must not know of my return. Otherwise he would make me prisoner. This fat-faced one slipped through the guard lines. There may be others." He grunted. "They do not dare kill me. For I—" He threw up his handsome head proudly.

"For you—" encouraged Peter.

"Must hide my identity," finished Kahn Meng with a little laugh. "But Naradia—they object to her. They have attempted to kill her, so many times. Naradia, how many?"

"A score of times," she said darkly. "Tonight they nearly succeeded. I am not wanted. I am a half-caste—a Chinese father, a poor French mother. They desired him to marry of the—"

"Hush!" cautioned her husband, for Naradia was almost hysterical and was willing to prattle on. Kahn Meng smiled tenderly. "Naradia," he continued, lowering his voice gently, "now that Peter Moore and I are at last together, will you excuse us? You must be exhausted, my dear—after this unpleasant affair. Will you retire? Remember, little Chaya, in another week this terror will be at an end. Mr. Moore and I will begin planning instantly."

Naradia laid her hands upon his and smiled sweetly. "Good-night!" she said, obediently. "Good-night,"—she lifted her brows archly—"Peter the Brazen! I do hope that you are not a dream!"

They watched the pink silk of her gown flit into the corridor, whereupon Kahn Meng took Peter's arm companionably and guided him to the window.

A keen, soft wind, tempered with the fragrance of ripening pepper trees, came in to them in delicate puffs. A mysterious light twinkled distantly upon the river. The moon was sinking into a void, and the night was becoming black.

Kahn Meng was extracting from his satin blouse a gold-and-black cigarette case. Peter accepted one of the white cylinders and struck a match. In the flare he found that Kahn Meng was studying him shrewdly, dispassionately.

"In the first place," began Kahn Meng, "let us settle the important matter of price. I will promise you whatever you desire. I want you." He spat into the darkness. "Why are you in Ching-Fu? I believed you to be in America, but I could not find you. What brings you here? Surely you were not planning to enter Len Yang again alone?"

Peter shook his head. "I came on another errand, which has nothing to do with Len Yang. But"—he threw away the half consumed cigarette—"you have made a mistake, Kahn Meng. The first matter to settle is the more important one of identity."

"Take me just as I am," pleaded Kahn Meng earnestly. "We have one desire, I know, in common—to clean up that horrible city! You have visited Len Yang. You know the wretched condition of the miners—slaves, poor devils. Perhaps you have seen them at nightfall coming from the shaft, dripping with the blood-red of the cinnabar, starving—blind!"

"I have seen all that," agreed Peter, grimly.

"Ah! But are you acquainted with that man's methods? Do you know that his corrupt influence has extended into every nation of Asia? His organization is more perfect than any eastern government. His system of espionage puts those of Japan and Germany to shame! You must know! You have encountered his underlings. Oh, I have heard of the Romola Borria affair. Your escape was masterly! I believe you astounded him."

Kahn Meng paused and puffed long at his cigarette.

"Think, Kahn Meng, what might be accomplished," said Peter fervently, "if the power he wields, that tremendous human machine—hundreds and thousands of men—were devoted to the proper ends! Think what could be done for China!"

Kahn Meng turned quickly. His eyes seemed to shine above the ruby glow of his cigarette.

"I wanted you to say that!" he exclaimed, enthusiastically. "The thing has been in my mind for years—ever since I was a child! We can do it! We can!"

"Yet one thousand men cannot enter Len Yang. It is a fortress."

"There is another way into Len Yang—by the mines. It cuts off three days of the journey. I remember it as a child. Tremendous black ravines lead to the entrance from the merchants' trail, and the opening is so small that you could pass it a thousand times without suspecting. Will you accompany us, Peter Moore—Naradia and I and our followers? We leave at dawn." He waited anxiously.

Peter shook his head regretfully. The song of adventure was musical to his ears, but he could not leave with Kahn Meng in the morning. There was Miss Lorimer—in Kialang.

"I cannot leave Ching-Fu until tomorrow night."

"That will be as well, perhaps," assented Kahn Meng after a moment's thought. "We will rest for the night in the Lenchuen Pass. It is to the right of the black road. My sentries will be watching for you."

CHAPTER XI

Peter shot the bolt and listened to the sad grumble of the river as he endeavored to adjust this strange incident to the stranger events of the very full evening.

Not until the mysterious Kahn Meng had said his good-night did Peter realize how exhausted he was.

He looked at his watch, a thin gold affair, which had ticked faithfully during all of his adventures, and was exceedingly astonished that the night had already flown to the hour of four-thirty.

Dawn would come very soon, and with the first peep of the sun he was to start for Kialang and Eileen.

The lamp smoked sleepily overhead; far away the great river sang its bass song.

He must be up at dawn. What a question-mark was Kahn Meng! A Harvard graduate—and a native of the red city! And what an adorable creature was the girl Naradia! Her eyes were like jade, her lips like poppy petals....

A crash of sound, a blaze of golden light, aroused him. He sat up, dodging a sunbeam which had flicked his eyelids. Shrill voices came from a distance. The odor of manure exhaled by the caravan sheds floated into the room, and Peter jumped up front the couch with an angry grunt. His heart was heavy with the guilt of the man who has overslept.

The watch ticked, and the neat, black hands had covered an amazing amount of ground; it was nearly tiffin-time.

The shrill, distant voices continued. Curiously, Peter looked out.

It was a beautiful sunlit morning, as clear as spring water. Miles away the sun shone on the yellow haunches of the range, altering them to a range of heavy gold; and gleamed tenderly on the paddy fields, black and ripely green.

Peter lowered his eyes to the square formed by the intersection of a number of alleys some distance beyond the caravansary. A sizable mob was collected in this enclosure; he estimated that there were at least a thousand pagan-Chinese assembled, in ring formation—a giant ring, dozens deep, and centered upon a small focussing spot of white.

The spot of white occupied the precise center of the square, and Peter studied it for some moments out of idle curiosity. Crowning the white object was a smaller spot of chestnut-brown. He dashed out of his room and down the stairs without even pausing for his hat.

Peter gained the edge of the crowd, and he bored into it, scattering protesting old ladies and chattering old men as ruthlessly as if they had been unfruitful stalks of rice.

It was a desperate fight to the center of that mob, for others were as curious as Peter. Then, over the swaying shoulders he caught a second glimpse of the chestnut-brown. It was a woman's hair, and it was familiar in arrangement.

He broke into an arena not more than nine feet in diameter in which were three objects: a wooden cask, upturned, a leather hand-bag, and a small and exceedingly pretty young woman. Her cheeks were flushed, her eyes were gray and sweet, and her mouth was like an opening rosebud.

"Eileen—" he cried.

"Why, Peter Moore!" she gasped.

He rushed to take her, but she held up her palms, retreating.

He laughed. "What under the seven suns are you doing in Ching-Fu—and Kialang—and China? What's the meaning?"

He observed that a snow-white apron extended from her dimpled chin to her small ankles.

"This is my office hour," she said severely.

"But what does this mean—this?" he exploded, gesturing wildly toward the circle of attentive onlookers.

"My clinic!" She smiled.

"You're not practising medicine out here—in this street!" he ejaculated.

"Indeed I am," she replied. "Some of these people have been waiting their turns since daylight. I returned from Kialang an hour ago. And I'll work until I collapse. I must. I wish I could multiply myself by a thousand. There's not another doctor within miles. You can watch, if you'd like," she added, then called shrilly.

An old woman appeared, and went scurrying, returning immediately with a clean, wooden bucket filled with hot water.

Eileen removed from the hand-bag what appeared to be a wallet. Stripping a rubber band from this she revealed a row of shining surgical knives. Then she produced from the black bag several bottles and a roll of absorbent cotton.

"Eyes," she told him as her hand was swallowed again by the black bag.

A child, a river boy, was pushed forward by a squinting mother. Quaking fearfully, he sat down on the cask at the girl's feet.

She turned to Peter. "This child has been without sight for a month. Without this operation he would remain blind forever. Tomorrow he will see again."

"You're wonderful!" Peter exclaimed.

At the gentle touch the child's loud whining ceased. She lifted one of the swollen lids. The boy did not flinch.

"Filth caused this," she explained. "The Chinese are the dirtiest race on earth, anyway," she added, dipping a clump of cotton into an antiseptic wash and rinsing the patient's eyes. "Where there is too much dirt, there is blindness. One-fourth of the population in this section of China are blind. They go to 'fortune tellers,' and they remain blind. In nine cases out of ten the simplest of operations followed by care will cure this type of blindness."

"Good enough; but will they be careful afterward?" Peter was curious to know.

"Once their sight is given back to them, they follow directions to a T. I'm leaving behind me a trail of the cleanest Chinamen you ever laid eyes on!"

She became silent, and so did Peter, who watched, hardly daring to breathe, the swift, sure dartings of the tiny knife in her white fingers. It was done in a jiffy; and there seemed to be on pain.

"Shouldn't you have an operating-room?" inquired Peter, as she bound up the child's eyes in gauze.

She gave him a bright, professional smile. "Peter, I've learned to operate with a thousand hooting infidels crowding closer than this. In Nanking I was nearly mobbed."

Peter looked concerned. "Did they harm you?"

"Oh, no! They wanted their children, their wives, and their virtuous mothers to see the light of day again."

"Eileen, you're an angel!"

"Be careful, Peter, or I'll kiss you in front of all these people." She blushed and smiled. "I think I was very bold to come up here all alone. Don't you?"

Peter grumbled something which escaped her.

She sat down wearily on the cask and looked up at him forlornly. "I thought it would be a lark; but it isn't. It's the hardest kind of work. There seem to be so many blind people—and I get tired—furious!"

"Can't we break away from this mob and have a little chin-chin by ourselves?"

"You're not anxious, Peter?"

"This is not Shanghai," he rejoined sententiously. "Ching-Fu is not a healthy spot for me—or for you. I've been watched. Perhaps, this very minute—" He stopped and looked at the dour faces pressed about them.

She shrugged. "Are you going on to Len Yang this time, Peter?"

He nodded slightly. "Perhaps."

"With me?"

"Without you," he stated firmly, dimly conscious of a stir on the fringe of their audience.

"It isn't fair," she murmured; "I've come all this way—" She touched her lips with the tip of a pink tongue. What she might have added was forestalled by rising confusion on the edge of the crowd. There were harsh voices, shrill voices; then these sounds were dwarfed by the thunder of furious hoofs.

White with the dust of the lower trail a troop of Mongolian horsemen, riding high in their jeweled saddles, swept into the square, shouting. Lashing their horses, they drove into the gathering with the fury of Cossacks.

Peter was thrown to one side by a tall man whom he had taken for a peasant. He tugged at his pocket, but the coolie was fighting his way toward the horsemen.

Indifferent to her struggles and screams, this giant carried Eileen in naked, brawny arms.

Peter leaped after, shouting and cursing at those who stood in his way. Some one tripped him. He regained his footing, shot his fist into the jaw of an argumentative youth, and struggled on.

The onlookers were scattering with loud and frightened squeals, running into one another, gathering in bewildered groups, darting for doorways, like sheep attacked by a wolf pack.

Then a black horse swept so close to Peter that the stirrup stripped the buttons from his tunic. A heavy whip stung him across the shoulders.

When he recovered from this blow the struggling girl was yards away, still struggling, but no longer screaming. She had been transferred to the arms of a giant Mongol, who evidently was the leader of this pack.

Peter whipped out the automatic and let go a burst at the horseman who now blocked his way; and the Mongolian, in the act of lifting a knife from its holster-scabbard, dipped across the animal's flank, with his eyes rolling toward heaven, his foot caught in one stirrup.

The horse, frightened, leaped up and spun about, twisting the fallen rider about his heels. And Peter had clear way for another few feet.

Another horseman swept down upon him. Peter brought the gun up and brought it down with fury. Twice he shot, and then this interference was removed.

The troops were gathering into crude formation, evidently for another charge. Eileen had disappeared.

Peter, knowing that she was somewhere in that quadrangle of rearing horses, struck forward, stumbling over fallen bodies, slipping in mud. His lungs burned, and he choked in a consuming rage. And suddenly he heard her scream his name.

The leader of the desert pack held her across his saddle, with his mighty arms pinioning her. He saw Peter, shouted, jabbed down with his spurs, and his mount fairly leaped. The others wheeled gracefully, and they vanished in thunder toward the plain.

Peter discovered the horse of one of the fallen warriors and leaped to capture him.

And in the next moment he was groping in blindness.

CHAPTER XII

Lingering in his vision was a leering face.

Mud had been thrown into his eyes, and the filth was plastered from eyebrows to nose. In a flash he recognized the face. Months ago he had thrown that Chinese from the deck of a steamer into the shark-infested waters of Tandjong Priok, the harbor of Batavia, Java.

Such amusing spectacles as the struggling unbeliever with rich mud plastered in his eyes have a tendency to evoke keen appreciation from the yellow races, who are supposed to be devoid of a sense of humor.

Shrill and explosive laughter was arising on all sides of him.

Light came slowly to his tortured eyes through a thick, yellow film. All of his muscles were tensed; any instant he expected to experience the long anticipated thrill of cold steel between ribs—or at his throat.

Some kindly Samaritan had taken him by the hand. Mucous breath assailed him. He distinctly heard a thud, a grunt, a screamed order.

No words were spoken, yet the mysterious hand tugged urgently at his wrist. Peter knelt down and raised handfuls of water to his eyes from a tub. He looked about for his benefactor and met only the leering countenance of a highly amused group of urchins, men and women, diverted as they had probably never been diverted before.

And in the meanwhile he realized with a torn heart that the thundering hoofs were receding farther with each flitting instant.

Peter knocked down one man as he struck out through the amused circle. The square was now all but deserted. Two bodies lay in the mud, unattended. Examination proved these to be the earthly remains of the two Mongolian horsemen—the two he had shot down. The two horses were unattended. Peter mounted the nearest.

The air was growing cold. A keen, ice-edged wind was moving northward from the range, and the sky was graying with storm clouds.

His horse was moving like the wind, perspiring not at all, a thoroughbred, a mount for a prince! At his present rate he should catch up with the Mongolian rear by nightfall; otherwise the pursuit was certainly lost. And then Peter fell to wondering what tactics he would pursue when he reached the band. How could he, alone, armed only with an automatic revolver, hope to overpower professional riflemen who numbered at the least forty? It was a nice problem; yet he could reason out no simpler solution. He was bent on a task that might have won applause from a *Don Quixote*.

The sun was settling upon the golden roof of the range, sending out monstrous blue shadows across the valley.

Mountain darkness soon enveloped the world. A dazzling star appeared with the brilliant suddenness of a coast-light. The wind was winy with the flavor of high snows.

And suddenly the horse stumbled. Peter jerked on the reins. The horse whinnied, dancing awkwardly on three legs.

Peter dismounted. A foreleg was crippled. He groaned. Fate, long his ally, was laughing at him. The chase was ended.

Suddenly hoofs thudded on the firm dirt; a shadow darted by, nearly colliding with him. There was a trampling. A lantern frame clicked, and a lance of yellow light rippled upon his face, broadened.

He glared into the anxious brown eyes of Kahn Meng.

CHAPTER XIII

"You are in time!" He gripped Peter by the shoulder.

"Have you stopped them?" gasped Peter.

Kahn Meng indulged in a bitter laugh. "Only the wind could overtake them." He shrugged. "They came—they broke through our lines—and again they broke through! If they had stopped for battle," he added grimly, "there would have been a different tale to tell."

"And they have taken her to Len Yang?" Peter suddenly recalled that Kahn Meng probably knew nothing of Eileen.

"The doctor? Yes," assented Kahn Meng sadly. "One of my men was in Ching-Fu when the troop drove through. He was looking out for you. He arrived only a few moments ago. By Buddha, how you have traveled!"

"I intend to go on."

Kahn Meng sighed. "It means only death."

"I am willing."

"But you cannot catch them with any horse. You would be killed. We can arrive in Len Yang sooner," Kahn Meng pleaded. "Everything is ready."

"I'll follow," Peter stated grimly, "on the condition that you answer two questions. What is your relation to the man at Len Yang—"

"On my word of honor," Kahn Meng interrupted him with emotion, "I am a friend. Won't that suffice until the morning? If I were an enemy, if I were on his side—"

"I realize that," Peter stopped him. "Very well. I'll wait. My other question is this: Why does that beast search the world for beautiful women—and consign them to the mines?"

Kahn Meng was silent. Reluctantly, Peter was allowing himself to be led through the darkness over broken ground. A pale dot of light emerged from the night.

"I do not know," said Kahn Meng finally. "It is hideous. I have seen them. That will be stopped!" he added tensely.

Under the lantern they paused, and Peter found his strange companion to be examining his features intently.

"I can add nothing to what has been said," Kahn Meng went on. "I have much to attend to now. We are starting immediately. At present will you trust me as I trust you?" He extended his right hand, and Peter clasped it silently.

The ripe old moon of Tibet was creeping from its bed, tipping the pointed tents with a soft glow.

On such another night as this Peter had first dared to enter the City of Stolen Lives, and the faint, mysterious sounds of a caravan at rest stirred up old memories.

The probable treatment of Eileen at the hands of Len Yang's king was too terrible for him to contemplate. And he was as helpless at this instant as though he were on the other side of the Pacific Ocean.

A hot flood of anger welled up in his breast. His palms began to sweat. Each minute was drawing her closer to the moldy walls.

He could picture her struggling in the arms of the giant Mongolian. He could see the great drawbridge swinging down to the white road in the moonlight or the blistering heat of noonday. And on the hill, like a greedy, white vulture, he could see that solemn palace with minarets stretching like claws to the sky, crouching upon the red slime vomited forth by the mines.

A cool voice startled him. Kahn Meng came out of the darkness.

"Two hundred men will accompany us. The others will remain here in case an attack is made on our rear. There may be trouble. Of course, I could go, unharmed, into Len Yang by the mountain road; but as soon as I entered I would be helpless—a prisoner forever. He knows I am returning. He is expecting me. But he does not know that half his garrison are loyal to me. The yellow-whiskered one will not be glad to see me," he added with a malicious grin.

The night seemed to be filled with silent, wakeful coolies, armed with rifles. The grim and watchful silence of the procession, the black mystery of the night with the sinking, cold moon aloft, and the uncertainty of the whole affair, set Peter's nerves to tingling; and his heart was beginning to react to the high excitement of it.

He was elated, yet anxious. Tonight's business was no quest of the golden fleece. The size of his undertaking, now that he stood, with only a few miles between, at the threshold of achievement, was overwhelming. He had pledged himself.

How he would proceed if the present venture succeeded was another matter. Fate or opportunity would have to shape his next steps. Perhaps in Kahn Meng, the mysterious, might rest the solution. Peter was an adventurer by choice, and an engineer by profession. Under given conditions he knew what to expect of men and machines. Before he had taken to the seas as a wireless operator he had had some experience as a railroad builder. He had laid rails in California, and Mexico. A successful career in that profession had been foregone when the warm hand of Romance laid hold of him.

He wondered how he could adjust himself to the routine of his old profession again, if that was the opportunity awaiting him in Len Yang. Governmental problems, he knew, would have to be given to more specialized men, such perhaps as Kahn Meng.

He looked behind him, at the long line of men stretched down the narrow ravine like the tail of a colossal serpent. Occasionally a stone, dislodged, clattered down into the crevices. Above them the rock stretched and lost itself in the cold purple of the night. The moon carved out vast shadows, black and threatening.

They emerged at length into a broader valley, jagged with spires flashing with gleams of the moon on frequent mirror-like surfaces. Ten thousand men could have been concealed in this desolate cavern. Yet it rang with emptiness as, far arear, a steel prod struck powdery fire from the flinty path.

Hours seemed to pass as they advanced, descending constantly. At times the granite walls nearly met above them, and then a shaft of moonlight would cast freakish shapes across their vision.

Once they paused for rest near a torrential stream. Some lingered to drink. The blackness in the sky was yielding itself to the spectral glow of the new day when Kahn Meng gave the order to halt.

He took Peter aside and explained his procedure. His plan was to send fifty men through the tunnel to the main shaft to subdue the guards; the remainder of the armed coolies, numbering about one hundred and fifty, would follow, forming a protective chain to the black door, an underground entrance.

"There should be no trouble, no confusion—a bloodless revolution," he added with a nervous, elated laugh. "I will occupy the place—you will follow. Wait ten minutes."

Peter nodded.

"A tunnel, fairly straight, leads from here directly to the black door. Have your revolver in readiness. My men may not make a clean job. The mine guards carry clubs. Each of my coolies has a rifle." Kahn Meng's eyes in the light of a torch were glittering excitedly. He grasped Peter's nearest hand in his enthusiasm.

"We are so near! Only a step!" He laughed wildly, lifted his voice ecstatically to a sing-song and chanted from Ouan-Oui: "Then—

"'Let us rejoice together.
and fill our porcelain goblets
with cool wine!'"

CHAPTER XIV

Now Peter was an emotional young man. And wrathful notions were kindled in him before he encountered the only guard Kahn Meng's men had over-looked—may the bones of that one rest gently!

He saw little children clawing in red muck; he saw young girls with sunken breasts, their former beauty a wretched caricature, carrying dying babes upon their backs. He saw tired old men, and women, crippled, blind, with red fingers and wrists, as if they had been dipped in blood. He saw plenty to enrage him.

Kahn Meng's guards bowed gravely as he passed them at tunnel passages. He had walked perhaps three-quarters of an hour generally in a single direction, bearing a torch, when he collided with a smooth, flat obstruction.

Somewhere in the earth distantly behind him occurred a metallic rumble, followed by a gust of soft wind, fragrant with the outdoors.

He was staring at blackness, the varnished blackness of a great wooden door. He was at the threshold! Somewhere on the other side of that enormous wooden barrier was the man of Len Yang!

Chalked boldly upon the surface was the legend:

P. M.—straight on—K. M.

Pulling with his fingers and bracing his feet in the rough floor, the mass moved monumentally toward him. It swung wide, on great, concealed hinges.

Peter's adventurous heart was beating an excited battle call. His burning eyes strained beyond the ruddy luminance of the torch, and examined—white marble! He was at his journey's end—somewhere in the palace of the Gray Dragon!

Peter dragged the great door softly shut behind him, and found himself in a chamber of vast proportions, built of what had at one time been purest white marble, discolored entirely now by the red taint of the bloody ore. The floor was perspiring redly.

Going on tiptoe to the center of the space, he searched the blank walls, listening breathlessly.

He heard nothing but the faint patter of the dripping slime, and he went swiftly to the end of the musty antechamber and discovered at the distant end the fourth wall, hitherto unseen. Reaching from the left corner of the scarlet tomb was a narrow staircase built also of marble.

Dropping his hand nervously into his right-hand tunic pocket, he went up and pushed open another door. He found himself now in a snow-white corridor, faintly lighted by grilles overhead. The hall reached gloomily into gray distance, and it was quite vacant. An unseen fountain was playing near by. At his left was another door, closed.

The closed door attracted him. Certainly there was no other course now than a detailed exploration.

Bracing himself for a surprise in this palace of hideous surprises, he flung open the door, and entered black darkness.

Carelessly he closed the door behind him, listening and sniffing. At first he heard nothing, but he smelled altar-incense faintly.

A deep-voiced gong suddenly reverberated while Peter tensed himself. The sonorous melody lifted and crashed, subsiding into countless unmusical overtones. Lighter metal rang upon wood.

Then lights—electric lights—by the dozens, hundreds—thousands—blazed with a violent suddenness, a suddenness that Peter could compare only with that of a tropical sun leaping out of the ocean; and Peter blinked upon green. It was a hideous green, a green of diabolical intensity. He shivered. It seemed to creep, to writhe, this green.

At first he could not absorb this insane color idea; and he stood there, with his heart sinking.

He discovered that he was occupying an oblong green rug of satin. He was dazzled by the green glare of a cluster of quartz lights in front of him, and he stared, first at a monstrous green Buddha, squatting on a thighless rump between flashing green pillars, and finally at the most hideous individual he had ever gazed upon, a human, who occupied a throne carved solidly from green jade.

The glimpse was like stepping from a dark dream into the center of an aquamarine nightmare. And in the instant following his partial digestion of the viridescent scheme he was possessed with the notion that the occupant of such a chamber of horror must certainly be insane.

That was the first idea to possess Peter. He was not surprised to find that he was unafraid. Anticipation is much more fearful than realization. He had experienced many panicky moments in looking forward to this meeting; and yet in the presence of him he was cool.

The Gray Dragon of Len Yang?

From the tail of his eye he detected a man with folded arms backed against the door. At either side of the green throne stood Mongolian guards, armed with rifles. They struck the only dissonant note of the picture, for they were garbed in desert brown.

Evidently all ways of escape were closed. For two years he had contrived to elude the tracers, the killers, sent out by this creature, and now he had deliberately walked upon his swords. Death? Where was Kahn Meng?

Possessed with a feeling akin to cat-like curiosity, Peter walked slowly to the beryl throne steps, where he paused, with his fists gripped tightly in his pockets, his chin up, and his shoulders back.

Close scrutiny did not soften the bestial cruelty of the face of Len Yang's ruler. It was a startling face, as gray as fresh clay, sharply wrinkled. The nose was exceedingly long and sharp, with a crooked joint. Dirty-yellow mandarin mustaches drooped like wet sea-weed from the sides of a curling, sneering mouth.

And it was dominated by a pair of very small, very bright green eyes, set deep and exceedingly close together.

But the tenor of the face was gray, the gray of living death, and from this emblem, Peter suddenly decided, the man had been given his descriptive name.

Long, gray talons reached out from the folds of a mandarin jacket and toyed nervously with a strand of gray hair which jutted from the pigtail winding over the slanting shoulder.

The green eyes blinked as they completed the survey of Peter Moore. The curling lips were moving.

"Peter Moore!" he rasped. "The most daring foreigner who has yet visited my city! Peter the Brazen, with a reputation of breaking the hearts of beautiful women! You are late. I have been waiting upon this visit for two years!"

He leaned forward, and Peter retreated a step.

"What have you done with her?" Peter snapped.

The Gray Dragon sank back with a sigh. "Ah! Would you like to gaze upon that which can never be yours?"

"May I see her—once—before I die?"

"That is a wise statement. You are altogether wise—astonishingly so! Wisdom is a rare gem in one so young." He chuckled in an irritating treble. "Look about you again, youth. This is known as the room of the green death. Few men leave the room of the green death alive. My hounds bay when they enter.

"The young woman is here—safe. If you will answer my questions, I may permit you to gaze upon her just once before you die! Perhaps I may be so lenient as to allow you to die together. Does not that appeal to you?" he demanded, as if anxious. "You—who are so thirsty for the gold of romance?"

Peter glared at him silently, and his fingers were twitching.

His host tapped the resonant gong. Some one stepped behind Peter, for he distinctly heard the seep of silken garments.

The man on the green throne muttered, adding to Peter: "I am granting your wish. You may gaze upon her before you die. I, too, will gaze, for I prize her highly, as you know."

He sank back meditatively, and in that moment the gray face became oddly sane.

"Peter Moore, seldom do I permit men who have troubled me so sorely to escape alive. Perhaps, in face of what has happened, you are foolishly taking unto yourself credit. And still, for a reason unknown to me, I hesitate.

"Listen to me closely, youth! For these two years I have watched you with my thousands of hired eyes—you cannot realize how closely! Because I was deeply interested. You are a riddle to me. You have the emotions of a woman, and the cunning of a *hu-li*.

"Times without count word has gone forth from this green room that your death must take place. Childish curiosity to stare just once upon the foolish adventurer has caused that word to be revoked! Do not assume credit for bravery that was not yours, Peter Moore! You are not heroic; you have been a plaything. The gods are through with you.

"Harken to me, Peter the foolish. Within these green walls daily are inscribed the names of men and women who must die. Your name has been spoken, yet never once has it been written. When it is written—" He paused with a portentous hush.

"Today, when I realized you were at last coming to me, when spy after spy ran to my feet to say that at last—at last—Peter Moore, the unconquerable, was coming to pay his long-overdue call—I hastened with that daily quota of names of those who are doomed, so that I could attend you with undivided attention.

"Can it interest you? Nine men are doomed. Within two weeks from this hour a mandarin will die by the knife, an ambassador at the court of Peking will expire by poison, an indiscreet Javanese merchant—" He waved his skinny arms impatiently.

"Those whose names are written must inevitably die. If the name of Peter Moore had but once appeared on the green silk—I could have forgotten you—and rested. But I was restrained by a most curious impulse." He looked at Peter eagerly.

"You have perplexed, almost fascinated me. Tell me first, what was your power over Romola Borria?"

Peter only grunted, angrily astonished.

"Wait!" cautioned the curling lips. "I am not ridiculing you. I am keenly desirous of knowing." He frowned, pondering. "I will tell you about that woman. Romola Borria was sent to me, and I employed her. For certain difficult tasks she was all that I desired—more beautiful than sunset on the Tibetan snow—a glorious woman, yet as cold, as unfriendly as that same snow. Her spirit was one of ice, yet fire.

"And her heart was stone—or snow also. I sent her directly to communicate a certain thing to you—to kill you in the event that you declined. Shall I tell you how many men she has put out of the way at my bidding before and after she met you? No matter.

"Romola Borria was proof against love. No man was created for her to love. Yet that snowy heart melted, that precious coldness vanished, when she met—Peter Moore!"

The Gray Dragon paused, and the cessation of his metallic voice, the quick relinquishing of the evil glint in his small, green eyes, left Peter with a deeper feeling of revulsion than previously. It had been his imaginative belief that the Gray Dragon was utterly without human traits; yet he possessed that lowest of them all, a bestial curiosity.

"I can all but read your thoughts," he went on, lidding his green eyes a number of times. "You are saying what my victims invariably say when I grant them these rare audiences before they die. Over and over you are repeating—'Beast! Beast! Beast!' Is that not true?"

"That is absolutely true!"

Malice seemed to hover about the glittering green eyes, and was gone at once. "Peter Moore, to gaze at you is like gazing into a crystal. In you I witness that supreme quality which was denied me in my youth. I can have anything in the world but that supreme, that sublime quality. I can buy anything in the world but that." The voice stopped.

Peter shifted his glance momentarily to the armed attendants who guarded this evil life. An inner whisper counseled him: "Not yet! Not yet! There is time!"

"Yet there is a chance that I may reconsider; that I may permit you to continue to live—perhaps in the mines. But certainly, Peter the foolish, you must not yield to that present impulse. Of course, you are armed. But do not move! Two feet behind you stands an excellent shot with a pistol aimed at your backbone. Men with cracked spines do not live long!" He chuckled.

"What was I about to say? Ah, yes! If I could purchase from you that quality—if I could, I say, anything in my kingdom would be yours—everything! It is the one thing I have been denied. Holy wheel! It is strange, this way I am talking! I have rarely had such an interested audience. Most of my captives at this stage are cringing, are kissing my feet."

The snarling grin left his lips again, and his mood became strangely soft, like dead flesh, so Peter thought, as he waited—with that pistol at his backbone!

"I intend telling you an amazing story, which you may or may not credit. I am telling it—this confession—partly because I dislike the look in your blue eyes. Like everyone else, you loathe me. But I will erase that look. I intend to show you I am even more human than you!

"By Buddha, I will tell that story to you—you, Peter Moore, the most fortunate man in all China this hour. Think, before I begin, of that mandarin, that bungling Javanese merchant, who, also, are about to die. Then forget all else—and listen.

"This took place many years ago, when I was a young man, like yourself. I, too, loved a woman. Can you understand me? I, too, once loved a woman, a maiden of the Punjab. I can conceive her in the veil of my memory still. Eyes like dusty stars, skin the color of the Tibetan dawn, the dawn that you may never again look upon.

"Her heart was gold, so I thought. Yet it was dross. On a night in spring-time, in the bazaar at Mangalore, we two first met. I have not forgotten. That night I fell in love with the white orchid from the Punjab. She was more beautiful to me than life or death, a feast of beauty.

"Len Yang was mine then, and I was a rich prince, but not so rich as now. Drunkenly I was casting my gold about the bazaar when we met. She saw me—and she smiled! It was the first time any woman had smiled upon me, and I was alarmed and troubled. I was no more handsome than now. I was the man that no one loved. *Chuh-seng*—the beast—was my name even then, among those who tolerated my friendship because of my fluent gold.

"And when the Punjab maiden smiled upon me, I thought to myself: '*Chuh-seng*, love has come at last to sweeten your bitter heart.' What should a young lover have done? I—I bought the bazaar and presented it to her—on bended knees!

"She confessed that she could love me, despite my ugliness, this white orchid of the plains. Peter Moore, do not look at me. You can believe—if you do not look. She kissed me—on my lips! Again she said she loved me. Had I been a thousand times uglier, she would have loved me a thousand times more passionately! Heaven had joined us. And I forgave my enemies, renewed my vows at the wheel, and blessed every virgin star!

"Love had come to me at last! Me—the most hideous in all of Asia. And I believed her. What would you have done, Peter Moore—you who know so well the heart of woman? Never mind. I believed everything.

"We lingered in Mangalore. But I did not know then of the Singhalese merchant—the trader who owned three miserable camels. He possessed not handsomeness, but the romantic glamour which you possess, Peter the Brazen! Reveling in my love, I was as blind as these imbeciles in my mines. Our child was born.

"She could have taken more, had she not been so lovestruck. She could have had my all—my gems, my pearls, and rubies, and diamonds, more colossal than the treasure of any raja—my mines which dripped with the precious mercury!

"Yet she stole only my gold which was convenient, and went out into the starlit night with the Singhalese trader, to share the romance of the blinding desert—the Singhalese trader, a man of no caste at all! Love? That was my love!"

The hideous, gray face retreated behind talons as though to blot out the thought of that ancient betrayal. When the talons again dropped down, the dead softness of the face was replaced by the former sneer.

This change was quite shocking.

The beast was laughing harshly. "If I could not have love, I could at least have hate! I have hated more passionately than any man has ever loved!"

Peter said nothing to this, although the gray lips closed and the green eyes looked at him expectantly, almost demanding comment. Surely this creature was insane, with his room of the green death, his wild tales of love of a Punjab maiden, of wholesale hate.

The Gray Dragon seemed irritated. "What have you to say now?"

"I was only wondering," said Peter, as if suddenly tired, "when that pistol is to explode at my back."

"There is yet time," muttered his host. "No man has yet left this room in contempt of me! Can you believe I have lied?" he snarled. "Why, you fool!" he croaked. "I will teach you! What do you suppose has become of that other one whom you met at the *weng* into the hills? Do you imagine my men were not in his camp? Every inch of the way you two were watched.

"And what has become of your prudence? You who defied me, who escaped me—undone by a woman! She is why you are here. Because you are such a fool you shall die. I might have relented. I thought you were proof against love. Is any one? Is any one proof against it but me? Ah—"

He looked eagerly beyond Peter, and Peter heard a frightened sob, then a little cry, as the door closed heavily.

CHAPTER XV

She flew across the room to him, and pressed her hands to his cheeks. Her eyes were sparkling with tears, and her face was very pale. Only her lips, which were everlastingly bright, gave color to that distressed young face.

"Peter!" she moaned. "Oh, I was so afraid!" She lowered her voice. "What is to become of us?"

He looked down at her and forced a smile to his lips.

"We who are about to die—" he began grimly.

She gave him a twisted smile as his arms tightened about her. He loved her for that courage.

With his arm at her waist he turned. He had observed that the Gray Dragon had spoken truly as regarded the armed coolie at his back.

Their captor bent forward and fixed upon them the most curious of glances. His merciless, green eyes ran from Eileen's tumbled chestnut hair to her small, tan boots—then he regarded Peter with the same intensity, and thereupon he seemed to be weighing the doomed lovers as a unit, or as an idea.

A devilish smile cracked his lips.

"So this is love?" he cackled. "This is the young woman to whom you have thrown your life away—after most splendid resistance—you, Peter the Brazen! Do you still love her?" He pointed a crooked forefinger at Eileen. "Tell me, would you desert him, in this first flush of your maiden love, for a handsomer man—and steal his gold, after he laid the earth at your feet? Would you do that?"

Methodically the talons stroked the sea-weed mustache.

"You are too anxious for death. You are romantic. Youth does have such ideas. Even I, *Chuh-seng*, have such notions. Death? Why does your little mind single out such simple punishment—you—lovers? Romantically you long for death, because in the next world you would come together again—in the lover's eternity of heaven.

"But I have a far more imaginative scheme. Separation! How does that appeal to you?" He leaned forward and watched them. "I have an excellent plan. One of you shall work until the end of his life in this mine, as beautiful captives in the past quarter century have slaved and died; the other shall labor until the end of life in my quarries, not more than one hundred miles from Len Yang.

"Then you will not speak of death. You will struggle and you will grow old long before your time, as the others have done, hoping that vain hope of again meeting. And I shall grant your wish! Years from now, when youth and the divine passion of youth have flown—when only the bitter dregs of that rapturous love remain—then you shall be reunited." He cackled humorously in his treble.

"O Buddha! How long have I waited for such an opportunity? How long? How long? Is it twenty years—or forty—or a thousand—since that night in the bazaar at Mangalore?" His green eyes rolled to the green ceiling. And his mood underwent another vast change, this creature of monster moods.

"Are you grateful to me, you two? You should be! It was I who brought you together—I, the cruelest man in all Asia! It must have been a divine night, that night on the great river, Peter Moore, when she came into your arms. Love blazed in your hearts that night; and this gray-eyed witch said, with downcast eyes: 'I like you, Peter Moore!' What difference what she said? Any words would have dripped as much with love!"

He sprang to his feet, groaning, his evil countenance undergoing convulsions, as of terrific inner spasms.

"You shall not have that!" he shouted. "You shall not have love! What I have done, I shall undo! You shall live apart. Love has been refused me; love is refused all who come within my reach! That is my decision. Nor shall you have death. One of you to the quarry—the other to the mines. I shall be generous. You may make your choice. And *that* is my decision!"

The lovers stared at him. The vicious plan had gripped Peter's imagination. Gone was all thought of the pistol, which lay even now in the palm of his hand. One shot would have silenced the beast forever; but he had forgotten such things as bullets and pistols.

He could realize only that, even before their first kiss had been exchanged, they would be torn apart.

The color had receded from Peter's skin and eyes; he looked very much nearer forty than thirty. And Eileen was reflecting that despairing attitude. She could think only of him toiling wretchedly in the mines or quarries, striving against a fate as unfriendly, as unyielding, as a wall of cold granite.

The Gray Dragon sank back, with his chest heaving. His features were working. The spasm had exhausted him; and the green brilliance gave his gray skin a ghastly pallor. He lifted a small silver hammer and brought it down upon the belly of a large bronze gong.

There was a stir behind them.

With the same cold hate in his expression as he addressed himself again to the lovers, who clung together like small children, pitiful objects indeed in this hall of pitiless green.

"The others are coming; their fate will be yours—you lovers!"

He turned to address words in dialect to the Mongolian on his right, and in the space Eileen's breath came warmly upon Peter's ear.

"Are you armed?" she whispered.

His nod was hardly perceptible. He dropped his hand into his pocket, and at that instant his arms were pinioned. The revolver was snatched from his fingers.

The malicious green eyes were staring beyond them.

Peter heard a low sob, instantly stifled. Naradia, with bloodshot eyes, was searching his face in distress. Her black hair had been arranged in a heavy braid, which ran down her back in a glistening rope.

Kahn Meng's sad eyes lingered on Peter's for a moment, sparkling with guilt, and his face was crestfallen. Plainer than any words could have said, his expression cried out: "I have failed! I am sorry."

Then he advanced to the throne, taking his stand at the Gray Dragon's side, a maneuver which was thoroughly mystifying to Peter.

The Gray Dragon seemed to ignore his presence. To Peter he said: "You recognize your companion of last night? The man with a legion of a thousand loyal men at his back?"

Peter nodded, muttering.

The Gray Dragon waved Kahn Meng to one side. "He is my son. He is my son by my faithful wife! Do you understand that, Peter Moore?"

"Your son? And he will carry on your work?"

"Precisely that! You have expressed it neatly, Peter Moore. The Gray Dragon will carry on the work of the Gray Dragon!"

The mystery of Kahn Meng was cleared aside. Fury directed at his treachery swelled in Peter's breast and burst. It was as though a torch had been applied. The flame of an ancient ancestral fire, when men fought for their lives and their loves with clubs, and nails, and teeth, burst into his brain and into his breast. The muscles under his tunic-sleeve, which clung to his arm from the moisture of perspiration, rippled and flexed and hardened.

His face—the clean, handsome face of well-lived youth—was quite dreadful to look upon—flushed to a fiery red and distorted. His lips were skinned back over his white teeth.

The thunder of his roar fairly shook the green quartz pillars, between which the smug, green Buddha smiled complacently, impervious to the rages of foolish mankind.

Peter sprang upon the heels of that roar like a mass of wonderfully controlled steel at the crouching figure, a figure whose countenance was suddenly wet and white.

He tore the carbine from the fingers of the nearest guard before that one could collect his wits.

The Mongolian sprawled over backward, and in the second instant the heavy butt of the carbine came down with a shuddering crash upon the skull-cap of the man who would no longer rule Len Yang!

With such tremendous vigor was that blow delivered that the walnut stock, as tough as iron, shivered into splinters, which swam in the bursting brains of the victim.

Screaming, Peter swung the stock again, and again, as if he would beat his wretched victim to a pulp. Nothing but the barrel and breech mechanism remained.

His murderous intention seemed to be to remove, to obliterate for all time, the hideous face, to wipe out by means of his brute strength the gray countenance.

Suddenly he sprang away from him with the elastic stride of a panther. Kahn Meng, the traitor, was next.

And as he leaped Kahn Meng slipped from his own pocket a revolver and dodged Peter's blow.

Peter staggered backward, reaching the center of the room, dragging the bloody and bent carbine barrel in a red trail. There he stopped, swaying, toppling.

Darkness was assailing him. He was sinking into a pit. And the heart was fluttering, laboring treacherously under the poison created in his blood by fury.

The green lights spun.

He threw the carbine barrel at the complacent Buddha, where it clanked to the marble flags. And he withered like the lotus, sprawling upon his back with his eyes tightly shut, the color fast disappearing from his complexion.

And his head was reclining upon the small, tan boots of Eileen.

CHAPTER XVI

Somewhere in the distance a sweet-voiced temple bell resounded dreamily. Vague odors of sandalwood and wistaria swam in the soft, cool air. A ray of warm sunlight fell upon Peter's inert hand, and he opened his eyes.

Memory came slowly back to him. He remembered that he had killed. The last thing he distinctly recalled from that moment of ungovernable fury which had taken hold of him was that Kahn Meng, the traitor, had drawn a pistol. As a natural consequence he should be dead. Perhaps he was.

Slowly his brain became clear, although queer vapors arose in it.

Soft footsteps crossed the stone flagging with a clicking of dainty heels. Small fingers, exquisite to the touch, brushed the tousled hair from his forehead. These were cool and pleasant.

"Old Sweetheart!" said a happy voice.

The cool fingers crept underneath his chin and lingered there. Others crept under his neck. A warm, satiny cheek floated down to rest upon his forehead.

Dozens of questions swarmed out of the wreckage of his waking consciousness.

"You are safe? Where are we? What happened to that scoundrel, Kahn Meng? Why did they bring you here? Did they harm you? Who hit—"

A silvery laugh interrupted him. "Yes, yes—yes!" said the voice that was sweeter to him than all of the music in Christendom with heathendom thrown in for good measure.

"I am safe. I was kidnapped and treated with all respect due a famous doctor—because a dead monster was suffering from neuritis. We are alone, in a tiny glass house on the roof of the ivory palace, and dawn has this very moment come. Such a glorious dawn, Peter!

"Are you rested? I never saw any one so completely burned out. Such fury! Gracious, what a man! But why, Peter, did you attack poor Kahn Meng? He's the best friend you have in the world!"

"The Gray Dragon!" muttered Peter, clenching his fists.

"Peter, Kahn Meng would lay down his life for you. Of course, he is the Gray Dragon; but that is only a name now. He is the Gray Dragon, and he has you, and you only, to thank for it.

"The title is hereditary, and he is the last of his line. He knew what that monstrous father of his was doing, and he has been helpless—until you freed him. And the dreadful secret, Peter, is that that beast was not Kahn Meng's father. A Singhalese trader, murdered years ago, was his father, and his mother, a beautiful woman of the Punjab, was for a time the wife of the beast!

"The entire organization has now come under Kahn Meng's control. He is the Gray Dragon of Len Yang, and it is a title that from now on will be a power for good, for construction!

"You can't imagine what wonderful plans he has. He's a genius—that young man is, Peter! And you—you—are to be his chief executive, the viceroy of Len Yang! The chief of mines, of transportation, of labor! He told me that millions of dollars of capital are at your disposal.

"Last night we planned a great railroad line, running from the mines to Chosen and Peking and Tientsin! Think of it, Peter! What opportunity!

"While I," Eileen went on blithely, "am to start a hospital. No more blindness, no more sickness, in Len Yang. And shorter working hours. And an age limit. And schools. And good food, and lots of it!

"From now on our work is to assume a world-wide importance. Word came over the wireless late last night that Germany has finally started the long-expected European war. Kahn Meng believes every nation will be drawn into it. So there is another menace for you to help stamp out—the Dragon of Europe. Kahn Meng says these mines, and the copper and iron mines, nearer the coast, can help—wonderfully!"

Peter felt vastly happy, too enthralled to believe that the state could endure. He stood up from the cot and looked down into the bright face of the one woman in the world. It was radiant, very pink, now, and her round eyes were tender and meek. Perhaps she was a little frightened by the fierceness which had developed in his expression.

She opened her arms with a little laugh. He crushed her close. Their lips met and clung.

He pushed her away, and his blue eyes were impassioned.

Eileen smiled. "Look!"

The white snow on the high peaks across the valley glowed with the heavy gold of sunrise. Far below them, midway to the green wall, he saw a great mass of people. There were hundreds packed about the mouth of the shaft. He wondered why they were waiting; then the shrill voice of a crier penetrated the cool morning air. The thousands waited in silence.

Peter wondered at their dumbness in the face of the news that the man who had ridden them into blindness, into starvation and death, was no longer to tyrannize over them.

The crier continued to shout his singsong.

How would the spirit of that mob react to the announcement?

The singsong halted, and for a breathless moment the miners, too, were silent.

Then a great volume of sound disturbed the morning hush. It swelled in volume, rose in key—a great thunder, the thunder of laughing voices, the hysterical joy of a people made free! It filled the valley and overflowed into the hills, a prolonged wave of happy tumult.

www.ingramcontent.com/pod-product-compliance
Lightning Source LLC
Chambersburg PA
CBHW010805250626
47156CB00010B/3007